MW01200059

COLONY MARS SERIES

BOOKS 1-3

GERALD M. KILBY

OUTER PLANET
MEDIA

Published by GMK, 2016 - 2017

This book has been edited for US English.
Version us1.2

For notifications on upcoming books, and access to my FREE starter library, please join my Readers Group at www.geraldmkilby.com.

CONTENTS

COLONY ONE MARS

COLONY TWO MARS

COLONY THREE MARS

ABOUT THE AUTHOR

Gerald M. Kilby grew up on a diet of Isaac Asimov, Arthur C. Clark, and Frank Herbert, which developed into a taste for Iain M. Banks and everything ever written by Neal Stephenson. Understandable then, that he should choose science fiction as his weapon of choice when entering the fray of storytelling.

REACTION is his first novel and is very much in the old-school techno-thriller style and you can get it free at geraldmkilby.com. His latest books, **COLONY MARS** and **THE BELT**, are both best sellers, topping Amazon charts for Hard Science Fiction and Space Exploration.

He lives in the city of Dublin, Ireland, in the same neighborhood as Bram Stoker and can be sometimes seen tapping away on a laptop at the local cafe with his dog Loki.

You can connect with Gerald M. Kilby at:
www.geraldmkilby.com

COLONY ONE MARS

PROLOGUE

What follows is the last known communication from Colony One Mars:

Sol #1:435 COM ID:N.L-1027.

This may be our last transmit for some time, we cannot spare the power. Sandstorm continues unabated, it will never end. We are down to 17% energy levels and have deactivated all non-essential systems. Solar array unable to recharge batteries due to darkened sky, running at only 7% efficiency. Plutonium power source has failed and attempts by EVA to find the fault have proved fatal. Those who have ventured outside to investigate have not returned. If the storm does not clear we will run out of power in approximately fourteen sols.

To add to our woes, a strange malaise has overcome many of us who still survive. A disturbing psychosis now affects one in three. We are prepared as best we can. We all know what is coming. We wait in hope, even though that now seems futile. Send no more.

1

DESCENT

In less than fifteen minutes Dr. Jann Malbec would be either walking on the surface of Mars or be dead, and there were plenty of ways for her to die. She could burn up in the atmosphere if the heat shield failed or be smashed to pieces on the surface if the thrusters didn't fire. In any event, it was going to be one hell of a ride.

After months of floating around inside the Odyssey transit craft en route to Mars, the moment had finally arrived for the six crew of the International Space Agency (ISA) to enter the lander and descend to the planet's surface. The habitation module was already in situ along with a myriad of equipment and supplies. The mothership would now be parked in orbit where it would wait patiently for their return.

Jann strapped herself into the seat, gripped the metal armrests tightly and tried to breathe normally. Ahead of her, at the flight controls, Commander Robert Decker and First Officer Annis Romanov cycled through the systems check routines.

"Detaching in five... four... three..." The voice of the first officer squawked in Jann's helmet and she felt a thud behind her as release bolts retracted. The lander detached itself, floating free from the mothership. A moment later thrusters fired to align it for the correct injection trajectory. Jann felt the force propelling her forward. Her grip tightened on the armrest. It bit through her gloved hand; it comforted her.

Gravity began to tug at the craft as it commenced its downward spiral. It shook. Gently at first. But with each passing second the vibration intensified and deepened until the entire vessel rocked with a violent cacophonous rage. The first officer began to shout out the descent velocity and elevation vectors.

"Mach two point seven. Altitude fifteen point six kilometers."

Jann tried not to think about the searing temperature building up on the craft's heat shield as it ploughed through the upper atmosphere. She gripped the armrest tighter and hung on.

It should have been Science Officer Patty Macallester sitting in this seat instead of her. But four weeks before the launch, Macallester started feeling unwell. An examination by the ISA medical team quickly diagnosed a viral infection. Not life threatening, but she would not be fit for the mission. So, after much deliberation and hand wringing by the ISA directorate, Dr. Jann Malbec got the call. She was officially next in line and checked most of the boxes for most of the stakeholders but she was least experienced in terms of astronaut training. Jann knew the journey here was the easy part. The real test was beginning now. She would soon find out if she had what it took, or if she was simply an impostor.

The craft accelerated through the thin upper atmosphere and Jann felt a sickening wave ripple through her gut as her stomach began to form a closer relationship with her throat. The staccato voice of the first officer echoed in her headset as she checked off stats. "Mach one point seven, altitude ten point one, lateral drift two point two. Get ready, deploying chutes..."

With that, three enormous chutes exploded from the top of the descent craft and the vessel slowed down dramatically. Jann felt like she was being vacuum packed into her seat as they all took heavy G, as they hurtled towards the surface at extreme velocity. The thin Martian atmosphere—only 1% of Earth's—was grossly insufficient to slow the craft down for a soft parachute landing. At best it took just enough sting out of the free fall to engage the retro-thrusters.

"Detaching heat shield in three... two... one..." Jann felt the thump of bolts as the shield fell away from the base of the craft to find its own way down to the surface.

"Prepare for chute jettison..."

For a brief moment Jann's stomach resumed its relationship with her throat before she was vacuum packed to the seat again.

"Retro-thrusters engaged... one point eight kilometers... targeting on HAB beacon... lateral drift still at two point two." The first officer and commander traded data, ticking off the distance to the surface and speed of descent.

"One point six... one point one... drifting..."

Slowly Jann's body resumed some ability to move and she shifted in her seat to reassure herself that she could still do it.

"Five hundred... three fifty... two seven five... hold on to your butts... here we go..."

The craft thumped down onto the planet surface. Landing gear took the strain and there was a brief moment when the stanchions held the full force before springing back to a complete rest. The thrusters shut off, the noise stopped and the craft was silent.

Stillness permeated the interior as the crew adjusted to the realization that they had landed, and that they were all still alive.

"Holy crap," it was the Chief Engineer, Kevin Novack, who broke the moment. Then followed a multitude of cheers and hand slapping. There was a palpable air of excitement mixed with intense relief that they had all survived the ride of death.

"It looks like we're about one klick from the HAB beacon." The commander pointed to a flashing blip on the main screen. " If our calculations are correct then the sandstorm should be about five kilometers west of us. Plenty of time to reach the Habitation Module."

They had been tracking the storm for some time while still on board the Odyssey. After much deliberation with ISA Mission Control it was decided to land now before the storm had chance to grow. If left too long it could engulf the entire area, making descent too risky and mean waiting weeks in orbit for another window.

It was a sandstorm that proved the undoing of Colony One, the first human settlement on Mars. It raged for over six months during which time all contact was lost. That was three and a half years ago. The crew of the ISA Odyssey was here to find out what had happened to it—and the fifty-four people who had called it home.

Annis ran through the lander shutdown sequence, flicking off switches and putting the craft into sleep mode. When the time came to return to Earth, it would be woken up, refueled from the methane/oxygen plant already on the surface and prepped for reuse as the Mars ascent vehicle (MAV) to rendezvous with the Odyssey orbiter.

"Prep for pressure equalization."

A chorus of *'check'* echoed in Jann's helmet as each crewmember confirmed the integrity of their EVA suit. Jann lifted her arm to adjust her helmet. It felt like lead. After so much time spent in zero gravity her body struggled to adjust to a new way of working. She managed to activate the heads-up display that gave her a status on vitals: pressure, oxygen, temperature and a raft of other biometric data. The others were also moving very slowly, readjusting to the one-third gravity.

"Okay, let's do this." The commander unfastened himself from his seat, opened the door to the Martian atmosphere and headed outside. In a well-practiced routine they followed in turn. Jann was last to leave. She felt totally uncoordinated as her body tried to remember how to move without floating. She clambered out backwards through the small hatch and fumbled to find the foothold that should be there—somewhere.

"See that on the horizon? It doesn't look good," said Annis.

"Damn, I thought we had calculated it was moving north of us." The commander was agitated. "Malbec, hurry up. We've got that storm heading our way."

"Sorry, Commander, can't find the foothold."

"Good God, would somebody please help her."

She felt a hand on her boot and her foot was guided to the rung. She scrambled down, stumbled on the final step and ended up facedown on the surface. She felt like she was glued to the dirt. *Gravity's a bitch*, she thought.

"Come on Malbec, move it." Decker was getting impatient.

Jann sat up, and with the help of Medical Officer Dr. Paolio Corelli and Mission Seismologist, Lu Chan, she was bundled upright.

"Thanks," she managed.

They were in the Jezero Crater, a forty kilometer wide basin situated near the equator. It was a desolate, barren wasteland washed with a rose-colored hue. It had a terrible beauty. Ahead of them, somewhere to the west, lay the HAB, placed there by an earlier mission. It was their destination, their home for the next few months.

"We've got to move. Look." Paolio pointed over towards the horizon. Rolling across it was a vast billowing sandstorm. It was moving fast—in their direction. Commander Decker checked his holo-screen, a red blip pulsed out the HAB's location. He pointed off into the distance. "That way. Let's go."

They moved slowly, but with purpose. The last thing they needed was to be caught out in the open. Jann's sense of balance was fragile and she struggled to put one foot in front of the other. She felt like an ancient deep sea diver, trudging along an ocean floor hunting for pearls, weighed down with brass and lead.

"Malbec, pick up the pace, let's keep it moving," Decker's voice echoed in her head.

"Yes, commander."

Annis looked anxiously at the encroaching storm front. "We're not going to make it. Dammit. Looks like we figured it wrong. Anyway, we're committed now, no going back. Come on, we need to move faster."

Jann dug deep and found a rhythm of sorts. They moved in silence, all focused on one objective, get to the HAB before the storm hit. She looked up at the ominous billowing cliff of dust as it moved and reshaped itself ever closer. Annis was right; they weren't going to make it.

"There it is." They could see the white squat cylinder of the HAB off in the distance, just before it was swallowed by the oncoming maelstrom.

"Stay close, we'll lose visibility shortly, everybody stay tight, keep everyone else in sight."

The storm charged across the crater's surface with impressive speed and Jann braced herself for impact. But the impact never came. The Martian atmosphere was so thin that she barely felt anything. It was eerie. Fine dust swirled everywhere and blocked out the world. Encapsulated in her EVA suit Jann had a strong feeling of dislocation. It was like she was not physically here. Like a ghost. She lost sight of all but Paolio and forced herself to move faster. Her balance failed, she tripped and tumbled forward.

"Help! I've fallen. I can't see anyone."

"Malbec, is that you? Goddammit, we don't need this now. Everyone stop exactly where you are. That includes you Malbec, don't move, we'll come to you, just stay put."

"I can't see anyone..." She managed to stand up again but had lost all sense of direction. Everywhere she looked was a dense murky sea of dust. She turned this way and that, arms outstretched. She was blind. Fear rose up inside her, she fought to control it. The sound of her own breathing began to reverberate in her helmet. She was beginning to panic.

A hand grabbed her elbow. "It's okay, Jann, I got you." It was Paolio. "Are you all right?"

Her breathing calmed. "I'm fine... just got a bit... I'm okay..." The others came into view, materializing out of the ghostly dust.

"Follow me, we're nearly there." Decker moved off again. The rest fell in behind. Jann stuck close to Paolio.

They walked for only a short time and finally the HAB rose up out of the dust like a lost ship in a fog. They found their way to the airlock door and one by one crossed the threshold and into safety. Decker hit the controls to pressurize the airlock. As soon as the alert flashed green the crew started to remove their helmets and breathe their first taste of HAB air.

"Holy crap," said Novack, "let's do that again."

2

JEZERO CRATER

For three days the vast Jezero Crater was immersed in dust as the crew waited it out, cocooned in the relative comfort of the HAB. It was a two story pressurized cylinder approximately eight meters in diameter and the same in height. The HAB was the culmination of intense design and redesign over thousands of hours and hundreds of iterations, each one inching it ever closer to ergonomic perfection. The ground floor housed the main operations area, a small galley dining space, and a utilitarian medlab sickbay. There was also a large airlock with enough room for all six crew along with EVA suits. An open column ran up the center of the HAB with a ladder and a small standing elevator, giving access to the top floor. It was divided into eight sections, sliced like a pie. It gave some private sleeping space for each crewmember along with a 'slice' each for exercise and sanitary. Compared to the cramped confines of the Odyssey it was palatial.

For Jann the sandstorm was a blessing in disguise as it gave her body time to adjust to working in one-third gravity. More than once she positioned an object in midair, expecting it to float, only for it to fall crashing to the floor. It also gave her mind time to contend with the enormity of the responsibility that lay before her. She spent much of this time in the privacy of her room studying mission protocol and mentally rehearsing many of the technical procedures.

By the morning of the fourth sol (day) the storm cleared, moving off eastward away from the crater basin. Jann sat in the HAB galley reading through the last known communication from Colony One. The message was sent over three and a half years ago by Nills Langthorp, the thirteenth human to set foot on Mars.

"What do you think he meant by that last line on the message?" Jann directed her question at Dr. Paolio Corelli, who was making his second espresso of the morning. The HAB had its own fresh coffee machine, courtesy of the Italian Space Agency. Paolio, being a native, was very proud of it and relished any opportunity to instruct the others as to its operation.

"Who... what line?"

"Nills Langthorp, the Mars colonist. His last message had the line Send no more."

Paolio waved his hand in the air. "Who knows? Many people have debated that over the last couple of years."

"I know, but what do you think it means?"

He sat down across from her and sipped his coffee with all the theater of a true connoisseur. "Most people think it meant send no more colonists. But I have another theory." He poked a finger in Jann's direction. "I think the message was cut off." He sat back.

"So you think there should be more to it?"

"Absolutely. I think what he was actually saying was send no more of that horrible Dutch coffee." He laughed.

Lu Chan stepped into the galley. "We'll be ready in ten for a preliminary mission brief."

"That gives me just enough time to show you how to use the espresso machine, Lu." Paolio jumped and grabbed a little cup from a storage unit.

"Paolio, show me later. I have to get ready for the brief."

"Nonsense, you have plenty of time."

Lu sighed. "Oh all right." She looked down at Jann. "Better let him show me so he doesn't keep going on about it." She rolled her eyes.

Lu and Paolio were close; they had a relaxed way with each other. Jann had considered it would be difficult for a relationship to survive the rigors of space travel. But they made it look easy. A part of her envied them. Paolio fussed and fiddled with the machine and a few minutes later Lu emerged from the huddle with a dainty little espresso. "Come on guys, time for the brief." She brought her coffee with her.

THE SIX ISA crew gathered around a large display table in the operations area of the HAB and waited for Lu to start the session. She tapped an icon and a map of the Jezero Crater radiated out across the table surface. She tapped again and the map rendered itself in three dimensions. It gave the illusion of hovering above the surface of the table. She rotated it.

"This is us here." Lu pointed to a red marker overlaid on a 3D rendering of the HAB. She zoomed in. "Over here is the lander and that's our fuel processing plant."

"Okay, let's see Colony One," said Commander Decker. The map zoomed out and they could now see most of the western side of the crater.

"That's Colony One, about two kilometers west, near the crater's edge." She rotated the map and zoomed in on the site. A wire frame 3D model ballooned out from the display table. "I can overlay this with our latest orbiter imagery to give us a better idea of what we can expect."

The Colony One site slowly rendered itself in photo-quality detail. It was a sizable facility comprised of a large biodome where the colonists had grown most of the food that sustained them. Radiating around this was a number of smaller domes and around these were dotted a series of interconnected modules, arranged like petals on a flower. These were the landers that each batch of six colonists arrived in.

"As you can see, the roof of this dome here has caved in, and the same with this one. We have major sand ingress here and here. Also several of these modules are damaged or missing completely." They looked at the model as it rotated slowly. It was more detailed than anything they had seen before.

"How can modules just disappear, could they have blown away?" said Jann.

"Impossible, the atmosphere is too thin for even the most vicious sandstorm to do that. The only explanation is they moved them or maybe they dismantled them for some other purpose," said Lu.

"These long humps in the sand are more grow areas, right?"

"One is. The other is soil processing for water reclamation and resource extraction—and it looks like that has also collapsed." Lu zoomed out from the main structure to take in more of the surrounding area.

"Over here, on the edge of the site is the main solar array field—looks about eighty percent intact. Here, up on the crater's edge is the plutonium reactor. We need to be very careful of this, in case it's fractured. The power cables run down along here and across here.

"I presume that's the last supply ship?" said Decker.

"Yes, still exactly where it landed, untouched for over three years."

In the months after contact was lost with Colony One, an unmanned ship was sent packed with emergency supplies, in the vain hope that some of the colonists might be still alive. It was still there where it landed, gathering dust—literally.

"I count six bodies, but none near the reactor or along the cable routes."

"I wonder why they're all scattered around like that?" Paolio waved a hand around the 3D map.

"If they went out during the sandstorm there would have been very poor visibility. They probably got disorientated. A bit like Malbec did when we arrived here," said the commander with a laugh. Jann said nothing.

"Lu can you zoom in a bit more on this body here?" said Paolio. The map model ballooned out and picked up on the prostrate form of a dead colonist. It lay flat on its back.

"I could be mistaken, but he, or she, looks to be missing an arm."

"Well the image at this detail is poor so it could just be a buildup of sand around the body obscuring the arm." Lu leaned to examine the image.

"I don't think so," said Paolio.

"Why?"

"Because... I think that's it over there." He pointed to an arm shaped smudge a few meters from the body.

The others looked at the forlorn figure with a mixture of fascination and horror.

"Well, we'll find out for sure soon enough." Commander Decker reached over and shut off the map. "Okay, listen up. I want all system checks done on all the equipment as soon as possible. Once everything is nominal we can proceed to the site. You all know what to do, this is what we trained for so lets get to it." He clapped his hands together.

"And Malbec..."

"Yes, commander?"

"I need you to stay sharp. I know you haven't had a lot of training but I still want you focused."

"Yes. Of course, commander."

~

"WHY DOES he give me such a hard time?" Jann and Lu were in full EVA suits, outside on the planet's surface, running diagnostic tests on the two utility rovers.

"He just wants to keep on top of the mission. Take my advice, don't take it personally." Lu disengaged the rover locking mechanisms to wake them up.

"Maybe you're right."

"I *am* right. You try too hard, Jann. No one's expecting you to be perfect at everything. Just keep your head down, stay focused and you'll be fine."

"I wish I had your confidence."

Lu stopped and looked over at her. "Believe me, underneath this elegant, swan-like exterior there's a lot of paddling going on." She laughed.

"Okay, I get it, head down, stay focused."

"Exactly... and chill out."

"And chill out." She nodded and smiled at Lu.

"That's the important bit."

That said, Jann was finding it difficult to concentrate on

the task at hand. In fact, both of them would get distracted, and stop and look around at the Martian landscape. It was the first time that Jann really had a chance to truly look at her surroundings. The trip from the lander to the HAB had been one of sheer terror, not a time for sightseeing.

"It's incredible, isn't it?" she said.

"Yes, truly awe inspiring." Lu was staring off into the distance. The topography of the crater basin was mainly flat with dips and valleys undulating across it. They could see Isidis Peak off to the east. To the west, the rim of the crater looped around the horizon. They stood there for quite some time, soaking in the vista.

After a while they turned back to their work. Lu hit a button on her remote control display and the first rover rolled out from its compartment onto the dusty soil. These were heavy-duty utility vehicles used for transporting equipment, supplies and samples. They were not designed for driving around in by crew. Just simple robotic mules, the space exploration equivalent of flatbed carts. Jann poked a button on her remote and the second rover rolled out. She drove it out a few meters from the base of the HAB and set to work doing a full systems test. Both rovers had robotic arms but one mule also had a drill for seismic research. The colonists had discovered cave systems in the area, so this rover was here to find and map these. It could drill down to a depth of several meters and deposit an explosive charge. When it detonated, the resultant shock wave would be analyzed and a detailed chart rendered of the subsurface.

They were also designed to be autonomous. You could load one up with all your gear, set a beacon on your EVA suit and the rover should follow along wherever you went—like a faithful donkey. Jann was now testing this; she walked away from the HAB and the rover dutifully followed.

However, the terrain around the HAB was hard and flat, easy ground for the rover. What she needed was something more rugged to truly put the machine through its paces. Jann looked out across the vast crater basin and marched off in search of more testing ground.

After the months of confinement onboard the Odyssey, on top of months of intensive training before that, she now felt a wave of exhilarating freedom wash over her. The vast plain stretched out as far as the eye could see: desolate, empty and inviting. She felt like a child again, wandering off across an expanse of old family farm. She moved with a steady, easy pace, soaking up her surroundings as she went, lost in her thoughts.

"Jann, where are you off to?" Lu's voice broke into her reverie.

"Oh... eh." She had to think for a moment to orientate herself. "I'm just testing the rover... taking it for a walk."

"You don't have to take it to the other side of the planet. Try and remember the focus part, Jann."

"Okay... yes. I'll head back." She took one last look out across the crater before turning around.

"Focus, I really need to keep focused."

3

COLONY ONE

It took most of that morning to get all the system checks complete. Once finished, Decker reported back to mission control, and by late morning they received a go to proceed with a preliminary reconnaissance of the derelict Colony One site. An air of excitement rippled through the crew as they suited up in the airlock.

"Comms check." Decker's voice squawked in Jann's helmet, followed by a ripple of verbal affirmations by the rest of the crew.

"Listen up. I want a tight line, no wandering off and no falling behind, Malbec. Understood?"

Jann nodded and they exited the airlock, stepping out onto the Martian surface. They wasted no time in loading up one of the rovers with the necessary equipment and, with final checks done, Decker gave the command to move out. The six crew of the ISA Mars mission marched off in the direction of the crater rim, the location of Colony One.

Reconnaissance imagery depicted the crater basin to be smooth and flat, but on the ground it varied widely. The terrain ahead undulated with dips and valleys, while underfoot it shifted from hard cracked regolith to soft sandy dunes. Rocks and boulders of varying size and composition were scattered across the entire site. Walking in one-third gravity took some getting used to and Jann, as usual, had difficulty keeping pace. It didn't help that she would get distracted by the landscape and slow down to take it all in. More than once Decker halted the procession just so she could catch up.

"Hey... check this out." Chief Engineer, Kevin Novack, looked down at the ground and toed some object in the dirt.

"What have you found?" said Annis.

"If I'm not mistaken, it looks like litter." He reached down, tugged the edge of a plastic bag buried in the soil and pulled it out. "A component wrapper of some kind." The others gathered around. They could just make out the faded Colony One Mars (COM) logo on the outside. Decker paid no attention to the artifact, he was busy scanning the horizon.

"There it is... over there," he pointed in the direction of a rock formation nestled in front of a low line of dunes. Through a dip in the line they could just make out the top of the biodome.

"Let's keep moving." He started off again.

Novack wasn't sure what to do with the wrapper. In the end he just let it fall out of his gloved hand and it drifted back down onto the sand. They moved off towards their destination.

After a while, it became apparent to them that the rock formation in the foreground was not natural. It seemed to have been constructed by someone, a colonist presumably. Annis was first there to investigate. "It looks like a small hut, crudely built with rocks, like an old stone wall." Annis paused, gently ran her hand over the stones and then continued with her commentary. "It's around two meters high and the same wide... with a domed roof. There's an opening on this side. I'm going in."

"Wait, Annis! It may be unstable, you shouldn't take any unnecessary risks just yet." Jann's voice squawked in the first officer's comm. Annis hesitated for a moment, looked over at Jann and then back at the hut. It was like she was considering a reply, but thought better of it and entered the stone hut regardless.

"There's a body in here... just sitting in the middle of the floor," she announced.

Jann was next over to peer inside, although she stood some way back, just in case her futile warning to Annis turned out to be prophetic.

A colonist in a full EVA suit sat cross-legged in the center of the small space, its head slumped down a little on to its chest. The nametag on the left breast read Bess Keilly. They all gathered around the strange alien mausoleum for a time, in silence, taking turns to peer in at the dead occupant.

"It's a beehive hut," said Kevin after a while. This seemed to snap them all out of it.

"What is?" said Annis.

"The little building here." He waved a hand over the hut.

"You mean for bees?" said Lu.

"No, not for bees—for monks," said Kevin. "There's a tiny remote island off the westernmost tip of Ireland—Skellig Michael it's called. A group of monks set up housekeeping on it back in the 6th century. They lived in huts built just like this one. They're called beehive huts because of the shape." He waved an arm around again. "The island was regarded as the most remote place in the known world."

"I don't get it, why would anyone build such a thing here?" said Lu.

"It's a sculpture, I suppose. A piece of art. It obviously has no useful purpose," offered Kevin.

"Well they did have a lot of time on their hands. Seems completely pointless to me," said Decker. "Okay, let's keep going."

They left the grim Celtic crypt and climbed up the back of a high dune. The sand was loose and their boots sank in as they progressed up its side. It made for tough going. Jann was last to crest the dune. She stopped at the peak and looked in awe as the entire Colony One site sprawled out before her.

"Wow, it looks way bigger than I imagined," she said. Jann could now see where some of the domes had caved in. Sand had also built up around the derelict site and it looked like Mars was reclaiming it, inch by inch, a little bit more with each passing year. It was like discovering the remains of some long lost alien civilization on a far off planet. And, in many respects, that‘s exactly what it was.

One by one, they descended the side of the low dune into the basin of the site and fanned out across its expanse. Jann felt like she was entering an abandoned mining town. Equipment strewn here and there, along with odd rock formations and sculptures of one kind or another. Most were in a state of collapse and partly covered in sand. On the far edge of the site, out past the solar array field, Jann could see the last supply lander, still sitting where it came down, untouched.

For a time they wandered aimlessly around the site in a kind of dazed wonder. Like how Howard Carter must have felt after entering the tomb of Tutankhamen.

"Found another body." Dr. Corelli's voice reverberated in

Jann's helmet. He was bending over the prostrate corpse of a dead colonist. It was lying face up, visor smashed, and was missing an arm just below the shoulder.

"It looks like a clean cut..." Paolio was examining the injury. "...done with something very sharp."

By now some of the other crew had gathered around. "Seems you were right, Doctor," said the commander. "The arm is over there." He pointed at the dismembered limb a few feet away.

"What the hell happened here?" said Annis.

"Well it wasn't the sandstorm, that for sure," said Jann.

"Obviously," replied Decker. "Okay, we need to stick with the program. I want everybody on heads-up. The commander thumbed a button on his suit sleeve. The others did the same. On her visor Jann could now see an illuminated three dimensional wire-frame overlay of the site. It followed the contours of the buildings as she moved, giving detailed information on each structure. There were also five flashing markers tracking each of the other crewmembers.

"Paolio, Lu, Jann, take a route around the northern perimeter of the structure. Myself, Annis and Kevin will explore the area on this side. We'll meet up over at the main airlock." He pointed off at a group of modules attached to the main Colony One dome. "Let's get to it."

"What about the mule?" said Jann.

"Just keep it tagged to you, we may need it on the other side."

"You're not planning on going inside the facility today, are you?" said Annis.

Decker considered this. "We'll see... after we do an inspection. It's a derelict site so it may be too dangerous. Anyway, let's get a move on."

They split up. Paolio took the lead and they walked over towards what remained of humanity's first ever planetary outpost. The structure was dominated by a massive bio-dome. Around this were the smaller domes, and around these were attached the crew landers and supply modules that the colonists and equipment arrived in. These were cylindrical, around five or so meters wide and the same tall. They each had two doors and some also had airlocks. They could be attached together and reconfigured into different arrangements. Somewhere on the far side of the structure were two long grow tunnels, partially buried in the sand. One of these had collapsed.

The first lander module they came to Jann's heads-up display identified as simply EVA/Maintenance, an entrance in and out of the base for work crews. A sand ramp had been built up to the height of the airlock entrance and the outer door was wide open. She walked up the ramp and peered inside. The inner door into the facility was sealed tight. The interior, having been exposed to the Martian weather, was covered in a thick buildup of sand and dust.

"Come and have a look at this." She waved her arm to signal Paolio and Lu. Inside the airlock, bolted to the floor, was a rudimentary windmill, fashioned from recycled materials. Its crude blades sat motionless in the still atmosphere.

"Weird. What do you think that was for?" said Paolio.

"Generating power, I think. Look there's a wire leading in through the door seal," Jann traced the cable with her gloved hand.

"But there's no wind."

"Not today, but during a sandstorm there would be plenty of wind. See the size of the vanes, big to catch as much as possible. They must have been desperate to generate more power," said Jann.

"Looks like it, although they wouldn't get very much from this. To generate any sort of meaningful power on Mars it would need to be massive." Lu was examining the motionless blades.

They moved away from the airlock and continued their circumnavigation of the facility perimeter. "Over here," said Paolio as he waved to the others. "It's an old rover."

A small, six wheeled machine was partly buried in sand. Two circular solar panels extended from its back, giving it the look of a winged insect. It was covered in grime. Jann wiped a hand over a panel to brush the dust off. She thought she saw a green LED flash momentarily and jumped back in fright. "Holy shit. I think it's still working."

"You okay?" said Paolio.

"Fine... just a bit jittery."

Lu laughed. "That rover hasn't functioned in years. It's totally dead, for sure."

As they moved away, Jann looked back at the little machine, half expecting it to awaken and crawl out of its sandy grave.

The three were now close to the base of the main biodome. It had a wall about two meters high made of a type of concrete produced in-situ from the local regolith. It was robotically manufactured and had been layered down by large industrial sized 3D printers. The upper dome structure consisted of a super-tough, semi-transparent membrane stretched over a lattice framework, its complex molecular structure engineered to provide radiation shielding. It was essentially the same material used in one of the many layers of the crews' EVA suits.

Jann walked up the edge of the wall where the sand had

built up, in the hope that she could see in. But so much grime had accumulated on the surface that it was impossible to make anything out.

They moved on towards one of the smaller domes where the roof had collapsed. The support members were bent and crumpled. Jann's augmented reality display overlaid a wire-frame of the last known facility configuration. On the readout there should have been three modules attached, tagged accommodation. But they were missing.

"See, the wall here has been sealed up. So they must have moved the modules," said Paolio.

"I wonder where are they?" said Jann.

"Recycled maybe, broken up and used inside for something."

As they worked their way around they could see several more modules were missing. On the far side of the facility, leading from the base of the biodome, the two long grow tunnels extended outward. These were partially covered in Martian soil. This was one of the oldest parts of the colony, built even before the first colonists arrived. They had been robotically constructed prior to human habitation so that the early settlers would have sufficient infrastructure to maximize their chances of survival.

Jann had considered simply walking over one in the hope that she would be high enough to get a glimpse through the main dome membrane, but thought better of it. The tunnel was probably fragile and one of them had already collapsed. Also the weight of the mule following along behind her might be too much for it. She instead walked around the tunnels. It was difficult to know where they ended as they seemed to just merge into the surrounding dunes. The crew gave them a wide berth nonetheless.

By the time they headed back to the main dome they could see Decker and the others approaching the cluster of four modules grouped together. A sand ramp led up to the main airlock. But unlike the others they had inspected, the door was shut tight.

"Malbec, bring that mule over here," said Decker. "Tell me we brought the laser cutters, Kevin."

"We did, why, what are you planning?" replied the engineering officer.

"A little breaking and entering."

Jann untagged the mule so it would stay put and not follow her around anymore. Kevin started to unload equipment cases.

"I don't think that will be necessary." Annis pulled the recessed handle on the airlock door and it swung open. She stepped through and examined the inner panel.

"That's odd."

"What is?" The commander was now beside her in the airlock.

"It's got power."

"Well that's possible, since the solar array field looks mostly undamaged."

"It's not just that... it looks like... well, it's pressurized inside."

"Let me see." The chief engineer was now examining the panel. He rubbed a layer of dust off the small screen and stood back in amazement. "I think you're right."

"All right," said Decker, "here's what we're going to do. Kevin, bring that cutting gear in here. We'll need to close the outer door before we can open the inner one. If we can't get it open, we'll cut it open. If we get stuck in here, we'll cut our way out. The rest of you wait outside until I give the all clear." He stopped for a moment, then looked at each of them in turn. “You all need to prepare yourselves for what we’ll find in here. There’s probably going to be a lot of dead bodies. It isn’t going to be pretty so be ready.”

They all nodded. Jann had not given this much thought. But now that the time had come, it was clear that it would be a hellish tableau that greeted them on the inside. She imagined the desperate colonists huddled together in some corner of the facility, eking out the last of their precious resources, all hope lost, waiting for death to come.

Decker, Annis and Kevin stepped inside the airlock and closed the outer door. Jann and the others could hear the conversation through their helmet comms. She looked over at Lu and Paolio. They exchanged a glance that spoke of excited apprehension.

“Outer door sealed, okay... let’s see if this works.” It was Kevin’s voice. “Look, it’s pressurizing, there must really be air in there, incredible. Sixty percent... eighty... hundred. All right, here goes... opening inner door.” There was a pause in the chief engineer’s commentary as he surveyed the interior. Jann, Lu and Paolio waited anxiously for him to resume.

“Looks like a storage area... boxes piled up on either side. Some old EVA suits... torn... parts missing... no helmets that I can see. Moving into the next section. Seems to be a common area... seating... tables. Wait a minute... that’s impossible!”

“What, what is?” said Lu.

“Eh... you guys better get in here and see this for yourselves,” said Decker.

4

EXPLORATION

Jann opened the exterior airlock door and stepped in, followed closely by Lu and Paolio, who shut the outer door behind him and spun the locking wheel. Jann hit the button to equalize pressure. It took a few anxious moments to complete the cycle and for the green alert light to illuminate. "Okay, here goes," she said, as she swung open the inner door. They passed through the airlock and Jann, Lu and Paolio stepped into Colony One.

They passed through the entrance into a room lined with broken and damaged EVA suits. They hung along the walls like abandoned marionettes. Ahead of them the area opened out and pale orange sunlight filtered down through the domed roof, illuminating a large circular space. It looked like a junkyard. Every available flat surface was covered with machines and components in varying states of disassembly. Balls of wire sprouted from containers and spooled out across the floor. Tubes and pipes snaked around the area in all directions. Yet, it was clear that a routine had been well worn into this apparent chaos.

They spotted the others just ahead.

"Over here," Kevin beckoned to them and pointed at something on one of the benches. "Have a look at this."

They gathered around and inspected the object that had so startled the commander. Resting on a plate, beside a small box of fresh fruit, an apple had been cut in two, a bite taken from one half. Kevin held the knife up and they could see the juice ruining down along the edge. "It's just been cut."

There was a stunned silence for a moment as the implications began to sink in. Jann reached down, picked up the partially eaten apple and held it up close to her visor so she could give it a better examination. It was fresh, no doubt about it.

"There's someone here, still alive. That's incredible," said Jann. "How is that possible, after all this time?" She put the apple back down on the bench.

By now, they were all looking around, expecting the ragged survivors to come through a door or emerge from some darkened alcove at any moment. Jann considered that the joy of the crew's arrival could be overwhelming for them. Like a group of deserted island castaways rescued after many years of isolation. So they waited with ever mounting anticipation—but no one showed.

"Where the hell are they?" said Annis.

"Maybe they're afraid?" ventured Kevin.

"Of what?"

No one had an answer.

"Okay, there's someone still alive here, that much is certain. So, if they won't come to us then we'll just have to go to them. We need to do a full search of this facility, every inch of it if necessary, starting with the biodome over there."

Decker pointed towards an open tunnel at the far end of the space. "Let's go." He marched off.

They picked their way through the junkyard detritus towards the entrance and passed into the low connecting tunnel. One by one, they entered into the biodome into a sea of verdant vegetation. Row upon row of food crops radiated out across the vast space. Densely packed grow-beds were built into racks stacked one on top of the other—three, sometimes four layers high. Tubes coiled around each bed bringing water and nutrients to the plants. A confusion of power lines and ducting arched overhead. Grow lights hung from beneath each row to augment the pale Martian sunlight. It was a machine for growing food. Everywhere was ordered and meticulously maintained, in complete contrast to the mayhem of the previous area.

"Wow, just look at this place, it's incredible," said Lu as the six ISA crew stood around in awe at the lush surroundings.

"We should split up," said the commander. "Paolio, Jann, take that side, and check out that long grow tunnel. But be careful, though. It may be structurally compromised. Kevin, Lu, you search along the opposite side, over there. Annis and I will take this central area. Let's see if we can find some life forms in here other than plants."

A PATH WOUND its way around the inside perimeter of the dome; Jann and Paolio followed it. Along the inner wall were stacked storage boxes of one kind or another. Jann opened one, it was full of some sort of biomass, and she wasn't sure what it was without testing.

"Potatoes," Paolio pointed at long neat rows of plants.

"And carrots." They walked through the rows for a while, identifying some as they went. "I recognize this," said Paolio. Jann looked at the leafy plant. "Is that what I think it is?" she said as she touched a leaf.

"Cannabis. Presumably it's legal on Mars," said Paolio.

Jann laughed. "I suppose the law is what you decide yourself up here. Looks like someone brought some seeds with them. They're healthy plants, so whoever is here is looking after them."

Paolio looked around. "So we're looking for a bunch of Martian stoners—wherever the hell they are."

"Come on, let's keep looking."

After a while it became evident to Jann that there were a great many plants she simply did not recognize. These, she suspected, were genetically engineered specifically for Colony One. Designed to produce food in the weak Martian sun. Plants that would never be allowed free reign on Earth, due to concerns over genetic contamination. But here, there were no such fears. As a biologist, she had followed the development of some of these new botanical species with avid interest. Colony One was a geneticist's playground, with a totally controlled eco-system, and not bound by the ethics of Earth. There really was no law on Mars but your own.

THEY ARRIVED at a point along the dome wall where it opened into one of the long buried tunnels. It had a wide airlock, but both doors were swung fully open.

Jann took a cautious step inside. It was wide, with dim overhead lighting. Two long rows of clear plastic water tanks receded into its depths. They could see that each one contained a different species of fish. The tanks all looked to be well stocked. The fish looked to be perfectly healthy.

Towards the back of the tunnel she found several low, shallow beds used for spawning.

"This is very impressive. It takes a lot of skill and knowledge to be able to do this," said Jann.

"I wonder if they're genetically engineered?" Paolio was leaning over a tank looking down at the swimming fish.

"That's a possibility. Although I didn't hear of it. Still, they were very secretive about what they were doing up here."

"If you're finished your sweep, meet us in the middle. There's something here you should see." Decker's voice echoed in Jann's helmet. She nodded over at Paolio and they both made for the rendezvous point in the middle of the dome.

"It's getting very hot in this suit." Jann was looking at the temperature readout on her helmet's biometric display. The EVA suit was designed to keep the occupant warm on the surface of Mars, where it could often be minus sixty. But in the hot and humid environment of the biodome the suit was having trouble maintaining a comfortable level. "We're going to have to get out of here soon."

"Yeah, I'm boiling up."

As they moved closer to the middle of the vast space, the neat rows of hydroponics gave way to an overgrown wilderness. The plants in this section had been let to run rampant. Yet here and there could be seen a deliberate planting structure. Someone designed it this way. Tall trees and grasses lined the path and, as they neared the center, branches began to hang down and form a tunnel. It was covered with trailing vines.

"It's like a tropical glasshouse in some botanic garden,"

said Jann, as she brushed her gloved hand along the hanging tendrils.

The path ended and they stepped out onto a large central dais. It was wide and flat. At the far end it sloped into a sizable pond, with a three meter high waterfall that sparkled and danced in the pale sunlight. The others were gathered around a hammock slung between two trees. Below it, on a low table, was a control interface of some kind. Kevin was down on one knee investigating.

"This is amazing," said Jann looking around.

"It's like Paradise Island," replied Paolio.

"Decker looked over at them. "Anything?"

"No, nothing. Just fish."

"Maybe they really *are* hiding from us," ventured Lu.

"Someone's here—somewhere." Decker was looking at a schematic of the facility on a small tablet screen.

"I'm burning up in this suit, we can't stay here much longer." Annis was also getting uncomfortable.

"Dammit, I don't want to report to mission control that the place is functioning and colonists are still alive but we can't find them," said Decker.

"We may have to. We need to get out of here and back to the HAB. We can do a better search tomorrow." Annis was moving off towards the airlock.

"Wait a minute." With that, Decker reached for the side of his helmet to flip open the visor.

"No... wait... don't do that. The air could be poisonous in here. We need to do some analysis first."

"It's fine, Paolio. Someone's alive in here so they must be breathing good air, right?

"You don't know that for sure."

Decker ignored him and popped his visor open. He held

his breath for a second or two and then took his first gulp of Colony One air. The others waited. He smiled, laughed and breathed again. Then he sniffed. "It smells like... like a forest."

Annis was next to pop her visor. She took a deep breath and then removed her helmet completely, shaking out her long hair. "Oh my god, that's better. I was beginning to feel like a hot dog in a water bath."

Kevin was next and soon they all had their helmets off. Jann was last to open her visor and breathe the fragrant air. Decker was right. It smelled of botanicals and biomass. It was strange that a colony outpost, on a far off planet, should have such a smell. It reminded Jann of an exotic garden.

Decker removed his gloves. "Okay, this gives us a lot more time to do a thorough search of the facility and find these people." He was back to consulting his screen.

"I don't think they want to be found," said Jann.

"That doesn't make any sense. Why not? They've just endured three and a half years isolated here with no communication," said Annis.

"Maybe they've gone insane—you know, and think we're a bunch of aliens invading the planet," offered Kevin.

Decker ignored these comments. "We still haven't searched any of the modules along these other sections. I suggest two of us stay here and keep an eye on the door into the dome. The rest of us will continue the search."

I'll stay here, if that's okay," said Lu.

"Fine, Kevin can keep you company. The rest of you... let's go, let's find these people."

There were a myriad of other modules connected to smaller domes, all grouped in different configurations. The first group they came to seemed to be used for refrigerated storage of some kind. Jann opened one of the large doors. "There's no point in that, Jann. We're not looking for a snowman." Decker laughed at his own joke. Then he stopped, gripped his abdomen and bent over with a low groan.

"Commander, what is it?" said Paolio.

He stood upright again. "It's nothing, just a bit dehydrated I think."

"Let me have a look at you."

Decker brushed him away. "I'm fine, it's nothing." With that he doubled over again clutching his stomach."

"You're not fine, let me see you." Paolio examined the commander as best he could. He felt his pulse and then put the back of his hand on Decker's forehead. "You're burning up. We need to get you back to the HAB—right now."

This time the commander didn't protest. He was leaning against the module wall, slowly sliding down onto the floor.

"Jann, give me a hand here." Paolio was throwing Decker's arm around his shoulder. Jann grabbed the other side and they helped him up.

"We need to go," said Paolio, as he and Jann helped Decker walk back to the entrance airlock.

"Lu, Kevin, you both better get out here," said Annis. There was no mistaking the note of urgency in her voice.

"What's happened?" said Lu when she saw them holding Decker up.

"The commander is not feeling well. Everyone put their helmets on—now. We're heading back to the HAB."

They carried Decker into the airlock. He was conscious but seemed to be having intermittent cramps and would double over in pain when they struck.

Once the crew were all back outside on the surface

Annis hit a button on her remote. The rover awoke and started across the site towards them. They bundled the commander into the back of the rover and started off. "We'd better hurry," said Paolio. The rover bumped and rocked over the Martian terrain as they all pushed hard for the HAB. Decker was bounced around and lapsed in and out of consciousness. Jann watched all this from her permanent place as last in line. No one spoke.

ONCE INSIDE THE HAB they got the commander out of his EVA suit and laid him on a bed in the tiny medical bay. He was now unconscious. Paolio shooed the others away and started his examination. The crew retreated into the operations area.

"Anyone else feel unwell?" Annis had assumed command now that Decker was non-operational, as she put it. Grunts and head shakes rippled around the crew as they eyed each other like a clandestine group seeking out a spy in their midst. They were all okay—for now. The crew sat in silence for a long time, waiting for the verdict from Paolio.

"So what the hell is it?" Annis was pacing; it was a habit of hers. The doctor had finished his examination and re-entered the operations area.

"I think it's possibly an allergic reaction. But he's stable now and I reckon he'll be okay, once it passes."

An audible sigh of relief emanated from the assembled crew.

"Do you think it was the air in the Colony?" Annis continued.

"I don't think so, since everyone else seems fine. But, it's not possible to know for sure without some further analysis.

Now, if you don't mind, I need a stiff coffee." He moved off to fire up the espresso machine.

"Everyone else is okay, aren't they?" Annis looked around at the rest of the crew. They all nodded. Yet Jann knew they were all thinking the same thing. "Only time will tell."

5

VANHOFF

Peter VanHoff, president of the Colony One Mars consortium, stood watching the snow fall from a window high up in his isolated Norwegian mansion. It swirled and danced under the garden lights, accumulating where it lay, like a soft duvet blanketing the earth. He turned away from the window and set about poking the log fire that was burning in the hearth. Sparks flared up with each thrust of the fire iron. He hung it back on its stand and sat himself in a high-backed leather armchair. Winter had thrust its first icy fingers into the landscape. He liked this time. The natural world slowed down, hibernated. He felt it resonated with his condition and held it in check.

Born with a rare genetic disorder akin to progeria, he aged at an accelerated rate. He was only thirty-eight, yet he looked fifty plus. Peter touched the back of his hand, the parchment skin, the genetically flawed epidermis—an ever-present reminder of his affliction. Was it improving? Was it getting worse? He couldn't tell. At least maintaining the status quo was better than succumbing to the inevitable entropy of his condition.

Yet what would have been a curse for some, Peter VanHoff turned into a crusade, dedicating himself to the genetic understanding of the aging process, becoming one of the foremost experts in the process. His research corporation made numerous early breakthroughs, resulting in lucrative patents and a considerable fortune for VanHoff. However, his greatest strides were made through the association with the Colony One Mars consortium, COM for short. This commercial partnership enabled his corporation to conduct research on Mars that simply wasn't ethical on earth.

His ruminations were interrupted by the chime of his holo-tab. The screen flickered with a muted illumination and an icon rotated above its surface. He had a call—Nagle Bagleir, vice president of COM. What could he want at this time of night? Several disaster scenarios ran through VanHoff's mind as he waved a hand across the screen. Nagle's avatar shimmered into existence in the air over the tablet's surface, and spoke.

"Extraordinary news, Peter. It looks as if Colony One is not as dead as we thought."

Peter sat bolt upright and fumbled with his glasses. There was a moment's silence as he considered this revelation. "What... alive... are you saying there are colonists still alive up there?"

"Not quite. But we've just got a report in from the ISA crew. A significant portion of the facility is still intact and functioning. It also looks like there are signs of survivors, but we have no confirmation on that just yet."

"After all this time—but this is impossible." The implications of the discovery began to filter through Peter

VanHoff's stunned brain. "What about the research lab? Is that still intact?"

"We don't know anything about the lab just yet. What we do know is it's going to be all over the news in less than an hour. The ISA have scheduled a press conference for 1:30am, your time."

"This is incredible." VanHoff stood up and began to pace. "If that lab is intact then there's a possibility that the research data still exists."

"My thoughts exactly."

Peter's voice became hushed. "We can't let that fall into the wrong hands."

"As in the ISA?"

"You know who I mean. Everything the ISA does is in the public domain. Anything they find up there can't be kept hidden."

"Well, it's a bit late for that now. You know as well as I do that after the collapse of the colony we had no option but to hand it all over to them. Otherwise we wouldn't be back up there now." Nagle's avatar shimmered as it spoke. "That said, we do have some contingencies on-site, Peter. But yes, I agree, we wouldn't want it becoming public."

"This is extraordinary. If that data still exists..." VanHoff didn't finish the sentence.

"There's another thing. It may be nothing, then again..."

"What?"

"One of the crew has become ill."

"Not our agent, I trust?"

"No, the ISA Commander, Decker."

"Is it the same symptoms as... you know?"

"Let's not jump to conclusions just yet. Like I said, it could be nothing."

There was a pause as VanHoff considered all this

information. Nagle continued. "In light of these developments, I suggest reconvening the board."

"Agreed, absolutely."

"You are of course aware that there will be certain members getting jittery with this news, Peter. You know who I'm talking about."

VanHoff grunted. "That research may be more significant to humanity than the discovery of alien life."

"Be that as it may. But we've been all working under the premise that it was dead and buried—forever. This changes everything."

VanHoff stopped pacing the floor. "You're right, Nagle, let's not be too hasty. Let's see how things develop. After all, we have our agent on site. That may prove to be a very wise decision after all."

"Yes, it may. I must sign off now; I need to alert the others. I'll keep you posted on the meeting." The avatar that was Nagle extinguished itself like a church candle in a draft.

Before Peter VanHoff took over control of COM, the original members were an eclectic mix of Mars enthusiasts, scientists and captains of industry that shared a common dream—to establish a human colony on Mars and lay the foundations for mankind as an interplanetary species. It had helped that most of them were newly minted tech billionaires. Yet, this in itself was not enough to launch a mission to the red planet. The complexities, and cost, of sending and returning humans had been such that no national space agency, at that time, could entertain it with any real vigor. NASA tried but its timelines kept being pushed out further and further. As one commentator put it, "We're ten years away from landing on Mars. And regardless of what decade you ask me this, we'll still be ten years away."

But COM had the advantage of being a private company, not bound by the politics of electoral consensus or the restraints of governmental budgets. They were also increasingly frustrated by the lack of progress in manned space exploration since the first moon landings. And so they conceived of a radical plan to establish a human colony on the red planet. Its success pivoted on one simple operational premise—remove the need to return. They would send humans to Mars, but they would not come back. The colonists would live out the rest of their natural lives looking up at Earth from 140 million miles away.

Of those early colonists, some said they were naive. Others said they were the embodiment of the human spirit. But many simply regarded them as crazy. Who in their right mind would go to Mars in the full knowledge that they could never return? Yet, potential colonists applied in their thousands and the stage was set for the greatest human adventure of all time.

In the early days, COM sought to fund these missions by turning the colonization of Mars into a reality TV show. They broadcast and streamed everything from the selection process and training, to the first liftoff and daily life on the red planet. It was a slow start but it proved to be an inspired move. As far as the viewers were concerned, it was people power writ large in the heavens, and boy did they love it. As ever more colonists made their way to Mars, their every word, every thought, every mundane activity was recorded, digitized, broadcast and analyzed by the masses back on earth. Everyone who watched these incredible events had an opinion, and not all of them were favorable. Yet, in the end, even the most strident critics of the Colony One Mars adventure eventually succumbed to reluctant admiration. There was no denying it was the dawn of a new era for humanity, an era where the zeitgeist reveled in the optimism for the future of the human race. Just think, if we the people could do this then there was nothing that we couldn't do.

For a long time this mood prevailed as Colony One grew and prospered. Until the mother of all sandstorms hit. It darkened the sky and blasted the colony for a full six months. Communication became sporadic in frequency and erratic in content. There were rumors of colonists suffering mental breakdown, going crazy even. Concern was building back on Earth, and as the weeks and months passed, this concern grew into fear. Fear that Colony One, and those who called it home, were being etched off the surface of the planet, one grain of sand at a time, like an hourglass running down.

Attempts at satellite imagery during this period were futile. So it was a full six months after the storm when the first high-resolution images of the site were released to the public. They showed devastation. Worse, bodies of several colonists could be seen lying around the facility. It was clear that Colony One had totally collapsed as a human outpost. That was three and a half years ago.

An hour after Peter VanHoff finished his call with Nagle Bagleir, the news of the discovery broke on an unsuspecting world. It was a media frenzy.

6

HAB

Jann couldn't sleep. She tossed and turned, and thumped her pillow a few times to try and beat some comfort into it. It didn't work. She lay on her back and stared at the roof of the HAB for a while, but there wasn't much to look at. The sleeping compartment was cramped, like all the others. Some would find it even a little claustrophobic, but that wasn't something she suffered from. Being an astronaut was not a job option for anyone who had a fear of enclosed spaces. She sat up. There was no point in forcing it. If she couldn't sleep she might as well get up and raid the galley for some comfort food, not that there was any. Unless you counted coffee, but it was a bit late for that. She still had hopes of a few hours sleep before taking on the trials of tomorrow.

She clambered out of bed and made her way to the access column, descending the ladder to the main deck below. In the dim light she could see Paolio sitting at the low galley table. He looked like he was reading.

"Jann, can't sleep?"

"No, I've given up, for the moment."

"Like an espresso?"

"God no. I'd be even more wired."

"This is a myth, I can drink coffee any time and still fall asleep."

"That's because you're Italian—anyway, you're still awake."

"Ha, yes... it's because I've not had enough coffee yet to put me to sleep." He laughed lightly.

Jann smiled. She nodded in the direction of the slumbering commander. "How is he?"

"Good, I'm just keeping an eye on him. But I think he'll be fine. His vitals have stabilized."

Jann took a juice and a small oat bar from a storage compartment and sat down across from the doctor. She sighed.

"So how are you doing, Jann?"

"Fine, no symptoms... none that I can tell anyway."

"I didn't mean physically. How are you doing up here?" he tapped the side of his skull with his finger.

She sat back in her seat and cocked her head to one side. "Are you trying to psychoanalyze me, Paolio?"

"Hey... just talking to a friend." He gave a lopsided grin. "So how are you coping?"

"So far so good. I've only fallen over once and I've managed not to get anyone killed, yet—so that's a plus."

Paolo didn't reply. Instead he gave Jann a long look. Jann stayed quiet for a moment, examining the drink in her hand. "Well... if you really must know, ever since landing on the surface, I feel like a bit of a spare part. Like I'm just getting in the way."

"I see." Paolio took off his glasses, folded them and tucked them in the top pocket of his shirt. He sat back. "And why is that?"

Jann smiled. "See, you *are* analyzing me."

"Well, I have a soft spot for you. And it's as good a time as any. Here we are, two doctors having a chat on the surface of Mars." He spread his arms out and smiled.

"You're the doctor, Paolio. I have a doctorate in biology; it's not quite the same thing."

"You're right, it isn't. And that makes you probably the most important 'spare part' on this mission—right now." He leaned over and pointed out in the direction of Colony One. "We've just uncovered a dome full of biology out there, where we didn't think anything was still alive. No one planned for this. They all thought it was dead. Now we've got a really big puzzle to solve and I think you are the one that's going to play a vital part in solving it." He sat back again.

Jann thought about this as she fingered her drink. She looked out the HAB window at the night sky. "Yeah, no one saw this coming. I really hope I'm up to the task. I feel like there's a lot of responsibility thrust on me, that I hadn't planned for."

"Yes, well, sometimes we choose for ourselves and sometimes fate chooses for us, Jann."

"Like me being on this mission in the first place. I chose to enter the training program but, if Macallester hadn't dropped out at the last minute, well... I wouldn't be here, would I?"

"And how do you feel about that?"

"Unworthy, I suppose... I mean they selected me because I fit a profile, not because I was fully trained for the mission —and now, I just don't know."

"It seems they picked the right person, then."

Jann laughed. "Ha... we'll see. But somehow I don't get

that impression from..." she didn't finish the sentence. She just sort of nodded at the sleeping commander."

"Ahhh... the Alphas."

"The what?"

"Alpha males, and females for that matter. It's not their job to like you, Jann. In fact they neither like nor dislike you. That's irrelevant to them."

"So you're saying I'm just being paranoid?"

"Is that the way you feel?"

Jann looked over at the canny doctor. She liked Paolio, felt comfortable around him. He was always there to talk to. Still, she felt he was keeping an eye on her. Maybe that was a good thing.

"Is that the way you think I feel?"

He laughed. "Ah... you're getting wise to my ways, playing me at my own game." He looked down, like he was thinking, and then slowly leaned in across the table and spoke to her in a precise tone. "What I'm saying, Jann, is do not underestimate yourself. And do not let your perceptions of what other people think cloud your judgment."

Jann let this resonate in her mind. "Well, I generally don't. I just wish that..." she sighed.

"What?"

"That the commander, and Annis, would give me a goddamn break."

"Ahhh... so there it is," he sat back.

"They have their job to do, they *are* alphas. In any successful group there's always the leader who charges ahead and whips everyone else in to shape. But they are seldom the smartest, no?" He touched a finger to the side of his nose. "The smart ones are the ones you never expect, they're the ones still alive when everyone else is dead."

"Like whoever is still in that colony."

"Yes, exactly." He sat still for a moment looking out the HAB window, not that anything could be seen. "They're hiding from us, don't trust us, probably."

"Maybe they have a good reason."

"Perhaps—odd though." He stood up and went over to the coffee machine. "Sure you don't want one?"

"Oh, what the heck, okay. Just a small one. Not going to get any sleep now anyway."

Paolio fiddled with the machine as it hissed and spluttered. He brought the coffee back over to the table and presented it to Jann with all the flourish of a seasoned waiter in a Michelin starred restaurant.

"Et voila, Madam."

Jann sipped the astringent brew for a while. "You know Paolio, I actually applied for the Colony One Mars program, back in the day."

"Really? I did not know that."

"Nobody does. You're the first person I've ever told—outside of COM."

"You kept that very quiet."

"Yeah, I had this romantic notion of being part of the great colonization experiment, being in the vanguard of humans as an inter-planetary species."

"Didn't work out too well for them. Nothing romantic about suffocating to death on an alien world. So, tell me, what happened?"

"I got accepted into the ISA astronaut program around the same time. Seemed like a much better option."

"And you never told them?"

"God no. Didn't want them to think I was a flake of some kind." She sat forward and took another sip of her coffee. "Sometimes, I think, in reality, it was me just copping out."

"What do you mean?"

"Well, let's face it, the possibility of me actually going to Mars by joining the ISA program was less than one percent. I knew that when I joined. I think it was just a way for me to dream but not actually commit."

"Well, here you are."

Jann looked around. "Yeah, be careful what you wish for. Because sometimes it might come true." She stood up. "I'm going to try and get some sleep. Big day tomorrow."

"For sure."

"Thanks... for the talk."

"My pleasure, Jann. Anytime. And remember, the difference between us and those colonists is we get to go home."

Jann turned around as she stepped on the plate elevator to ascend to the sleeping quarters. "Let's hope so, Paolio."

7

A NEW SOL

The discovery that the Colony One site was still functioning, at least technically, sent shock waves through ISA mission control back on Earth, not to mention the public media channels. Mars was now a twenty-four hour story with non-stop speculation and debate. All this was interspersed with an endless loop of archive footage of the early colonists, from liftoffs and interviews to daily life on the planet. The general consensus had always been that the colony had collapsed as a self-sustaining facility and that all fifty-four colonists were long dead. The brief for the current mission was simply one of survey and assessment of what was thought to be a derelict site. Not anymore, everything had changed.

Commander Decker was still laid out in sick bay, and still unconscious. The rest of the crew had assembled in the operations area to review the overnight report in from mission control. The audio-visual on the main screen was that of ISA Mission Director summarizing their assessment of the discovery and advising on next actions.

"The top priority, as we see it, is to find whoever is still alive in the colony. If we can do that then we can get answers to all the other questions such as how did they survive, and why they didn't try to contact Earth. This is now a mission imperative." The ISA director droned on. *"Regarding Commander Decker, we understand that he is still unwell and as a precaution we strongly advise not breathing the air in the facility. Stay in your EVA suits at all times when surveying the site..."*

"That's bullshit," said Annis. "Everyone else is okay. We could get much more done by not having to bake in an EVA suit inside that place," she shook her head and sighed.

"...we are currently working with the COM people to get you as much data as we can on the ecosystem within the colony. But you have to realize that nobody thought we would ever need this information, so it's taking time to put together. In the meantime, we have sent you all the current data we have. As mission biologist, please have Dr. Jann Malbec review this data, it may prove useful..."

Jann had already downloaded the information sent overnight by ISA onto her tablet. She was quickly scrolling through it as she listened to the director. She sipped her second coffee of the morning, trying to wake herself up. She only had a few hours sleep the night before and was feeling it. The others seemed to be all fresh and alert, even Paolio. He was obviously made of stronger stuff than her.

The ISA Director droned on for a while but they were all losing interest and started to discuss the plan before the report ended.

"Okay, it's pretty clear what the objective is. Find whoever is still alive in there." The first officer, Annis Romanov, had assumed command since Decker was still incapacitated. "That means a full and thorough sweep of the entire facility. Every module, every compartment, every nook and cranny. I want no stone unturned."

"What about the commander?" said Lu.

"I'll stay here and keep an eye on him," said Paolio. He was refilling his coffee cup.

"No, Paolio, we'll need you at the site in case we find someone and have to assess their health. Anyway, the commander is out of danger, you said so yourself." Annis was being adamant.

"I'll stay," said Jann. "I need to go through all the data sent from mission control, so it's as good a time as any to do it." In reality she was seriously considering going back to bed when they all left.

"Okay, that's settled. Malbec will stay. Everyone else get ready to EVA in one hour."

THROUGH THE SMALL window in the HAB, Jann watched as the four crew marched across the Martian surface towards Colony One. She sat there for a time, watching them trail off into the distance. She wondered how long it would take to find the elusive colonists? And if they were found, then what? After a while she turned away from the window, sat down in the operations area and started studying the Colony One eco-system in earnest.

It soon became obvious to Jann that much of the information sent by the ISA was old and out of date. It was data that anyone with an interest in the Colony One Mars program could find out with a quick internet search. However, there were a number of interesting schematics of the facility. The one that caught her eye was the layout of the research laboratory. She studied it for a while and realized that there were a number of anomalies that she couldn't quite put her finger on.

Eventually, Jann got up and went over to the display table in operations and activated the current 3D map of the site. She brought up the schematic and zoomed in on the location of the research lab. On the charts that ISA had sent, it was a single module attached near to the biodome, at the functioning side of the colony. She flipped on the hi-res satellite image to overlay it on the schematic. The image now showed an additional large dome with four modules attached. This meant it had been greatly expanded at some point. It was now a major part of the facility. Perhaps this accounted for some of the missing modules, but not all of them. "I wonder what they were up to in there?" She switched off the display and went back to the reports.

Most of these were about plants that had been genetically modified specifically for the colony. Included was a group of reports which dealt with bacteria, genetically modified (GM) bacteria. The biggest stumbling block to the colonization of Mars was not water or oxygen, but soil. It was not possible to grow food crops in the Martian regolith as it contained a high concentration of perchlorates. Toxic to humans. At high doses it could cause thyroid problems. So it needed to be decontaminated first and this magic feat was performed by a genetically engineered bacterium. They converted the perchlorate into useful compounds including oxygen, and in the process cleaned up the soil so it could be used for food production. This was just one of the many GM bacteria in use in Colony One. But most of this information Jann knew already. There was nothing new in any of this. After a while fatigue got the better of her. She folded her arms on the table and slumped her head down. Within a few minutes, she had dozed off.

. . .

Jann awoke some time later to the sound of a low moan. She lifted her head up and listened intently. She heard it again. "Decker?" She couldn't see him from where she was sitting. He had been afforded some privacy in the small sick bay by virtue of a curtain. Jann stood up from the table and cautiously walked over to look in on him.

He was flat on his back, still out. *It must be eighteen hours now*, she thought. His breathing was normal, as far a she could tell, but his face had a pained contorted tightness. She leaned over to get a better look at his skin. His eyes flashed open. Jann stepped back in shock—not far enough. The commander grabbed her wrist in a viselike grip. She tried to twist free but he was too strong. His eyes were wide and wild. Then he spoke—just one word—"Contamination." He released his grip, his eyes closed, and he was still again.

"Holy shit." Jann rubbed her wrist and moved back against the wall of the HAB. "Robert?" She ventured a tentative step forward. "Commander, are you okay?" No answer. He was out for the count again. *Jesus, what was that about?* she thought as she stood there for a moment and considered what to do. *Contact Paolio, let him know.*

She hurried quietly back into the operations area, all the time trying to rub some feeling back into her wrist and keeping one eye on the commander. He didn't move again. She sat down at the communications desk and started thinking of what she was going to say, and how best to phrase it. She didn't want to sound like a frightened idiot. "Focus," she said to herself as she leaned into the desk to press the transmit button. She caught her reflection in the blank screen in front of her and thought she saw some other movement. She spun around, Decker was standing right behind her.

"Robert, you're awake."

He didn't reply, he had a vacant, glazed look in his eyes. He seemed confused as to where he was. He kept looking this way and that.

"Are you okay?"

"Contamination."

"What?" Jann was now backing away and putting some distance between herself and the commander—just in case. He advanced toward her. "I must get rid of this contamination."

"What are you talking about, what contamination?" Jann hadn't noticed at first but now she could see that he was carrying a heavy metal bar of some kind. He raised it over his head. Jann backed up, pressing herself against the HAB wall. "Robert, you're scaring the shit out of me. Put that down, put it down NOW!" She drove some authority into her voice and for a moment Decker stopped, like he was considering the situation. He looked at the tool briefly as if wondering what it was doing in his hand. Then he sprung forward and smashed it down, aiming for Jann's head. But she was too quick for him and darted out of the way as it clanged off the HAB wall.

"Robert... Christ, what are you doing?"

"You are a contaminant that must be eradicated."

Jann slid along the wall to put more space between them and realized she was beside the airlock door. She opened it and dashed inside. But as she tried to shut the door the commander managed to get his arm inside, she couldn't close it. She pulled with all her might. Decker's arm swung about wildly and tried to grab her. It was no good. She couldn't get it closed—there was only one thing for it. She pushed open the door and swiveled a kick into Decker's stomach. He stumbled back and the bar fell out of his hand. She slammed the door shut and locked it.

Jann backed into a corner of the airlock. Her breathing was heavy. Adrenaline coursed through her body. She had never kicked anything other than a punching bag in her whole life. Part of her was concerned that she might have hurt the commander. No sound traveled through the airlock door. "Oh shit, what if I've injured him?" She had visions of Decker lying on the HAB floor, blood pouring from a head wound or some other injury he may have sustained as he fell. Still no sound.

Her breathing slowed and eventually she moved over to peer through the little window in the airlock door into the HAB. There was no sign of the commander. "Shit, what do I do now?" She could go back in and try to contain the deranged Decker. She could wait it out here until the crew returned, but that would be many hours from now. Or she could get out now—and run.

Jann hurriedly got into her EVA suit and started to depressurize the airlock. Before the sequence had completed, the commander's face appeared on the other side of the window. Jann was momentarily relieved that he was okay, before he started shouting. She couldn't hear. It looked like he was mouthing 'contamination.' Then he started bashing the door, over and over again. She could feel the force vibrating through the entire HAB.

"Come on... come on." The status light on the airlock finally illuminated green. Jann opened the outer door and jumped onto the planet's surface. She ran as fast as it was possible to run in a bulky EVA suit in one-third gravity. It wasn't beautiful, but it was probably a record.

She was quite a distance from the HAB when she

realized she should have jammed something in the outer door so the commander couldn't get out. Once the airlock was repressurized, the door to the HAB would unlock. Would he come after her? Too late, she was not going back now. She kept on running.

8

JUST THE FEELING

The four ISA crew, led by Annis Romanov, had spent a number of hours investigating the deserted Colony One facility, searching systematically, ticking off areas as they went. Here and there lay the scattered evidence of recent activity: crumpled clothing, scraps from a half-eaten meal, food in the process of being stored—but no colonists. They also discovered areas that were not in use at all: sealed off, closed up, shut down. This was not surprising considering it was a facility designed for a hundred souls that now sustained just a few—somewhere.

Yet, their search was not completely in vain. It did pull back a veil on the mysterious Colony One survivors. It was evident that they were skilled at engineering. The crew found many areas with equipment being repaired or recycled, or in the process of being fashioned into something else.

After two hours of methodical investigation they reconvened in an area inside a small dome that looked to be a common room of some kind. It had worn and tattered seating. Crude drawings depicting Martian landscapes adorned the walls. It also had strange homemade furnishings and lighting that gave it a kind of scrapyard chic. It had the feeling of someone's home. But that someone had vanished, all that remained now was the feeling.

"There must be more to this base, a hidden section perhaps. Maybe some of the derelict areas are still functioning?" Annis had long given up on keeping herself cocooned inside an EVA suit, as had the others. They had become too hot and uncomfortable after the first half an hour inside the colony. So, one by one, they stripped off the bulky EVA suits down to basic flight-suit clothing.

"We've been everywhere, there's nowhere else to look. Nowhere that's got life support, that is." Lu sat down on one of the tatty armchairs. "It's obvious, they simply don't want to be found."

"But why? It doesn't make any sense. You'd think they would be jumping for joy at the prospect of being found alive after all this time." Paolio had joined her on another armchair. "Maybe they've been hiding for the last three years," he continued.

"What do you mean?" Annis was pacing.

"Think about it. The colony is presumed dead after the sandstorm, no message, no communication, not even an SOS scrawled in the sand outside, nothing. But someone is still alive, still living here—somewhere. Do you not think that's just a little weird?"

"And what about the others? There were... what... fifty-four colonists alive up here before the storm. There are six outside," ventured Lu.

"Seven. You forgot the one in the beehive hut," Kevin corrected.

"Okay seven. Then there's one, maybe two, hiding out

here somewhere so that makes forty odd unaccounted for. No bodies, no EVA suits, so where are they?"

"Maybe they're compost, you know... recycled as plant food," said Kevin.

He was just about to sink his teeth into a colony apple when he stopped and thought better of it.

"All right, let's split up and see if we can find some better clues as to who's here. Paolio, take the medlab, Lu take the galley and accommodation modules. Kevin, I want you in the operations room and I'll do another sweep around the biodome. We'll meet back here in an hour."

"So what are we looking for this time?" Lu reluctantly got up from the armchair.

"Anything that will give us an idea of who's still here—and where they might be. Make a note of any computer terminals you come across. We can do a more forensic analysis later."

They all nodded and slowly wandered off to their appointed tasks.

THIS WAS Paolio's second time examining the medlab. The colony's sickbay, so to speak. It consisted of two connected modules, one of which was shut down, its door control panel dead. Conserving power, he assumed. He didn't find anything the first time so he was not expecting anything this time around. Mostly, he spent his time opening compartments and detailing the contents. It was well equipped and reasonably stocked with supplies of antibiotics, painkillers and a host of other medicines.

It was very quiet, dimly lit, and just a little creepy. Every now and again some machine deep within the bowels of the colony would start up and Paolio would get a jolt. On more than one occasion, he could feel his heart race as some eerie feeling got the better of his rationality.

"Anything?"

He jumped. "Jesus Lu, don't sneak up on me like that."

"Sorry, didn't mean to give you a fright."

"Nothing here. Weird isn't it? It's like the Mary Celeste."

"What's that?"

"It was the name of an old sailing ship found abandoned off the Azores, back in the late eighteen hundreds."

"Never heard of it," replied Lu.

"The thing is, when they boarded the vessel it was completely deserted. But there were plates on the galley table, like someone had just eaten. Yet, they searched it top to bottom and found no one. It's still a mystery to this day."

"I see what you mean."

"Anyway, I thought you were supposed to be searching the galley?"

"Eh... just didn't want to be on my own."

"I know how you feel."

"Funny, isn't it? We spent all those months cooped up on the Odyssey, getting in each other's space and now... well I get freaked out if I'm alone," she moved closer to Paolio.

"It's perfectly natural to get a bit freaked out in this place." He waved an arm around. Lu came closer still and started to shake. Paolio embraced her. "Hey, it's okay." She held him tight and he could feel her heart beat against his chest. She tipped her head back, gave him a long look and then kissed him.

"Paolio." The voice of First Officer Annis Romanov squawked in his headset. *"I just got a message from the commander, he's awake. But we have a problem."*

"Shit." Paolio pulled his head away.

"What is it?" said Lu.

"It's Annis." He tapped his earpiece. "Decker is awake."

"Can't you just ignore it?"

"No, I can't. There's a problem." He pressed his earpiece again. "Annis, yes. How is he?"

"He's fine, a slight headache, that's all. But it seems Malbec has gone AWOL."

"Jann? What happened?"

"He says when he woke up the HAB was deserted, didn't know what was going on. I explained to him we left Malbec there to keep an eye on things, but she's gone and her EVA suit's gone too. You better go talk to him—and meet us in the common room right away."

"Okay."

"What is it?" Lu looked anxious.

"Jann's gone missing. Come on, Annis wants us in the common room." Paolio tapped his earpiece again, but this time to contact Decker.

"Commander, this is Dr. Corelli."

"Doctor, go ahead."

"How are you feeling?"

"Fine, feel great actually. But I got a bit of a scare when there was no one here."

"Where's Dr. Malbec?"

"No idea, the HAB was empty when I woke up. Look, I'm heading over to the colony. I'll talk to you there."

"Are you sure you're physically up to it?"

"Yes, fine. We need to find Malbec, though."

"Okay, we'll see you here." Paolio was concerned for Jann. She didn't strike him from their conversation the previous night as someone ready to abdicate responsibility. Then again, he wasn't sure he knew what the hell was going on anymore.

. . .

THE OTHERS HAD ASSEMBLED in the common room by the time Paolio and Lu arrived.

"I knew she wasn't ready for this mission. I don't know why they picked her in the first place, she's a liability." Annis was waving her hands in the air, pacing up and down.

"Have you tried to contact her? If she's gone EVA she should have her comms on."

"Tried that, no joy, nothing."

"The commander is on his way," said Paolio. "Let's just stay calm and try to find her."

They all turned as they heard a sound from the airlock; it was depressurizing. "Decker?" said Kevin.

"No, he was just leaving the HAB, it's too soon," said Paolio.

"Maybe it's a colonist?" said Lu.

They looked from one to the other and waited. The outer door opened and someone entered, the door closed and the airlock began to pressurize again. The green alert flashed, the door swung open and out stepped Jann Malbec. She collapsed to her knees on the floor. Paolio rushed over and helped her remove her helmet. She was sweating and breathing hard. "Jann, what the hell is going on?" She struggled to get her breathing under control as she spoke.

"The commander, he's gone crazy, attacked me with a metal bar or something, tried to bash my head in, I had to escape, run, talking crazy shit, contamination." She put her head in her hands and shook. They looked blankly at her. Annis knelt down beside her putting her hand on Jann's shoulder. "We've just been talking to Decker and he's perfectly okay, nothing crazy about him."

Jann's eyes widened and she backed away from Annis. "No, seriously, he's crazy, dangerous."

"He didn't sound that way to me, Jann," said Paolio. "What the hell happened in the HAB?"

"I told you."

"Tell us again, from the top."

Jann regained some composure. "He woke up suddenly, grabbed my wrist and said something about 'contamination,' then conked out again. I went over to the comms desk to call you and he was standing behind me, looking crazy. Then he attacked me, with a metal bar, I think. I barricaded myself in the airlock. He was trying to bash the door down so I got into my EVA suit and ran here. That's it."

Annis stood up. "Hmmm, well he sounded totally rational to me. He's on his way over now."

"What? No, you can't let him in, no way."

"Calm down, don't get hysterical, get a grip," said Annis.

Jann stood up with the help of Paolio and Lu. She looked at him, pleading. "I'm not going crazy, it happened like I said."

"It's okay, Jann, no one's saying you're crazy."

The airlock light flashed red, it was depressurizing again. Decker had arrived. Jann moved away from the entrance and behind a workbench. "Paolio, stay with her, keep her calm, don't let her go crazy."

"I'm not goddamn crazy."

He moved over to where Jann was standing and watched her closely. "Just stay cool, Jann."

The door opened and the commander walked in. He took off his helmet and looked over at Jann. "So you showed up finally. Where did you get to?"

Jann said nothing. She just stood wide eyed.

"How are you feeling Robert?" said Paolio.

"Fine, although I'd be better if I knew what the hell was going on."

"What do you remember?"

"I remember waking up alone." He walked towards Jann. "Where did you get to, you were supposed to be keeping an eye on me."

Jann backed up. "Don't come near me... stay away." She grabbed a knife off the workbench.

"Woah... easy now Malbec, put that down, we don't want anybody getting hurt."

"Just stay away."

Paolio moved over to where he left his doctor's bag beside the airlock entrance. From it he took a syringe with 5cc of cyclophromazine. It was small enough to conceal in his hand. He moved back towards Jann, and while she was distracted fending off the commander, he slipped in behind her and jabbed her in the neck. Paolio grabbed her around the waist as she collapsed, unconscious.

"Jesus Christ, she's gone nuts, this is all we need," said Annis.

"Can someone please tell me what the hell is going on?"

"Lu, help me get her into the medlab." Between them they carried her in and laid her on the bed. Paolio checked her vitals. "She'll be out for a few hours."

"What happened to her?" said Lu as she brushed the hair from Jann's face.

"I don't know, I really don't," he shook his head a few times.

Once he was satisfied that she was okay, they returned to the common room. Annis was in the process of explaining to Decker what had happened.

"It makes no sense," said Decker. He looked over at Paolio. "What do you think?" Paolio didn't know what to think. He was glad that the commander seemed well again but now this breakdown of Jann's was a major concern. "She'll be out for a few hours. I can try and make an assessment of her mental health once she wakes up. But even if she seems fine we'll have to keep a very close eye on her."

"I'll not have her mess up this mission, it's too important. Christ, this is all we need." He was rubbing his head. "Speaking of which, have you found anything?"

"Nothing, at least no colonists. We've searched everywhere we could. We found lots of evidence of recent activity, by at least one person. But where they are is still a mystery," said Annis.

"There are still quite a number of areas in the colony that are intact but shut down. So maybe that's the next place to look," offered Kevin.

"Show me where we've searched so far and what's left."

"Sure." Kevin produced a tablet and laid it flat on the common room table. He activated it and a 3D schematic of the Colony One site ballooned out across the table surface. "All these areas here in green we've searched. The ones in red I've identified as derelict. Probably structurally dangerous. We'll need to be careful entering any of those areas. All these areas here are offline but still intact, as far as I can tell. They're shut down, no power or life support."

"What's this area here, looks pretty big." Decker was pointing to a small dome with a number of modules attached at the other end of the main biodome.

"Research lab."

"Might be worth getting in there and having a look around."

"Tricky."

"Why's that?"

"There's no outer airlock so we can't just EVA in there. We'd have to power it up and pressurize it first."

"I see." The commander rubbed his head again. "Annis, what does mission control know?"

"That the place is not dead and that you are feeling ill."

"You need to send them an update on what we've found so far. And let them know I'm fine now. We'll keep quiet about Malbec for the moment, okay? I don't want them getting too concerned."

"Will do."

He breathed a sigh and rubbed his head again.

"Are you all right?" said Paolio.

"Yeah, just a bit of a headache."

"I'll get you something for it."

"That would be great, thanks."

"So what's our next move here?" said Kevin.

The commander thought about this for a moment. "We assess the infrastructure, find out what's working, how it works and what resources are available. We'll do a complete inventory on all Colony One systems."

"That's probably going to take weeks to do."

"Well you guys better get to it. Me, I'm actually going to lie down for a little while, I feel a bit woozy."

"You're still not a hundred percent, Robert. Come, I'll show you where there's an accommodation pod, you can rest there," said Annis.

"I'm just going to check on Jann," said Paolio. "Lu, do you want to join me?"

"Eh... I need to get back to checking the galley again." She gave a little shrug of her shoulders.

"Okay." Paolio headed back into the medlab and looked down at the unconscious figure of Dr. Jann Malbec. "Well Jann, you sure as hell know how to ruin a person's day."

9

COM

Peter VanHoff scanned the report from First Officer Annis Romanov. It was brief, yet interesting in that it was from her and not Commander Decker. Nonetheless, it seemed that he had recovered from his mystery illness, which was a major relief. Still, Peter could not help feeling a certain unease that the commander was not fully operational, so to speak. His uneasiness stemmed from memories of the mayhem that preceded the demise of Colony One. The final communications from the stricken outpost spoke of a deep psychosis affecting a number of colonists. Ever since, the question in many people's minds had been: was it this that caused the destruction of Colony One and not the sandstorm? The question, of course, was still unanswered.

He put the report aside and pulled up the site schematic that the first officer had sent. A good deal of Colony One was still intact, including the research lab. This was a section of the facility that he was acutely interested in. Nevertheless, if the lab were to be brought back online, how much of the scientific data would realistically still be viable? It was a question that greatly occupied VanHoff.

Shortly before Colony One went dark, the scientists working there hinted at a major genetic breakthrough. But the data was never transmitted as the colony started to come apart at the seams. So he had all but given up on acquiring this information. Now though, it seemed he had been given a second chance. But it was a double edged sword, he needed to be careful. What went on in that research lab was for COM eyes only. It would be very damaging for them should it become public knowledge.

VanHoff looked at his watch, time for the board to convene. Who could he trust? Initially he had considered that Rick Mannersman might be a problem. But the media frenzy surrounding the discovery was keeping him very busy—at the center of attention. The fact that Mannersman was motivated simply by greed and self-aggrandizement meant he was relatively easy to manipulate, as long as he was distracted. Most of the others were inconsequential and easy to handle. But could they be relied on if tough decisions were required?

Leon Maximus, on the other hand, Peter admired. He was motivated by a seemingly sincere desire to advance human civilization. To make it an interplanetary species. To establish a Planet B, as he liked to call it. He was a rare breed indeed. None of this would have been possible if were not for him and his genius. His company had developed the rocket technology to get the first colonists to Mars. Still, it was a slow tedious process. It was an eight month trip and, with the way the planets orbited each other, a tight two year launch window.

In the end, it was Leon's near maniacal insistence on the research and development of an exotic device known as an

EM Drive that changed the numbers. A bizarre contraption that defied normal engineering convention. As far as Peter understood, it was essentially a microwave in a cone shaped box. How it worked nobody could really explain to him without delving in to the realms of quantum physics. Ultimately, it was an extraordinary breakthrough. Here was a simple engine, with no moving parts, not subjected to enormous forces, that worked simply by electricity. With enough solar panels strapped to your spaceship you could have thrust on tap any time you wanted. Swap the solar panels with a small nuclear reactor and all of a sudden space became a much smaller place.

This radically changed the nature of a mission to Mars and ultimately the economics of Colony One. The journey time went from over eight months to just under seventy days. Now more missions could be sent: more supplies, more equipment, more colonists. And, coupled with Leon's inspired reusable main stage design, it came in at a fraction of the initial cost.

Nonetheless, after a few short years and twenty odd colonists later, the excitement was beginning to fade and COM was finding it hard to generate revenue from the media rights alone. This was when Peter VanHoff entered the scene. But he was not interested in some grand vision for humanity. That, he left to the dreamers. No, it was his passion for genetic research and his quest to crack the complex process of aging that involved him in the COM consortium. He realized early on that there were things one could do on Mars that were simply not ethically possible on Earth. Particularly in the area of xeno-combinant genetic research and genome manipulation. And, as a bonus, there were a great many corporations willing to pay good money for the ability to do this, far from the prying eyes of legal scrutiny. So he convinced Leon Maximus and the others in COM of the opportunity for building such a biotech research facility. With failing media revenues due to faltering public interest, they had really no other option. They bought into it and Peter VanHoff took effective control of COM.

HE PUT THE REPORT AWAY, stood and looked out across the snow capped mountains in the distance. His mind considered the implications of this report from Romanov. It was full with possibility, uncertainty and not a little danger. They would need to tread carefully. He shook his head and walked back into his study and touched the controls on the holo-tablet. A small illuminated screen materialized in midair, less than an arm's reach in front of him. It moved as he moved. He reached out and touched a virtual icon on the screen. Several avatar symbols appeared and floated in the space before him, one for each member of the board. They arrayed themselves around Peter VanHoff's field of vision like dead relatives in a Victorian séance. The meeting was about to begin.

"Good evening gentlemen." There was a collective murmuring of greetings and acknowledgments as the ghostly figures moved and shifted in the space before him. Peter VanHoff continued. "You all know by now that the crew of the ISA Mars mission have successfully landed on the planet's surface—and that the colony is not as dead as we thought." This was met with various nods and grunts from the avatars representing the board members of the Colony One Mars consortium.

"To recap, the ISA crew entered the colony facility to discover that it is still functioning and there is possibly at least one survivor. To facilitate a more comprehensive search they removed their helmets and operated wholly within the colony environment. A short while later Commander Decker became ill."

"What? Why did nobody warn them?" it was Rick Mannersman who voiced this concern.

Peter ignored it and continued. "According to First Officer Annis Romanov's latest report the commander has made a full recovery."

"But what if it's happening again?"

"We don't know that yet, so let's just stick to the facts," insisted Peter.

"What about the research lab?"

"Ah, the lab, yes. Well it's still intact, although not online." With that, there was a general air of excitement within the group.

"I'm sure you'll appreciate that there is eh... sensitive information in that laboratory that is not for public consumption."

"I knew we shouldn't have got into bed with ISA. If they were to get an inkling of the research that went on up there then there would be all hell to pay," said Mannersman. His avatar bobbed and bristled as he spoke.

"Well they're not."

"How can you be so sure?"

"Because we have our own agent on site, remember? So they can see to it that it does not fall into the wrong hands. Furthermore, we now have an incredible opportunity to return this research to Earth."

The avatars shifted and murmured. They were all salivating at this prospect.

"Do you really think it still exists?"

"If the information we have received is correct then there

is every possibility that the... eh, Analogue is intact." It was Nagle who responded. As the COM member assigned to ISA mission control he was in a unique position to validate all expedition data.

"We are moving our own satellite back into position over the Colony One site and running full communications diagnostics on it as we speak. Assuming our agent performs their duties then we will soon know if what we seek is indeed viable."

"I trust I don't need to remind you all of what this will mean to the future of humanity, if we succeed." Peter decided to up the ante.

"You're all forgetting one major issue. What if it's happening again? What if the unfortunate Commander Decker is succumbing to the same malaise that brought the colony down in the first place?" said Mannersman.

"You don't know that for sure."

"You're right, I don't. But if it *is* happening again, then this may be the last we hear from the crew of the ISA Mars mission."

10

MEDLAB

Paolio wandered into the medlab to check on Jann. What happened to her? he wondered. What made her flip like that? There had been no indication the previous night. She was a little anxious perhaps—but then again, that was understandable considering the circumstances. He thought back to the time they spent on the Odyssey en route to Mars. There had been no sign then either, at least none that he could discern. Nothing to indicate Malbec's potential mental frailty.

Another issue was the commander. Paolio was still not convinced that Decker had fully recovered, although outwardly he seemed remarkably alert. He had given him something for the headache and he was now resting in one of the accommodation modules. This concerned the doctor, considering the commander had just spent eighteen hours asleep.

As for the others, Lu had gone back to doing a search of the galley and accommodation modules. He would check in on her later. Kevin, the mission engineer, had ensconced himself in the operations area, a section of Colony One given over to control systems. He was busy trying to get a sense of how the colony functioned: power supply, environmental controls, life support. Romanov had gone off to file a report to mission control. They would be pleased to hear that the commander was on the mend. But they were still no further along in the search for the survivors. With Jann now a concern, it seemed to Paolio that bit by bit, little by little, the mission was losing its way.

HE SPENT some time checking Jann's vitals. She looked comfortable enough even though she was still encased in her EVA suit. Paolio had considered stripping it off and taking her out of it, he didn't want her to overheat. But she would be awake in a while so he just removed her boots and gloves, pushed a pillow under her head, and left it at that. He stood back from his handiwork and surveyed the rest of the medlab module. It was in fact two modules connected together. But only one of them was operational. He walked to the far end and checked the door into the disused section. The control panel was dead. He fiddled with it for a while but it was pretty obvious it was never going to open, not without power. There were quite a number of these areas in the colony: shut down, offline, disused. They would soon have to start investigating them. But not before they had a better understanding of the colony control systems.

Along one wall of the medlab were a number of terminals. Paolio swiped a hand over one of the control interfaces—no joy. He hunted around the workbench looking for a power source. Eventually he found a bank of switches that looked like they might control power. He flicked one marked 'terminals' and the area illuminated followed by a number of beeps. He waved his hand over the control interface again and this time it came to life and rendered a 3D animated COM logo just above its surface. He touched the logo and it split up into a myriad of icons for programs and files. What he really wanted to find were medical records. Something to shed a little more light on the colonists that lived here. It might give him an idea of what happened to them in those last desperate days.

Paolio had always been of the opinion that there was more to the demise of Colony One than just the sandstorm. The last communication from Nills Langthorp had intimated at deeper psychological issues affecting the colonists. Perhaps this had hindered their ability to maintain sustainable life support? Yet it was never discussed within COM, or the ISA for that matter. Any mention of this line of enquiry was quickly dismissed as unnecessary speculation. Nevertheless, it had always been in the back of his mind. He wondered if this was the same illness that had afflicted the commander. He dared not mention his concerns to the others, in case he raised the paranoia levels unnecessarily.

Then there was Jann. Was she also affected? He put that thought out of his mind and went back to studying the terminal. He touched on various icons looking for anything that might help shed some light on the mysteries of Colony One. After a short time he finally came to a gallery of colonists. There was a headshot for each, tagged with a cryptic alphanumeric reference. He was about to touch one to open it when he heard a series of screams emanating from deep within the bowels of the colony. He jumped up from the terminal. "Lu!"

Paolio ran out of the medlab heading for the galley to check on Lu. He frantically searched to no avail. "Lu?" he shouted. No answer. "Damn where is she?" He moved out of the galley and into the main workshop. “Lu, are you there?” Still no answer. He turned around and about five meters behind him stood Commander Decker. He had a vacant expression and seemed to be looking up somewhere towards the ceiling. Paolio took a tentative step forward. “Commander, are you okay? Did you hear that scream, have you seen Lu?” Decker didn't reply. He fixed his gaze on Paolio with an intense, questioning look. Paolio was about to move towards the commander when he realized Decker was holding a long steel bar. Its end was covered in blood, some of which was dripping onto the floor. “Jesus, Robert. What’s going on?”

Decker slowly raised the bar. Paolio backed away. Decker lunged. He was too quick for the doctor and struck him square across the shoulder—with force. “Contamination. It must be eradicated.”

Paolio heard his collarbone snap as white-hot pain rifled up his neck and into his brain. The second blow connected with the side of Paolio's head. He lost his balance and went flying over a pile of workshop junk, landing hard on the floor and banging into the side of a tall rack. It rocked and tottered and finally came crashing down on top of his leg. He heard the snap and more pain than Paolio had ever known in his life coursed through his body. He cursed and screamed and looked around to try and see where Decker was. But the area was now dark. “Has the power gone?” Paolio couldn’t move, he waited for Decker to come and attack him again—but he didn't. Had he moved off somewhere else? It was deathly quiet.

Paolio tried to get some control of his mind and calm himself down. His body screamed with pain, his head throbbed and his vision was blurry. With his good arm, he managed to drag himself backwards into a corner and hide.

It was all he could do. It was very dark. He was sure the power must be out. Then he heard it. Another scream, and another, and then silence. "Lu, no, not Lu." He couldn't bear the pain, it was too much. Then he saw a muddy pool of his own blood seeping out from under him. The break in his leg must be bad, very bad. He was a doctor so he knew what happened next—he was bleeding to death. His vision began to dim, his thoughts dulled and his eyes slowly closed.

11

COLD, SO COLD

Jann's eyes snapped open. It was cold, her breath condensed and she shivered even though she was still in her EVA suit. She sat up and looked around. Her gloves and helmet were on a bench on the far side of the medlab. There was no sign of anyone. Then she remembered what had happened. She had really lost the plot, freaking out like that and waving a knife around. Could she really blame Paolio for what he did? Too late anyway, the damage was done. Now she would be regarded as the *crazy one.*

"Hello, anyone there?" No answer. *There's no power*, she thought, must *be why it's so cold. Where is everybody?*

She swung her legs over the side of the bed and stood up. She was a little shaky and took a few moments to find her balance. The light in the lab was dim, but she could still see well enough. What time was it? How long had she been out? Jann made her way over to the bench, took her gloves and helmet and put them on, just in case. If there was some emergency she could get life support from the suit almost instantly. Probably a good idea. She strapped on her boots but left the visor on her helmet open.

She stood in the medlab for a few moments considering what to do next. Silence. Cold, dark silence. Not a sound. She listened; not even the pervasive low hum that comes with space travel, an inevitable consequence of the need to be permanently encased in life support. The hum that you only notice when it's gone. Maybe they're trying to restore power? But then, why didn't Paolio, or anyone, stay here for when I woke up? "Hello?" she ventured into her helmet comm. "Malbec here, anybody please respond..." Nothing. Maybe she should go look for them. Or maybe she should get out and make for the HAB. She checked the time; there was still another hour or so of daylight left. But the Martian night came quick. It would be pitch black out on the surface, no moon to illuminate the way. She did have the HAB beacon so she could follow that if necessary and her helmet had a powerful floodlight. Jann thought about arming herself with a weapon of some kind. A baseball bat would be good, or a knife. Then again, maybe not. It didn't work out too well the last time she tried that. So she left it, no point in exacerbating the situation.

After deliberating her options for some time, Jann cautiously moved out of the medlab and into the main common area. Pale daylight filtered down through the domed roof, enough to illuminate her way. "Hello?" she listened. Nothing. "Where the hell are they?" She jumped as she heard a cracking sound from high up in the dome superstructure; it was adjusting to the change in temperature. Metal contracting and shifting causing a creaking that echoed around the facility. Jann made her way towards the biodome, all the time looking around for anything that might give her a clue as to the whereabouts of the crew.

She stopped at the entrance of the short tunnel that led to the biodome. Ahead of her, she could make out a crewmember sitting on the floor, their back resting against the tunnel wall. “Hello?” They didn’t respond; she moved closer. It was Lu. Her head was covered in blood from a serious gash on her skull. Her eyes were wide—and dead. “Lu, Jesus... Lu!” Jann rushed to her, removed one of her gloves and checked Lu’s pulse. Nothing. She slumped down onto the floor opposite the lifeless Lu Chan, and cried for the loss of her friend. “Lu, what happened?” But Lu had nothing to say.

SOMETHING FAST MOVED between the rows of vegetation inside the biodome. Jann caught a fleeting glimpse in the corner of her eye and she froze. It moved again. She stood up slowly, keeping her back to the tunnel wall and moved in through the entrance to investigate. It came at her like a freight train and something heavy hit her hard on the side of her head. The force knocked her forward and she went careening over a grow bed and crashed to the ground on the other side. Her suit helmet had taken the blow and held, otherwise she would be dead, or dying. She rolled over onto her back. Commander Decker towered over her. He stood motionless, glaring down at her with a demonic stare. She lifted herself up on her elbows and tried to shuffle backwards. She was dizzy from the blow. “Decker, what the hell?” He stopped and tilted his head slightly to one side like he was considering her. He then looked over at the grow-bed, pulled a long sharp metal stake out of the ground and hefted it like a spear. He advanced. Jann frantically kicked out but it was a futile action. He raised the spear, aiming to skewer her through the abdomen. Jann screamed and held her arms out in a last desperate act of self-preservation.

From nowhere, Kevin Novack appeared and struck the commander across the back of the head with a heavy bar. Decker reeled and lost his balance. The engineer hit him again, this time on his shoulder, and Decker went flying over a grow-bed and collapsed on the floor. He stayed still. Kevin looked at the prostrate commander, ready to strike again. Satisfied that he wasn't moving he reached down to help Jann up.

"You okay?"

"I told you he was deranged."

"I know, I know... you were right, what can I say?"

"What happened?"

"He was perfectly fine then he started talking crazy. Lu tried to talk to him, and he just... killed her. I couldn't get to her in time. Then he ran off. I've been stalking him since."

"What about the others? Paolio?"

"I don't know, it all happened so fast. I don't know where they are."

"Hello, Malbec here. Paolio, Annis... please respond?" Jann spoke in her comm. Nothing. "Is no one wearing a headset?"

Kevin shrugged. "I took mine off in the operations area."

"How long has the power been out?"

"Shortly after Decker went crazy."

"Shit, look..."

She pointed at the spot where the commander had been —he was gone.

"Come on, let's get out of here... now!" Kevin grabbed Jann and moved her towards the tunnel exit. He pushed her through the door and then started to close it. It was stiff.

"Shit, give me a hand, Jann, we can close him in here if we get this shut." The short tunnel between the main biodome and the common area was designed as an airlock so each section could be sealed off. But the doors had been rigged to stay open. Jann had just turned back to help when Kevin's eyes went wide and a large dark bloodstain spread across his abdomen. A metal spear protruded from its center. He dropped to his knees. "Kevin... no..."

Decker stood behind the stricken Novack holding the bloodied metal shaft. He looked at it with a vacant curiosity, like it was something alien. He seemed mesmerized by it. Jann backed slowly down the short tunnel. She grabbed the door at the far end and put all her weight behind it. It moved, but slowly. It was stiff and needed all her strength to operate. Decker's head jerked up as he noticed the swinging door. He shot forward with frightening speed. But Jann had her shoulder to the heavy door—it was gaining momentum and clicked closed just as Decker crashed into it. She bounced off it with the force and slid across the floor, but the door held. She rushed back and spun the locking wheel, grabbed a bar from one of the scrap piles and wedged it into the handle. Just in time. She could see it rattle as the commander tried to open it. He stopped and for a brief moment silence returned to the colony. Then there was a massive crash as the door shook, and another, and another. He was throwing himself against it in a crazed frenzy. The entire facility resonated with the force, but the door held. Jann backed away.

The banging stopped. Jann wasn't sure if that was a good thing. It probably was, but now she didn't know what he was up to. The daylight was also fading fast. She needed to get out now and make a run for the HAB. Like she did this morning, running from the demented Decker.

She was about to flip her visor down and make for the airlock when she heard a low moan. She froze. It came from over by the workshop. There it was again. She picked up a heavy metal rod from one of the scrap tables and cautiously headed towards the sound. She kept low, moved behind a mound of disassembled machines and peered in. On the floor, in a gap between a row of storage boxes, she saw a pair of bloodied legs. She shifted closer to get a better view. The legs were attached to Dr. Paolio Corelli. He was sitting on the floor with his back resting against the dome wall, hiding as best he could. "Paolio."

His face was bloodied but he was still alive, still breathing. She shook his shoulder. "Paolio, it's me Jann." His eyes opened slowly. "Jann." He coughed and spat a bloody gob on the floor. She crouched down beside him. "Paolio, can you move?"

"My leg... broken, collar bone... ribs I think."

"Decker is trapped in the biodome, for the moment. We need to get out of here."

He grabbed her by the arm and pulled her closer. "Lu... where's Lu?"

"She's... dead, Paolio... so is Kevin. I don't know about Annis.

Paolio let out a long, gut-wrenching moan. "No... not Lu." Then he let go of her and slumped back. "I'm sorry, Jann. I screwed up... thought you had gone off the rails." He spat again.

"It's okay. You probably saved my life, Paolio. If I wasn't out for the count I might be dead by now. Come on." She put her arm under his and tried to help him up.

"Ahhhhh..." he collapsed again. "It's no use, I'm too broken."

"Don't give up on me now, just get your shit together."

She raised her voice and put some sting into it. Anything to get him to move. "We've got to try and get to the HAB. If you can get outside I can call the mule and you can ride it there. You've got to try."

"Okay..." He steeled himself and, with Jann's help, managed to stand up on one leg. He was weak and unstable, but seemed to revive a little now that he was upright and had purpose.

"Where's your EVA suit and helmet?"

Paolio rubbed his head as he balanced himself against the wall. "Over by the airlock... I think."

Jann put his arm over her shoulder and propped him up. "Okay, ready?" He nodded, and they shuffled off. Paolio hopped on one leg, he could put no weight on the other. They made slow progress.

"Hold it... I've got to stop. Oh god, I'm a total mess." He balanced himself against a workbench, breathing hard and looking deathly pale. "I don't think I can make it."

"Yes you can, just keep going, come on."

"Jann, I'm a doctor, I know the story. I'm losing a lot of blood. I've already passed out once. Unless I get it stopped soon, I'll bleed to death. I'm screwed, Jann."

It was clear to her that Paolio had a point. Their only option now was to head for the medlab and take their chances.

"The medlab then. You can make it that far. Come on."

"No Jann. Every thing's gone to rat shit, leave me, get out of here, get off this planet... do you hear me? Get off while you still can... go now."

"I'm not leaving you here, you can forget that idea. And I'm not leaving Annis either." She threw his arm around her shoulders and hoisted him up.

"She may be dead too, Jann."

"Move, we're wasting time."

JANN HELPED him onto the bed in the medlab and rushed back to shut the door. She needed to find something to wedge into the closing mechanism but time was running out for Paolio, so she left it and went back to him. His leg looked bad. His flight suit was saturated with blood. "I'm going to have to cut this off." She hunted around for some surgical instruments and found several trays. She grabbed a set of cutters, probably designed for this exact job. She surveyed Paolio's leg more closely. He had managed to apply a tourniquet to his upper leg just above the knee. Best not touch that for the moment.

"Are you sure you want me to do this?"

"My leg's not much good to me if I'm dead."

"Okay." She started cutting. It didn't take long to reveal the wound and to realize that it was worse than she thought. He had a large gash on the inside left calf, and the bone protruded from a gelatinous mass of blood. "Oh shit." She hadn't meant to alarm him, it just escaped out of her mouth. Paolio lifted himself up on one elbow and assessed the damage to his body. "Shit." He collapsed back down again.

She found some gauze and started cleaning around the wound. Paolio groaned in pain. "Stop. Jann. Wait." He raised himself up again and this time took a longer look at the wound. The bleeding seemed to have stopped, which was something at least. But he knew the score, what he wanted Jann to do next would either save him or kill him. It was fifty-fifty, at best.

"Jann, listen to me. Here's what I want you to do..." before he could finish they heard an intense banging from across the dome. Jann ran to the lab door and looked out.

Decker was trying to get the main biodome door opened. She could see the bar she used to wedge it closed was working itself loose with the vibration. They didn't have much time.

"Jann!"

She shut the medlab door and this time jammed a long, hardened steel surgical instrument in to the locking mechanism. It would buy them time, nothing more.

"Jann!"

"Paolio, Decker's breaking his way out of the biodome."

"Jann, listen to me, listen to me."

She stopped. "Sure Paolio."

"I want you to reset the bone and stitch me up."

"Are you serious?"

He grabbed her arm and brought her face closer to his, and gritted his teeth. "Do it. Do it now before I change my mind."

"Okay, okay. I'll need to find some clean bandages first." He released her arm and sunk back down on the bed. Jann backed off and started opening drawers and doors and pulling out everything she could find. She knew what he was asking. Resetting the bone would mean starting the bleeding again, as well as the excruciating agony. He might just pass out from the pain... if he was lucky. She found some bandages, still packaged so still sterile, if that actually mattered in the rarefied Colony One environment. There was loud crash outside. Decker was out of the biodome. She ran back to Paolio. *If there was ever a time to get focused this is it. Do it now*, she thought.

"Paolio, ready?"

"No," he sighed. "Yes, yes." He managed a hint of a smile.

She surveyed the wound as best she could, but there was no easy way to do this. She placed one hand gently on his leg just below the knee. Paolio screamed. She whipped her hand away, Paolio held his forehead and moaned. "Here, bite down on this." She pushed a plastic handled instrument between his teeth, not that it was going to do much good, it was more psychological. She readied herself at the foot of the bed to reset the bone. "Ready in three." Paolio groaned and nodded. She grabbed his calf just above the ankle. "One... " and jerked it back with a twist. Paolio screamed in agony. The bone retracted back in through the open wound. She could feel it grind around inside as she tried to feel it back into place. Paolio raged and roared and she was sure he was going to pass out. Blood oozed out of the wound and pooled all around, it dripped on to the floor and her hands were wet and slippery. She couldn't do this to him any more, when she felt it was right she stopped. "I think that's it." Paolio didn't respond. She quickly wrapped his leg with a tight bandage to close the wound. It wasn't pretty, but they were way beyond that now. She finished the bandage and the blood flow had lessened. He looked deathly white, his body drenched in sweat and his breathing shallow. *He's still alive,* she thought, *but for how much longer? I've probably just killed him.*

She sunk down on to the cold floor of the lab and cradled her head in her hands, rocking back and forth, like some long-term inmate of a desolate gulag whose mind had been eroded by eternal hopelessness. How did everything get so messed up so quickly? Lu and Kevin were dead. Killed by the unhinged Decker, and Paolio, what hope was there for him now? Annis was probably dead as well. Soon, there would be just her.

Even if she were to run now there was no way out. She wasn't going to leave Paolio. And there was no way she could get him into an EVA suit before Decker got out. They were stuck here. What's more, with no power in the colony it was only a matter of time before the air became so saturated with CO_2 it would be poisonous. How long, she had no idea. Hours, days, weeks? It didn't matter; Decker would get them long before that.

But there was no respite, the lab shook and reverberated as Decker tried to get in. She jumped up, "Shit," and backed away as the door rocked again. There was nothing for it; she would have to make a stand—here, in this lab, on this desolate planet. It would be her end and she knew it. Jann swept the lab with the light from her helmet in search of anything she could use as a weapon. The door reverberated again. She picked up a long, sharp surgical knife and held it with both hands out in front of her. She hoped to God it would not be the instrument of her own death. Her body shook and sweat streamed down her face, stinging her eyes. She could smell her own fear. *Hold fast old girl,* she thought, *focus.*

The banging stopped and Jann entered a twilight zone of the unknown. At least with the noise she knew where he was. Once it stopped her anxiety ratcheted up, notch by notch, as she waited for the inevitable onslaught of the crazed commander. She held fast.

Time passed and the light from her helmet grew dim, soon she would see nothing but total blackness. She had stood rock solid just back from the door ready for the attack, But now, her legs began to shake as the initial surge of adrenaline began to ebb. How much longer could she keep this up? She rubbed her eyes. It seemed like the light in the lab was getting brighter. Was the power back on? She shook her head and blinked. Yes, it was much brighter, coming from behind. She spun around and standing in front of her was the strangest man she had ever seen.

. . .

He was thin and ragged with wild hair and a thick scrub of beard. The light came from behind him so she could only see him in silhouette. He had come in through the door from the other section of the Medlab, the module they had all assumed to be sealed and derelict. Then came a low buzzing noise and a small robot moved in beside him. It was a little over waist height. It stopped at his side, like a faithful dog.

"Is your colleague still alive?" He pointed over at the unconscious doctor.

"Yes, I think so."

"Gizmo, would you be so kind as to look after the unfortunate individual."

The little robot swung its head around to look up at its master, then it spoke.

"Certainly, Nills." It whizzed over on sleek tracks, extended two arms under the body of the doctor and lifted him up with ease.

"Wait, stop... where are you taking him? Who are you?"

Nills paused and extended his hand. "If you want to stay alive, then you'd better come with us."

12

NILLS & GIZMO

Jann had no real choice. Either stay and face the homicidal Decker, and certain death, or follow the enigmatic colonist and his robotic sidekick to possible safety. So she followed them tentatively through the door and into the wide, brightly lit module. It was empty save for a large section of flooring, hinged up to reveal a long ramp sloping down into the subsurface. The little robot descended first. Nills turned to Jann and waved his hand towards the tunnel. "Quick, follow Gizmo."

As she descended she could hear him closing the floor panel behind them. The light extinguished and the tunnel grew dim, lit solely by illumination from an open airlock door just ahead. Jann had a feeling that she was entering the proverbial rabbit hole.

They passed through the airlock and into a spacious underground cavern. It was hard to take it all in at once as it was dimly lit, with only patches of illumination here and there. The floor was flat and solid, and looked to be fashioned from some type of concrete. The sections of cave wall that Jann could see shimmered and glistened like they had been coated with some sort of sealant. The area was furnished like a workshop with equipment and machines of indeterminate function. Computer racks and monitors rested on scattered workbenches.

"Gizmo, would you be so kind as to place the injured human over there."

The little robot wheeled around and set Paolio down on a bed with an uncanny gentleness. The doctor was still unconscious. He badly needed surgery on his broken leg and he needed blood, none of which was going to happen. There was not much Jann could do for him. His fate was in the lap of the Gods. She took her helmet off and looked over at the ragged colonist. "You're Nills Langthrop."

"Yes, and you are Dr. Jann Malbec. Science Officer with the International Space Agency Mars expedition."

"Yes, how did you know that?"

Nills didn't answer. Instead, he turned and waved a hand towards the little robot. "This is my friend Gizmo." It rocked its head and spoke.

"Greetings Earthling," said Gizmo.

"Eh... pleased to meet you," she replied, a little uncertain. She turned back to Nills. "Where are we? Are there any more colonists?"

"All in good time. For the moment you are safe."

"Why were you hiding from us? We've been searching everywhere."

He went quiet and scratched his beard. "It's a long story."

"Nills, I think the infected Earthling is getting ready to leave." Gizmo was over by a bank of monitors. Nills rushed over, followed by Jann. On screen was a video feed from the main Colony One airlock entrance. Decker was putting on his EVA suit. They stood in silence for a while and watched.

"You know what's wrong with him, don't you?" said Jann.

"He's infected. You all probably are." He turned to face Jann who was visibly shocked. "But don't worry, it only affects some. You're okay, as is your colleague," he nodded over at the unconscious Paolio.

"This is what you were talking about... in your last message."

Nills nodded. "So you got that, interesting."

"There must be something we can do."

"Wait, just wait. Come, are you hungry?" He stood up and gestured in the direction of a makeshift galley.

"What? No. It's not exactly high on my list of priorities at the moment. What about Annis, do you know if she's still alive?"

"Patience, we have plenty of time." He walked off, the little robot followed after him. Nills sat down at another row of workstations and started looking at readouts on several monitors. Jann had so many questions going around in her head it was hard to know where to start. But it was clear that Nills was not going to respond well to an intense interrogation. She would have to take it slow. She was not in any immediate danger, as far as she could tell, so there was that at least. Jann also got the impression that Nills had the situation under control, as far as possible. So she decided to take a different tack.

"Yes, I'm really hungry."

His face lit up. "Good, come on, follow me." He jumped up from the workstation and gave a kind of a nod to Gizmo. The little robot reciprocated by rocking its head as they moved over to the galley.

"Gizmo, perhaps you would be so kind as to decant some of that cider we've been saving for a special occasion."

"Excellent idea, Nills. Now would seem like the perfect

time. Considering that we have guests with us," the robot replied.

Jann watched it go about its task. It had a kind of scrapyard construction with bits attached here and there. It rode around on tri-pointed tracked wheels and had a speed and grace of movement that spoke of superb engineering skill. She had never seen, or heard of anything like it before.

"Do you like fish?" Nills was staring into a tall storage unit, like a teenager surveying the contents of a fridge.

"Fish would be lovely." She wasn't sure if it would be lovely. But it seemed to be the best way to engage with the enigmatic Nills.

"Excellent. We have some top notch fish pie left over from our last baking day."

"Good choice, Nills. It should still be well within optimal safety limits for human consumption," the robot interjected.

Nills and Gizmo busied themselves bringing food and plates over to a table. The both moved with a practiced ease, they knew each other's ways. For Jann it was like watching a surreal ballet.

"Come, sit... and tuck in."

There was fish pie, fruit, bread and an assortment of other food of uncertain provenance. As she sat, Gizmo poured her a cup of cider.

"We call it colony cider." Nills raised his cup to her. Jann did likewise and they clinked.

"To new friends," said Nills.

"To new friends." She took a sip and was surprised to find it was absolutely delicious. She downed the whole cup in no time. Gizmo refilled it for her.

"Thank you Gizmo," she said.

"Not at all, my pleasure. It's good that you are enjoying it."

"Yes, it's... delicious." Jann had just entered a whole new world. One where she was having a conversation with a robot, over dinner.

"Your robot is extraordinary."

Nills looked at his creation. "He's my friend."

"Its language skills are remarkable. I'm used to robots saying things like *'stand clear of the doors'* or *'mind the gap.'*"

"Indeed," he nodded. "Tell me, what do you think of the pie?"

Jann was cognizant that, at the same time as she was tucking in, the psychotic Decker was still at large. Kevin and Lu were dead and Paolio was... dying, not to mention the whereabouts of Annis. But, to get anything out of Nills and his robotic friend she would have to work at his pace, on his terms, and that meant trying some pie first. Then a thought crossed her mind. "Maybe he's the cause, maybe he's trying to poison all of us?" Prolonged exposure to isolation can do strange things to the human mind. "Perhaps he's the one who's really mad. Or am I just being paranoid?"

Nills took a forkful of pie and proceeded to eat it, with relish. Comforted by this, Jann placed a tentative morsel in her mouth and ate it. "Mmmmmm... this is absolutely amazing." And it was. After spending months living of ISA prepackaged rations it tasted fantastic.

"Do you hear that Gizmo? She loves it."

"But of course, Nills. I have always said your culinary skills were bordering on the epicurean."

"You flatter me, Gizmo."

"Well, credit where credit is due, as they say. More cider, Doctor Malbec?"

"Eh... sure... okay. Thank you."

"Not at all, it's my pleasure. Please... drink up." It gestured with its free arm at her cup. Jann sat transfixed by the quirky robot. It was more polite and considerate than a lot of dates she'd been on. She began to relax and eat. Hunger got the better of her paranoia. It helped that the food was delicious and she didn't stop until she had cleared her plate. All the while sipping on the colony cider between mouthfuls of fish pie. This seemed to please Nills no end as he kept smiling and nodding at Gizmo, who reciprocated with a kind of Indian head wobble. Then it beeped, and its head turned to look off into the distance, like it was thinking. "What is it?" Nills asked.

"The ISA Commander, Robert Decker, has left the colony," it said.

"Excellent, come, let's get the power back on and get to work." Nills jumped up from the table and scurried over to the workstations. His fingers danced across a keyboard and he muttered to himself as he inspected screen readouts.

"So it was you who switched the power off." Jann had just finished off the last of her cider.

"Yes, yes." He waved a dismissive hand in the air.

"Why did you do that?" Jann ventured.

"The infected. The drop in temperature quiets them down for a while, they become more rational, less volatile." He turned back to his workstation. "How are we doing Gizmo?"

"Rebooting sequentially as planned... all sectors nominal... optimal temperature in approximately twenty two minutes."

"Good, keep an eye on power distribution."

"Biodome ranging at two point seven"

"Watch acceleration drift."

"Compensating."

"Sub-system deviance?"

"Standard, minus oh point three."

It was evident to Jann that Gizmo was somehow connected into the Colony One systems. Like a sort of remote control unit that monitored and gave feedback to Nills. They also seemed to have established a strange evolved lexicon that only they could understand.

"The commander, where's he going? Where's Annis, is she still alive? Jann was getting more animated.

Nills stood up and surveyed her with a quizzical expression. "I understand you have a lot of questions. We're pretty certain your commander is heading back to your habitation module. We will now lockdown the colony so he can't get back in, at least not easily. We don't know where your first officer is. But once we have power restored, we can do a full sensory analysis of the facility, we'll find her then. Come, we need to look after your injured friend, and Gizmo and myself have many things to tend to in the garden. We can talk later and I will do my best to answer your questions then. In the meantime you're safe."

Jann was taken aback by this uncharacteristic flood of information. "Okay, thank you. I understand." She walked over to where Paolio was lying. He was regaining consciousness and started moaning and twisting with pain. "We'll need to bring him back up to the medlab so I can do a proper job on that leg."

"Gizmo, can you do the honors?" Nills waved at the injured doctor.

"Certainly," replied the robot as it lifted him up and whizzed off towards the airlock.

13

ANNIS & MALBEC

With power back on in the facility the temperature had risen, it was no longer as cold. Gizmo placed Paolio back on the operating table in the medlab and started a full body scan. A large donut shaped apparatus moved slowly along the length of the table, producing a narrow ribbon of light across his body as it traveled. The resultant image rendered itself on a nearby monitor.

"Fractured collarbone, two fractured ribs," Gizmo zoomed in on Paolio's leg. "You did a good job resetting that fibula."

Nills took his leave. "I need to get to operations and do a complete check on all colony systems. I'll leave you in Gizmo's good hands. He knows where everything is."

For over an hour they worked on Paolio: giving him morphine, setting up a plasma transfusion, stitching up his leg. The little robot moved with a fast, fluid confidence —Jann was mesmerized. It had the ability to rotate its body three hundred sixty degrees around its tracked base. It had two arms, each with a great number of articulations, giving it the ability to do things no human arm could possibly do. On one, it had a hand of sorts, three fingers and a thumb. On the other, it had the ability to snap on and off different tools which were attached to its body. Its head, if you could call it that, also had the ability to rotate completely and consisted mainly of sensors and antenna. After awhile, she noticed it had no real front or back. Whichever way it pointed its head was front. It would zip over to the operating table, perform some function, rotate its head a hundred and eighty degrees and zip back the way it came.

BY THE TIME they had finished, Paolio's face had regained some of its color, gone was the deathly pallor. The attention they had given the stricken doctor was evidently having a beneficial effect on his physiology. They had pumped him full of morphine, so it would be quite a while before woke up again. But at least he was out of danger. Gizmo surveyed his handiwork. "Your colleague is maintaining a status compatible with life. I would say he has an 86% chance of surviving the next twenty-four hours."

Jann looked at the quirky little robot. It had such a strange way with words. Symptomatic of its programmer's eccentricities, no doubt.

"Thank you Gizmo—for what you did for him." Jann wasn't quite sure why she kept thanking it. What would its silicone brain understand of gratitude? But it seemed like the right thing to do.

"Don't mention it; it is my pleasure to assist. I would advocate a lengthy rest period of six to eight weeks for the patient. After which he will require some physiotherapy to regain strength in the damaged member."

"Indeed. Tell me Gizmo, how long have you been, eh... aware?"

"Aware of what?

"I mean, when were you switched on?"

"Ahh... yes, you need to ask me a direct question for a direct answer. Otherwise my responses may be as obtuse as the question is vague."

"I see."

"One thousand, one hundred and fifty-eight sols... approximately."

Jann did some quick mental calculations. "Three years. So you were created after the collapse of the colony."

"One thousand, one hundred and fifty-eight sols... approximately," it repeated.

It was built as a friend to keep the castaway sane, his very own Man Friday. "Why did Commander Decker go crazy and start killing our crew?"

"I possess insufficient data to answer that."

"You need to frame a question carefully to get the best response from Gizmo." Nills entered the medlab. He had cleaned himself up and donned a new jumpsuit. Perhaps, before the arrival of the ISA crew, he had no motivation for personal grooming. But now that he had guests, it jumped several notches up his to do list. He looked younger than his thirty-six years and very healthy. A diet of fresh fish and vegetables would probably do that to a person. He turned to face the little robot. "Gizmo, extrapolate probable causes of ISA crew member Commander Decker's psychotic behavior."

"The most likely cause is he succumbed to the very same malaise as the previous members of Colony One"

"Well that doesn't tell us much," said Jann.

"No, but it's the correct answer. He can only work with

what he knows already. And I created him after all the mayhem so he has no specific knowledge of it."

"He's an incredible creation nonetheless, with an extraordinary turn of phrase."

"Ha, yes. Sometimes I regret using the complete works of Oscar Wilde as the basis for his grammatical syntax."

"So that's where he gets it. Must have taken you quite a while to build him."

"Well, I did have a lot of time on my hands. He started just as a service bot, for lifting and moving. After a while I integrated him into the colony systems so he could monitor status and alert me to any malfunction. Eventually I programmed him with self learning, neural-net algorithms." He turned and placed an affectionate hand on Gizmo's shoulder. "He's my friend, he's my sanity."

The little robot looked up at its master, like a faithful dog. If it had a tail it would be wagging it right now. Then it twitched and spun its head around, like it was looking off into the distance. Jann had seen it do this once before when Decker left the colony. "Temperature anomaly in fish farm, third quadrant."

"Extrapolate." replied Nills.

"It is consistent with a human life form—it's also moving."

"Annis!" shouted Jann, and she rushed off, with Nills and Gizmo trailing in her wake.

SHE RAN INTO THE BIODOME, past the remains of the door that Decker had broken through. The entrance to the fish farm was strewn with smashed up electronics. She picked up a broken circuit board and showed it to Nills. "The remote comms unit. Annis was using this to send her report back to mission control."

They heard a moan. "Annis?" Jann ventured down the long tunnel and spotted the first officer sitting on the ground with her back to the wall. "Annis... are you okay?"

The first officer looked up and glared. "Malbec?" She held one hand to her head in and Jann could see it was covered in blood.

"Decker's gone crazy... attacked me with a steel bar... totally berserk." She looked up and her eyes widened with fright. She shifted and started to back away. "Malbec, there's someone out there!" She pointed towards the entrance.

"It's all right, Annis. This is Nills Langthorp, a colonist."

Nills waved.

"Is that... a robot?"

"Yes, that's Gizmo."

Gizmo raised his hand to wave. "Greetings, Earthling."

Annis stared at the pair for a moment. "So he's the ghost we've been hunting."

"Yes, he was hiding out."

"And where's that crazy bastard Decker?"

"Gone. Left the Colony a few hours ago. Went back to the HAB."

"The others?"

Jann hesitated. "Paolio is pretty banged up. Kevin and Lu are... dead."

"Oh shit." Annis slumped down and held her head. " What a mess."

"Come, let's get you to the medlab." Jann helped her up.

As they moved out into the biodome Nills approached them. "We have work to do in the garden here. I'll check in on you later."

"Sure, thanks."

. . .

THE FIRST OFFICER sat on a seat in the medlab as Jann tended to the wound on her head. She brought her up to speed on all that had happened. Like Jann, Annis got lucky. Decker attacked her in the biodome while she was sending her report. She retaliated by throwing the comms unit at Decker. This seemed to distract him and the unit now became the threat in Decker's deranged mind. He proceeded to smash it into tiny pieces, giving Annis time to hide out under a tank in the fish farm—where she eventually passed out from the blow to her head.

"We should really do an x-ray to see if there's a fracture," said Jann.

Annis brushed her aside. "I'm fine." She stood up. "No time for that now. We need to deal with that crazy Decker or he'll destroy this mission."

Before Jann had time to answer Nills and Gizmo entered the medlab. "How are you feeling?"

Annis stared at them for a moment, looking from one to the other. "I'm fine. You got any ideas what the commander is up to now?"

"Gizmo, extrapolate possible current scenario for ISA crewmember Robert Decker," said Nills.

"Based on the historical data sets available, subjects tend to engage in a repeated pattern of deep sleep, followed by psychosis, then by a short period of rationality. Your commander has a 72.6% probability of being asleep at this time. But this is based on the limited data at my disposal."

Annis was visibly in awe at the response from the little robot. It took her a moment to adjust to this new reality.

"Well, if that's true, then it doesn't give us much time," she said.

"Why? What are you going to do?" said Jann.

"You mean what are *we* going to do. Well, it's simple. We're going to kill him."

"What? No, you're joking, you can't do that."

"That would indeed increase your mission success probability by a factor of 82.6%. Allowing for other unforeseen events," offered Gizmo.

"No way, I won't do it."

"Listen, Lu and Kevin are dead, Paolio's in bad shape and I'm getting seriously pissed off. So you better start growing a set of balls, Malbec. We're going to do this—we have to do it—and, if that robot thing is right, we're running out of time."

Jann thought about it and Annis had a point. If what Nills told her about the progress of the condition was correct, then the commander would only get worse. What alternatives did they have? The only other option was to somehow contain him safely, for both the rest of the mission here and on the long journey back. Cooped up on the Odyssey transit craft for two and a half months with a psychotic Decker was not a prospect that anyone would relish. But to kill him—that seemed brutally cold to Jann. "There has to be a better way."

"Like what? Appeal to his feminine side?" snapped Annis.

"Your first officer is right," interjected Nills, who was in the process of opening drawers and lockers looking for something. "His condition will only deteriorate. He'll drift in and out of psychosis until eventually he will be completely insane." He was reading the labels on various packages he had liberated from one of the medlab lockers. He looked over at Jann and Annis. "There is no hope for him now. You must realize he is beyond redemption."

"I can't accept that. There must be something we can do for him," said Jann.

"Like what, find a cure?" said Annis.

"Nills, you must know something about what causes this."

"I've told you all I know. It only affects some people, male and female equally. They go mad with rage, become crazed psychotic killers. I don't know how or why." He scratched his chin as if he had thought of something. "If I were to hazard a guess I'd say it's a bacterial infection."

"What makes you think that?" said Jann.

"I don't know... it's just a... feeling."

"Enough of this. We're wasting time. Do you have anything we can use as weapons?" said Annis.

Nills tossed a small plastic package over to her. "Here. It's cyclophromazine. There are three doses in there, each in separate syringes. That should be enough to kill him."

"Wait a minute. If it's bacterial then have you tried just using a dose of antibiotics?"

Nills paused before answering, "Well, no. We were too busy trying to stay alive. It's hard to play doctors and patients when the patient is trying to bash your head in."

"So it might work?" Jann looked at them both in turn.

"Attention... Commander Decker is on the move," squeaked Gizmo.

"Quick. Follow me... this way." Nills raced out of the medlab and into the main Colony One operations area. He flicked a display table to life and a 3D rendering of the northwestern area of the Jezero crater ballooned out from its surface. They could see the colony on one side. Farther out were the HAB and lander. A red marker flashed beside the HAB. Nills pointed at it. "That's Decker. Gizmo's right, he's left your HAB module."

"Of course I'm right."

Annis turned to the quirky robot. "I thought you said that he would sleep for hours."

"Gizmo did, but it came with a 72.6% probability caveat. So this action is in the other 27.4%."

They all watched the blip as it moved away from the HAB and then stopped. "What's he doing?" said Jann.

"He probably doesn't know himself," said Nills.

"We're wasting time. We need to get out there and take him in the open." Annis was heading over to get her helmet. Jann was now looking at the package containing the cyclophromazine. "There's no way this is going to penetrate an EVA suit. The needle is too short."

"Shit," said Annis. By now the blip was on the move again. "Looks like he's heading this way." Nills pointed to the marker on the map.

Jann considered what to do. They should at least try and contain the commander. That way they could help him and maybe even shed some light on the source of the affliction. "I think we should attempt comms, try and assess his state of mind."

"Are you joking? That might be just a red flag to a bull."

"Dr. Malbec has a point," said Nills. "If he's semi-rational then you might be able to contain him more easily. If he's not, then it's not going to make any difference."

Before Annis could answer Jann had strapped on her suit headset and pressed broad transmit. "Commander Decker, this is Dr. Malbec, what's your status, over."

There was silence. Jann tried again. "Commander Decker, this is..."

"I hear you. Where is everybody? What's going on?"

They all exchanged looks, like partners in crime, a conspiracy unfolding. Annis grabbed her headset, put it on and listened in. "We're in the colony. How are you feeling?"

"They're crawling all over me... I can't get rid of them... gnawing at my brain... I need to scratch them out... this... this contamination."

"Just stay calm, we'll help you."

More silence. "Commander?" Then there was a sickening cry from the comms. Jann and Annis exchanged looks. Nills wore a concerned face, tinged with an experienced acceptance—he'd seen it all before.

"Decker, can you hear me?" Silence. Jann whipped the headset off and flung it down. "We'd better get ready."

"What's he sound like?" said Nills. "Batshit crazy, going on about 'contamination.' It makes no sense."

Jann looked at the blip on the 3D map. It was moving steadily towards them.

"Can we trap him in the airlock?" Annis directed her question at Nills.

"And then what? Wait till his air runs out?"

"Is that possible?"

"No, wait, let's think. If we can contain him and get him sedated, then maybe we could find out what's causing this," said Jann.

"Jesus, Jann. If we let him in here he'll kill us or we'll get seriously injured before we can take him out. No way."

"We just need him to take his helmet off before he leaves the airlock. Then we jab him in the neck, he'll go down in a few seconds."

"Gizmo thinks the probability of successfully containing your Commander Decker without sustaining injury is 0.1%," said the little robot.

"Thanks for the analysis," replied Jann.

"Don't mention it, my pleasure. I'm here to help," said Gizmo.

"We're going to need some weapons. What have you got, Nills?" said Annis.

"Knives, heavy tools, steel bars."

"Okay, show me." They moved over to the workshop and in a few minutes Annis returned holding a long sharp knife in one hand and a heavy tool in the other. "Here's the deal. If he doesn't take his helmet off he stays in the airlock. If he does, and you don't get that syringe into to him, then the first step he takes I'm going to gut him, no hesitation. Got that?"

Jann nodded. The red blip was almost at the door.

10CC OF CYCLOPHROMAZINE would be more than enough to drop a large man in seconds. 20cc and it would be fifty-fifty if he lived. 30cc and he's dead—no question. It was 5cc that Dr. Corelli jabbed into her when she lost it in the colony. Things had changed since then. Two crew were dead and the tables had turned. She broke the seal on the package and fumbled with the hypodermic. It seemed a very insubstantial weapon in the face of such a raging bull as the demented Decker. "Hold fast old girl—focus," she said to herself.

"At the door!" Annis had taken up position right at the interior airlock door. She had the look of a warrior, the long knife held at the ready. Jann looked around to find that Nills and Gizmo had disappeared. "Where's Nills?"

"Screw him, we don't need him. This is our shit to sort out. Are you ready to do this, Jann? Because if you're not then we keep him in the airlock and watch him die."

Jann hurried over to the door and steeled herself. "Okay,

ready." They heard the *whirr* of the pump as it started to depressurize. The alert indicator flashed red as the exterior door opened and in stepped Commander Decker. It was a tentative step at first. Like a wild animal sniffing out a strange box in the forest. Driven on by scent, held back by fear, uncertain of its surroundings. The door automatically closed behind him as he spotted Jann and Annis through the interior door observation window. He raced forward and crashed into it. They jumped back. Jann was shaken by the ferocity of the attack. He banged at the door several more times and then paused.

"Jesus, he's pretty pissed. I say we just go with plan A and keep him locked in there until he runs out of air."

"Do you know how to switch off the air?"

They both realized that they didn't know. The only one who did was Nills and he had gone back into hiding. "Shit, no."

"What's he doing?"

Annis peered through the little window again. "Just standing there. Wait a minute, I think he's taking his helmet off." Jann came back to the window and joined her. His face was blotchy red and scratched. Blood had congealed along his forehead and matted his hair. He looked at them but didn't move. He seemed to be in pain and his face contorted as he brought his hands up to cradle his head. He mouthed a scream and dropped to his knees, he shook his head like he was trying to get something out that was gnawing away at his brain.

Jann looked on in horror at this forlorn figure. A pale and tormented shadow of the Decker that commanded the ISA Mars mission. There was no rethinking this. She needed to help him if she could. Somewhere inside that tortured creature was still the soul of a human, one that needed to be saved, not killed. She looked over at Annis. The first officer was ready to kill him to save the mission. It was simply a matter of calculating the odds with her. The mission came first. The human second.

Jann readied herself. Time to do this. "Okay, let's open the door now he's down. I'll stick him in the neck with this and that should take him down."

"You really want to do this?"

Jann nodded and placed a hand on the door release. She held the hypodermic high, ready to stab down at the first opportunity. Annis stood to her left, ready to end his life if need be.

Jann hit the door release and slowly began to ease it open. Then something must have clicked in Decker's tormented brain because he lunged at the door with tremendous speed. Jann was sent tumbling backwards across the floor with the force of impact. The syringe fell from her hand and skidded under a mound of workshop parts. "Damn."

She tasted blood in her mouth, her face hurt like hell and her right eye was closing up. "Shit." Annis failed to counter Decker's attack and he grabbed her knife hand at the wrist, the other hand on her throat, pinning her down to a workshop table. She kicked and fought but it had no effect. Decker was simply too strong and too crazed. "Shit, where's the syringe?" Jann got on all fours and tried to find it. She had better hurry or Annis would be dead. She spotted it, picked it up and bounded over to Decker. He saw her coming, turned and literally threw Annis at her. In one-third gravity she sailed through the air like a rag doll. Jann ducked as Annis crashed down across a pile of machine parts. Decker grinned. Jann stood her ground. They faced off.

He lunged. But it was primal, there was no fighting skill there. Simply the wild flailing of a rabid animal. Jann, on the other hand had a skill, kickboxing. It was a hobby, a way of keeping fit, nothing more—until now. She saw the way he moved, his momentum. She twisted sideways and brought the needle down on his neck—except she missed, the needle hitting the metal neck rim of his EVA suit. Decker careened past her and crashed to the ground. He slid along it with the force of his own momentum. The needle was broken.

"Shit." Jann rummaged in the pockets of her flight suit to extract another one. But Decker was already on the attack. Again she dodged but this time she swung a kick and caught him across the side of the head. He felt it because he crashed face down on the floor and took a moment to recover. Annis was now back on her feet and looking for the knife. Before Decker had time to get to his feet, Jann swung another kick to the head and again he went down. Annis found the knife and was ready to dispatch him when Jann finally jumped on Decker and jabbed him in the neck with the hypodermic. He looked at her with a kind of shocked surprise, then his eyes closed and he slumped to the floor.

Jann rolled off him, breathing heavily and shaking with adrenaline. Her face hurt like hell. Annis came over and offered her a hand. Jann grabbed it and pulled herself up. "Where did you learn to kick like that?"

Jann shrugged. "I work out."

"You're one real badass—respect." She patted Jann on the shoulder.

They looked down at the forlorn Decker. "That bastard nearly killed me." Annis kicked him hard in the gut a few times. Decker didn't move. "Is he dead?"

"No, but he's out for the count for a few hours. Come on

let's get him tied up before he comes around. Drag him into the medlab."

PAOLIO, still unconscious, occupied the only bed in the medlab. But his injuries paled in comparison to the torment that afflicted Decker, so Jann had no qualms about relocating him to the floor, while Decker took up residence in his stead. Fortunately, the medlab operating table had restraints built in. Why, Jann didn't know, nor did she care. They laid him out, strapped him down, and double checked. Then Nills showed up.

"Well, where the hell were you? Hiding in your hole, no doubt." Annis was pissed.

"It's served me well in the past. In case you haven't noticed. I'm the only one left alive in here. I see you have managed to incapacitate the afflicted crewmember."

"No thanks to you," replied Annis.

"Enough," said Jann. Her face hurt when she talked. She was exhausted—mentally, physically and emotionally. She sat down, grabbed a mirror and brought it up to her face. It wasn't too bad. Not as bad as it felt. Just a lot of bruising. Could be worse, much worse. She could be dead.

Annis sat across from her rubbing her neck. "You know, I need to get a report back to mission control. They'll be wondering what the hell is going on up here."

"We have no comms unit, remember? Decker smashed it to pieces."

"I'll do it from the HAB."

"Can't it wait?"

"No, it's got to be done. I'll take the mule, let it drive me." She stood up and stretched her shoulders. "Let's hope Decker hasn't trashed the HAB."

14

CAVES

Jann set up an IV drip to keep Decker sedated—to keep his violence in check. He was comatose and she hoped he would stay that way until she got a handle on the cause of his psychosis. And if she didn't, then what? Let him die?

"Come, I'll show you where you can sleep." Nills beckoned to Jann from the medlab entrance. Gizmo gently lifted Paolio off the floor. They weren't going to leave him here, not on the floor and certainly not with Decker. The doctor was beginning to come around, he moaned and cried out as Gizmo carried him. Jann held his hand. "It's all right Paolio, we'll get you comfortable." They all moved off to an accommodation module and the medlab was locked down —just in case.

There were several of these modules dotted all over Colony One. Nills had powered up a unit just off the main common area. It was designed for twelve. They put Paolio in one of the bunks and settled him in.

"There's a shower in here, if you want to freshen up."

Jann slumped down on a bunk opposite Paolio. "Thanks Nills."

"Okay, we'll leave you alone now. If you need anything, I'll be in the biodome." He left, Gizmo trailing after him.

"*Malbec?*" Jann pressed the headset closer to her ear; the signal from Annis was distorted. The Colony One radiation shielding was playing havoc with the comms.

"Annis, yes, I'm here."

"The HAB is trashed. That crazy bastard wrecked the place."

"How bad is it?"

"He must have gone berserk inside, smashing things up. It's still got integrity, life support is okay. Mostly it's just the equipment inside, things strewn everywhere. The coffee machine is history."

"Paolio's not going to be happy to hear that."

"Well that's the least of our problems. The comms unit is dead."

"What?"

"We have no way to contact mission control."

"Can it be fixed?"

"I don't know. I'm going to run some tests and do an audit on the damage. I'll touch base with you in the morning."

"Are you staying in the HAB tonight?"

"Damn right. I'm not spending any more time in that colony than I have to. If you want to stay over there and play mommy, that's your problem. I'll see you in the morning—assuming you're still alive."

The comms disconnected. *Jesus*, thought Jann. *A whole new level of obnoxiousness—great.*

. . .

HER SLEEP WAS fitful as her mind spent most of the night contemplating the malaise that had turned Decker into a homicidal maniac. She rationalized the obvious first. It manifested itself as an altered mental state, probably due to a chemical imbalance within the brain. This could be caused by drugs, but she thought that unlikely. The other possibility was an infection, viral or bacterial. Either one could theoretically cause an imbalance. Nills had intimated that it was bacterial. But this was not based on any scientific analysis. It was simply an assumption on his part. Of course, Jann couldn't rule out the possibility that it might be of alien origin.

"DR. MALBEC, WAKE UP." Nills shook her gently. "Dr. Malbec..."

"Eh... what..." Jann opened her eyes and stared up at the strange figure. As her sleep-fogged mind cleared, she remembered where she was. "I fell asleep. How long was I out?"

"Eight hours. I was going to wake you earlier but you looked so peaceful so I left you."

She sat up rigid. "Decker?"

"Still there... still comatose."

She sighed, relaxed a bit and then realized Paolio was also awake. He was alert and sitting up in the bunk talking to Gizmo—in Italian.

"Paolio!"

"Jann, you're still alive I see," he smiled. He was in good spirits, gone was the deathly pallor of the previous day. He was anxious to learn all that had happened, so they talked for a time. Nills and Gizmo left them to it, but returned a short while later with a homemade, motorized wheelchair.

"Here. This might be useful. We made it... eh... for Marcella, I think. Long time ago now. She injured her ankle doing some stupid low-gravity stunt... can't remember what it was exactly. Anyway, I checked it out and it still works pretty well."

Jann lifted Paolio out of the bunk and helped him into the wheelchair. She found the low-gravity tremendously empowering. To lift such seemingly heavy weights just didn't get old for her. Paolio's broken leg was kept extended by virtue of a metal truss attached to the seat. He played with the controls to gain some familiarity with their function.

"I should go check on Decker," said Jann.

"I'm coming with you."

"You should really be resting, Paolio. Not taxing your body any more than necessary."

He looked up at her and smiled. "Who's the doctor here? Anyway, I think I've got the hang of this thing, let's go. Lead the way." He tapped the joystick and followed Jann to the medlab.

The commander was still strapped on the operating table where they had left him the previous night. His life drawn out on the monitors in green and blue phosphorescent waves. Paolio spent some time examining him and checking his vitals. "Well, he's not going anywhere for a while," he said when he had finished. "How do you think we should proceed?"

"Let's start with blood, that might give us some clues." Jann looked around the medlab. "This place is reasonably well equipped. It's got everything we need to make a start. And then there's that research lab, on the other side of the facility. That may prove useful if it can be brought back online. I wonder what they were doing in there?"

Paolio shrugged his good shoulder and smiled. "Research?"

"Greetings." Gizmo whizzed in. "Nills has requested you join us in the common room for some breakfast—at your convenience, of course."

Jann looked down at Paolio. "Hungry?"

"Starving."

"Come on then, Decker's safe enough here for now. Let's get some food."

NILLS AND GIZMO had been busy. They had set out an array of food on the main table in the common area. Standard colony fare: fresh fruit, salads and fish. There was also a good supply of colony cider. Nills sat in a battered chair eating a bowl of porridge.

"Just so you know," said Nills between mouthfuls of food, "The bodies of your deceased colleagues have been stored in an exterior unit, where it's subzero."

Jann sat down and put her head in her hands. Paolio leaned over and patted her back. She grabbed his hand with both of hers, pressed it against her cheek and sobbed. It had finally sunk in, the tragedy of it. She couldn't control it, and it all came flooding over her and her body shook.

"Dr. Malbec?" Gizmo's voice was surprisingly low, as if the little robot could somehow sense the emotion of the moment. Jann lifted her head, released Paolio's hand and rubbed a moist eye. "Yes?"

"Would you like some tea?"

She managed a smile and nodded. "Sure, thanks."

"Make that two," said Paolio, he too was visibly emotional. The death of Lu was particularly hard for him.

He patted Jann's back one last time as the moment passed and they both regained some composure.

"Tell us what happened here, Nills. You've seen all this before, haven't you?"

Nills put down the now empty bowl and scratched his chin. "I have, it seems a long time ago now. It's what destroyed the colony—well almost."

"So what the hell is it? We need to know. Two of us are dead and our commander is a raging psycho. What do we do?" Jann's frustration was bubbling to the surface.

"There's nothing you can do, except run and hide."

Gizmo arrived with mugs of tea and Jann took a tentative sip. It was surprisingly good. She relaxed, got some control of her emotions. She needed to get the story out of Nills, but it was evident he would do it in his own time. There was nothing to be gained by pushing him. Nills sipped his tea, took a rolled up cigarette out of his pocket and lit it. He blew the smoke out in a long satisfying plume. He offered it to the others. "Fancy a toke?"

Paolio reached over and took the joint. Jann looked over at him. He waved a hand and shrugged his good shoulder again. "Hey, pain, you know."

Nills opened up. "It started after the second phase of the colony was built, after the research lab. We don't know why it happened or what caused it. But some of us just started going off the rails. In the beginning it was like... just one or two people. The symptoms were a type of psychosis that affected just the individual. I mean, they had no desire to kill anybody. The first colonist to die was Peter Jensen. He suffered very badly from this illness. And then, one day, he just walked into the airlock without an EVA suit and depressurized it. It took us days to clean him off the walls."

"Days, really?" said Jann.

"Well, no. That's a bit of an exaggeration, but let's just say it wasn't pretty."

Paolio coughed and passed the joint back. Nills took another drag, blew out the smoke and continued. "COM knew all this, of course, but they were at a loss as to what was causing the colonists to go stark raving mad. Eventually it got so bad that a few of them decided to decamp to the mining outpost."

"The one over at the far side of the crater?" said Jann

"Yeah."

"But I thought that had only minimal life support?"

Nills scratched his chin again and looked from one to the other like he was considering something. "I don't suppose it matters now, so I might as well tell you." Nills waved a hand in a vague direction. "The mining outpost is around ten kilometers north east of here. At the base of a cliff over by the crater rim. It's a vast, mineral rich cave system. It had a relatively small entrance so over time it was sealed with an airlock and pressurized. Once that happened, people began to stay there, and eventually we moved a lot of equipment and many of the modules over there. It was quite impressive. We also had this crazy idea that if anything happened to this place we could survive there."

"How come we didn't know about this?" said Jann. Paolio was coughing again as he passed the last of the joint back to Nills.

"We kept it secret." Nills inspected the butt. "You have to understand, that back then, living here was like living in a fish bowl. Every single microscopic detail of our lives was broadcast to a million different digital media channels back on Earth—twenty-four seven. No one had a private life. So, we just kept it quiet. No cameras, no intrusion, it was our private space."

"Are there still people there, maybe someone still alive?" said Jann.

"No, definitely not. They're all dead."

"How do you know for sure?"

"Look, I just do, okay? The outpost ran using solar panels so they would have run out of power during the storm. If there was someone still alive they would contact me here. No... they're all dead. There's just me and Gizmo left now." He took a last drag of the joint and stubbed the butt out on a metal plate. Then he just sort of zoned out. Jann wasn't sure if he was thinking or had simply stopped talking.

"So what happened during the sandstorm?" she prompted.

"Oh, eh... yes, the sandstorm. Well that was a total mess if ever there was one. It wasn't a big deal at the start, we were used to them. But after the first month we had the bright idea to start conserving power. That's when people really started to go nuts —like your commander. People were dying as we fought to get the crazies under control. But as soon as one was dealt with another would go nuts, then another and another. It was mayhem. We managed to get some contained in the far dome, that's when the plutonium power source failed." He clicked his fingers. "Just like that, bang, gone. Now we were in real trouble. If we didn't get it back online then all we had for power was the solar array and that was worse than useless during the storm."

"So what did you do?"

"We assumed it had been damaged or sabotaged by the crazies. Some of us ventured outside to try and trace the cables back out to the source—find where the problem was.

But they never returned. Some got lost, some were killed... I don't know. Meanwhile, the power was getting critical and more of us were succumbing to the illness. It was scary as you didn't know who would be next. They destroyed the far dome, one of the tunnels and a whole bunch of other stuff."

"How did you survive?"

"Back in the beginning of the colony, we used to process soil on the surface but we accidentally discovered caves," he laughed, "right under us. It was just luck. Anyway, we sealed them up and started using them for soil processing. Much easier than outside on the surface. So, when everything went to rat shit it was a good place to hide." He stopped and seemed to be thinking again.

"So you holed up down there, for how long?" Paolio had now progressed on to a mug of colony cider.

Nills had zoned out again. "Eh... where was I, oh yes, the cave. Three months we spent there. They couldn't find us, too dumb. We would sneak up when they were asleep, when they had stopped trying to kill each other and wrecking the place. We'd grab stuff and bring it back down. Eventually, they all killed each other up top, there was only one left. So we blew him out the airlock."

"And then what?" said Paolio.

"By now we were living off fumes. Very little power left and the facility was ripped apart. Life support was barely functioning. The storm still raged outside."

"So... The windmills in the airlocks..." said Jann.

Nills laughed. "Yeah, that was my bright idea. It helped a bit. But what saved us in the end was a power control system reboot." He started laughing and shaking his head. "It was just so dumb. I was trying to conserve as much power as possible by hacking the software on the mainframe, switching things off that it regarded as essential. I took the risk of doing a cold reboot—and what do you know?" Nills was on the edge of his seat now, waving his hands. "The goddamn plutonium power source came back online." He started laughing hysterically. "We were just a bunch of dumb idiots, we never thought to try it before, kept thinking it was the crazies that were causing it." He collapsed back in his seat. "And that was that. We survived."

"We?" said Jann

Nills went quiet for a time, eventually he spoke again. "I don't want to talk about that... not now, some other time... maybe."

"Why didn't you contact Earth and let them know?"

"The storm destroyed the uplink antenna."

"But you could have written an S.O.S on the sand or something."

"And then what? What would happen?"

"Well Earth would send people and supplies."

"Yes. That's exactly what they would do. And look how that turned out." He looked across at Jann and Paolio. "Not so good, don't you think? Two of your crew are dead." He sat back. "No, there was no way we wanted any more people up here. Not until we found out what was causing this psychosis."

"So did you discover anything?"

"Not much. I suspect it's some type of bacterial infection. It started a while after the research lab was built. New people came, geneticists. The rumor was COM was even going to return them to Earth. That didn't go down well with the rest of us." He waved a dismissive hand in the air. "I don't know, maybe it was just crazy talk."

"So what were they doing, these *geneticists*?" Jann kept prompting Nills, now that he was in talkative mood.

"Playing God, screwing with organisms, making money

for the Colony One Mars consortium. Although, to be fair, without GM this place wouldn't function."

Jann stood up and started to pace. "There must be more to it than a rogue bacterium, how come only the commander was affected?"

"It only affects some people, and there's no pattern that we could see. Nills downed the last of his tea.

"So, I've told you my story, what about you? You're not COM people."

Jann took up the question. "No, this is an International Space Agency mission. We're here to investigate what happened, gather up a few rocks while we're at it and return to Earth. It's a three month mission."

"Return to Earth?"

"Yes."

"Where is COM in all of this? After all, this is technically their facility."

"Not anymore. They handed it over to ISA."

"That sounds uncharacteristically generous of them. Forgive me if I don't believe it."

"Well, nobody was going to come back here on a one-way ticket and COM didn't have the resources to start all over again. So it made sense to do it this way."

"Let me see if I have this straight. The COM consortium hands over all their assets up here to the ISA, which don't amount to a hill of beans since they all thought it was derelict. And then, gets national space agencies to spend taxpayer money to get them back up here."

"This is not a COM mission," insisted Jann.

Nills laughed. "Want to know what I think? I think you've all been taken for a ride." He stood up. "Look, do what you need to do. I really don't give a shit anyway." With that, Gizmo seemed to wake up.

"Earthling approaching airlock."

A FEW MOMENTS LATER, First Officer Annis Romanov strode into the common room and straight over to Nills. "Our comms unit is dead in the HAB. We need you to fix it for us."

Nills looked at her with eyes like laser beams. Yet it was Gizmo that spoke. "Nills does not go outside on the planet's surface."

Annis was not sure what to make of this response. She looked at the robot and then back at Nills. "Hey, this is a serious issue. We have no way to contact our mission control.

"Nills does not go out onto the planet's surface," repeated Gizmo.

Before Annis could react Jann interjected. "What if we brought it here, could you look at it for us?"

Nills nodded. "I could do that. No guarantees, though."

"Forget it. I'll fix it myself, said Annis.

"Can you do that?" said Paolio.

"I think so. It will be quicker than taking it apart and bringing it here."

"Problem solved, then," said Nills. "Now if you all don't mind I have a garden that needs attending to." With that, he and Gizmo headed off to the biodome.

Annis slumped down in a chair. "You're all still alive, I see."

"Sleep well, did we?" said Jann.

Annis scowled. "In case you haven't noticed, Kevin and Lu are dead and Decker is a vegetable. As first officer that puts me in command of this mission now, and we need to keep it on track."

"Eat some breakfast and chill out."

She looked at the food with disgust. "How do you know he's not trying to poison us?" I don't trust him—or that goofy robot."

"Actually, when I get back to Earth, I really want one of those things," said Paolio.

"That's assuming we get back," said Jann.

"Look, we've had a major setback, but there's no reason we can't salvage what we can from the mission. The colony still functions and a survivor has been found. This is major and we need to get this information back to COM."

"You mean ISA," Jann was pouring herself some colony cider.

"Yes, yes, I mean ISA." Annis paused for a minute, like she was considering something and looked from one to the other. "Just so we're all up front," she finally said, "if either of you start going off the rails... I won't hesitate to kill you."

"That's nice of you, Annis. You're such a sweetie," replied Jann.

15

BLOODS

Paolio felt extremely fatigued after the morning's breakfast with Nills. No doubt, the two mugs of colony cider and the smoke had a lot to do with it. Nevertheless, he was still physically fragile after what Decker did to him, so he went back to the accommodation module to rest. Jann headed into the medlab to check on the commander. As for Annis... well Jann wasn't really sure where she went.

There was no change in Decker. His breathing, heart rate and temperature were all still elevated. His skin was a heightened pink color and his body was drenched in sweat, like he was running a high fever. Earlier, Paolio had cleaned up the wound around his forehead. Jann leaned over to inspect the Italian doctor's handiwork. The scratches that Decker had accumulated all over his face were healing fast. In fact, they were nearly gone. Perhaps the injuries weren't as bad as she had originally thought. Lifting up the bandage covering Decker's head wound, Jann was startled to find that it had also begun to heal. Better mention it to Paolio when he arrived. No doubt he would have an explanation for this seemingly remarkable healing power.

She let him be and turned her attention to the equipment in the medlab. Before embarking on any tests she first needed to do an audit of what was available to her. As a medical surgery it was well equipped and stocked. But for in-depth analysis, she would need something more sophisticated. Possibly the research lab on the other side of the facility had what she needed. But that was offline for the moment. Maybe Nills could be persuaded to get it back up and running. In the meantime, she had a reasonably good microscope at her disposal here, so she could start doing some preliminary investigations.

By late morning she had taken a blood sample from Decker, as well as a number of other swabs, and was now incubating a series of test cultures. If there were any invasive bacteria roaming around in the commander then these tests would go a long way to finding it. However, they needed hours, possibly days, in the incubator before any conclusive results could be ascertained, so she had time to kill. Rather than waste it she made up several slides with a drop of Decker's blood using different stains. She placed the first one under the scope and peered through the lens. She delicately moved and shifted the focus point around the sample, not really expecting to find anything out of the ordinary.

It contained the usual mix of healthy blood biology. She would try and get an approximation of cell count, giving her a base to chart any rise or fall over time. Then something caught her eye. A darkened area; she focused in. A cluster of elongated cells came into view. Jann marked the spot and continued with her visual scan. She found another, and another. She wouldn't need the incubated cultures after all. Decker's blood was teeming with bacteria.

Her first thought was it might be tetanus, a fairly typical blood infection, usually picked up from soil. But it didn't have the right features for her to be certain, and this being Mars, it wasn't in the soil up here. Yet, there was something very familiar about these cells, the elongated rod shape, the waxy surface... she had seen this before. Then it hit her. "Impossible... it can't be."

She sat back and contemplated this discovery. Was this the cause of Decker's psychosis? She stood up and was about to go find Paolio, to give him the news, when another thought entered her head. Maybe she should check her own blood. She wrapped a tourniquet around her upper arm and bit down on the loose end to pull it tight. She clenched her fist, felt her forearm for a suitable vein and identified a candidate. She flicked the cap of a syringe with her thumb and jabbed it in. Jann retracted the plunger and drew up her own blood. Once the plunger could go no further she gently extracted the needle and released the tourniquet. She prepared a slide with a drop from the syringe and placed it under the microscope. After a few moments of searching she sat back in the chair and breathed a sigh of relief... she found nothing. But that didn't mean she wasn't infected. It might still be there in much lower levels. Too few for her to detect with such a tiny random sample. She considered making up another slide, but it would be better to incubate a culture. If there were any bacteria it would grow and multiply in the petri dish. But it would take a long time for a clear result—assuming this was what she thought it was.

Jann heard the whirr of a motor and turned to see Paolio drive in to the medlab in his scrapyard wheelchair. "How's our patient?" he said.

"No change. But have a look at this." She directed him to the microscope and hit a button to bring up a snapshot of Decker's sample on the monitor.

"What am I looking at here?"

"A blood sample from Decker."

Paolio examined the image. "Looks like a pretty bad bacterial infection, any idea what type?"

"I've seen something like this before. But not in blood, only in skin tissue."

Jann looked at Paolio for a moment like she was considering what she was going to say next. "Paolio, how familiar are you with *Mycobacterium Leprae*?"

He thought about this. "*Leprae*?" He tapped his chin with a finger as he thought. Then it dawned on him. "Leprosy! Are you saying this is leprosy?"

"Do you know anything about the disease?"

Paolio screwed up his face as he delved into the recesses of his memory, trying to resurrect any snippet of information he had stored away. "Let me think. Not something that a medical practitioner comes across these days. I know it's bacterial, affects the nervous system and that around 95% of humans have immunity to it. Other than that, not a lot."

"You're correct, it's bacterial, and it attacks nerve cells. But it can perform a very remarkable trick. What it does is turn nerve cells into stem cells, cells that can become anything: muscle, bone, organs... anything. Not only that, it also alters the human DNA within the cell, a bit like a retrovirus."

"No, I didn't know that."

"As you can imagine, this is of great interest to geneticists. Here's a bacteria that can manufacture stem cells and alter DNA at the same time."

Are you sure that's what it is?"

"I did a thesis on it, that's how I recognized it."

"So, this is leprosy?"

"Well... no. It's something very like it. A lot more virulent for one."

"A mutation?"

"More likely it's been engineered. Probably right here."

"Holy shit." Paolio looked over at the unconscious commander.

"Why? For what purpose? He was looking at the image on the monitor more intently now.

"If you wanted a way to re-engineer a human from the inside. '*Mycobacterium Leprae*' gives you the tools. A bacteria that creates stem cells with your very own DNA payload."

Paolio stared wide-eyed at Jann. "Jesus."

"Yes, exactly. Playing God."

Paolio looked back at the image and pointed to the cluster of cells. "Do you think that is the cause of the commander's psychosis?"

"Well, it would seem to be a likely candidate. Then again, it could be something else entirely. If we could get the research lab up and running then I'd be able to do more in-depth analysis. I might be able to sequence it, or at least part of it.

"That could take a while."

They both looked back at the image on the monitor and said nothing for a time.

"What about trying some antibiotics, see if that kills it? It's old-school, but it's just bacteria after all."

"Worth a shot."

"Okay, I'll check what they have here and what we brought with us and see if one of them can kill it. If it does then we might just be able to bring him back."

"I've also checked my own blood."

"And..."

"I found nothing. Nevertheless, I'm doing a culture test, just in case. I'll need to check everyone, though."

Paolio rolled up his sleeve. "I'm sure mine is 80% caffeine."

"Sorry, I feel guilty about taking a blood sample from you. You lost quite a bit already." Jann unpacked a new syringe.

"A few ccs more isn't going to make any difference now."

When Jann had finished Paolio grabbed two more syringes and stuffed them into a pocket. "I'll go and get samples from the others."

"Okay. Oh... before you go, can you have a look at this?"

She walked over to where Decker was lying and lifted the dressing from his head wound. Paolio leaned in and examined him. He looked up at Jann with a raised eyebrow. "That's almost healed. Quite extraordinary."

"That's what I thought, and see here, all the scratches on his face are gone, too." Paolio sat back in his wheelchair and rubbed his chin. "I've never seen anything like it. It's like his body is in overdrive."

"What could cause that?"

"I really don't know." Paolio was about to replace the dressing but there was really no point now. He backed up his chair and sighed. "Things are getting weirder around here." He rolled across the medlab heading for the door. "No point in concerning ourselves with it now. I'll go get samples from the others."

"Paolio."

He turned back. "Yes?"

"I think it would be best if you didn't go mentioning *leprosy* to the others, for the moment."

"You mean Annis." He nodded.

"That's exactly who I mean."

16

WALKABOUT

First officer Annis Romanov felt, rather than heard, the hiss of the main Colony One airlock depressurizing through the thick laminate of her EVA suit. The outer door opened and she stepped out on to the dusty Martian surface. Ahead of her, to the east, lay the ISA HAB module. The others had effectively abandoned it now. With Paolio injured, Decker turned in to a lab rat and Malbec playing nursemaid, the decision had essentially been made for them to relocate to Colony One. After all, it had no shortage of space and food. Nevertheless, it was vital for Annis to establish communications with Earth, and it gave her a valid reason to spend most of her time in the HAB rather than in the contaminated biology of Colony One. She didn't trust the place; the less time spent there the better, as far as she was concerned. Fixing the comms unit was as good a reason as any to isolate herself in the HAB. However, she wasn't going to fix it—she didn't need to. Fortunately she had a plan B. It was part of her mission brief with COM from the very beginning. And now was as good a time as any to execute it.

She looked out across the dunes towards the location of the ISA HAB. Its marker reflected on the heads up display on her visor. Another marker, farther from the HAB, identified the location of the fuel processing plant. And another outlined the Mars lander. This also doubled as the Mars Ascent Vehicle, the MAV. It served both to land on the planet's surface and lift off again to rendezvous with the Odyssey transit craft, still in orbit. To return to Earth they first had to refuel the MAV with supplies from the processing plant. But that operation was a long way off, a few more months at least.

Annis was not heading for the HAB this time. Instead, she took a few paces out from the colony airlock and turned north towards the location of the old supply lander. This had been sent in the aftermath of the disaster, when all contact from Colony One was lost. It contained emergency supplies of food, medicine and survival equipment. There was one item that she had been instructed by COM to utilize once she found an opportune moment early on in the mission. These were instructions to her directly from COM —they were not part of any ISA mission plan.

It was clear to Annis that the mission had already suffered a major catastrophe with two dead, Paolio injured and Malbec's crazy notion of helping the psychotic Decker. He should have been killed. He was still a danger and no amount of probing and poking by Malbec was going to change that. He had been contaminated by something in the colony and it was only when Annis left that she felt safe. If she had her way, they would leave this godforsaken place now. She was the first officer, the de-facto commander of the mission now that Decker had been compromised. She would not be brushed aside as if she were a minor entity, a bit player.

Annis moved across the dusty crater's surface, picking her way through the detritus of abandoned equipment. Every now and then she would pass the body of a dead colonist, a graphic reminder of the horror that had befallen the great Colony One adventure. After a time she left the main site behind and entered into the solar array field. Hundreds of black panels laid out across the crater, each slightly elevated to catch the maximum amount of sunlight. She looked up. A pale orb hung low in the Martian sky, bathing the solar array with life giving photons. She examined one of the panels. It was remarkably dust free. They had their own self-cleaning system, but they still needed regular manual maintenance to function at optimum levels. And the only way that could happen is if Nills went out onto the planet's surface. "So he *does* EVA." She was beginning to mistrust him even more. She moved on.

It took a full fifteen minutes to get through the array field and arrive at the location of the old supply lander. Its squat form rose out of the landscape like the conning tower of a submarine breaking through the ice. The bright red COM logo emblazoned on the side was still visible. The three and a half years of Martian dust and sand had still not etched it clean.

Annis located the hatch and worked the levers to open it. Once the bolts retracted she grabbed the handles, lifted the entire door off and set it down on the sand. The inside was jammed with equipment and supplies. She started unloading bags and boxes. None of these were of any use to her, what she was looking for was the emergency communications unit.

When this supply mission was being put together, it had been considered that the comms might be damaged, and that any survivors would need a way to communicate with Earth. COM still had its satellite in orbit around the planet, targeted on the colony site. All the comms unit had to do was connect with that satellite and two-way communications could be re-established.

It didn't take her long to find what she was looking for. Two suitcase sized units, one a satellite uplink and the other the comms unit. She dragged them out of the modules and put them down on the ground outside. She then brought up her 3D display and tapped out the commands to call the rover to her location. It would take a few minutes so she repacked the supply module and replaced the outer hatch. Annis then moved the satellite uplink unit to the far side of the supply module so it would not be visible from the colony, unpacked it and extended the solar array. Having spent three years inside the supply module it was unlikely that it had any charge, in fact she was doubtful that it even worked.

She waited. Every now and then she would check the satellite unit to see if it showed any signs of life. She was beginning to think that it was totally dead when the unit responded with an orange charge light. So far so good. After a few more minutes the charge light turned green. *Okay, time to see if this puppy works.* She extended the dish antenna and hit the search button. The unit was now slowly tracking across the sky seeking out the communications satellite, and it didn't take long to find it. The small screen came to life and showed the connection and signal strength. *Excellent,* thought Annis. In about thirty minutes time the old COM control center back on Earth would see the connection.

By the time Annis had finished establishing the satellite link the rover was already in sight, rolling across the surface, tracking to her location. Setting up the satellite link was only half the job. She now needed to unpack and power up the comms unit. Only then could she send a report. This however, could only be done inside. So when the rover finally arrived she threw the unit onto it and headed for the HAB. All going well, she should now be able to re-establish communication with Earth and talk directly to COM, without ISA snooping in on the conversation.

THE CLOSER TO the HAB she got, the less paranoid she felt. It had become her safe zone. A place where she felt insulated from the malignancy of the Colony One environment. She unloaded the comms unit from the back of the rover and entered the airlock. She waited as it repressurized and decontaminated her EVA suit, removing any dust and particles that had accumulated. She wished it would decontaminate her as well. She was beginning to feel like her body was invaded by the contamination from the colony. The light went green and she wasted no time in stripping off her EVA suit before entering the HAB interior. The place was still a mess after Decker had trashed it. She should really clean it up. *Some other time,* she thought. In the operations area she hoisted the unit up onto the bench, opened it up and spent a few minutes connecting power from the central HAB source.

The screen illuminated and showed a schematic of the satellite's position and strength of signal. Everything looked good. Time to send her report. Annis kept it short and to the point, it was done in a few minutes. Nevertheless, it would take at least thirty minutes for it to reach Earth, and at least another hour before COM could digest her message and formulate a reply. She had time to kill, so she decided to take a shower and wash the colony grime from her body.

The prevailing paranoia that rumbled beneath the surface of First Officer Annis Romanov's sanity was one of contamination. If Decker had succumbed to it then maybe it was only a matter of time until they all met the same fate. Yet none of the others had shown any signs of mental instability—at least no more than normal. And Nills said it only infected some. But then a thought struck her as the hot shower beat down on her back. *Maybe he's the one infecting them, maybe he's picking them off one by one—him and that robot sidekick.*

Her arm hurt and she realized that she had been scrubbing it until it was red raw, trying to wash the contamination out of her. She stopped the shower and got out to dry herself. She still didn't feel clean. It was like it was inside her and no amount of scrubbing was going to shift it. She dressed, tied her hair back and went over to the operations area to check on the comms unit. A message had come through. It was direct from Nagle Bagleir and started with the usual bullshit. Annis carefully listened to the message twice, to ensure that she understood what they required of her. When it finished she sat back in the chair, ran her fingers through her still wet hair and laughed. "That crazy hippie's not going to like this."

17

THE ANALOGUE

All had gone dark—again. It looked like Rick Mannersman's premonitions were turning out to be true. There had been no communication with the ISA crew now for over twenty-four hours and anxious eyes in mission control scanned satellite imagery for any clue as to surface activity—there was still hope. Peter VanHoff's tablet pinged and the avatar that was Nagle materialized in front of his field of vision and spoke. "Some interesting developments, Peter."

"This better be good news."

"Good and bad. The good news is our agent, First Officer Annis Romanov, has re-established communications by utilizing the emergency comms unit, sent up on the last supply lander."

"Excellent."

"Indeed, it means we now have direct communications with her, outside the sphere of ISA influence. The bad news is that our worst fears may have been realized."

"Don't tell me... it's happening again."

"I'm afraid so. The ISA Commander Decker has

developed a violent and destructive psychosis. So far he has killed Chief Engineer Kevin Novack and Seismologist Lu Chan."

"Oh dear God, no."

"Nonetheless, our agent has seen fit to contain the commander. He is strapped down in the medlab and suitably sedated. She has also set Dr. Malbec the task of establishing the cause."

"Is that wise?"

"Only time will tell. What I do think would be wise is if Romanov redirects any analysis back to us, so we can get some clues as to the nature of this affliction."

"Hmmm. I see. Does ISA know any of this yet?"

"The commander has also destroyed the ISA comms unit in the HAB, hence the reason there have been no reports to ISA. So no, they are still in the dark and we have not informed them, as yet. But there is another significant development. A survivor has been found."

"You're kidding me, after all this time?"

"Nills Langthorp, colonist number thirteen."

"How in God's name did he survive this long?"

"From what we know of him he is a highly skilled engineer and very resourceful."

"Well, I suggest we see how things develop before informing ISA. Because once we do, there goes our control again."

"My thoughts exactly."

"Has Romanov located the *Analogue*?"

"Not yet, the research lab is shutdown. They will need to bring it back online first."

"Can she not EVA in there and retrieve it?"

"Difficult. If the entire facility were derelict then yes, she could. I know that was our initial plan, but the fact that it's not makes the operation risky. We have to make it operational first."

"I don't like it. We can't have them poking around in that lab. Particularly if this Dr. Malbec is involved in the analysis. That lab would be an Aladdin's cave for her."

"It's a risk we have to take if we want the Analogue."

Peter VanHoff paced, a habit of his when he was thinking. He turned back to the avatar that was Nagle. "Fine, if we must. But once the Analogue has been retrieved that lab needs to be destroyed. No one must know what went on in there. Is that understood?"

"Yes. I will instruct Romanov on how to proceed."

"Ensure that she is suitably motivated. She may be required to go well beyond the initial mission brief before this is over. Particularly if Malbec gets too nosy—or lucky."

"Understood." The avatar that was Nagle extinguished itself.

18

NO RETURN

Jann opened the door to the incubator and inspected the petri dish cultures. One from each of the remaining ISA crew and one from Nills. It was plainly obvious, from the multitude of blots populating the agar gel, that they were all infected. Yet, Jann checked them anyway, one by one, under the microscope just to be certain. And there it was, the same elongated bacterium that had infected Decker, and possibly morphed him into a deranged psychotic. It was present in all the crew samples. However, it was only Decker that had developed the devastating psychological transformation. The good news, if she could call it that, was their infection load was much lower. It seemed that all but Decker had some way of fighting the infection, fending off the biological invasion and keeping them sane.

Nills, on the other hand, was clear. Even though he had been exposed to this for years, his sample looked to Jann to be completely free of the bacteria. Perhaps she made some mistake in preparing it. She would need to check again to be absolutely sure.

The implications of these results began to percolate in Jann's mind. The bacteria were highly virulent and once infected, you either went psychotic or your body figured out a way to live with it. This meant that there was only one option now—she had to find a way to kill it. And if she failed, then none of them could leave the planet. Ever.

The risk of carrying this plague back home and infecting Earth was unthinkable. It had the potential to devastate the human race. A pandemic bordering on apocalypse. Of course, she was assuming that this bacterium was in fact the cause. Jann had no real proof of that—as yet. She looked over at Decker. His chest rose and fell as the monitors drew out his life in luminescent peaks and troughs. He had been lying in stasis for a long time now. His consciousness held in check by the drip-drip of drugs. *How long would he last like that?* she wondered. A month, less? It was slow death by starvation. Perhaps Annis was right. Killing him might have been better—more humane. Yet, she had to try. It had gone beyond simply Decker now, they were all in this, all infected. If she was to ever see the blue planet again then she had to find a solution. A way to kill it.

Since it was a bacterium, it might be as simple as administering a course of the appropriate antibiotic, as Paolio had suggested. The lab was well stocked, although how much was in date would impact on its effectiveness. But they had others in the HAB. It would help if she knew more about the type of bacteria she was dealing with here. It was engineered, that much she was certain. But how and why she had no clue, unless she could dig deeper into its DNA. For the moment at least, she had no way to perform those kinds of test. Not that it mattered in reality. Decker would be the guinea pig. If the antibiotics worked on him they would work on the rest of them. In the meantime she would repeat the culture test on Nills. If it still proved negative then here at least was a potential source of biological answers—maybe even an antibody. But she was getting ahead of herself.

On the bench, beside the microscope, a red LED blinked on her comms headset. She picked it up, placed over her head and hit the receive button. It was Annis.

"Malbec, nice of you to answer. You'll be happy to hear I managed to re-establish communications with Earth."

"That's great, you fixed it. What was wrong with it?"

"Eh... look I don't have time to get into the technicalities. Suffice to say, I managed to send a report back to Earth."

"And?"

"And the upshot is they want to get the research lab back online. They reckon it will help you in your investigations."

"That's fantastic."

"Now listen. We need to get that hippie on board with this. I've been sent the boot-up routines and schematics, but it would be better if he and that goofy robot of his help us. He knows the systems better than anyone."

"Okay, when are you coming back here?"

"I'm on my way."

"Well bring some food... and coffee."

"Malbec, we've got more important things to concern ourselves with than food."

"If you want to get Nills on board then there is no better way than to come bearing gifts. He's been living on a diet of fish and plants for years. He may well be in need of a change —even if it's just for the novelty."

"Fine, I get your point."

"And Annis..."

"What?"

"When you get here, be nice."

"Jesus, Malbec. Next you'll be asking me to seduce him with my womanly charms."

I wouldn't worry about that. You don't have any, thought Jann as she switched off the headset.

ANNIS DUTIFULLY BROUGHT BACK SUPPLIES. They consisted of some standard ISA food rations and a few pouches of ground coffee. Nills was tucking into a portion of Chicken Tikka Masala. "This is just amazing. I had forgotten how good it tastes."

"Consider it an Indian takeout, with a 140 million mile delivery," said Paolio. "To be honest, we're pretty tired of it after three months."

"And this coffee is simply ambrosial." He sipped the thick black beverage. "You know, we tried to grow the Arabica plant up here. Not very successfully. It's a difficult and temperamental plant to grow, even on Earth."

"What did mission control have to say?" Jann was prompting Annis to get to the point now that Nills had been softened up.

"They want the research lab brought back online."

Nills stopped eating and looked wide-eyed at Annis. "No way. It's too dangerous. And besides, there's every possibility that none of the equipment will work after all this time."

"Well that's what they want us to do—with or without your help," said Annis.

"What's the difficulty in bringing the research lab back online?" asked Jann.

Nills sighed and sat back in the battered armchair. "There are lots. For one it's a power suck. That's the reason we shut it down back during the storm. It uses a whack load of juice. Two, it's been sitting in deep-freeze for over three years so if things start shorting then it could cause more serious power problems back along the line, jeopardizing the main colony life support. Not something to take lightly."

"But I thought parts of it are still up and running?"

"Yes, there are systems in there still powered up. They can't be shut down, I don't know why, but they were obviously important."

"We could isolate all the ancillary equipment circuits, use a standalone power source, bring life support up first, then power up the machines one by one as needed," offered Gizmo.

Nills gave him a look as if to say *'traitor.'* He scratched his chin and then poked at the Indian takeout with his fork. "Maybe. But we would still need to recycle the air supply a few times to clean it out while keeping it isolated. That's assuming there are no leaks, you know, that the modules can still hold one atmosphere of pressure. And the condensation buildup doesn't short anything out."

"We have to try. There's probably a lot of specialist equipment in there that might help us find answers to this infection."

"Assuming that's what it is, an infection. Who's to say it not related to the Martian gravity or contamination in the soil or a whole lot of other things?" said Nills.

"What were they doing in there anyway? We've got no record of it in our initial brief. In fact it doesn't even show on anything we have." Jann flicked through a sheaf of ISA notes and diagrams.

"Genetic research, at least that's what they said." Nills was now biting into an apple. He wiped his mouth with the back of his hand, leaned in and looked at them intently. "Four of them... they were a breed apart. They came shortly after the biodome was built and started creating the research lab. Dr. Venji and three others. Said they were developing new bio-organisms for the colony. But there was something about them, kept themselves away from everyone else. They had their own accommodation module, ate their own food, seldom mixed with the rest of us. Rumors started that COM was planning to return them back to Earth after... whatever it was they were doing was finished. I don't know if that's true or not. But one thing is for sure, they were up to lot more than they let on." He sat back and waved the apple core in the air. "To be fair, they did bring a lot of advanced medical equipment and supplies with them." He dumped the apple core into the remains of the Tikka Masala. "About six months into their stay here they started doing tests on all the colonists. Medical checks they called them. They got more frequent as time went on."

"What sort of checks?" said Paolio.

Nills waved his hand. "Checks, I don't know. They would lay us out in the medlab and wire us up. Told us we were in perfect health, and all that."

"We need to get that lab back online, and then maybe we can find some answers," said Jann

"I doubt that any of it will still work." Nills shrugged his shoulders. "But hey... if you think it's worth trying then Gizmo and I will give it a go." He stood up. "We'll have to run a lot of diagnostics first, so that's going to take a bit of time."

"How long?"

"I don't know, several hours at least. Then we can try. But first, I have other work to attend to. What with all these extra mouths to feed." He got up and moved off towards the biodome, Gizmo following faithfully behind.

. . .

Paolio sipped his coffee. "He's probably right, you know."

"About what?"

"About none of the equipment functioning."

"Maybe." Jann wondered if now would be a good time to break the news. "I've done some preliminary tests on our blood samples."

"And?" said Annis, sitting forward.

"I've found traces of the same bacteria in Decker in all of us."

"Shit," said Annis. "You mean we're all infected?"

"Except for Nills. He seems to be clear, as far as I can tell."

"I knew it. Don't you see, he's infecting us?" Annis was standing up pointing back in the direction of the biodome.

"That's crazy. He's just built up an immunity to it. He probably doesn't even know himself." Jann was now also standing, facing off with Annis.

Annis seemed to back off a bit. "Maybe, but I still don't trust him." She started to pace. "Do you know what it is?"

Jann hesitated, she wasn't sure how Annis was going to react. "It's a genetically modified variant of *Mycobacterium Leprae*."

"What the hell is that?"

"Leprosy," said Paolio.

"Leprosy? You mean this is a goddamn leper colony?"

"No, it's a derivative, not the same thing."

"So how do you get rid of it? Annis was leaning into the table now.

"We're trying some antibiotics, but none have worked so far," said Paolio.

"Well that's just great, just goddamn great." She sat down again shaking her head.

"It's impossible to know with what we've got in the

medlab, Annis," said Paolio. "That's why we need the research lab up and running."

"There's one other thing," said Jann. She might as well get it all out on the table, so to speak.

"What now?" said Annis.

"We can't leave this planet until we find a cure."

Annis was back on her feet again. "That's bullshit."

"No, seriously, we can't afford to bring this back to Earth."

"No way, I'm not staying on this rock any longer than I have to. I didn't sign up for this crap." She was moving around, waving her hands in the air. "Screw this," she said, and stormed out of the common room.

JANN AND PAOLIO SAT IN SILENCE FOR A MINUTE.

"I thought she took that pretty well, all things considered." Paolio said finally.

"Where's she off to? Back to the HAB?"

"I'll talk to her later, once she settles down a bit."

"She's losing it," said Jann.

"She's just under a lot of stress, we all are."

"There's one other thing," said Jann.

"I'm not sure if I can take any more. What now?"

"It's Annis. Her infection load is much higher than the rest of us."

Paolio picked up his coffee cup from the table and looked over at Jann. "You think she's a risk?"

"I don't know. It's nowhere near Decker's, but it's much higher that than rest of us."

Paolo looked into his empty cup. "I think I'm going to need a lot of strong coffee." He swung his wheelchair in the direction of the galley.

"I'd better go and talk to Nills." Jann stood up and headed for the biodome.

Paolio turned back to her with a smile, "Oh, and Jann..."

"What?"

"Remind me never to have dinner with you ever again."

19

BIO-DOME

Jann went in search of Nills and found him deep inside the biodome. He was in an area where he had created the garden, as he liked to call it. It was a rustic vegetable patch, no hydroponics, no hi-tech lab equipment, no use of any twenty-first century technology. Of course, this belied the fact that all plants were bioengineered, the soil was treated with specially manufactured GM bacteria to cleanse it of Martian toxins and no pests would ever come to blight this crop. Nevertheless, it had the outward appearance of a typical kitchen garden, an oasis of low-tech simplicity in an environment of hi-tech engineering.

He was digging potatoes and piling them into containers. His fluid movements told of long practice at this very task. Jann watched him for a while from a distance, peering through the gaps in the overgrowth. His simple unhurried movements had a calming effect on her. Eventually, it was he that spoke first. "I won't bite, you know."

"Sorry, I didn't mean to spy." She came out from behind

a large hanging vine. He stopped and rested an arm on the handle of his spade and gave her a bright smile. If it hadn't been for the latticework of the domed roof in the background he looked just like any artisan gardener, working in his allotment back on Earth.

"Want to help? It's good for the spirit."

Jann considered this for a moment. Paolio was talking to Annis, getting her head straightened out—hopefully. Decker was going nowhere and there was not much else she could do until the research lab was brought back online. "Sure, why not."

"Here, let me show you." He picked up a short handled fork. "You dig in like this, not too hard, so you don't skewer a spud. Then lift out the earth and give it a shake." Four potatoes of varying sizes were resting on the fork. He leaned over to pick one up. "These bigger ones we store for eating, these smaller ones go into this container and we'll keep them for replanting." He handed her the fork. "Think you can manage it?"

"Hey, you're talking to a farm girl here. I grew up tending vegetables." She took the fork and went to work. Nills was right, it was good for the spirit. After a while they got into a rhythm. Nills went ahead and pulled up plants as Jann followed by digging out tubers. They harvested quite a bit in the time they were at it.

"Okay, I think that's enough for now." He wiped the sweat from his forehead. "Let's get these stored." They carried the boxes between them as they traversed the biodome over to a processing room. It was small and crammed with machines, most of which seemed to be of Nills' own making. They laid the boxes on a long bench. Jann watched him as he fiddled with one of the contraptions and started it up.

"Did you ever get lonely up here, all those years on your own?"

"Yea, sure. Well... at first there were three of us, after we got rid of the last crazy."

"What happened to them?" Jann continued, now that Nills was ready to talk again.

"Jonathan... died of natural causes, not sure what exactly. He simply wasted away over a few months. It was hard to watch him go like that, after all he'd been through. That left myself and Bess."

"Bess? Bess Keilly?"

"Yes, did you know her?"

"No. We... eh... came across her... body, in the stone hut, out past the big dune."

Nills stopped sorting the potatoes and hung his head. He said nothing for a while, then spoke in a soft tone, almost a whisper. "So that's where she went. I should have known." He looked up at Jann again. "We were close. But the isolation began to get to her. She became more and more depressed as each day passed. Eventually, she just went out the airlock one morning and never came back."

"Oh... I'm sorry, I didn't mean to..."

Nills shrugged. "It's okay."

After a moment Jann continued. "Did you ever try to look for her?"

"Yes, but I started to get panic attacks when I went EVA. They got worse and worse each time I went out. Eventually I just stopped trying."

"So that's why you don't go outside?"

"Yeah. Fortunately Gizmo can go out for me if something really needs to be done, like cleaning the solar panels, that sort of stuff."

"It must have been hard on you."

He waved a hand. "Ah... it's just this place, what happened, everything. It tries very hard to kill you, one way or the other. Physically, mentally, emotionally.

"Do you ever miss Earth?"

"In the beginning I did. But after a while I realized what I really missed was the physical Earth, the natural beauty of it. What I didn't miss was humanity's desire to destroy it." He turned back to the machine and adjusted some dials. "But tell me... would you miss Earth?"

Jann sighed. "If I don't find an answer to this infection then I don't think we'll be going home. So, ask me again if we're still here in a few months."

"Ahh, I see. Sorry if I don't look surprised. I could have told you that the first time we met." He proceeded to empty the harvested potatoes into a hopper on the machine and started it up. It made a horrendous racket. He signaled to Jann with a nod of his head to move back into the biodome. Jann waited until they were in a quiet spot before telling him her news. "I've run some tests on the blood samples we took. We're all infected, except you."

He stopped. "I see. Do you know what it is?"

"I think your hunch was right, it's caused by a bacterial infection."

"And you say I don't have it?"

"No, not as far as I can tell, but I need to do more tests to be certain."

Nills considered this for a moment. "You know, this all started to happen after the research lab was in operation."

"Is that why you don't want to reactivate it?"

"What do you think? Whatever is in that lab doesn't need to get out again."

"But if that's where it came from then we may have a

chance of finding out what it is... and maybe find a way to kill it."

Nills scratched his chin again, like he couldn't get used to not having a beard. He had shaved it off a while ago and it made him look even younger. Jann and the others still couldn't quite get over his youthful appearance. Paolio had put it down to diet. He also postulated that maybe the one-third gravity had a beneficial effect on aging. But this was all speculation. Nonetheless, Nills looked like a twenty year old, not someone the wrong side of thirty-five.

"If it's bacteria then surely antibiotics would kill it?"

"We've been trying various types on Decker's samples, but still no luck. It seems to be highly resistant to anything we've thrown at it so far."

"Like it was engineered that way?" He stopped and looked at her.

"Yes, that's what I'm beginning to think. We're dealing with something that was engineered rather than evolved here. You have to remember that bacteria can evolve relatively fast. I had thought that it was something designed for the ecosystem here that had mutated."

"But now you're not so sure?"

"No. That's why we need to get into the research lab and take a look."

As if on cue, Gizmo sped into the biodome. "Nills, I've done the diagnostics and run through a number of activation sequences. My best scenario has a 78% success probability."

"Thanks, Gizmo." He turned back to Jann. "Are you sure you want to do this?"

"Yes, it's the only option... if we're ever going to be able to return to Earth."

"It's not so bad here. After a few years you might even get to like it." He laughed.

Jann smiled and looked around her. He did have a point, even if he was just joking. It had a beauty to it, like an oasis in a world gone mad, even if that oasis was 140 million miles away. "Yeah, I might."

"Although it's better when you have someone to share it with." He smiled and at that moment Jann found herself quite attracted to this enigmatic soul. He radiated calm and serenity and Jann felt herself drawn in by its glow. She stopped short and looked away. "I should go and check in with Paolio, see how the commander is doing. Maybe he has some good news with the antibiotics."

"Okay, sure. Gizmo and I need to... eh, run through some more stuff, anyway. If everything checks out then we'll start reactivation tomorrow."

"Great." She walked out of the garden, heading for the medlab.

HER MEETING with Nills had left Jann feeling more optimistic, or maybe she was just less pessimistic. Either way she no longer had a tight knot of apprehension in her gut. She decided not to go and find Paolio just yet. He might still be talking to Annis and she didn't want to interrupt that dialogue. Instead, Jann sat down in the common area on a battered armchair and took some time out.

Along the wall were pinned a number of sketches and artworks, presumably created by the colonists, back in happier times. They all depicted scenes from Mars. Some were landscapes, some portraits of people, some were even quite accomplished. One caught her eye. It was a well crafted landscape sketched with some type of brown charcoal. In the foreground two colonists in full EVA suits embraced. She stared at it for a while.

What was the worst thing that could happen? They would be stranded here. Was that so bad? Jann began to think the unthinkable and the more she thought about it the more she began to feel giddy. Was it so strange to imagine a life in a botanical paradise, shared with the radiant Nills? She shook her head, she was getting soppy. But then again, if this was worst case scenario, it wasn't so bad after all, at least not in her mind. But what of the others? Paolio and Annis?

Yet there was something else she was not considering in all of this. What was it? Jann couldn't put her finger on it. It was there in her subconscious trying to get out, a new danger, a deeper threat. There was something she was missing. The knot returned in her gut and gripped it tight. Was it the infection, malignly working away to undermine her sanity? A shiver ran through her body. The thought of it repulsed her and dispelled any romantic notions she had of this place. Then another thought exploded in her mind. Could she end up like Decker? A deranged homicidal maniac? "Oh dear God, don't let me lose my mind."

"JANN." Paolio buzzed into the common room on his motorized wheelchair. "Did you speak to Nills?"

"Yes, he thinks they can start the reactivation of the research lab tomorrow."

"Good."

"How's Annis?"

"She's returned to the HAB."

"Why won't she stay here? We really need to stick together."

"I know, but there was no stopping her. Anyway, I've given her all the data from our sample analysis. She's going to send it through to mission control tonight. Maybe the boffins back on Earth can shed some light on what it is."

"And Decker?"

"The same. No change."

Jann sighed and slumped back in the chair. It was late and she was exhausted. They sat in silence for a moment. Then Jann leaned forward and spoke very low. "Paolio. I want you to do me a favor."

"Sure, name it."

"If… if I should go like Decker, you know… succumb to this infection. I want you to… kill me."

"Jesus, Jann, that's a bit dramatic… anyway, it's not going to happen."

"But if it does, you promise me you'll do this."

"It's not going to come to that."

"Promise me."

Paolio looked at her for a moment. "You know I can't promise that. I'm a doctor. My duty is to save life, not end it."

Jann slumped back in her chair again. "I'm sorry, I shouldn't have asked you, it's unfair of me." She looked back at the wall of paintings. "Maybe you're right. Maybe it won't come to that."

"Let's hope not."

20

RECALIBRATION

Nills examined the rows of overripe tomatoes. Some had already fallen from the vine and would be good for nothing except composting. He should have picked them at least three days ago. The beans needed tying up and he really should check the herb garden to see which plants had seeds ready to save. His carefully scheduled tasks were falling behind and now he was playing catch up. The arrival of the ISA crew had thrown a spanner into his world and created stress where before there was harmony. The rhythm that he and Gizmo had grown accustomed to was disrupted. A new dynamic had entered colony life and new demands were being placed on its resources. Deep down, he knew this would happen sooner or later. New people would come to investigate what had happened, or simply tempted by the lure of adventure. Still, it was good to be able to talk to another human. For a long time he was uncertain of his own sanity. Had he gone mad after all these years? That uncertainty had been put to rest now, as he had truly survived—with his mind intact.

He thought of Jann, or was it Bess? He shook his head.

He needed more time, it was too soon to contemplate such emotions. "Put it out of your mind," he said to himself.

"Put what out of your mind?" said Gizmo, who was shadowing him as he worked.

"Oh, nothing, I was just thinking aloud," he said as he snipped a bunch of tomatoes and placed it in a box that Gizmo was holding for him. He stopped for a moment, looked around him and considered what he had achieved here in those three and a half long years.

In the beginning, the agriculture at Colony One had been utilitarian. Scientifically calculated to maximize yields. The plants where the vegetative equivalent of battery hens. The biodome was a factory simply for producing food. But since the demise of the colony population high yields had become unnecessary, so Nills had set about creating more of a garden than a factory. Slowly but surely he had given over more space to his Eden. And slowly but surely it gave him purpose and fortified his spirit. He would sit for long hours, surrounded by the lush vegetation, listening to the sound of the water flowing in the pond and stare up through the dome roof into the nighttime sky. It was at these moments that he realized you can take the human out of the Earth but you can't take the Earth out of the human. He might be living on an alien planet, but all around him was the very essence of Earth, of nature itself, of what it meant to be a living creature. He was more in tune with the ecosystem on this dusty godforsaken rock than he ever had been back home. It had taken him 140 million miles to get back to the garden.

He wiped a bead of sweat from his brow with his sleeve and set to work again. Both he and Gizmo spent their time harvesting and tending to the tomatoes as these were the most urgent. Then Nills turned his attention to building up the soil around a newly sprouting crop of potatoes as Gizmo went off to store the night's harvest. The little robot returned just as Nills finished the last of his work.

"They are related, you know."

"Who are?" replied Gizmo.

"Tomatoes and potatoes. They're both from the nightshade family, which includes *Deadly Nightshade*, a highly toxic plant."

"Interesting. I will make a note of that. Perhaps it may be a useful tidbit to regurgitate when I am next put upon in polite company, and find myself wanting for a fascinating fact to toss into the conversation."

Nills cocked an eyebrow and the little robot. "Indeed," he replied. "I think we're done here for tonight, Gizmo."

"The strawberries are sprouting new runners, should we not get these staked down?"

"Time enough for that tomorrow. There's been too much excitement around our little garden these last couple of days."

"Yes, it has been a rather dramatic interlude."

"I'm tired now. Come, let's sit a while and talk." Nills put away his garden tools and walked into the center of the dome. The little robot whirred along beside him. He sat down on a low chair fashioned from wood he had pruned from the fruit trees in the biodome over the years. It had a rustic artisanal look and felt perfectly in keeping with the verdant surroundings. Beside it was a low table made from the same materials. Nills waved his hand over the holo-tab that was resting there. A three dimensional control interface rendered itself above the surface and he tapped several of the icons in quick succession. A series of screens materialized, showing charts and data of the colony systems. Nills studied them for a while. "I see you have compensated for the additional oxygen requirement, Gizmo."

"Yes, Nills. Several adjustments needed to be made to accommodate the additional Earthlings."

"Very good. Everything looks nominal."

"I would suggest we need to recalibrate our food production process at some point. They could eat us out of house and home."

Nills scratched his chin. "This is a concern. However, they *have* brought their own supplies. Enough for a hundred days I understand. Since two are dead and one incapacitated then this could stretch for longer. So that gives us some time to increase our planting."

"Do they know yet that they will not be returning to Earth?" said Gizmo.

"It is only beginning to dawn on them. The problem will be how they are going to react when they do finally realize."

"Will they be disappointed?"

"Hopefully it's just disappointment and nobody starts getting crazy—doing something stupid."

"Yes, that would be most unfortunate."

Nills was now looking at a recording from one of the many cameras in the biodome. It was from a few hours earlier and showed Annis Romanov jogging around the path along the inner wall. She was panting and pushing hard. He studied her face as it swept into full view; he paused it. "We need to keep a close eye on her, Gizmo."

"Is she dangerous?"

"Unpredictable. And we don't like that do we?" He turned and looked at the robot.

"No, we like a place for everything, and everything in its place."

"Exactly." He returned to the screen and tapped another

icon. The recording of Romanov extinguished and was replaced by a direct video feed from the accommodation module. It was of a naked Dr. Jann Malbec preparing to have a shower. Nills flinched, his finger hovered over the camera control to switch it off and not intrude—but he lingered. He was drawn by the beauty of her poise, the arc of her neck, the curve of her spine. A memory stirred within him.

"Is she dangerous, too?" said Gizmo.

Nills tapped the off icon. "No, no, she's just... never mind." Nills' head slumped and he looked at the ground for quite some time before reaching up to wipe a tear from his eye.

Gizmo moved closer to his master and spoke in a surprisingly low tone. "Is it Bess again? Your eyes always water when you think of her."

Nills cocked a smile and the quirky robot. "Yes, Gizmo, I miss her and... well, she reminds me of her." He wiped his face again, shook his head and tapped another icon. This time a feed from the medlab showed Paolio examining the stricken Decker. Nills sat back in his chair and watched it for a while. From a pocket in his flight suit he took out a small metal box. He carefully opened it up and proceeded to roll himself a joint. He lit it, took a long drag and settled himself back into the wicker recliner. He watched the doctor take a blood sample from the commander and prepare it for more tests.

"Gizmo."

"Yes Nills."

"I think tomorrow it's time to give you an upgrade."

"Excellent, what sort of upgrade?"

"I think maybe a weapon or two might come in handy."

"Splendid, I do love playing with new gadgets."

21

LIES

Peter VanHoff scanned the lab report sent by first officer Romanov in her most recent communication. It was a blood sample analysis done by Dr. Jann Malbec on the ISA crew and the sole colonist Nills Langthorp. It was Malbec's identification of the bacterial infection that interested him most. He was impressed. It was clear that his geneticists on Colony One had been busy, as this was evidently their work. What intrigued him, however, was the fact that Nills Langthorp showed no signs of the infection. And what made this even more interesting was Romanov's observation of his youthful appearance. Clearly then, this bacteria had been an earlier attempt. They had come close, but the side effects were disastrous. He put the report aside, stood up, and paced.

The intention had always been to return the science team. There was only so much that could be done remotely. Although that turned out to be quite a lot. Nevertheless, acquisition of the active biology was the end game. The other reason was that it was difficult to get a team with any depth assembled if the mission was one-way. They just wouldn't go. But offer a return mission and then COM would have its pick of the best talent. They had been working on developing their own return mission for quite some time. But all that stopped when the colony fell apart. And with no more money coming in, it was left to wither on the vine. Getting into bed with ISA had been the only option left.

He waved a hand over the holo-tab and touched the icon to summon his second in command. A few moments later the avatar that was Nagle materialized in Peter VanHoff's field of vision and spoke.

"Good evening, Peter. How are you feeling today?"

"I told you not to keep asking me that."

"It's just a greeting, nothing more."

Peter grunted. "Have you seen the infection loads in the report?"

"I have."

"The survivor Nills Langthorp is clean."

"I noticed that, very interesting."

"This is all the evidence we need. I suggest we move forward our plans."

"I concur. I have also come to the conclusion that the mental state of our agent is deteriorating. At this rate we may not get another chance."

"Yes, I did notice her load was higher than the others, barring the commander of course. How is she holding up?"

"So far, so good. But that status may change very quickly the longer she is exposed. She is becoming more paranoid of Langthorp and the colony in general. She keeps referring to it as a leper colony. Also, Malbec is trying to convince her that returning to Earth would be catastrophic."

"Yes, well it would be—if we were going to let her live."

"My thoughts exactly. So I think we need to act now to secure the Analogue and complete the mission."

"You have a plan then?"

"Yes, it is as simple as it is elegant. Fortunately, Romanov's current state leaves her exposed to straightforward psychological manipulation. In essence, I plan to lie."

"Excellent. It's time to bring home the bacon, then."

ANNIS PACED the HAB floor with a deep primal rhythm, back and forth, back and forth, back and forth. She waited out time in measured steps. Each one closer to a reply from Earth. It should come soon.

The comms unit chimed an alert. A message had arrived. Annis broke her step, wheeled towards the unit and tapped receive. The avatar that was Nagle materialized before her and shimmered like a fiery beacon, a light in the darkness of an alien world. It spoke...

'We understand your concern, first officer Romanov, and concur with your hypothesis that the colonist, Nills Langthorp, is in fact the cause of this infection. We have long suspected that he may have even instigated the collapse of the colony. From Dr. Malbec's analysis, which you sent back in your report, we have ascertained that he, and the rest of your crew, are now all contaminated with a highly malign form of leprosy. However, you may remember the inoculations that our medical team administered to you before you departed. These were to provide a certain level of biological protection. Suffice to say, they are working and fortunately you are not contaminated—thus far.

Nevertheless, the longer you stay on the planet the less effective this protection will be and your life will be in increasing danger.

Therefore, it is imperative that you acquire the Analogue now and prepare the MAV for your return to Earth. You must also ensure all contaminants have been eradicated by destroying the research lab. Forsake all thoughts of the others as they can no longer be saved. You must save yourself. You are all that is left of the mission. We have the utmost faith in your ability to fulfill this difficult operation and return to Earth with the Analogue.

Good luck and God speed.'

The avatar that was Nagle faded and extinguished itself. In its place was left an empty space that was now being filled with the frenetic thoughts of First Officer Annis Romanov. *Return to Earth, leave the others, destroy the colony? Did she hear that right?* She paced over and across the HAB floor, bisecting it in a steady even pace, all the time thinking on the new mission requirements. She was not contaminated—Malbec was lying. She could still get out of this alive, and she could get out now.

Assuming that the research lab came back online, acquiring the Analogue would be simple. Preparing the MAV for launch without alerting the others would be a much more difficult task. What she needed was a distraction in Colony One, something to keep them all busy and buy her enough time. She required around thirty minutes to prepare the craft, another hour to move the six fuel canisters from the manufacturing plant and attach them, then another twenty minutes or so to run the prelaunch diagnostic. Around two hours in all.

She moved into the HAB airlock and donned her EVA suit. Time to head back to Colony One, hopefully for the last time. She closed her visor and hit the button for the outer door. Once the pressure was equalized she stepped out on to the surface and walked towards the seismic rover, its surface already covered in a layer of dust. From the rear storage hatch she extracted four explosive charges and placed them into a pocket in the front of her suit. "This should be enough of a distraction."

22

RESEARCH LAB

Nills and Gizmo were in the operations area studying a three-dimensional schematic of the research lab systems. They had been working on it all morning. Each time they tried to power up the lab, fail-safe circuits would kick in and power would die. And each time they would analyze the results and try to isolate the problems. Nills zoomed in on one of the four modules attached to the main research lab. "This seems to be the problem area, something in there is tripping the power every time we try and boot up."

"If my analysis of the circuitry is correct, and it generally is, then I would have to postulate that it already has some power," said Gizmo.

"Well, we've known for a long time that the main lab has been using a little power... for something, God knows what. But this is new." Nills looked over at his robotic friend. For a long time his careful husbandry of Colony One resources concluded that the facility used more power than he could account for. He made many attempts to identify this anomaly, to no avail. In the end he and Gizmo simply factored it into their calculations and lived with it. "Could this be the source of the power suck we've been seeing all this time?"

"I think you could be right. It is consistent with the 2.1% additional power loss we have been calculating."

"It's no wonder we couldn't find it. What the hell is going on in there?"

"Something so important that required it to be integrated with the low level life support. Something they did not want switched off."

Nills looked back at the schematic and drew his finger along a circuit line, pointing out the power connections to Gizmo. "I think we need to disable here and here, and reroute through here. Then we can try life support again."

"Roger that, Captain," said Gizmo. "Reconfiguring circuits now—ready."

"Okay, here goes." Nills tapped a few icons on the table and full power was again routed to the research lab. The schematic lit up with a series of red alerts all across the power circuits. "Shit. Well that didn't work. We're still getting a lot of shorts. I suppose it's to be expected with a unit as complex as this lying in deep-freeze for the last three and a half years. Gizmo, can you identify the new problem area?"

"Working on it." Circuits on the schematic flashed and danced as Gizmo reconfigured lab systems and rerouted connections. This went on for quite a while. "Okay," it said. "Try it again."

This time no alerts flashed. "Looking good, Gizmo. I think you've done it. Modules two and five are running hot, though—wait, looks like they're stabilizing.

"I estimate with the current power consumption we would have thirty five hours and forty six minutes of supply from the remote power unit we've set up," said Gizmo.

"Very good, let start with repressurizing the area." A graphic sea of illuminated bar graphs appeared over each module on the 3D holo-table. They all started to drift upwards and the research lab received its first taste of air in over forty months. The atmosphere now cycled through air scrubbers as they worked to clean it of moisture and contaminants. "Looks like we have a minor integrity issue in number four. Can we compensate?"

"We would have less than two point three percent deterioration over one full sol."

"I think we can live with that." Nills looked at the stats that were now streaming in. "Okay, it's going to take a few hours to cycle enough air through the lab before we can enter."

"Three point three two five, to be exact."

"Okay, you can let it roll. We'll check back on it later. Come, let's get back to the garden."

"Roger that," replied Gizmo.

A LITTLE OVER three hours later, Jann and Paolio were in front of the research lab door as Nills entered the code to open it. "Well, here goes."

They heard a thump as the locking bolts retracted followed by a slight hiss as the door opened forward. Nills stood back and waved his arm. "It's all yours." Jann stepped in first, followed by Paolio. The main lab was a large circular domed space, with racks for scientific equipment lined up along the walls. The center was crisscrossed with workbenches. A ring of pale green light illuminated the area, giving it a strange alien feel.

"There seems to be a lot missing," said Jann. There were obvious gaps both on the floor and in the racks where nothing remained except for a bunch of wires and tubes. Jann crouched down and examined the floor where one such unit was no longer. "Look, you can see the indents where something heavy stood here." She stood up. "Where has all this equipment gone?"

"I know they took some over to the mine," said Nills.

"But so much? More than half the equipment is gone," said Jann. "What were they doing over there?"

Nills just shrugged. "Mining?"

"Look at this." Jann ran her hand along the surface of a large machine, still bolted to the lab floor. "A DNA Sequencer. If this works it could prove very useful."

Around the perimeter of the research lab dome a number of additional modules had been attached, and Nills and Gizmo were examining the door into one of these. She could sense there was something about this module by the way they were discussing it. While Nills fiddled with the door keypad, Jann came over.

"What's in here?"

"It's an anomaly, it still had power going to it." He looked over at her. "It was never offline." Nills had taken apart the keypad, wire spooled out as he probed its innards with a small screwdriver. They heard a thump, and the door unlocked. "Okay, let's go check it out."

Bright fluorescent lights flickered on as they entered. Around the walls were what looked like server racks. Column after column, arrayed side by side all around the circular room. Each column had maybe twenty or so pizza-box sized units stacked horizontally, one on top of the other.

"Looks like a datacenter." Jann examined a unit, running her finger along the cryptic identification number on the slim fascia. She heard a click and jumped back as the unit silently slid out from its housing, the top gracefully opening as it moved. They gathered around and gazed into its mysterious interior. Inside, a myriad of strange illuminated circuitry, rendered in glass or some crystalline plastic, shimmered and pulsed with a slow hypnotic rhythm.

"What's this, some sort of bio-server?" said Paolio.

"Yes, you could say that," said Jann. "It's a biological analogue. A combination of electronic and living circuits—see here and here." Jann pointed to different areas of the strange circuit board. "Each of these sections are a facsimile of different organs: lungs, liver, kidneys. And here, look, the heart... see how it pulsates.

"Incredible."

"They're generally used for drug testing." Jann moved back and pushed the front of another of the units. It slid out and opened, just like the first. "As you know, drug testing is an enormously expensive exercise, and that's before it even gets to human trials. So if you could test a drug on an analogue then a pharmaceutical company could potentially save billions."

"I've heard of these, they've been talked about in medical circles for years. I always thought they were just fantasy." Paolio pushed another one out and was peering into its innards.

"So they were drug testing, that's how they got so much investment."

"More than that, they were doing human DNA engineering." Nills was pushing open more units and peering in. "We suspected it but, they were so secretive about what went on in here, it was mostly just speculation."

Jann suddenly realized. "Oh my God—they're human—they're colonists."

Paolio looked around at the panorama of racks, "There's a lot missing. Look at all these empty spaces. Still, there must be hundreds here. But there were only, what... fifty odd colonists?"

"There's probably at least three or four for each colony member. One would be a control, and could be used to create a genetic replica for experimentation."

"How would they even create such things?" said Paolio.

"Biopsy samples."

"But they would have to slice open all the colonists."

"Or stem cells." Jann looked over at Paolio as they both felt a piece of the puzzle fall into place.

"Stem cells, of course. The bacterium is how they created them. My God."

They all stood for a while just looking around, taking in the horror of what this room represented.

"You're probably in here somewhere." Jann said after a while as she looked over at Nills.

"Yes, but which one? We would need to get the IT systems up and running first to find out. But I don't suppose it matters that much now anyway."

Jann pushed the units back in. "It does if we want to find out what has afflicted the commander, and how to kill it."

"Gizmo's working on getting some of the IT up and running soon. We'll have a better idea then."

Jann's headset beeped. She touched the side of the unit to receive—it was Annis. "Yes."

"Malbec, any word on that research lab yet?"

"It's open for business, mostly. You'll never believe what they were doing in here."

"I'm sure I won't. Anyway you can tell me when I get there. I'm on my way."

"Did mission control come back with anything useful?

"Eh... no, nothing yet. See you there in a while." She shut off her comms unit.

"Annis?" asked Paolio.

"Yeah."

"Any update?"

"None. She'll be here shortly."

"Wonderful." He gave a wry smile.

OVER THE NEXT few hours Nills and Gizmo worked to restore function to various systems within the lab. Jann's priority now was the IT system, or at least what was left of it. The lab had been stripped of much of its equipment, moved to the mine according to Nills. *For what purpose?* she wondered. Not that it mattered for what she wanted to do; there was still a good deal of scientific apparatus remaining, enough for her purposes.

And with access to the IT systems, she might be able to gain some insight into the experiments that had been pursued by COM geneticists. But restoring power to this was proving problematic. So she remained in the research lab to assist Nills and Gizmo. Paolio retired to the medlab to monitor Decker; he had been concerned over his physical state. Annis had still not shown up.

PAOLIO CHECKED THE PATIENT. His chest rose and fell with a steady rhythm. His vitals all looked strong. The cuts and bruises he had acquired were all healed. If Paolio didn't know better, he would think the commander was as healthy as a pig. He spent some time checking the adhesion of the ECG pads on Decker. Then moved on to the drip. He made up a new batch and replaced the old one—it was nearly out.

Wouldn't be good to let that run dry. He thought about increasing the flow rate but decided to do a quick inventory first. They only had a limited supply of the drug that was keeping Decker subdued. How long would it last? He jotted down some quick calculations on a pad. Twelve days. Not much time to find a cure. And then what?

Decker twitched. Paolio jumped. "Jesus." He moved over to examine the readouts again. Then he took out a penlight and shone it into the commander's pupils, one at a time. He sat back. There was no doubt that Decker was growing stronger, not weaker. The current rate of drug flow was just enough to keep him under and no more. Should he increase it? If he did then this would just shorten the timeline for a more permanent solution. In the end he decided to leave it for the moment. He would check back later and decide then.

By the time Annis finally showed up it was late. They were all gathered around the table in the common room when Gizmo alerted them to activity in the airlock. Annis arrived carrying a bag. "Evening Annis, glad you could make it. What's in the bag?" said Paolio.

"Eh... I've decided to stay here from now on. I think it's best we all stick together."

Jann gave Paolio a glance. She was skeptical but maybe she should cut Annis some slack. "Come, join us. There's food here if you're hungry."

"No... thanks. I'm fine. Is the research lab operational?"

"Yeah, partly."

"I'm going to have a look." She walked off to investigate. The others followed her with their eyes as she left the common room.

"Don't," said Paolio to Jann.

Jann raised her hands. "I didn't say anything."

"No, but I know what you're thinking. Just let it ride. She's trying, okay?"

"Sure, fine." Jann bit her lip.

Nills stood up. "I need to get back to the garden. I'll show you where she can stay tonight."

"Just make sure it's far away from me," said Jann.

Paolio looked at her.

Jann raised her hands. "Sorry, couldn't help it. It just came out."

23

XFJ-001B

Annis considered the face of Commander Robert Decker as he lay unconscious on the medlab operating table. In the harsh glow of her flashlight she could see he was damp with sweat and flushed with fever as the infection raged inside him. She moved closer and leaned over the bed to inspect the injuries he had sustained to his forehead. They were all healed, and not a scratch remained. “Weird," she thought. She swept the narrow light along the wires that trailed from his body and into the machines that monitored his vital signs. She was about to disconnect them when she hesitated, they might set off an alarm if the status changed. *Best leave them. He can yank them out himself later,* she thought. What she was looking for was the pump that kept him supplied with sedative. The drug delivery system that stopped him from becoming conscious, and kept his violence suppressed. She found it and gently pulled it out of his neck. How long it would take for him to return to consciousness she wasn't sure, an hour, two hours? It was hard to tell. All she knew was that when he did, all hell would break loose. His body twitched and she jumped back in fright. She held her hand over her mouth to suppress any noise she might inadvertently make. She stood and watched him for a few seconds. Maybe he would wake sooner than she thought. "Better get moving, no time to waste."

Annis moved silently out of the medlab and picked her way across the common room floor. It was the middle of the night, 4:35am Mars time. Colony One was in darkness and all the others were asleep. Even Gizmo was docked in his recharge station in the operations room. Still, she couldn't be one hundred percent sure that the robot was totally offline and not monitoring some low level processes. She made her way to the research lab, tiptoeing as she went. The heavy boots of her EVA suit made hard work of keeping silent. The door was open and power was still on. *Good,* she thought. *This will make things quicker*. She scanned the dim interior with her flashlight and made her way to the racks in the module at the far end. These were the *analogues* and it was one of them that she was now searching for, sweeping her flashlight up and down the racks looking for the serial number that COM had given her. This was the *source analogue* that they so desired. Why they wanted it was of no concern to Annis. Other than it was her ticket off this planet. Her flashlight stopped over XFJ-001B. She pressed a button on the fascia and the unit slid out. She grabbed the sides, slid it out of its shelf and placed it carefully inside a rugged case. She thought she heard a noise and stopped, silence. It was just the creaking of the superstructure adjusting to the nighttime temperature.

From the front pocket of her EVA suit she took out one of the seismic charges and set the timer to its maximum. That should be around forty-five minutes. She wedged it in a gap between the racks. She set two more to take out the rest of the units. The last charge she placed against the exterior hull of the lab module. It would be more than enough to open the whole place up like a can of tomatoes in a microwave. "That should keep them busy for a while."

THE STEADY ORANGE LED on Gizmo's breast panel flicked green as he detached himself from the docking station. He spun around and whirred off at full speed to wake Nills. He found him lying in his hammock in the center of the biodome. One arm hung over the side, his hand hovering above a half smoked joint that was poised on the edge of an ashtray fashioned from a small rover dish antenna. Gizmo stroked Nills' arm gently with his metal hand. "Nills, wake up." His eyes snapped open. "Gizmo, what is it?"

"An Earthling has just operated the airlock."

Nills sat up in the hammock and jumped down. "Who?"

"Temperature coefficient of the accommodation modules indicates that First Officer Annis Romanov is not at home."

Nills was now checking the camera feeds on his holo-tab. He flicked through each of the modules. Annis' bed was empty. "What the hell is she up to?"

"I'm afraid I have no logical answer. Perhaps she couldn't sleep and decided to go for a walk."

"Come, let's find out where she is." They moved off together to the operations room.

DUST SWIRLED around Dr. Jann Malbec and engulfed her. It billowed and blew with a frenzy and blocked all sight. It formed into bacteria and they moved and shifted across her field of vision. She thought she saw a light flash from inside her EVA suit helmet. Where was she? She heard a voice calling her name. *'Jann... wake up Jann.'* She opened her eyes and Gizmo was beside her bed. She jumped up and clutched the blanket to her neck.

"So sorry to wake you, Jann, but Nills needs you in the operations room. It appears your colleague Annis has gone walkies."

She arrived to find Nills bent over a 3D map of the Colony One site.

"What's going on?

Nills pointed to a marker on the map. "Annis went EVA half an hour ago and she's spent the last few minutes inside the MAV."

Jann looked down at the green marker that was First Officer Annis Romanov. How much did she really know about her? Not much, it seemed. Then it started to move out from the MAV, but not back to Colony One. It was heading to the fuel processing plant.

Jann stared at the dot in disbelief.

"How long does it take to prep the MAV?" Nills had a concerned look.

"Around twenty minutes." Then it suddenly dawned on Jann. Annis was getting ready to leave. "Jesus, I don't believe this. She's planning to lift off. Why would she do that?"

"You've got to stop her. We can't let her get back to Earth carrying that bacterium."

Jann looked wide eyed at Nills. "Shit," was all she could manage.

"It would be chaos, if that infection gets loose. Armageddon, the end of human civilization as we know it."

"Shit, shit." The magnitude of the possible devastation that would befall humankind if Annis were to successfully return to Earth was beginning to dawn on her.

"How?"

"Any way you can, you stop her. She must not take off, you've got to stop her."

A nerve shattering scream emanated from just outside the operations room entrance, as the bloodied and broken body of Dr. Paolio Corelli sailed through the doorway and landed with a crash on top of the 3D display. The map flickered off and sparks flew as Paolio's lifeless body buried itself in the remains of the table. Jann turned away from the destruction just in time to see Decker swing a long bar and connect with Nills' extended forearm. He let out a scream and went flying across the operations room floor. Before she could react, Decker pounced on her and swung the bar down hard on her head. She dodged, but it connected with a searing crack on her collarbone. She dropped to the floor as the pain engulfed her. She tumbled backwards and cracked her head on something, blinding her momentarily. When she opened her eyes, Decker was standing over her with the bar held ready to plunge into her chest. But then his whole body started shaking violently. He dropped the bar and it clanged to the floor. Jann grabbed it with her good arm and jumped up. Two long coils of wire ran from prongs embedded in Decker's back to Gizmo's breast panel. A taser. Nills had fitted him with a weapon.

Decker shook. Smoke rose from his body, the skin on his skull blackened and his eyes boiled and hissed in their sockets.

"Gizmo, switch it off." With that Decker stopped shaking and dropped to the floor—dead. Jann turned and staggered over to the forlorn figure of the doctor. "Paolio, I'm so sorry, it's my fault." She touched his bloodied and battered cheek with her hand; tears welled up in her eyes.

"Jann, JANN! You've got to stop her, time is running out."

Nills was tugging at her shoulder. "Oh God, Nills, your arm, it's broken."

"It's all right, Gizmo will take care of it... go, go, you've got to go now."

"Okay." She wiped the tears from her eyes, took one last look at Paolio and headed for the airlock. She felt the pain in her shoulder as she donned the EVA suit. It was bad, probably broken. Jann was just about to flip closed the visor when Nills came over. He was holding his arm tight against his body as Gizmo raced behind him with what looked like a syringe. "Nills, be still. I need to give you this for the pain."

"Listen, Jann. You understand what's at stake here. Our lives don't matter. You need to do whatever it is to stop her taking off."

"I know Nills. I know what I have to do now." She reached out and touched his face. "Hey... if... if I don't see you again, it was nice meeting you."

He smiled. "Likewise, it was a pleasure."

The research lab exploded.

SMOKE AND FLAMES burst out from the lab and the force of the blast threw them both across the common room floor. It engulfed them and Jann began to cough and splutter as she tried to orient herself. She looked over at the lab door as a new force hit her. The smoke was being whisked back out into the lab. When it cleared she could see why. There was a black hole where the lab used to be—it was open to the Martian night. Air was being sucked out of the colony at an alarming rate and they were being dragged along with it. Jann slid along the floor with the force of the escaping atmosphere. She grabbed at a table leg and hung on. She could see Gizmo spinning wildly on his back with no apparent control. "Nills, where's Nills?" She saw him sliding past her as he made frantic efforts to grab on to something before he got ejected into the void. She reached out and grabbed him, pulled him in.

Then Jann's EVA suit detected the drop in pressure and automatically closed her visor. "No, no, Nills, no." She looked into his eyes as he struggled to breathe. He clawed at his throat as the oxygen was sucked out of the colony. "No, Nills, goddammit." The force was too strong, she couldn't hold him. He slipped from her grip—and he was gone. Sucked across the floor, through the doorway and out into the Martian night. Jann screamed. She tried to look out through the hole at the far end of the research lab where Nills had been ejected. But the force of the escaping colony atmosphere was such that she was being lifted horizontally off the floor. She clung to the table leg with all her strength to keep from being sucked out.

Nills was gone, Paolio was dead... Decker, Kevin... Lu—all gone. She tried again to look back out through the gap as the facility was being vacuumed clean. She saw Gizmo wedged in an alcove, he didn't seem to be moving. "Even Gizmo is gone," she thought. It was just her now. And Annis, who was now trying to return to Earth, carrying with her the potential destruction of humanity.

HER HAND SLIPPED OFF the table upright, she scrambled to catch it again but the force was too much, she was torn away. Jann rolled and banged her way across the floor, her arms flailing about trying to grab onto anything still screwed down. She bounced off something hard, cartwheeled through the air and slammed into the wall beside the open door to the Research Lab. The air was still rushing through, bringing with it the contents of Colony One. Objects hit off the walls and banged around her head. Jann felt for something to grab onto and found she was pinned against the door of the Research Lab. It was fully open and flat against the wall, held there by the force of the evacuating atmosphere. She inched her way to the outer edge of it, grabbed the inner handle and planted her feet against the wall. She pulled on the handle with all her strength to try and get the door moving. She had it off the wall about two feet when it was hit hard on the side by some heavy flying debris. This added to its momentum, enough for the rush of the air to catch in behind it. She had no time to react. The door swung over with a sudden violence and crashed closed. The shockwave reverberated through the colony superstructure and Jann lost her grip as she was flung across the research lab floor. She spun and slid, then stopped.

She lay there stunned for some time, looking out through the gaping hole in the lab wall, straight at the night sky. All was still and eerily quiet. Slowly Jann sat up and looked around. The lab door was closed and held shut by the inside atmosphere, or what remained of it. She was now effectively outside in the near vacuum of space. She did a quick check of her EVA suit for damage. All looked okay. No warnings, no alerts. She stood up and flipped on her heads up display. Was she too late? Had Annis lifted off? A 3D map illuminated in her field of vision. The markers for the HAB, MAV and the fuel plant hovered over their respective locations. She rotated in their direction. Annis was still on the surface, moving towards the MAV.

She headed for the hole in the Research Lab wall and picked her way through the detritus of the cryo-rack module. It was little more than a shell, split open on all sides. She moved through it, careful not to damage her EVA suit on any of the sharp metal of the walls. At the edge she jumped down onto the surface and swiveled in the direction of the green marker that was First Officer Annis Romanov. She had made her choice, for better or worse she was going to try and save the human race. She ran.

24

MAV

Jann crested the dune and looked out across the Jezero crater. Overhead the nighttime sky sparkled with the light from a universe of suns. Far off in the distant blackness she could just make out lights moving across the planet's surface. It was either one of the rovers or possibly the lights from Annis's EVA helmet. Her first thought when dropping down onto the surface from the wreckage of the research lab, was to switch her own lights on. But she thought better of it as she would rather not announce her arrival. Progress was difficult in the darkness. She wasn't sure of the terrain and had to take it slow so as to not lose her footing. She could tell from the heads-up display that Annis was refueling the MAV. The rover lights correlated with the display markers. She didn't have much time. She moved faster.

Jann hadn't given much thought to how she was going to stop Annis. Perhaps she would just talk to her, try and reason with her. But then again, the first officer had just tried to kill them all and destroy Colony One. And she had achieved pretty much all of that. Only Jann was left. The others were all dead. As for the colony, the damage had to be extensive, possibly even beyond saving.

By now Jann could see the silhouetted figure of the first officer, walking along beside one of the rovers, two large fuel canisters up on top. *How many more did she have to go?* thought Jann. Maybe these were the last. The MAV needed all six to take off. But with only Annis onboard there was a huge weight saving so maybe just four would do. Jann cursed herself for not paying more heed to all the engineering training she had been given. As an astrobiologist she hadn't deemed it necessary. Then again, she never thought she would be in this position. She thought about disabling the MAV in some way, removing some vital part or sticking a proverbial spanner in the works. But again, her lack of engineering knowledge meant she couldn't be sure if what she did would work. Also, it was now becoming clear that Annis would get to the MAV first. In the end the choice was made for her as her EVA suit comms burst into life.

"Jann, I know you're out there. Sorry, but you can't come with me. There's only room for one on this trip."

"Annis, what are you doing?"

"What do you think I'm doing, I'm getting off this contaminated planet."

"Are you crazy? You can't go back, not carrying that infection, it's too dangerous."

"Bullshit."

"No Annis, you have to stop. Annis, for God's sake, listen to me."

"Go screw yourself. You should never have been on this mission in the first place. You never had the smarts for it."

Jann felt a slight tremor underfoot and looked around. Too late. The seismic rover plowed into her at full speed and sent her flying through the air. She landed heavily on the ground and tumbled. That bitch Annis was setting her up all along. Maybe Annis was right; she didn't have the smarts for this. She rolled on the dirt just as the rover drove into her again and rolled over her already damaged left arm. She heard a crack and her body was convulsed by excruciating pain riffling up and across her chest. She screamed.

"Annis, Annis, for God's sake stop." There was no reply. Jann tried to move but the weight was too much. She banged at the rover's paneling with her good arm, but it was pointless. She twisted and squirmed to try and get some movement, but the pain in her side made it impossible.

Suddenly, the robotic arms of the rover sprang to life. Jann tried to fend the grabber away with her right arm but it moved for her throat and pinned her down even more. She banged and pushed. The drill arm started up. "Oh shit." She could see the short drill bit spin furiously as it pointed and moved closer and closer to her helmet visor. She tried to move her head, but it just shifted inside her helmet, which was now firmly held down. The drill tip corkscrewed across her visor as it tried to gain some purchase. It skipped and skated as she frantically banged at it with her free arm. It was now stabbing down, bashing against her faceplate. It didn't need to drill a hole, just a crack would do.

Then Jann saw it, the emergency shutoff panel right above her on the front base of the rover. She raised herself up to flip the cover but struggled to reach. If she could get to it then maybe she'd have a chance. The drill banged down hard and she heard a crack. "Oh shit." Alert lights flashed inside her helmet, to warn her of deteriorating suit integrity. Jann forgot about the pain of her broken bones and frantically pushed with all her strength to flip open the shutoff panel. The rover shifted and slid a little to the left, like one of its wheels had been resting high on some rock, and with her frantic efforts it had slipped off. Her hand reached the panel; she flipped open the cover and punched down on the emergency shutoff. The rover stopped, its drill spun down, its arms lost power.

Jann stopped squirming and she could feel herself breathing hard. She checked the alerts. "Shit." Her faceplate was cracked and she was losing air. The suit tried hard to compensate for the loss in pressure and was using up excessive supplies of nitrogen to rebalance. "Thirty minutes." She had thirty minutes of air left. Thirty minutes before she died. Thirty minutes to save the world. She laughed. It was an odd feeling. It was not that she was scoffing in the face of death. She was laughing at the absurdity of the situation. The awkward, geeky farm girl. The girl who shouldn't even be here, look at her now. She rolled over and sat up. A stabbing pain shot up her side. "Dammit." She couldn't walk, she would just have to crawl. Jann knew that as soon as Annis realized she had lost remote control of the seismic rover she would be over to finish her off. So she scanned the ground around her, looking for something she could use as a weapon, a sharp rock maybe. But there was nothing obvious to hand. She looked back at the MAV, half expecting to see Annis approaching, but she didn't. Instead she was heading back to the fuel plant with the other rover to get the last of the tanks, presumably having decided that Jann was no longer a threat. And from where Jann was sitting, that would be an accurate assessment of the situation.

She slumped back onto the ground and looked up at the heavens. Above her the vast expanse of the universe was spread out in all its celestial glory, as if to mock the insignificance of her very existence. What could she do?

Maybe it was better to let Annis go. Maybe the decimation of the human race would be the best thing for the planet. A cull of a species that was destroying their own home. Too many, too greedy, too stupid... or just simply too successful.

She could hop or maybe crawl back to the HAB in the time left to her. "Twenty-three minutes." She could save herself... maybe, if she went now. It would be cutting it fine, even with that. She sat up again and tried to stand. The pain in her leg was excruciating now that the initial rush of adrenaline had worn off. She reached over and pulled herself up using the deactivated seismic rover for help. She stood there for a minute, gathering the remains of her strength, trying not to breathe too much. She rested her head in her arms on the top of the rover and looked down along its side. The bright ISA logo seemed to fluoresce in the Martian night. She stopped, and looked again. Beside the logo, on the door of a storage compartment on the side of the rover, were marked the words *caution, seismic charges*. Jann looked at it for a minute as an idea began to formulate in her mind. "Twenty-one minutes." Up ahead, Annis was still en route to the fuel dump.

Jann sat back down again so she could get better access to the rover's storage compartment. She flipped open the door, reached in and took out a charge. They could be detonated remotely; she just needed to tag the charge to her control. She held it in her hand for a moment and contemplated the consequences of what she was planning. Being able to detonate it meant nothing unless she could get the rover to the MAV, or the fuel dump. Or should she just kill Annis? "Twenty minutes." It also meant she would not be able to reach the HAB before the oxygen in her suit dropped to a point where she would lose consciousness and die. She looked over again at Annis. In the darkness she could see the beams of light from her helmet bob along the Martian surface towards the fuel dump. If she was going to do this she needed to do it now. It would mean her own death but, as Nills had said, what did that matter against the enormity of the devastation that would be wrought if this bacterium made it to Earth?

She flipped the cap on the charge and tagged it to her control. She set it back in its compartment along with all the others and closed the door. She then crawled around to the back of the rover where the control panel was and switched it on. The screen illuminated, displaying options for rover operation. Jann deactivated all remote control functionality so that Annis could not hijack it again. She then tagged it to Annis' suit. Now, as soon as she switched the power on again, the rover would dutifully roll off to rendezvous with the first officer. It was now or never. Jann hit the power button and moved back. The rover took a few seconds to orient itself, read its new instruction set, and then it moved off to find Annis. "Nineteen minutes."

The first officer had reached the fuel plant and was loading up the last of the canisters. She stopped when she noticed the seismic rover moving in her direction.

"Jann, are you still alive out there?"

It was Jann's turn not to reply.

"What are you trying to do, run me over? Well, that's pathetic. But then again you always were a total waste of space."

She could hear Annis laugh at her own joke.

"Too late anyway, it's time to go."

Annis hefted the last canister and started off. The seismic rover noticed the change in direction and turned to follow. "Twelve minutes." The rover closed the gap, Jann flipped on her 3D control interface.

"I'm sorry Annis, but you leave me no choice." She hit

detonate.

An explosion in the thin atmosphere of Mars is a strange phenomenon. There's virtually no sound. It was just a slight tremor that Jann felt as the nighttime sky illuminated in a fiery ball of methane/oxygen rocket fuel. The light was blinding and she covered her visor with her arm and looked away. There was a brief moment before the debris rained down, peppering the entire area with dust and rocks and shards of metal. It was some time before Jann ventured to look again after the last of the destruction had stopped falling. She couldn't see much, just an enormous plume of dust. She switched on her helmet lights but even they could not penetrate the murky darkness. She switched them off and rolled onto her back. *Nine minutes, well this is it,* she thought. Now it was time to die. She had prevented the decimation of human civilization and no one would know, no one would care. It was her time now, her work was done.

The EVA suit blinked a new alert to warn its occupant of the impending low oxygen emergency. From her training, she knew it would now try to maximize the remaining reserves by substituting nitrogen. This way her body would still feel like it was breathing, even though there would be less and less oxygen in each breath. It was a calm way to die; she would simply drift into unconsciousness and never wake up.

"Five minutes."

As her mind drifted, she had the feeling of being lifted up towards the canopy of twinkling stars. They began to move, *or was it her that was moving*, like she was being transported somewhere. She felt no fear, no pain and no care. Her eyes closed and she drifted off into the heavens.

25

THE GARDEN

The sudden loss of atmosphere from Colony One could have been the end of the facility, save for the fact that Jann had managed to close the lab's inner door while she was being ejected. By this action she had averted a potential catastrophe. As soon as the tsunami of evacuating air had ceased, Gizmo was able to right itself and could now move into action. Since there were no longer any Earthlings in the colony it could get radical with the analysis of priorities. It shut down unnecessary sectors and killed power to all nonessential systems. It set about rerouting energy and reassigning all priority protocols to the biodome, trying to bring it back up to nominal levels and stabilize the fragile ecosystem. After monitoring the effects of its efforts it estimated it could save 67.3% of biomass and 71.2% of diversity. It meant that several plant species had now become extinct on Mars. However, this would still depend on it physically fixing the damaged infrastructure within the biodome. So it raced around righting hydroponics, untangling ducting and covering exposed root systems.

It was during these latter tasks that a new data stream entered its silicon consciousness. It was another life support system going critical. But this was not in Colony One, this was out on the planet's surface. At some point Nills had interfaced Dr. Jann Malbec's EVA suit with colony systems so that he, and Gizmo, would get feedback on her state. Gizmo considered its own internal instruction set for any preprogrammed routines that were to be executed for such an event and found none. However, after it ascertained that it had no preset actions to take, it did the next thing on its list of priorities—Gizmo analyzed the situation.

Its number one priority had always been to ensure the safety of Nills Langthorp, but he was now dead, blown out through the hole in the Research Lab wall. It also assessed that no other human was alive on the surface of Mars, save for ISA crewmember Dr. Jann Malbec, whose life was fading fast. But, it was precedence that tipped the balance for Gizmo. Nills had saved her life before, back when the demented commander tried to kill her in the Medlab. So this must have been a priority for Nills and therefore, by extension, for Gizmo. The final decider was its analysis that it had a 54.8% probability of saving her life. All this, its silicon mind calculated, in a fraction of a microsecond.

Gizmo made its way to a functioning airlock and exited out onto the planet's surface. Its tracked wheels enabled it to race across the dusty terrain at great speed. By the time it found her and lifted her up she was just losing consciousness. Gizmo finally got her back through the airlock just as the EVA suit shut down.

It took the little robot several attempts to resuscitate her on the medlab operating table, but on the fourth attempt Jann's body responded and she sucked in a long gulp of air.

She was still unconscious while Gizmo tended to her broken bones, and it was several hours later before she opened her eyes, looked around, and spoke.

"Gizmo, how did I get here?"

"I brought you here."

"I thought I died."

"Well, technically you did, I rebooted you."

She looked at the quirky machine for a moment. "Thank you, Gizmo."

"Don't mention it, the pleasure is all mine."

BUT THAT WAS a long time ago now and many months had passed. The colony's systems now hummed and sung with optimal perfection and the biodome had regained much of its lush verdant abundance. Yet it was different. A new wildness had taken over. More tropical forest than kitchen garden. Gizmo whizzed through the connecting tunnel and into the biodome. It zipped along the racks of hydroponics until it came to the edge of the forest area near the center of the vast dome. It slowed down so as not to cause damage to the velvety carpet that was the forest floor, a thick mat of mosses and grasses. It was a product of diligent bioengineering, hard work and time. It moved through the worn gap in the tall overgrown vegetation and out onto the central dais. The pond shimmered and the splash from the tall rock waterfall prismed the morning light into a myriad of twinkling colors.

Standing at the base of the waterfall, Dr. Jann Malbec held her head back as she washed her hair in the gently falling cascade. Gizmo watched from the edge of the pond and waited patiently. She stepped out, shook the excess water from her hair and waded across the pond, carp scattering as she went. She spotted Gizmo.

"Ah... good morning."

"Good morning Jann, I trust you had a good sleep."

"I did, Gizmo, thank you."

"I have brought you some breakfast. It's the last of the coffee, I'm afraid."

"Not to worry, I think there's some still left in the HAB. Next time we're outside we can bring back the remaining supplies." She bit into some toast and sipped her coffee. She was naked. Over the last few months Jann had found herself with little reason to get dressed. With no humans for more than 140 million miles there were a lot of things that don't seem so important anymore. Putting on clothes was one of them.

It took only four weeks for her bones to heal enough for her to use her arm again. A remarkably speedy recovery. During that time she had learned as much as she could from Gizmo on the state of the colony after the research lab explosion. Between them, they nursed it back to health and sustainability. It was another few weeks more before she finally ventured out on the surface again and made her way to the HAB. She found the COM communications unit and realized the extent of the first officer's deceit. They brought it back to Colony One, along with the satellite unit, and Gizmo reconfigured it to function for ISA transmission protocols. So, it was over two months before Jann sent a long report back to mission control.

It had been assumed on Earth that the colony was destroyed and all crew lost. With no communication all they had to go on was the satellite data. It showed images of the destruction at the colony and also the catastrophic loss of the fuel plant. The MAV was still intact, but with no fuel to power it, it was useless. Jann was stuck on Mars, there was no way to return to Earth, unless a new fuel manufacturing plant could be built and new canisters fashioned. Mission control sent her detailed plans on how to do this with materials available in the colony, but she was not great at engineering and, in truth, she was in no hurry to return. The next launch window was not for another year and a half, anyway. She was also beginning to fall under the same spell that Nills had talked about, and as the weeks went by she became more and more at one—with Colony One.

She replaced the hammock that Nills had used with a low futon and curled up on it at night, looking out through the dome at the infinite universe. During these nights she began to gain a deeper understanding of what it meant to be human. It was a kind of feral reawakening. A sense of wild abandon bubbled up inside her and she began to understand how Nills must have felt. And, like him, she realized the critical importance of Gizmo for maintaining her sanity. The human mind was a fragile thing, kept in balance only by the company of others. We are social animals, we feel safe in the herd, and desire its acceptance. Alone, the human mind wanders with no clear purpose, nothing to keep it in balance.

"WILL you be requiring clothing today, Jann?"

Jann thought about this a moment. Clothing did have one big advantage in the colony—pockets. Her daily dressing considerations had effectively been reduced to whether pockets would be useful in performing whatever tasks she had assigned for herself that day.

"Or would you prefer more time to think about it?"

"Yes, there's no rush, we can decide later." She sipped her coffee and sat down on a low chair to dry her hair.

"Tell me Gizmo, do you miss Nills?"

"Alas, poor Nills, I knew him well. A man of infinite jest."

"That sounds like Shakespeare."

"That's because it is. From Hamlet."

Jann laughed and sipped her coffee. "You have no concept of death Gizmo, do you?"

"I understand it is reality for living entities. I understand that Nills no longer exists."

Jann put the towel down and lay back on the recliner like she was sunning herself by the pool. "That's not, strictly speaking, true."

"You mean he's still alive?"

"In a sense."

"Explain. I hate to admit it, but I am confused."

"Remember when we checked the MAV and we found one of the analogues from the bio-rack in the research lab? Annis was trying to return to Earth with it."

"I do. Curious, that."

"Well here's the thing, I finally managed to cross reference it with data I had gleaned from the lab IT systems before it was destroyed, and guess what?"

"It's Nills."

"Correct. So in a sense, part of him still exists. Even if it *is* just a facsimile."

"The plot thickens."

"Indeed it does, Gizmo. For one, why did COM want Annis to bring this back to Earth? And second, what was it about Nills that was so special?"

"Again, I have to admit I have no answer."

Jann sat up on the recliner and looked directly at Gizmo.

"Did you ever notice any physiological changes in Nills over the time you were together?"

"Sure. Beard, no beard. Clothed, naked. Clean, not clean. There were many."

"No, I mean more subtle than that."

"Now that you mention it, I did notice that my recognition algorithm was losing accuracy by approximately 12.34% per year. This I attributed to aging and compensated for it accordingly."

"Well, as always Gizmo, you are correct. But he was not getting older. No, he was getting younger."

"My understanding is that is not possible."

"It's not probable. But in this instance, it would seem that it is indeed possible."

"Holy cow."

Jann laughed at the little robot and stood up.

"So what happens now, Jann?"

"What do you think?"

The little robot paused for a beat and then replied. "They will come for it. If they wanted it that badly, they will return here to get it."

"My thinking exactly. But that can't be for at least another year and a half."

"So we have some time."

"We do. And time that I need to find out exactly what was going on here. My guess is that COM were on the cusp of some major genetic breakthrough. They may have even achieved it. But all was lost when the sandstorm hit and the infection broke out. I intend to find out what it was that they were doing."

"Is that possible with the research lab destroyed?"

"Doubtful. That's why I think we'll need to investigate

the mine at some point. I would really like to know what was going on over there."

"When do we start?"

"Oh... there's no rush, Gizmo. Time enough for that." She looked around at the vast biodome. "Anyway, I don't really want to leave. I'm beginning to like it here too much."

COLONY TWO MARS

1

THE ANIMAL

Dr. Jann Malbec stood a little over knee-deep at the edge of the pond in the biodome of Colony One. She was still and quiet, her face to the sun so as not to cast a shadow over its surface and frighten the fish. She held a spear high above her shoulder and waited. After a while the fish would start to swim around her legs, sometimes even touching her. Jann held fast until the right moment and then loosed the spear. It knifed through the water, bending in the refracted light.

Damn, only one, she thought as she pulled it out. Her record was two in one throw, three was exponentially more difficult to achieve. The fish flapped and squirmed on the stick as she stepped out and brought it over to the campfire she had set up on the central dais. Grabbing the fish by the tail, she slid it off the spear and whacked its head on the hard floor to kill it and stop it flapping around. From a small mound of dry kindling Jann grabbed a handful of straw, placed it on the dying embers and blew gently to get it going again. Soon it was burning steady. It crackled and sparked as she threw more kindling on.

Sitting down cross-legged, she started to gut the fish with a sharp knife that she kept on a belt around her waist. The area around her was covered in the scattered remains of similar meals she had eaten in this place. As soon as the fish was cleaned she skewered it and set it on the fire to cook. Then she sat back and waited, turning it every so often to prevent the flesh from blackening.

Through the dense foliage all around her she could hear the robot going about its business: harvesting, maintaining, monitoring. She didn't speak to it much these days. It didn't seem to mind—it was a robot after all. In the beginning it was different, she had had long conversations with it. But after a while she grew tired of the rhetorical analysis of its dialog. The robot simply took in what she said, analyzed it and regurgitated it back in a reorganized form. It was like talking to a distorted mirror. Sometimes she even got angry at it, and banished it from her space. Then after a while, oddly, she would feel guilty and would seek it out again. How strange is the human spirit to feel empathy for a machine. Now though, she left it to its work. It managed the colony and there really wasn't much Jann had to do. The colony didn't need her input, it just needed the robot.

After the cataclysmic events of the ill-fated ISA Mars mission, Dr. Jann Malbec ended up being the only survivor. Nonetheless, since the Mars Ascent Vehicle (MAV) was still intact, she had a possible way home. Mission control had sent her details on how to fabricate new fuel tanks after the originals had been destroyed when she had immolated Annis Romanov in a fiery ball of rocket fuel. Jann and the robot had set about building these, but when they were ready, she had a new problem. As far as the ISA was concerned, she was still a potential biohazard, a Typhoid Mary, so to speak. They would not let her return unless she could prove she was not a contaminant.

So Jann worked to gain some understanding of the bacteria that had devastated the ISA mission, and Commander Decker in particular. But try as she might she simply did not possess the equipment to gain any further understanding. In the end she simply gave up. And with it, any hope of using the MAV to return to Earth. She had no option but to wait it out until the next ISA mission. The colony was self-sustaining and well resourced, so she was in no real danger.

But as the first year passed, messages from mission control started to include phrases such as: budget constraints, political apathy, low priority. Fear grew in Jann's mind that Earth was losing its appetite for Mars. It became clear to her that there was little desire, by any of the ISA member governments, to spend billions rescuing someone who could potentially devastate the entire population of the planet. So they had effectively abandoned her.

At the start she was angry, but as the second year passed she began to accept it. She couldn't blame them, really. By the third year, she had resigned herself to dying on Mars. The only problem was, like Nills, she was getting younger, not older. To die on Mars might take her a very, very long time. Unless it was by her own hand—and she began to realize it might come to that in the end.

So day by day, slowly but surely, the colony had changed her and made Dr. Jann Malbec just another part of its enormous biological ecosystem. It needed a human to complete its collection of flora and fauna, so it entered deep into her psyche and sought out the essence of the animal that lay within. By now, she wore little clothing and went barefoot. Her food she hunted by spear and gathered by hand. She ate by the fire and slept in a tree. Her hair had become a long mass of matted dreadlocks. The colony had claimed her for itself—and it had done a good job.

She had made herself a nest high up in the crown of the tallest coconut tree, and at night, looked out through the translucent dome roof at the vastness of the universe. What was she becoming? An exotic specimen in an equally exotic enclosure, to be peered at by the gods? Sometimes she would rise from her bed of straw and leaves and shake her fists at the heavens. She would rant and rage against her sense of insignificance and challenge the infinity of the void above her, like King Lear going mad on the mountain. "Screw you, space!" or words to that effect.

LIFTING the skewered fish from the fire, Jann set it down on a banana leaf to cool. She couldn't hear the robot anymore, it must have moved off to tend to some other part of the biodome. While she waited for her meal to cool she lifted up the spear and examined the point. It had become blunt with use; she would set about sharpening it later. Jann had become quite adept with it. She had taken to setting up targets in and around the biodome and would run through as fast as she could firing off spears, one after the other as she flew by. By now, she seldom missed. Once she got so angry at the robot she threw one at it. She missed that time.

Jann tested the fish; it was ready. She clamped the skewer between her teeth and scampered up the trunk of the tall coconut tree to her nest, where she could relax and eat her meal. From its height she had a commanding view over the whole biodome canopy. It felt safe. She had just finished the last of her meal and was wiping her face with the back of her hand when she heard the robot enter the biodome again. From the sound, it was moving at speed. It burst through the dense foliage out onto the central dais, stopped, scanned the area, and then tilted its head up at Jann.

"GO AWAY!" she shouted at it.

"Dr. Malbec, there is something important you need to know."

"I don't want to know, now go away." She picked up a coconut and flung it at the little robot. It didn't dodge, it simply caught it in its metal hand. It had uncanny reflexes. Jann was always impressed at how it could do this. Sometimes she would sneak up behind it and fire off a spear. It nearly always caught it. The only time it didn't was when it had calculated that whatever projectile Jann was throwing at it was going to miss. Jann had no idea how it could be so accurate and agile. But then again, it was a machine.

It placed the coconut gently on the ground. "Jann, this is important. Do I have your attention?"

Jann glared at it. "Oh, all right, what is it?"

"Another Earthling has just entered the airlock."

Jann felt like she had been physically kicked in the gut. She had to sit down.

"Jann, did you hear what I said?"

She tried to get words out of her mouth but they just wouldn't come.

"Jann?"

"That... that's... not... possible." She thought maybe the robot was playing a trick on her, getting its own back for her insensitivity and borderline cruelty to it. But it was a droid, it was straight and true, and in many respects, a better friend to her than many humans she had known.

"Okay... I need to think... I need to..." her sentence trailed off.

"I understand that this is an improbable event. But nonetheless, another Earthling has entered the airlock."

"How can this be?"

"I possess insufficient data to offer any useful analysis. What do you want me to do?"

Jann thought about this. "Can it get in?"

"It is a he, and he is already in. However, he cannot move as he appears to be barely alive."

Jann's shock was beginning to recede, enough for her to gain some control. "Okay, okay, I'm coming." She clambered down the tree trunk, slowly, as she was still shaken by this news. Near the base she jumped down onto the dais, grabbed her spear and ran off towards the main airlock. "Come on, Gizmo, let's see this Earthling."

JANN LOOKED at the forlorn figure lying on the floor of the airlock with a sense of incredulity. "Where in God's name did he come from?"

"That is a very good question, Jann," replied Gizmo.

She inched closer, still holding the spear high, just in case. But it was clear this human was no threat. He had passed out and his life was ebbing away. She put down the spear and knelt beside him. His suit was battered and filthy. Patched up to maintain its integrity and mechanically hacked to make it function. It was more steampunk than space age. But she could still make out it was from the colony.

"He's a colonist, judging by the design of the suit. Quick, help me get him in to the medlab."

With that, Gizmo lifted the unconscious figure and

brought him out of the airlock. They placed him on the table in the medlab, removed his suit and hooked up several IVs to get fluids into him as quickly as possible. His body had lost its ability to sweat and his core temperature was critically high.

"He's dangerously dehydrated; he could have a heart attack any minute."

After some time, Jann had managed to stabilize him. "Who the hell is he?"

"We could do a retinal scan and see if we get a match from the medlab database," offered Gizmo.

"Okay, let's do that. Then at least we might get some clues." Jann tapped a few buttons on the operating table control panel and an arm extended from the wall, positioning itself over his head. A thin line of light scanned across his face as Jann deftly pushed back one of his eyelids. Data began to display on the main monitor. As it searched, images of colonists momentarily flashed on screen, then it stopped. It had found a match. Thomas Boateng. Colonist number 27.

Jann read the data. "This can't be right."

"It has a 99.9% accuracy probability," said Gizmo.

"Well this must be in the 0.1% range because it says this colonist died over seven years ago."

"Intriguing," replied Gizmo. "I assume you mean Earth years?"

"It says here that he died on sol 6,348, due to a severe brain aneurysm as the result of injuries sustained in a mining accident." She looked back at the patient. "So this guy must be someone else."

"He cannot be someone else, the retinal scan is very accurate."

"Well he can't be dead and alive at the same time."

"Indeed. That would be very unlikely."

The bio-monitor screeched an alarm as the colonist's vitals went critical. "Dammit, he's going into cardiac arrest. Quick, get the defibrillator." Jann started ripping off the remaining clothes around the colonist's chest as Gizmo handed her the pads. She rubbed them together to get an even coating of gel and positioned them on his upper ribcage. "Clear." She hit the button and several hundred volts tore through his body. His back arched for a moment then he slumped back down. The alarm continued. "Shit, come on." Jann waited for the charge to build and tried again, and again, and again.

His skin was scorched and there was a distinct smell of burning flesh in the air. But no joy. Jann flicked the switch on the bio-monitor to silence the alarm. He was still. She stood back and looked at the colonist. "Well, he's dead now, for sure. We may never know who he was."

"He is Thomas Boateng."

"He can't be, Gizmo." Jann was beginning to get angry at its infuriating rationality, so she distracted herself by scanning through the medical records of the dead colonist. They were extensive. "It says here he should have a benign mole just above the left shoulder blade." She glanced over at Gizmo. "Let's take a look."

They raised him up and peeled away the remains of his tattered vest. "Holy crap," Jann was stunned.

"It seems this really is Boateng." Gizmo lowered the body down again.

"That's just not possible."

"It is not probable. But as you so rightly pointed out to me many years ago, it would seem it is, indeed, possible.

Here lies the evidence." Gizmo extended a mechanical arm towards the dead man with all the theater of a stage artist.

"There's one way to find out for sure and that's do a dental x-ray." Jann tapped a few buttons on the operating table control panel and a large doughnut-shaped ring started to advance along the table. It moved across the face of the dead colonist and the resultant scan rendered on the main screen. Jann now tapped the historical image from the dental records and the two images were presented together. "That's weird."

"What is?" said Gizmo.

"Well I'm no expert at dental forensics but the shape and layout of the teeth and jaw are identical. Except this guy hasn't had any dental work, not even a filling."

"Is that strange?"

"Yes, very. If I were to hazard a guess I would say this is a younger version of the same person."

"Like Nills?"

"Yes and no. Nills was getting younger, that's correct. But this guy would seem to have come back from the dead." She went silent for a moment. "The other big question is where did he come from?"

"The only possible place is the mining outpost, on the far side of the crater."

"That's a hell of a long walk."

"Indeed. Probably why he died in the attempt."

"But Nills said no one in the mine survived."

"It would seem Nills was wrong."

"Holy shit, maybe there are more people out there?"

"It is a distinct possibility."

Jann turned and rubbed her head. "I need time to think, this is all too much. For someone to show up like that after all this time is one thing. But the fact that this person already died seven years ago is... I don't know... mind blowing."

"There is something we could do to shed some light on the mystery."

"What's that?"

"Pay a visit to the mausoleum."

"You mean see if the original body of Boateng is still there?"

"Exactly."

"If it is, then what?"

"Then that means there are two Thomas Boatengs, impossible as that may be."

JANN SWITCHED off the main screen and stopped short as she caught her reflection in the blank monitor. She stared at herself in shock. Instead of Dr. Jann Malbec, Science Officer of the ISA Mars mission, what returned her gaze was a semi-naked, feral animal. Was this what she had become? "Christ, is that actually me?" She looked away. Maybe I truly have gone mad. Then a thought shook her to her very core. "How would I really know?"

She walked out of the medlab, making sure to lock the door. It was done out of paranoia, from the memories of what had happened there before. Then she did something she hadn't done in a very long time. She went and had a shower.

2

MORE THAN ONE

Jann sat in her wicker chair in the central dais wearing a crisp clean Colony One jumpsuit, which itched. She examined her thick matted hair in a small mirror as Gizmo waited silently beside her. "If I'm going to EVA out to the mausoleum my head is not going to fit in a helmet with all this hair. Will you cut it for me, Gizmo?"

"Certainly, Jann. How would you like it?"

"Just take it all off. Leave about a centimeter."

Gizmo moved closer, selected a suitable tool from its collection and went to work. It took only a few minutes for Jann's matted hair to form a large mound on the floor of the dais. When Gizmo finished she examined the robot's handiwork in the mirror. She rubbed her hand over her scalp and felt the tight crop. It was like a velvet mat. "Oh, that feels so much better. My head must be a few kilos lighter."

"My pleasure, I am here to assist."

"Okay then, let's go do this. Let's see if there really are two Thomas Boatengs."

. . .

THE MAUSOLEUM WAS FASHIONED from an old lander module and isolated from the main Colony One structure. It had no power or life support. There was no need for that in a place for the dead. Jann cracked the handle on the makeshift crypt and swung the door open. She stepped inside and scanned the racks. Paolio, Lu, Kevin... they were all here, the entire crew of the doomed ISA mission. It even housed what was left of Annis. A blackened husk was all that remained after Jann had incinerated her.

This module had been used by the original colonists as a place to temporarily store the dead before they were buried. But as time passed, they realized that in the rarefied atmosphere of Mars, bodies do not decompose. So they simply left them interred in here. As more dead were added it became the de facto mausoleum for Colony One.

The walls were lined with horizontal metal racks, floor to ceiling. On these lay the corpses of the departed. In the center was a raised circular table, holding artifacts of faith and no faith, as well as totems of remembrance. Jann considered that in some distant time, it might become a hallowed place. Venerated by the future citizens of Mars as a direct link to their foundation history.

She moved over to where the body of Thomas Boateng should be resting. It was still there, lying on a long metal shelf. A thin layer of dust had accumulated over it; it had been there a long time. She looked at the desiccated face. It was hard to be sure, but there was a vague resemblance to the recently deceased visitor. She judged this simply by a visual inspection of body height and facial structure rather than from anything scientific. Jann then considered looking for the mole on his shoulder but now that she was face to face, she couldn't bring herself to disturb the dead.

"*Satisfied?*" Gizmo's voice resonated in her helmet as the robot buzzed in beside her.

"Yes and no. If this guy died seven years ago, then who is the person on the operating table in the medlab?"

"*It is another Thomas Boateng.*"

"I find that very hard to comprehend." She sighed. "Come on, let's go. There's nothing more we can do here." They moved outside and Jann swung the door closed. Hopefully she would not have to visit this place again anytime soon.

In the early days of her life in Colony One, Jann had always considered the mine as an area needing more detailed investigation. A place where she might find some answers. But it was considerably farther than Nills had originally suggested—over thirty kilometers away on the other side of the Jezero crater. Much too far to EVA, as the dead colonist had found out to his detriment. So she had given the mine no further thought. Now, though, it seemed that it was not as dead as Nills had led her to believe —*something* was going on over there. Yet, even if she could not EVA to it, she could at least start to look in the Colony One archives and get a better understanding of its formation, and perhaps even its true purpose. So it was a reinvigorated Jann that set to work in the operations room in Colony One.

Much of what was contained in the archives was vague and sparse. Most of what Jann had learned had come from Nills.

She knew that the early colonists had discovered a mineral rich cave system on the other side of the crater rim. This much was common knowledge. She also knew that at some point, it had been sealed up and a pressurized atmosphere created inside. This allowed it to be used not just as a mine but also as a secondary colony—Colony Two.

Food production had been established inside and, over time, many of the original colonists had moved over there permanently. Nills intimated that this had been as a direct response to the increasing invasiveness of the reality TV model that had funded the initial colony. But what was of most interest to Jann was the fact that the geneticists had also relocated there, shortly before everything went to rat shit in Colony One.

She stood up from the workstation terminal and stretched her shoulders. She had been studying the archives for over three hours straight but had not learned anything she didn't know already. She rubbed her head again; it was becoming a habit. She liked the feel of her closely cropped skull and the lightness it gave her. She moved over to the newly repaired holo-table. The original had been damaged when the insane Commander Decker threw Paolio at it. Every time Jann used it she couldn't help but shed a tear for her dear friend. Her feelings for Decker were not quite the same. But in reality, he was just as much a victim as any of the others of the unfortunate ISA crew.

She brought up a map of the crater and zoomed out to get a broad view. It rendered itself in 3D so she could get a sense of the scale of the vast crater. Jann rotated it and found the location of the mining outpost. It was at least thirty-five kilometers away. *That's a hell of a walk to undertake in a battered EVA suit*, she thought. She zoomed in on the site and a wire-frame image of the structure began to render as it dialed in closer. It was big. Maybe twenty times the volume of Colony One, and that could accommodate a hundred people. But the wire-frame was sketchy, there was very little detail in it.

Jann looked up as Gizmo entered the operations room. "Gizmo. Have a look at this." She pointed to the location of Colony Two on the holo-table. "How come there's so little detail on the internal structure of the mine?"

Gizmo moved closer and examined it. "It does seem very incomplete."

"From my analysis there should be areas for food production, accommodation, operation, processing and a whole bunch of other stuff. But this is minimal."

"They obviously were not too interested in updating the data."

"Or they were trying to hide its true nature." She sighed and looked at Gizmo.

"Did you move the body?"

"Yes, he is now lying beside himself in the mausoleum."

"You're assuming that they are the same person, Gizmo."

"I never assume, Jann."

"Well, if you're correct—and let's face it, you always are —then that would mean only one thing. That this guy must be a clone."

"A genetically identical human?" said Gizmo.

"Yes."

"Interesting."

"What's even more interesting, Gizmo, is there are probably a lot more."

3

IN SEARCH OF ANSWERS

Jann sat in a battered armchair in the common room of Colony One. It was the first time she had done so in over a year. The table before her was laid out with dishes and utensils, as well as an ample array of food, all extracted from deep-freeze storage. She had not eaten like this in a very long time, she'd given up on such formal niceties. But, like a ship's captain of old on the far side of the world, taking tea from a fine china tea set, she felt she needed to reconnect with civilized behavior, lest she forget forever.

But it brought with it painful memories of friends long dead, of Paolio, Nills, Lu and Kevin. She raised her cup of colony cider. "Here's to you all," she said, in the memory of all those that she had lost.

Gizmo entered. "Is the food to your liking, Jann?"

"It feels weird, eating off a plate."

"Sorry, but I would not know."

Jann smiled at the quirky robot. "The food's fine, Gizmo. But it would be nice to share it with some friends."

"Well, if it is any consolation, I do enjoy your company."

She laughed. "Thank you, Gizmo. I know I can be difficult. It hasn't been easy for me... this last while."

"That's okay, you are only human after all."

Jann cocked an eyebrow at it. "Coming from a robot I'm not sure how to take that."

"Consider it a compliment."

"All right. I will." She raised her glass to Gizmo and nodded, then sat back. "Tell me, Gizmo, what are my chances of returning to Earth?" It was the same question she had asked of it a hundred times before. Whenever any new message came in from mission control, or when she gained some new insight into the bacteria, she asked this very same question of Gizmo, hoping that this new snippet of data would prompt a different response. It never did. Its reply was always the same. '*None,*' it would say. She understood that in Gizmo's lexicon, this meant anything with less than a 0.01% probability. But this time its response was different.

"Slim. Approximate probability of 2.7%."

Jann nearly choked on her drink. "Slim? How come? What's changed?"

"Quite a lot, Jann. Consider this: you can return to Earth anytime you want, your launch craft is still functioning and the new fuel tanks are ready. The only thing that is preventing you is the need to convince the ISA that you are no longer a biohazard. And the only way you can do that is to find a way to kill it."

"Well, since the research lab is destroyed I have no way to do that. The medlab equipment is not up to the mark for that kind of analysis. Anyway, you know all this, Gizmo."

"True, but what is different, is you may find something in Colony Two. It would seem from our visitor that this is still viable for human life support. And judging by his genetic makeup it would be reasonable to suggest that they have, or had, significant research facilities there."

"I don't know, Gizmo. Even if I was willing to take the risk of exploring it I have no way to get there and back again. An EVA suit just doesn't have the resources."

"You could take the exploration rover."

Jann sat back in her seat and rubbed a hand across her skull. "The rover. I had completely forgotten about that."

TOWARDS THE END of the first year of Jann's isolation in Colony One she was running out of projects to keep her mind focused. The tanks had been built and her efforts at gaining further insight into the malignant bacteria were growing ever more frustrating, hampered as she was by the lack of adequate equipment. This, coupled with the increasingly vague communication from Earth as to a date for the next mission, had prompted Jann to finally explore the derelict sectors of the great colony. It was, after all, the initial mission brief. So since she was going to be stuck here for a while, she might as well get on with it. She also considered that she might find something useful: another lab, or some scientific equipment that she could use.

It was during one of these excursions that she came across the old Colony One exploration rover. It was parked up inside a small derelict workshop dome on the western side of the facility, accessible only by EVA. It was one of two such vehicles, the other, it was assumed, was over in the mining outpost. The rover was non-operational, and had been for five or more years. Jann thought about trying to get it working again, but as time moved on, and her sense of abandonment and isolation increased, her excursions outside became fewer and fewer. By the early part of her second year she had given up on EVA altogether. So, as the colony tightened its grip on her psyche, she retreated into the biodome and spent more and more of her time with the garden: researching it, tending it, becoming one with it. By the close of the second year, not only did she not EVA, she seldom even left the biodome.

"BUT IT'S NOT OPERATIONAL, it hasn't been for a very long time, Gizmo."

"It could be made to function again."

Jann rubbed her hand across the top of her skull again, slowly this time. "I don't know."

"What do you not know?"

Jann sighed. "Even if we do get it working, I'm not sure I want to risk trying to go out there. It's been a long time... for me."

"Yes, it would be an uncertain venture with a high probability of death."

"Thanks, Gizmo, That's very comforting."

"My pleasure, I am here to assist."

"The other big question is: what would I find when, and if, I get there?"

"Unfortunately, I do not have access to sufficient data to give you any useful analysis. However, if Thomas Boateng made it here that would suggest there is life support. So there is a high probability of other life within its confines."

"But if there is, then why have we not heard from them before now?"

"I would suggest a few obvious scenarios: they had no way to communicate or exit the mine. In essence, they were trapped."

"Maybe, but if there are survivors over there the next question is, are they friendly?"

"One would assume that they would be glad of rescue."

"You really think so?"

"It is merely one of many possibilities. They may equally have descended into a barbarous cohort of violent animals who eat their young."

Jann sighed. "So what you're saying, Gizmo, is you really don't know."

"Too many possible outcomes to predict with any accuracy. The only way you will know for sure is to go there and see. In the meantime I suggest your best course of action would be to revitalize the exploration rover so you have transport should you decide to investigate Colony Two."

Jann thought for a moment, then stood up. "Okay, I suppose there wouldn't be any harm in taking a look at this rover again."

"Very little."

"All right, let's check it out it and see if it can be salvaged. Then we can decide."

THE GARAGE WORKSHOP, where the rover was housed, was on the far side of the Colony One site. There was no internal route to it, as the derelict areas had been sealed off a long time ago. Venturing into any of these sectors could be dangerous; they were structurally unsound. So the safest way to get there was to EVA. Jann checked her suit for power and resources as Gizmo waited patiently in the airlock. Being a robot it had no need for life support, it could go anywhere, limited only by the range of its power cell. Jann donned her helmet. It felt strange, now that she had very short hair. It had a roomier feel to it, more like wearing a dome than a helmet. She locked it in place and pressurized the suit. All biometric readings were clear, ready to go.

They worked their way around the perimeter of the facility until they finally reached the workshop. It was a small domed structure with its roof still intact. Along the exterior wall a large airlock protruded, big enough to fit a small truck. They brought a small remote power pack with them and Gizmo set about fiddling with the door's control panel. After a few minutes it had reduced it to a gaping hole of sprouting wires. "*Okay, here goes,*" it said as the door slowly rose up from the ground and slid into the roof. Jann was surprised by how much it looked and worked like a standard garage door. Then again, it was probably a very good design to begin with. The airlock was empty, save for another door at the far end. They moved inside and a short while later Gizmo got it open. They finally entered into the large workshop, and parked in the middle of the space was a six-wheeled, pressurized exploration rover. Jann rubbed her gloved hand along its side. "Well, looks like it's still here."

Over the course of the next few weeks Jann and Gizmo worked to restore power and life support to the maintenance workshop. But Jann still had to EVA to get access to it. They simply did not have the resources to rebuild the damaged structures linking it through to the main facility. All this activity was building up a new routine in Jann's life and imbuing it with a new sense of purpose, and as the sols passed, she felt herself becoming more and more reconnected with reality.

THE ROVER itself was powered by a methane internal combustion engine, the same fuel used for the MAV. It was old school, but made a lot of sense as the fuel could be manufactured easily on Mars. This also gave the machine a great deal of power. It was built to be a tough exploration vehicle with a range of over two hundred kilometers and a fully loaded top speed of sixty-five kilometers per hour. It could also accommodate six crew for a full thirty hours.

It took them another few weeks to get it to a point where they were ready to try and start it up. Jann sat in the driver's seat and surveyed the controls. It had a pretty basic joystick mechanism. The instrument panel was well laid out and clearly defined. It had obviously been designed so that even an idiot could drive it. That suited her just fine. She hit the power on switch. The instrument panel flickered into life, alerts flashed and data started to scroll down the main screen. Gizmo examined it. "Okay, looks like the main systems are operational. Time to see if it will start."

Jann pushed the start button and the rover engine burst into life. She looked over at Gizmo and gave the little droid a thumbs up. She let it run for a minute or two before killing the engine. Gizmo scanned the data readouts on the main screen. "You have fuel for approximately one hundred and eighty kilometers and oxygen for eight hours, twenty-seven minutes." It tilted its head at Jann. "I would say you are good to go, although I would advocate taking it for a test drive, first."

Jann sat back in the driver's seat. "So now I have a decision to make."

"Looks that way."

"Okay, let's get back. Nothing more we can do here this sol. I need to think."

. . .

It took Jann just one night of sleeping in her tree, staring at the stars, to finally make up her mind. To remain in Colony One was a route to insanity, of that she was certain. She was not Nills—she was not that mentally tough. The three years Jann had spent here had already eroded her sense of reality. She had only been brought back from the brink by this new sense of purpose. So she needed to go, not simply because she might find some answers, but because she would find none by staying here.

After several more sols of tests the rover was finally ready for the journey. It was agreed that Gizmo would stay behind and maintain the colony. Not that the little robot wouldn't be useful to her on this trip, but she was worried that some critical system might fail in her absence and there would be no one here to deal with it. The last thing she needed would be to return only to find her primary life support had succumbed to some catastrophe. She was confident there was nothing Gizmo couldn't handle in her absence.

Jann had made her decision and the moment had come. She clambered on board the exploration rover and, after a last systems check, she signaled for Gizmo to open the airlock. She started up the machine and waved at the little droid as the rover rumbled out of Colony One, and onto the barren planet's surface.

"*Good luck.*" Gizmo's voice resonated from the cabin speaker.

"Thanks," she replied as she pushed the throttle forward. The rover responded, picking up speed.

"For what it is worth, Jann, your probability of returning to Earth just increased to 7.3%."

4

COLONY TWO

The mining outpost was thirty-five kilometers northeast of her, so at a gentle twenty kph she would be there in less than two hours. That gave her plenty of time to investigate and still be able to make the return journey. She passed the solar array field and the old supply lander, and moved on towards the vast expanse of the central crater basin. It reminded her of her first days on the planet, when she went for a walk, testing out one of the small utility rovers they had brought with them. Back then she had felt a strong urge to just keep walking before Lu Chan called her back. Now, that same desire surged within her—to head out into the emptiness and just keep going. Maybe it was the years spent cooped up in Colony One or maybe it was something more primal. Either way, it was exhilarating. Jann opened up the throttle a little more and the rover replied, giving her a new sense of speed and purpose as it accelerated. She hit forty-five kph before she calmed down and let caution prevail. It was not a good plan to push it to breaking point and be stranded out here. She eased back and settled into a safe and steady twenty kph. It was Sunday driving, Martian style.

After an hour or so she began to make out the top of the crater rim on the far side of the basin. It grew in size and clarity as she moved closer. She checked her range and location on the main screen. Another thirty minutes and she would be there. According to the maps and diagrams she had studied back in the colony, the main mine entrance should be located at the base of a tall overhang in the cliff wall. This would make it hard to find without the aid of an accurate chart. Since there was no GPS or magnetic north on Mars, her calculations were done the old fashioned way, by simple trigonometry.

But she wasn't planning on using the main entrance. If one colonist was still alive then there could be others. She didn't want to announce her arrival before checking the place out first, and that meant finding other possible ways in. These were smaller airlocks, dotted farther up the crater rim, and could be accessed on foot. They were installed as escape routes for miners should there be a collapse at the main entrance. She would try one of these first. Hopefully sneak in and do some clandestine reconnaissance.

The crater rim rose up before her. Jann scanned the horizon looking for a natural valley carved out of the cliff. That should be where the main entrance was located. But it was hard to make out in the haze. She had to find it quickly and not spend too much time driving along the base of the cliff. She was pretty sure she was on the right course when eventually she spotted the dip in the crater rim. She aimed for it and stepped on the gas. The rover obliged.

It still took her quite a while to find it. The main entrance was so well concealed she was only three hundred meters away when she spotted it. She slammed on the brakes and came to a skidding halt. Jann waited for the dust to settle before utilizing the onboard camera to scan along the base of the crater's rim. When she found the entrance she zoomed in.

It consisted of one large airlock and two smaller ones. There was nothing out of the ordinary about them other than they were well hidden. She looked at it for a while, half expecting it to open and empty out a cohort of stormtroopers. But it was still and silent—and just a little ominous. Jann started up the rover again and moved off towards the cover of a large rock formation. She parked out of sight of the entrance and switched off the engine.

"Okay, old girl, this is it. Time to focus."

She snapped on her helmet, checked her biometrics and made her way through the airlock at the back of the rover, out onto the surface. The sun was high in the sky and she dimmed her visor to counter the glare. According to the charts, about half a kilometer left of the main entrance there should be a path of sorts, leading up the side of the crater rim for about a hundred meters to a wide ledge; the location of an emergency airlock.

She moved slowly, all the time endeavoring to stay behind whatever cover she could find. But after a few hundred meters the rock formation came to an end and she had no option but to cross to the base in full view. As she worked her way west the cliff face become less sheer and started to slope outward. The ground underfoot also became more rugged and broken as she picked her way between boulders and rocks that had crumbled down the side of the rim over the eons.

Then she saw them. At first she wasn't sure, but as she came closer there was no doubt. She was looking at a trail of footprints coming down the side of the crater and heading off in to the central wasteland. They were crisp and clean, clearly made recently. *The colonist,* she thought. *This is where he came out.* She followed the line of footprints back up the slope. There were places where she lost them over rocky terrain but managed to pick them up again as she progressed upwards. She was high above the level of the crater basin when she saw the entrance. Jann expected to see an airlock but instead it was a low tunnel carved out of the rock, the trail of footprints leading into it. She kept moving, ever upward, towards the tunnel.

THE TUNNEL WAS DARK, but thankfully short, only a few meters deep. At the end was an airlock, and judging by the illumination coming from the control panel, it was functioning. She advanced to face the door. A ripple of fear cascaded through her as she examined the panel. She pressed the *open* button and stood back. The door silently moved inward to reveal a surprisingly large area. It had an inner door at the far end but, oddly, two other doors on either side. Jann considered there might be several routes into this airlock from the mine. It made sense, as this was an escape hatch, presumably for emergencies. She stepped in. The floor was dusty but she could make out the footprints, heading from the door at the far end. She decided this would be her exit. The outer door swung closed and the airlock began to pressurize. Due to its large internal volume it took somewhat longer that the one back in the colony. Jann waited anxiously. She was committed, no going back now. Finally the light went green and there was a momentary pause before the inner door opened.

. . .

Four people stood at the entrance, in full hazmat suits. Jann froze as two of them rushed forward and grabbed her arms, pinning them behind her back. She struggled and kicked, but the bulky EVA suit made it difficult to move. They looped a metal band around her waist and she could feel it pulled tight, trapping her arms. She twisted and tried to pull them out, but it was no use.

When they were satisfied she was secured, a third person advanced. He reached up and unfastened her helmet, pulling it off her head. "Get me out of this," she shouted as she kicked out at her assailant, aiming for his groin. But she was too clumsy, and he sidestepped her easily. He raised an arm and Jann could see he held a small syringe. Jann struggled but the two others had a firm grip on her. She felt the needle jab into her neck. "Bastards," she managed, before all consciousness drained out of her.

5

INCARCERATION

Consciousness came to her in waves of ever increasing clarity: light, sounds, a sensation of being trapped. Jann woke to find herself bound to an operating table. Her feet, hands and body were strapped down tight. She turned her attention to her environment and saw that she was in a small room. It was stark, save for some medical equipment of indeterminate function. She lifted her head further to fully examine her situation. It was not good.

The wall in front of her was made from a semi-transparent glass, and she could make out the vague shapes of people moving around on the other side. She struggled against the bonds again, this time with such ferocity that the table shook with her rage. The figures noticed her activity and the glass wall became a little more transparent. She could now see several people sitting at workstations, facing her. One was standing looking straight at her. They all wore white lab coats and odd looking face masks. The standing figure spoke; Jann thought he must be in charge.

"Please, do not be alarmed. We need to restrain you for your own safety."

Jann strained against her bonds again. "Get me out of this."

"If you insist on struggling then we must sedate you again."

Jann stopped. "Who are you? What do you want from me?"

"All in good time, Dr. Malbec."

"How do you know who I am?"

"We know a lot about you. We have been observing you for quite a while."

Jann shook the table again. "Get these off me."

"That is not possible at present. You see, you are a biohazard and as such a contamination risk to us. Please remain calm. You will feel no pain while we conduct our experiments."

Jann fought her bonds with all the strength she could muster, the entire room shook with the violence of her struggle.

"I'm sorry but you leave us no other option." With that, the window dimmed and Jann heard a pump kick in. She looked for the source of the sound and found it was coming from a unit beside her head. From this she could see a clear tube running into her neck, a blue liquid flowing through it. She slowly felt her muscles relax and all consciousness drain out of her—again.

~

JANN WOKE with a start and sat bolt upright. Light blinded her and she shaded her eyes to look around. It was the same room but the operating table and the medical equipment were gone. She breathed a sigh of relief when she realized she was no longer restrained. She was lying on a small bed, a pair of soft shoes and a bottle of water on the floor next to her, and nothing else. She stood up, feeling a little shaky, and moved over to the window. It was dull and cloudy, she couldn't make out anything on the other side. She rubbed her wrists, they were bruised and cut where she had tried to free herself from the straps that restrained her. She sat back on the small bed. It was clear to Jann that Colony Two was very much alive and well.

THE SOLS PASSED, one by one. She could tell only by the light in her room dimming at night and growing brighter in the morning. It was a strange light. There was no specific point of origin, it seemed as if the entire upper half of the room glowed with an even luminosity. It had a reddish hue, like the daylight on Mars. At night the light didn't switch off, it simply dimmed slowly over time, like a Martian dusk. But it was never totally dark. At night she could make out the constellations of the nighttime sky. It was like camping out. At one point she reached up and touched the wall, just to check that she was not imagining it. That all this time, she was really outside, as if that were even possible. But she needed some way to anchor her mind to reality. It gave under the touch of her fingers and felt soft, almost velvety. Jann considered that it might be bioengineered. Some sort of phosphorescent living organism that grew across the roof of the room.

Food came to her through a hatch in the wall. The table would first extend then a side panel would open and a tray of food slid onto it. The first time this happened she cowered in a corner on her bed, then sat and looked at it for a while before moving over to check if there was anything she could use as a weapon. There was nothing, no utensils and the dishes were made from some flimsy paper-like material. She picked it up and flung it at the window. But by sol three, she was hungry and sat down to pick at the food. It consisted of salads and some vague, nutty rectangle, presumably protein. She took a tentative sip of water. It tasted fresh and clean, so she drank it all.

Sometimes she could make out vague shapes moving behind the dull window. She would scream and shout at them, bang her fist against it. But it was useless—there was no response.

IT WAS EARLY on the forth sol when the door finally opened and in walked a tall, dark, elegant man. Behind him were two others wearing black, one carried a tray of food, the other a long metal bar. They were male, Caucasian, and looked identical.

"Dr. Malbec, you're finally awake. My name is Dr. Ataman Vanji." He extended a hand towards her.

Jann froze for a moment. "The geneticist from Colony One?"

"Ahh, you've heard of me? Yes, one and the same." He shook her hand. "My apologies for the unfortunate nature of your welcome. But we needed to be sure that you were clean."

"Clean?"

"Please, eat." He signaled for the other man to bring forward the tray. He waved a hand over a wall panel and a small table slid out along with a bench on either side. He placed the tray on the table.

"We needed to ensure you were free of the infection. That's why we had to keep you locked up here."

Jann was finding it difficult to formulate any sort of a

reply. She stood with her back to the wall, ready to strike at the first opportunity.

"You know about the infection, don't you? Some of your crew succumbed to it."

"Yes," she managed.

Vanji waved a dismissive hand in the air. "It was an error on my part that allowed it to escape into the general environment, before it had been fully developed."

"You can kill it?"

"Oh yes, quite easily really."

"How?"

"As a biologist, Dr. Malbec, I'm sure you are aware of the toxicity of oxygen to certain life forms?"

"Well, yes."

"Expose the bacteria to a low pressure, one hundred percent oxygen environment for twenty-four hours and it is dead. Expose an infected human to the same for thirty-six and they too are free of it. Simple." *Pressure, of course. Why didn't I think of that?* she thought as she slumped down onto the edge of the bed. *How could I have been such an idiot not to have tried that?* Oxygen toxicity was an obvious experiment, and she had tried it several times, but not in combination with a variable pressure environment. All these years, all the hopeless experiments, and now she had her answer. Just like that.

"That's why we needed to keep you sealed in here for a few sols. Come, let me show you what we have done here. I'm sure you have many questions." He stood back and held the door open, inviting her through.

Jann took a moment to compose herself. The shock of what she had just discovered was still reverberating around her mind. Finally she stood up and looked from the door back to Vanji, and then at the two guards standing behind him.

"Come, you have nothing to fear, and as a biologist, I'm sure you'll be fascinated by what we've created."

Jann took a tentative step towards the door. Vanji had already walked out, leaving the two guards behind. She followed him out into a long, wide corridor hewn from the rock. The walls were rough. Above her, the roof was curved, with the same strange illumination. They walked side by side, the two guards following behind.

"How did you survive? All this time, it must be, what, six years since the sandstorm, since Colony One went offline?"

"We got lucky. Originally we only had solar power, but this whole area beneath our feet," he gestured towards the floor, "has considerable geothermal activity. Aerothermal, to give it its correct terminology, seeing as we are on Mars."

"You mean it's hot?"

"Not exactly hot, but there is a significant temperature difference between the surface and the lower galleries of this cave system. Enough for us to sink deep bores and create a heat exchanger—in fact, several of them. So we were able to generate our own power. That's what saved us. Not only that, it enabled us to create what I'm about to show you."

They came to a stop in front of a metal door set into the rock. Vanji swiped a hand across the control panel and the door opened to reveal a lift. They stepped inside. It was both wide and tall, its interior sleek and well engineered. Jann could feel the lift move a short distance before it came to a soft halt, then seemed to move sideways. Finally the doors opened into a large cave filled with desks, seating and personal items. It looked like Vanji's own private space.

"Please," he gestured towards an armchair. "Have a seat.

Are you hungry? I can have some more food brought to you if you like."

"No I'm fine, thanks. Where are we?"

"This is my humble office. It's where I live, really. Let me show you the colony." He moved over to long flat wall and swiped a control panel. Slowly the wall illuminated. Jann thought it was a screen at first. But it was a window, presumably made from the same material as the one in her room. She stood up, moved over to it, and looked out. "Oh my God."

"This is a window into our world. Down there is the soul of Colony Two."

BELOW HER, a vast cavern stretched into the distance. The floor was covered with vegetation and plant life. Here and there she could see small ponds and streams. It was like a lush parkland. Overhead, the cavern ceiling had the same strange illumination. The entire ceiling was light, a diffuse reddish illumination. Strange and incredible, it was like being outside. What startled Jann the most was the population. Throughout the cavern she could see groups of colonists going about their business: planting, harvesting, tending. With just a cursory look, she estimated there must be at least a hundred people down there. How could this be? She turned to Vanji. "All these colonists, where did they come from? There was only supposed to be a few dozen working here when the sandstorm hit."

"Ah, yes. This may come as surprise to you but most of these people are in fact clones. They are my most magnificent achievement: loyal, trustworthy and eternally young." He faced the window and opened his arms wide as if to embrace his creation.

Jann was silent for a while as she tried to comprehend this. So Gizmo was right about clones after all. She should have known, it always was. The colonist that arrived at the airlock at Colony One must have been one of these. But why did he go there? Was he trying to escape?

Vanji turned back to Jann. “I know it’s a lot to take in. But give it time and you will begin to understand the society we have created here.”

Jann looked up at him. “I’m sure I will, but right now I just want to get back to Colony One as soon as possible.”

“Ah… well, you see that’s not possible.”

Jann stiffened. “What do you mean?”

He looked down and rubbed his chin. “Your arrival here has created something of a dilemma for us. Our existence here is secret and… well, you jeopardize that.”

“But how?”

Vanji waved a dismissive hand. “The *how* is not important at the moment. What *is* important is your future here.”

“What? I’m not staying here.”

“That is not for you to decide. There are those on the Council who demanded you be recycled. But since you’re a biologist I think you will make a great addition to our team.”

“Recycled? You mean… killed?”

“Not a term we use here. We treasure life; it is a precious resource on Mars. We do not kill, we recycle. You see, our philosophy here is that the soul belongs to the person but their biology belongs to the colony.”

“So, what are you saying?”

“I’m saying that this is where you live now, until the time comes for you to be… recycled.”

6

BIOLOGY

After her meeting with Vanji, Jann had been taken, under guard, to a different room farther down the long corridor. She was unceremoniously shoved inside and the door locked. The room was like the corridor, hewn from the rock, a cave within a cave. It was spacious, but furnished only with a bed, a desk and a seat. All of which were fabricated from bio-plastic. The ceiling was high and had the now-familiar lighting covering the ceiling. Again she had the disjointed feeling of being outside. She presumed this was now her room for the foreseeable future, however long that future might be.

On the table was a handwritten note. *Place your palm over the touch plate on the desk to activate. To activate what?* she wondered. Inspecting the surface, she found it to be smooth except for a small frosted glass to one side. She placed her palm on it and a 3D image of Mars projected upward and rendered itself just above the desk. *'Welcome Dr. Malbec. Please relax and enjoy this presentation.'* The rendering of Mars grew larger and started to rotate. It zoomed in on the Jezero crater and then on the location of Colony Two.

'In the beginning...' The voiceover commenced. It was a history lesson. Jann sat down and paid attention.

THE MINE WAS FIRST ESTABLISHED by the early colonists, over ten Earth years ago. Initially they open cast for metals and silica but eventually sealed the cave system and created a pressurized atmosphere inside. This single act radically transformed the place and in many respects, as a Martian habitat, it was far superior to Colony One. It had heat from aero-thermal activity deep below the surface. The rock and regolith were free of toxic perchlorates, and the millions of tons of rock above made a perfect radiation shield. No wonder Vanji regarded it as being the perfect crucible in which to forge his vision of humanity. The vast cavern that Jann had witnessed from Vanji's lair was only one of many, a great many. What they had accomplished here was staggering. Not least the incredible advances that they had made in genetic engineering, particularly in human cloning.

YET, the know how to clone a human had already existed, at least in theory. However, it was the ultimate scientific taboo. No scientist in their right mind would touch it. The repercussions of such experimentation would, at best, destroy a career instantly. At worst it would come with a hefty prison sentence. It was banned outright. But of course, that was on Earth, this was Mars. *'The only law on Mars is your own.'* She remembered that first day in Colony One with Paolio, wandering around the biodome. "We've come a long way since then, Paolio," she said to herself.

. . .

When the presentation finished, Jann sat for a while digesting all that she had gleaned from it. What interested her most was not so much what was said, but what had been left unsaid. Even if Vanji and his team had successfully developed a human clone, it would be a mere baby. All the colonists she saw in the cavern were adults. So how was this possible? And the numbers suggested that there must be more than one clone of the same person. Multiple copies, all created from the same source.

Then there was the secrecy. No one knew this place existed as a functioning colony. Not even Nills. He seemed convinced that no one could have survived the great storm. Or was he also in on it, part of the conspiracy? He had tried hard to hide his own existence from the ISA crew, maybe he knew? But she realized this was not possible. Because what Nills knew, Gizmo would also know, and the little robot had scant data on Colony Two. She gave a thought to Gizmo, even felt a twinge of sorrow for it, tending to the garden in the vast biodome of Colony One, all alone.

Jann had no answers to any of these questions. So she turned her attention to examining the room. Specifically, how to get out. But after a brief period of testing and prodding she gave up and lay down on the bed. She needed to think.

On the plus side, she now possessed the knowledge of how to kill the bacteria that had so devastated her life. Oxygen toxicity she knew, and had tried. But not in combination with low pressure. How could she have been so dumb not to have considered it? She could have been home free by now. But there was no point dwelling on it. At least now she knew. It was her passport off this planet, her ticket back to Earth.

Yet even with this, she was further away than when she started. Trapped in a nightmare, with no escape. *There must be a way out*, she thought. At least her mind was beginning to focus now. It was clear to her what her mission was. She would find a way to escape or be *recycled* in the attempt. *What did that mean?* she wondered. Was it death or something halfway in between? Some form of termination that could only be conjured from the mind of a geneticist? It wasn't something she wanted to experience. No, what she wanted was to go home, back to Earth, and be done with Mars and all its insanity.

So, her number one priority would be to find out as much as possible about the inner workings the colony. Next would be to gain Vanji's trust and to a lesser extent, the trust of the Council. It was clear from her initial discussion with him that they were not all in favor of keeping her alive. Her stay of execution was prompted by Vanji regarding her knowledge as an asset. She needed to play along with this, and in truth, part of her was fascinated to learn all she could about the experiments being conducted here, especially regarding cloning.

In the end, she realized she had little choice but be a part of Colony Two and try not to get herself *recycled*. She remembered Vanji's words. *'The soul belongs to the person but their biology belongs to the colony.'* A shiver ran up her spine.

7

HOMO ARIES

Jann awoke to the sound of the door being opened. The light grew brighter and she sat up in bed with a jolt, her body taut, ready for action. The same two black-clad guards entered and took up positions either side of the doorway. They were followed in by a woman carrying a tray of food. Her head was lowered and she moved deftly, but in silence. She put the tray on the desk and retreated, without making eye contact. The two guards followed her out and locked the door again.

Jann relaxed, swung her legs over the side of the bed and stood up. *It must be morning,* she thought. She eyed the tray of food, picked up an apple and took a bite. It tasted good, so she finished it in four bites. She was hungry. Better eat as much as possible as who knows when she would eat again. As someone who had lived the hunter-gatherer lifestyle for the last few years she was not accustomed to eating only when food was available. She cast her eye over the tray again. There were baskets of fruit and bread, a jug of juice and a small platter with what looked like paté. She lifted it up, examined it, sniffed and was pretty sure it was synthetic, probably grown in a lab. Jann put it back and decided the fruit might be the safer option, and chose a pear. She noticed something odd at the bottom of the basket, and reached in to lift it out.

It was a small hard object wrapped in a paper-like material. She opened it to find a note.

'Our joy knows no bounds now that you have come. Your presence amongst us fills us with hope. This token will keep you safe. Tell no one.'

Jann examined the object. It was a small white stone, carved into the shape of the beehive hut near Colony One. Its base was flat and etched on the underside was the word '*Source.*'

She turned it over a few times, examining it. She could tell that it must have been carved some time ago as it was worn and unevenly polished, as if someone had kept it in a pocket. Dirt had accumulated in the word scratched in to the base. It was a strange artifact, its meaning obscure.

She dressed, ate and was back examining the object when the door opened and Vanji strode in. She shoved the object into her pocket before he noticed.

"Ah, Dr. Malbec, are you ready for our little tour? I have something very special to show you today. Come." Jann stood up and made her way into the corridor, sizing up the two guards. She reckoned she could take them, if she had the element of surprise as an advantage. Relieve one of his cattle prod and the other would go down easy. But she would only get one chance at that, and now was not the time.

They walked to the elevator at the end of the passage and entered. "So where are we going?" asked Jann as Vanji pressed a code into a touchscreen.

"We are going to witness an act of creation in the

birthing room." They descended, deep into the bowels of Colony Two. The doors finally opened on a short tunnel, opening out into a wide cavern. The roof had the same, all encompassing lighting. Rows of horizontal glass tanks, each the size of a large bath and filled with a thick, opaque liquid covered the floor. There was something inside but it looked dull and formless through the fluid. Wires and tubes snaked in and around the tanks and they all glowed with a muted luminosity. Vanji led her down a row towards a knot of people gathered around a tank, all busy tending to their tasks. They looked about twenty-five, but Jann doubted that was their actual age.

"Dr. Vanji, we're ready when you are." One technician broke away from the knot and approached them. She eyed Jann with a distinct air of suspicion.

"Excellent." Vanji turned to Jann. "You are now going to witness the birthing of a new life form." He waved his hand at the technician. "You may commence."

The technician retreated with a nod. Activity increased around the tank as the glow brightened. Jann could now make out the recumbent form of a human. Pumps activated and the level of liquid in the tank slowly decreased. She was close enough to witness the human breach the surface. It was male, fully adult, and also looked around twenty-five. Its entire body was covered in a thin wire mesh, and various tubes snaked from its orifices.

When the last of the fluid drained away, the sides of the tank detached and started to rise upwards into the space above. The technicians gathered around the body, removing tubes and wires in a well-practiced routine, all the time getting feedback on bio-status from monitors. After a few moments they all stood back down. The lead technician turned to Vanji. "He's ready."

"Excellent. You may proceed with the *kick*."

Again the technician nodded, and signaled to the others.

"All clear?" A chorus of confirmations echoed around the platform and the body appeared to be zapped with a high-voltage charge. Its back arched, muscles contracted and it shook, and banged, and vibrated for a few seconds before lying still. Steam rose from the body.

"Again." A technician shouted.

For a second time the body was racked with a high-voltage jolt, longer this time. Finally it stopped and there was a moment of silence. His fingers twitched, his back arched and he took in a long hissing breath. The technicians moved fast, he kicked and shivered and shook as they gathered around him: probing, testing, analyzing. They watched a large monitor: checking stats, verifying data, monitoring readouts. His eyes were wide and frantic, and one of them jabbed his neck with a syringe. He quieted down. They stood back and inspected the monitors.

"Subject's physiological and neural data looks excellent. We can proceed with processing." With that, the technicians started cleaning him before finally lifting him onto a waiting gurney and covering him with a thin sheet. When they were finished they wheeled him off.

JANN STOOD IN MUTE SILENCE, all the while clutching the totem that had arrived with breakfast. She rubbed its smooth face with her thumb; it comforted her. Vanji turned to her as she watched the huddle of technicians wheel the subject out of the birthing chamber. "You have been privileged to witness the creation of life itself. A new colonist to add to our ever-growing population."

Jann was speechless. What could she say that could in

any way sum up her emotions? In the end she simply said, "Holy crap."

Vanji threw his head back and laughed. "I fully appreciate your shock at witnessing this event. For the uninitiated it must be a surreal experience."

"So what happens to him now?"

"He will be processed over the next few months until he is ready to join our community."

"Processed?"

"Looks can be deceptive. He may seem fully grown, and in many ways he is, but his mind is like that of a small child. New members require counseling and processing before the full potential of the mind is realized."

"But how can you create a clone so fully formed, so complete?"

"Would you like to see how it's achieved?"

Jann thought about this for a minute. She had just witnessed the creation of a new life, the moment it became cognizant, and that new life was the product of science. Not of nature, per se, but through the genius of one man, Dr. Ataman Vanji. He had stolen the secrets of the gods, the knowledge and ability to create life. Part of her felt that this power was not right, not natural—not moral. But the scientist in her was fascinated. How was this even possible?

"Show me," she said finally.

Vanji stared at her intensely for a moment. Then he s smiled and said, "I was right about you, you have the soul of true scientist. That insatiable desire to know and understand. Let me show you."

They walked back along the rows of tanks until they came to a laboratory. Here again, a tank took central position. It was filled with the same opaque viscous fluid but Jann could see it was empty. From around its base ran a myriad of wires and tubes into machines and systems of indeterminate function.

"This is where the magic begins," he indicated the tank. "In here is a biological suspension of stem cells and nutrients. Into this primordial soup we introduce the zygote. It is then stimulated, using a complex radiation process with a specific harmonic frequency modulation. This accelerates the cell division process and as each cell starts to define itself, it gathers to it the raw materials—the stem cells it's surrounded by—and utilizes these to speed up the process of growth."

Jann touched the side of the tank and peered in. "How do you create these stem cells? I mean, there are so many."

"We grow them, and we also recycle."

Jann stepped back from the tank with a jolt. "So that's what you meant. The soul belongs to the human, but their biology belongs to the colony."

"You must understand, this is a barren planet, life is precious here. Nobody should die needlessly. It would be a waste."

Jann put her hand into her pocket and clutched the totem. "Are you creating genetic replicas of all the colonists who came here?"

"Not quite. You see, it is quite a traumatic experience, for an original human to come face to face with their clone. So we have only cloned those that are no longer alive."

"But there must be over a hundred people here."

"Our total population is nearing two hundred."

"So there are multiple clones of the same person?"

"Yes, there are secondary, tertiary and even quad clones. These do not experience the same emotional trauma at meeting their twins. But we are now embarking on a whole new phase. We're creating hybrids."

"Hybrids?"

"Yes, a genetic mix of different colonists. You see, clones are an exact genetic replica of their hosts. But with hybrids, we can introduce biological variation and new genetic enhancements. You see, Jann, we are creating a whole new species of human. We call this new species Homo Aires."

Jann shuddered as the implications of Vanji's genetic experiments with the human race began to sink in. "Oh my God." She stepped back from Vanji and stared at him in shock. It took every ounce of her will to keep it together. *Get a grip, old girl, don't let him see,* she thought as she clutched the totem in her pocket tighter.

"Ah, I see you are suitably impressed, as I knew you would be." He had mistaken her body language for admiration, not horror.

Jann looked around at the lab equipment to give herself some time to compose herself. Finally she said, "So tell me, why are there no children? Surely with everyone in the full flush of youth there must have been some pregnancies?"

"Ah, well the clones are sterile and, well... natural reproduction is... forbidden."

"Forbidden?"

"It is too harsh an environment for such fragile biology, and, let's face it, we have a better, safer way of doing it. We think of it as a major evolutionary step for humanity."

"But how do you prevent it? The need to reproduce is the very essence of life."

Dr. Vanji looked down at the floor for a moment. "I wasn't going to mention it right now, but since you brought it up I might as well tell you. All the females have a procedure to make them sterile. And I assure you it is quick and painless, you won't feel a thing."

"What? You're not serious."

"It is not a request, it's for the good of the colony. You must realize this after everything I showed you."

Jann began to feel even more trapped. She looked around anxiously, she wanted to run, to get out now.

"Just think about this," Vanji continued. "When you set foot on this planet for the first time you were in your early thirties. Now, three years later, you have the physical body of a twenty-five year old. This is the gift we have given you. What we ask is a small price to pay for this miracle."

Jann stayed silent and tried to keep from running.

"It is good that you found us, you were using your newfound youth and energy to live like a cavewoman. This was a complete waste of your talents."

"How do you know that?"

"Ah, we may be hidden from the world but there's not much we don't know."

Jann thought about how much had changed. She had gone feral, that much was true, but at least she had freedom, both of thought and action. Yet here, she could possibly be sacrificing her womanhood. In her mind, this was a very high price to pay. She forced herself to stay calm.

"So why all the secrecy, why hide all this from Earth?"

"Just think of what this technology could do to humanity if given free reign. It would destroy them, and possibly the entire ecosystem with it. It needs complete control and we are not ready yet."

Jann had to admit, he had a point. It would do nothing for the human race but sow the seeds of its own destruction. "But, why hide? Why not let them know you're all alive and prospering, but keep silent on the genetic breakthroughs?"

"Because if they know we're here then they will find out. And then they will come and they will simply take it. Do not underestimate the greed of humanity. The lure would be irresistible. So we must wait until the time is right, when we alone can dictate the terms and keep control."

"And when is that?"

Vanji gave her a long look as if considering how much he could reveal. "Soon, the time is very soon. And it is you that has made that possible."

"Me? How come?"

He waved a dismissive hand. "That's enough for today, I think. We can resume our discussion at a later date." He signaled to the ever-present guards. "Please see Dr. Malbec back to her room."

8

THE COUNCIL

Vanji sat at the head of a long table that had been carved from solid rock and polished to a high sheen. On either side sat the members of the colony council. They were all *alphas*, original colonists, and all had a youthful appearance that belied their true ages. No clones, *betas* as they were called, held positions on the ruling council.

He pulled at the cuffs of his robe of office, something he wore only when the council met. It conferred power and status and signified his authority. There was much to discuss, the assembled members were intrigued with rumor and counter-rumor concerning the latest addition to the colony. But, first things first, protocol needed to be observed. Vanji stood and signaled to The Keeper of Records.

"Can we start with the figures for the previous period?" he sat down again.

The Keeper consulted his screen and a 3D rendering of various datasets materialized in the center of the enormous stone table.

"First the good news. We've had a record number of

births this period, bringing our total population up to one hundred and ninety three." There was a cursory round of applause at this news. "If we continue at this rate we will reach a population of two hundred in the next period." The Keeper continued, "That said, the rate of discontent and insubordination continues to rise. We recycled three this period, and an increasing number of betas are requiring *correction*." This last set of statistics was met with muted murmurs.

"It seems that our Head of Harmony Sector is failing in her duty to fulfill the requirements of her office. This cannot be allowed to continue." Luka Modric, Head of Operations, pointed an accusatory finger across the table.

"I would challenge that it is our Head of Maintenance that is failing in his duty and is, in fact, the root cause of this discontent. These constant power outages are a cause for concern, not just for betas." Harmony reciprocated by pointing at Maintenance.

"We do what we can with what we have. Some systems are old and spare parts are not easily manufactured here in the colony. Betas still lack the skills to fashion what we need. The population is growing too fast." Maintenance fought back with a resigned acceptance of reality.

"My betas can make anything." Manufacturing slapped the table. "Anything you asked for, they have made. Have they not?"

"Enough of this bickering, it is not what we need right now." Vanji silenced the council members and then waved at the Keeper to continue with the data report.

The Keeper cleared his throat and continued. "Eh... mining output suffered a sharp drop due to... eh... issues with some of the processing machinery." This was met with silence around the table. "However, we have sufficient supplies in reserve to maintain manufacturing levels in and around those of the previous period."

Manufacturing directed a raised hand at Maintenance. "I rest my case." Manufacturing scowled.

"Food production is 5.6% higher overall, with increases seen in all areas, most notably in that of... eh... wine." This was met with several nods of approval.

The Keeper of Records droned on in this fashion for some time as the ups and downs of colony life were read out in numbers and percentages. When he finally finished the rest of the assembled council breathed a collective sigh of relief.

It was Luka Modric, Head of Operations, who spoke next, as was his right by rank. "So what is the current status of this... ISA crew member?"

"She is being kept under close guard at present while she undergoes a period of psychological readjustment," replied Vanji.

"Is that wise? If word of her existence here gets out, then the betas may become more unsettled. They would find this revelation hard to absorb. If not handled delicately it has the potential to upset the colony." Head of Harmony was concerned.

"It's bad enough that Boateng escaped and made the trip. Now we are living with the consequences of that," said Modric.

"Have we found out how Boateng got access to a functioning EVA suit?" The question was put to Daniel Kayden, Head of Hydro.

"Not yet, but rest assured, we will."

"He had to have help from someone, and it must have been from an alpha," Modric continued.

"Well that makes twenty people, if we include you in that," said Kayden.

"Are you accusing me of having some part in this?"

Kayden raised a hand. "I'm saying you are also an original colonist, as all of us here are."

Vanji leaned into the table. "His trip has proved fortuitous for us. If Boateng had not set out on his quest then the ISA crewmember would not have come to us. She is a biologist of some expertise, so a very useful addition to the colony."

"Yes, but at what cost? What if they have seen it?" Modric pointed skyward. "A satellite may have picked up all this activity."

"All the communication we have intercepted over the past few years indicates that Earth has given up on sending another mission here anytime soon. Even if they have seen something they can't know what it is. It's not going to prompt an invasion." Kayden was hitting his stride.

"Her presence here is a clear danger to the social balance of the colony. The betas already have a strong creation myth developed around Colony One and that beehive hut. That's why Boateng escaped, it's this obsession they have, it grows stronger every sol. Therefore, for the good of the colony, I proposed that she be recycled immediately." Modric was adamant.

Vanji raised a hand. "Let's not be so hasty, she could be very valuable to us. And may even help calm the betas."

Modric was having none of this. "I propose a vote, a show of hands. All in favor of recycling the ISA crew member Dr. Jann Malbec?"

A few timid hands were raised. "Well that settles it," said Vanji. "She stays."

. . .

Buoyed by this besting of Modric, Vanji considered that now might be a good time to get consensus from the council for his latest creation. He nodded to his Head of Genetics. “Lori, if you will. Now would be a good time to make your presentation.”

Lori Bechard tapped some icons on his screen and a 3D rendering of a human rotated above the center of the table. “This is HYB-Q003.” He waited a beat to increase the drama. “She will be the first quad-donor hybrid ever created.” This was met with interest.

“More hybrids, Vanji? I thought it was agreed by the council that this line of genetic experimentation was to be phased out?”

“It was never *agreed,* Modric. At best it was advisory. The development of hybrid humans is the future, as I’ve argued many times around this table. We are bringing into being an entirely new race of humans. This is to be celebrated, not denied.” Vanji was standing now, one hand on the table, looking directly at Modric. “What’s more, the twenty or so hybrids we have in the colony are the best resource we have for keeping the betas from getting ideas beyond their station. In short, Modric, we need them.” He slapped the table and sat down.

Lori took this his cue to continue. “HYB-Q003 will be birthed within the next few days and represents a new pinnacle in our genetic cloning program. For the first time, we now have a hybrid clone that is biologically capable of reproduction.”

The council erupted.

“What? That is going too far, we cannot allow it.” Modric was apoplectic. The others added to his outrage with their own outbursts.

“This is madness.”

"Have you lost your mind Vanji?"

"I for one, am not comfortable with this," said Harmony.

"This goes against everything we agreed on."

Modric stood up and raised his hands to quiet them all down. "There is a simple way to settle this once and for all. I propose another vote. A vote to ban all experimentation with hybrid clones, forever. For the good of the colony. All in favor?"

Hands shot up, save for the geneticists and Daniel Kayden.

"Very good." Modric turned to Vanji. "The Council have spoken. There will be no more of this line of experimentation. It is to cease immediately and this... hybrid will be recycled." He sat down.

"You are making a grave mistake." Vanji's face was tight, his body taut, his anger barely contained. "You are throwing away the future evolution of the human race."

"This is not our future, Vanji. Nor will it be. It has been decided. No more of this line of experimentation." Modric waved a dismissive hand.

Vanji seethed. He had been defeated, his ambition thwarted. He had played his hand too soon, grossly miscalculated. He looked around the table at the assembled councilors. They were fools, simpletons with no vision. But now he knew who was on his side.

9

INTRIGUE

Along one section of the upper gallery of the vast main cavern, a common rest and recreation area had been created over time, for alphas only. It was their exclusive domain and no clones could enter, unless of course, they were on the serving staff. It was long, with a low wall running along the edge like a balcony. Above this wall ran a window that afforded those who had sufficient rank to gaze down across the lush vegetation and busy industry of Colony Two. It was one-way, Alphas could see out, but nobody could see in.

When Kayden entered, he noticed that Modric was already there, sitting at one of the far tables facing the window, in a quiet and secluded spot. He played with a drink and looked to be deep in thought. He had asked to meet Kayden here, to discuss things, as he put it. Modric's way of finding out which side he was on, he presumed.

"Modric."

"Kayden, come, sit." He waved a hand at the seat closet to him. Kayden sat. "Drink?" he lifted his glass. "Sol 11,345, an excellent vintage, I would highly recommend it."

Kayden nodded and a glass was poured. Modric raised his own to him. "I would suggest 'to your good health' but that would seem a little self-serving."

"Indeed," replied Kayden, as he took a sip of the fragrant Colony wine. "That was a brave challenge you made, back at the council meeting."

"Perhaps you think it foolhardy? To overrule Vanji like that?"

"The thought had crossed my mind."

"Maybe I grow old. Maybe I tire of this place and this... existence." He looked back at Kayden. "Does it not feel strange to you, that your mind is that of a forty year old but the face staring back at you in the mirror is only twenty-five?"

"Far from it, Modric. I'm constantly amazed at what we have achieved here. Perhaps it's really something else that bothers you?"

Modric looked into his glass for a moment, then looked over his shoulder before leaning in closer to Kayden. "I feel we are living on borrowed time. I sense the betas grow more agitated with each passing sol. It's like we're sitting on a powder keg. Look at us, look around you. We live the exalted life as top dogs in the colony hierarchy. Yet we are few. Every time Genetics births a new beta we become more of a minority. And the history of societies ruled by minority elites never ends well."

"Ha, you're being paranoid." Kayden laughed and quaffed his wine, refilling his glass from the bottle on the table between them.

"Maybe. But you know this creation myth that the betas have developed around Colony One is getting very strong."

"Yes, I've heard rumors. Is it really true?"

"It gets more ingrained with them every sol." He sat

back. “It’s because of their dreams. Strange, don’t you think, that they should all have the memories of the alpha they were cloned from? Growing more lucid as they age.”

“Yes, but that’s what makes them so useful. Without these dreams they would know nothing, they would have to learn like children. It would take years before they are productive.”

“Well it’s a double edged sword, one I hope we don’t all fall on.”

They stayed silent for a moment and gazed down across the vast cavern. Betas were working away, planting, harvesting and maintaining the lush garden.

“It’s the reason Boateng escaped and tried to journey to Colony One. It’s this... desire that is awakening within them. It grows stronger and stronger.”

Kayden considered this, but stayed silent. Modric continued, “Look, it was bad enough that he got out. But now, the last ISA crewmember shows up at our door.” He pointed skyward. “They must have seen all this activity. Earth must suspect something by now, assuming they still have a working satellite up in orbit. We cannot remain hidden much longer.”

“I’ll grant you that, Modric. This is a concern.”

“We are entering uncertain times. This ISA woman is nothing but bad news. Why did Vanji allow it?”

“I don’t know. He sees something in her. She’s a biologist, apparently.”

“Her presence only serves to undermine the harmony we have maintained with the betas. She’s from Colony One, to them she is a God, don’t you see?”

They went quiet again. Each sipping wine, each deep in thought. After a few moments Modric refilled their glasses and sat forward.

"We have all toiled under the shared belief that we cannot let Earth have this technology: genetic manipulation, longevity, the ability to clone humans. The population would explode and ultimately destroy what's left of the planet."

"If they find out we're here they will come. They will simply take it; we are still not strong enough to stop them. You know this, Modric."

"If we are not strong enough now, then when? Do we need a population of three hundred, or five hundred, or what?" There is no clear plan that I can see. Meanwhile we can't venture out, we can't utilize the resources that we know exist in Colony One, nor can we receive supplies from Earth, even trade with them. In the meantime, we are fracturing. There are essential parts we simply cannot manufacture here. What happens when one of these fails, we all die? What good is the secret of eternal youth if we're dead?"

"You're being overly dramatic. We have power, heat, water and food a plenty."

"A society needs more than that to keep harmony, you know that as well as I do."

"We live in dangerous times, make no mistake."

"Indeed."

Modric looked around to check if they were alone and leaned in again. "Here's what I propose. We kill her. Before she has a chance to infect the minds of the betas. Do it now, while her presence here is still under wraps."

Kayden looked at Modric and took another sip from his glass as a way of giving himself time to think before replying. He placed the glass back down the table with a slow precise movement. "How do you propose we do this?"

"That, I don't know. I thought you might be able to offer

a possible course of action. Seeing as Vanji looks to you as an ally. You would be least suspected."

"No one could know of this, or we'll be the ones being recycled."

"I fear if we don't, then our days here as leaders are numbered."

Kayden stood up and leaned in to put a hand on Modric's shoulder as he spoke. "Let me sleep on it. That's all I can do for now."

"Don't sleep too long, or we may miss our opportunity."

10

HYDRO

In the sols following Jann's experience in the birthing rooms, she gained a little more freedom, or at least the sense of it. This was limited to short sessions in the bio-labs with the genetics team. She met few colonists save for Vanji, the two guards, and the woman who brought her food. Yet she learned a lot, not just about the complexities of human cloning but also the social hierarchy of the colony. The technology underlying this human outpost might be at the pinnacle of human achievement, but the social structure was medieval.

Alphas ruled. The twenty or so original colonists who had survived all that Mars had thrown at them formed the bulk of the council. They controlled everything. The workers were the betas, the clones. They were created from the *seeds*, as they were known. These turned out to be the Analogues that Jann and the original ISA crew had found in Colony One. No alpha living in Colony Two had been cloned, so the betas were the reincarnation of all those who had died. And there were multiples of each. So far Jann had only met one, the woman who brought food to her room.

She was Caucasian, young, and carried herself with a submissive deference, reminding Jann more of the polite manners of a Geisha, never looking her directly in the eye.

But like any technology, it never stood still and Vanji and his team had progressed to creating hybrids. This was more than just cloning, this was human genetic engineering taken to a whole new level. They had effectively created a new species, Homo Aries, Aries being the Greek god of Mars. The two guards were hybrids. Tall, strong, elegant—and silent. They never spoke, but Jann began to notice that, at times, they would look intently at each other, as if they were communicating. They would subtly nod or shake their heads along with almost imperceptible facial twitches. It was eerie to witness, and not a little unsettling.

At the top of this hierarchy was the imperial master, Vanji. He was like an Emperor, feared and worshiped in equal measure. He bestowed the gift of life and possessed the power to take it away with nothing more than a simple edict, a click of his fingers, so to speak. Most of the alphas feared Vanji and the betas feared the alphas. As for the hybrids, they seemed to be oblivious to everything. At least, that's how Jann perceived it.

After a few more sols of obedience they rewarded her with a window. Still confined to her room save for the odd excursion to the bio-labs, it was a blessing. It was something to break the boredom, and the increasing feeling of being trapped that was fermenting inside her. She had taken to pacing the room, bisecting it in a steady rhythm like the caged animal that she was. It was during one of these pacing sessions that the long smooth wall behind the desk became transparent. She stopped her pacing, crept forward and looked out. The entire vista of the main cavern was laid out below her, vast, verdant and industrious. She spent many hours just observing, following the patterns and rituals of the betas that toiled there. But in the end, all this anthropological study brought her no closer to escape. In fact, she feared she would somehow grow complacent, more accepting, and lose her desire for freedom, maybe even her will to live.

Eventually, on or around the tenth sol of her captivity, a new face entered her room. It was Daniel Kayden, one of the councilors. Behind him stood the same two guards. He smiled as he entered and reached to shake her hand. "Some good news for you, Dr. Malbec. We are paying a visit to a very special place this sol."

"Good, let's go, this room is making me demented. When am I getting out of here?"

"I don't know, that hasn't been decided yet."

"Why the hell not?"

"Look, please be patient, it's just politics." He opened his hands and shrugged his shoulders. "Come, follow me, we can talk as we walk."

Jann quelled her frustration. At least she was getting out for a while, why jeopardize it? They walked side by side in silence, the two guards following in step behind. Jann glanced back at them, their faces were a complete blank.

"Are they hybrids?" she jerked a thumb over her shoulder.

"Yes."

"They don't say much, do they?"

"No, none of them do."

"Are they engineered that way?"

"I'm sorry, I don't know. I'm not one of the geneticists."

"So, what's your story then?"

"I'm a geologist, Head of the Hydro sector."

"Water?"

"Yes, H2O, and I'm taking you to see some."

"Water?"

"Ah," he smiled. "Yes, water, but not like anything you've seen before."

They stepped into the elevator and descended. It felt to Jann that they were going lower than before, lower than the bio-labs. It was also getting noticeably warmer.

The doors opened into a short corridor that led into a pumping station. The sound of engines reverberated around the room. It was loud and mechanical. Large industrial pipes and ducts crisscrossed the space. At the far end was a control board with three betas monitoring the systems. At least Jann assumed they were betas.

"It's very warm in here."

"Yes, we are deep down, close to the aero-thermal engines. It gets even hotter the farther down you go."

"Well I hate to break it to you, but this is not very interesting."

Kayden turned to her and smiled. "Ah, just wait, you'll see."

As they moved past the control station, the three betas straightened and turned to her. She could have been mistaken but it looked to her like they all bowed.

"Are they doing that for you or me?"

"Both. But they do seem fascinated by you. It's the first time they've seen an outsider. You're something of a celebrity to them."

Jann looked back, they were just standing there staring at her as she passed. She nodded at them. This action resulted in their looking amazed and they bowed even lower.

"Come, just ignore them, this way."

They continued on through a short tunnel lined with

pipes that finally opened out into a large cave. The floor was sandy and the roof bright, but in the middle was something Jann never thought she would see on Mars. It was a large lake of flowing water.

"Wow."

"Told you."

"This is incredible."

The sandy floor of the cavern extended out to meet the water, like a beach. The lake itself seemed to disappear into a cloud of mist off in the distance. The cavern roof was peppered with long stalactites, and she could hear the water dripping down from their tips.

"The aero-thermal activity is more intense the farther in you go." Kayden pointed towards the back of the cavern. "That's what creates the mist. It's colder overhead so the moisture condenses and drips down, creating these huge stalactites."

"Like rain."

"Yes, like rain. On Mars."

At the edge of the sandy beach a small jetty with a floating pontoon tethered to the end extended into the lake. All along the water's edge seating had been set up.

"Is this where you go for a vacation?"

Kayden laughed. "Yeah, you could say that. Come, let's get onboard the pontoon and we can see the cavern from the middle of the lake."

They walked across to the jetty and Kayden held his hand out for Jann as she stepped onto the pontoon. It was flat and square with a low handrail on all sides. They hunkered down and Kayden picked up a paddle. "Here, you grab this, I'll cast off."

Jann moved closer to the center of the pontoon, where it felt more stable.

Two guards stood stiff and silent, watching. They became slightly more animated when Jann and Kayden cast off.

"It's okay, we'll only be a short while." Kayden shouted over to them. They relaxed.

"What's with them?"

"Just paddle. We'll take it out to the middle."

They moved with a graceful silence, the only sounds were the paddles hitting the water and the drip-drip from the cavern roof.

"Have you found any life in here?"

"You mean any microbial Martians swimming around?"

"Yes. It would seem ideal, water, heat and lots of complex chemical compounds."

"Sorry to disappoint, but no, nothing."

Jann looked back to see how far they had come. They had skirted the edge of the lake, around a rocky outcrop, and were now out of sight of the guards. They slowly paddled out from the edge, towards the middle of the steamy lake. Then a thought struck Jann. She knew next to nothing about Kayden, or his intentions.

She looked down into the water. "Is this toxic?"

"Yeah, but don't worry, it won't kill you if you fall in, as long as you get out quickly. That said, you could still drown in there. Hell of a way to go, drowning on Mars."

Jann withdrew her paddle. "If it's okay with you, let's head back, I've seen enough."

"Just a bit more, keep paddling."

She reluctantly resumed, but kept a tight grip on the paddle—in case she needed it as a weapon.

. . .

Mist began to envelop them before Kayden finally reversed his stroke. The pontoon came to a halt. "Okay, I think this should be far enough."

"Those guards back there," he nodded in the direction of the beach. "Are Vanji's eyes and ears. And what I have to say to you is not for them to hear. That's why I took the precaution of bringing you out here." Jann gripped her paddle.

"We don't have much time, so I'll be quick. Here it is. We have a plan to help you escape."

Jann was not sure if this was a trick or some test of Vanji's.

"Escape?"

"It may come as a surprise to you, but some of us don't like what's going on here. We want out, and that's where you come in. How would you like to get back to Earth?"

"Are you serious?"

"Yes."

Jann paused for a moment. "Go on... I'm listening."

"We know that the Odyssey transit craft is still in orbit, still functioning. And that the MAV is intact, it can still be used."

"It has no fuel tanks, they were all destroyed."

"We know the ISA sent you information on how to manufacture them. So we have everything we need to escape, am I right?"

Jann wondered how much Kayden really knew. "In theory, yes. They've been fabricated, but they still need to be filled, checked and transported."

"How long would that take?"

Jann shrugged. "I don't know, at least a sol."

Kayden considered this, as if he were recalculating his

escape plan based on this new information from Jann. He stayed silent, thinking.

Jann interrupted his thoughts. “How do you propose we get out of here? Just sneak out at night? I don’t think we’d get very far.”

“Look, it can be done.” Kayden seemed irritated. “But we need *you*, as you are the only one who knows the launch sequence.”

Jann thought about this for a moment. Escaping undetected might be possible—with the right help. And Kayden certainly fit that bill. After all, Boateng had done it. But what Kayden was suggesting regarding the MAV was reckless. They would first need to get back to Colony One, then transport fuel tanks back to the MAV, connect them, check all systems and then *hope* that it all worked when the button was pressed. It was insane. There was no guarantee that the MAV would not simply blow up with them inside. Considering it had sat there for three years it would need time to do all the proper preliminary checks. Furthermore, there was also a time issue in coordinating with the Odyssey orbiter, it all needed to be carefully set up. Perhaps Kayden didn’t fully understand this.

On the other hand, Kayden was offering her a way out of here. As for getting off the planet, well... she could just play along with that—for the moment.

He looked over at the edge of the lake. “We can’t stay here too long, the hybrids will be twitching. Are you in?”

“Okay, where do I sign?”

“Excellent.” He clapped his hands together. “Let’s head back. We’ll find another opportunity to talk more.”

They returned to the jetty. The guards had not moved. But Kayden was right, they were twitching a lot more than usual. They stood face to face, looking directly at each other, seemingly not noticing Jann and Kayden stepping off the raft and onto the jetty. "What are they doing?" Jann whispered.

"I honestly don't know. They all started doing this weird staring match with each other a few months back. Strange isn't it?"

"Has anyone *asked* them what they're doing?"

"They say they're just passing the time."

"Really?"

"You don't need to concern yourself with it. Best to just ignore them."

THEY MADE their way back to the upper galleries and Jann was escorted to her room. No more was spoken of the plan. She assumed they would meet again under some other pretext and the details would be outlined. In the meantime all she could do was wait. She sat on the small seat and looked out over the main colony. She felt her pocket for the object she had been given. It was gone. "Crap, where is it?"

She searched the room frantically, around the floor, on the desk, and through the pockets of the few clothes she had been given. It was gone, along with the note. "Damn, they must have found it."

She thought that possibly the beta who brought her food might get into trouble for it. Jann felt she had let her down, she should have taken better care of it. *Too late now*, she thought.

She sat in silence for a while, and watched the to-and-fro of the betas working all across the cavern floor. They moved in random patterns, in and out through the vegetation, planting, harvesting, tending. It had a hypnotic rhythm and Jann felt the stress being gently expelled from her body. Maybe now that Kayden had given her hope she could *stand down*, so to speak. She moved her gaze away from the betas and started to observe the hybrids. Before encountering the strange behavior today at the lakeside, she had not given them much thought, save for how she could take one down. Now though, she began to notice them, pick them out from the other colonists. From what she could see they made up around ten percent of the colony's population. They seemed to do nothing except monitor the betas, always silent, always watchful. But every now and then two or three would group together and do that same weird face to face communicating, their facial muscles twitching. Anytime this happened the betas would distance themselves. It was bizarre.

What was Vanji really creating? They were human, that much was true. But they clearly displayed traits incompatible with human behavior. They were a different species, a step up on the evolutionary tree. It was how a Neanderthal might have felt observing Homo sapiens communicating. They were the same—but different.

Then something extraordinary happened. The betas had all congregated in one area, just below her, and in unison, they all looked up—directly at her. Just for a moment, then they dispersed.

She jumped up. "Holy shit, can they see me?" It happened so fast that she wasn't sure it really occurred. Maybe she was hallucinating? Jann gripped the back of the chair to steady herself. "What the hell was that?" She retreated to her bed and curled up. She could take no more of this place. She just had to get out. The sooner the better.

11

RECYCLING

Jann tossed and turned, her sleep was fitful. She awoke to the shadow of a beta moving in the room. It was morning and they had come to bring her food, but it was not May, the woman that had come before, it was someone different. Jann sat up and rubbed the sleep from her eyes. "Where's May?"

The beta kept his head down and did not look directly at her. "She has been... eh, reassigned. Please eat. You will be required at the council meeting shortly." He turned and walked out. *Council meeting?* she wondered. Finally she was going to meet the rest of the original colonists. *Should be interesting.*

Jann got up and sat at the desk, eating and looking out across the main colony. She watched the betas going about their business, half expecting to witness a repeat of the previous evening's occurrence. But there seemed to be a different dynamic going on. She couldn't put her finger on it, but a different mood prevailed.

The door finally opened and the two guards stepped in.

One spoke, "Come with us, please." It was the first time she had ever heard them speak. It was deep and sonorous, and had a mellow soothing quality to it. Jann was so surprised that all she could do by way of a reply was stare wide-eyed and nod. They all moved down the long corridor, one in front of her, one behind, to a doorway near to where Vanji had first shown her the colony. They entered unannounced. Along both sides of a long stone table sat the Council. At its head was Vanji. Behind him was a glass wall with doors opening out onto a terrace. She could see the cavern roof in the background.

"Ah, Dr. Malbec, please be seated." Vanji pointed at a vacant seat at the far end of the long table.

The two guards took up position either side of her. Jann scanned the council members. They all wore similar off-white clothing. But each had a different color patch sewn on the breast. Vanji, however, wore a purple robe of some kind, perhaps as an indication of his rank and power. She noticed many of the council wore a patch of the same color. Jan wondered if these were the geneticists, presumably the highest ranked citizens of the Colony Two social hierarchy. They sat close to Vanji. She also spotted Kayden. He was closer to her and had a blue patch on his tunic. He didn't make eye contact with her.

"I have something to show you," Vanji began. From a pocket he took out the object that Jann had been given by the beta on that first sol. He carefully set it on the table. "We found this in your room. We would like to know how you came by it."

"It was in the fruit basket." There was no point in trying to hide it, Jann reckoned they knew already. But her response set off a ripple of murmurs around the table. Vanji raised a hand to silence them.

"Do you know what it is?"

"I'm guessing it's a replica of the beehive hut, out past the dunes near Colony One."

"You are correct. But it is also evidence of something we have begun to suspect."

"Which is?"

"Which is the existence of a creation myth amongst the betas." This brought more animated murmuring from the council members.

"This must be stamped out!" One member slapped the table. "We can not allow this to gain traction."

Vanji raised a hand and turned back to Jann. "You see, betas retain fragments of the memories of their alpha when they are birthed. Why? We are not sure. But that is irrelevant, the fact is they do. Now, this is very useful as they can be conditioned much faster and trained to utilize the technical know-how of their forbearer. But they also have memories, dreams, that become more lucid over time and these memories can drive them to seek out the past. It became a creation myth and it has the potential to undermine everything we are doing here."

"That's a bummer," said Jann.

"You may scoff, Dr. Malbec, but this concerns you, more that you think."

"How so?"

"Because rumor has it that they have a clandestine leader. One that unites them. Some say it's a deity, a god, if you will. If this *leader* were to become strong... well, let's just say the harmony of the colony would be in jeopardy."

"So what's that got to do with me?"

He picked up the object from the table, examined it for a moment, and put it back down slowly.

"We believe that you are this deity they worship."

Jann laughed. "Maybe I should be honored."

That sent the council apoplectic. "Quiet!" Vanji shouted above the clamor. They quieted down. Jann sensed an ugly mood developing.

"You need to understand that these *dreams* are of the past, of Colony One. They are becoming obsessed with it. They seek it, like a Mecca. It will drive them crazy. And you represent that to them. A visitor from Colony One is like a god descending on the multitude."

Jann was silent this time.

"She needs to be recycled."

"Yes, this situation is too dangerous."

"It has to be done."

"We should never have let her in here in the first place."

The table was erupting around her, they wanted her head on a plate.

Vanji raised a hand again and they settled down. "Kayden, what is your opinion? You have been very quiet so far."

Jann looked at the Head of Hydro, her fate totally in his hands. It seemed like an age ago when he had given her hope, a way to escape; now everything had changed.

Kayden looked down and fumbled with the sleeve of his garment. "In the light of these revelations, it would seem the only option is recycling."

"What!" She had been betrayed. She jumped up and her arm was grabbed by one of the guards. But Jann twisted fast and buried two knuckles into the guard's throat. He dropped; she knew she could take them down. She bolted out the door and into the corridor, but she didn't get far. She felt a sting in her neck and touched a small needle. She pulled it out and threw it on the floor. But it had done its job. Her head felt heavy and she quickly lost all control of her body. She collapsed on the floor, face down, Her eyes closed and she lost consciousness.

12

THE TANK

In the time after conception, cells divide and multiply, growing exponentially more numerous. It is from this clump of living matter that all of which defines our biological makeup stems. Hence the term *stem cells*. They possess within them the power to become anything and everything. The genius of Vanji was not the ability to choose what was created, humanity already possessed this knowledge. Nor was it the ability to speed up this process, although that too was a major breakthrough. No, it was the ability to reverse engineer.

How to take a clump of stem cells and turn them into an organ was known. But to take an organ and turn it into stem cells was knowledge of a totally different order of magnitude. This was the genetic alchemy that he controlled. This ability to biologically *recycle*.

It was Jann's fate that soon, she too would experience this biological transformation. Like a zygote in the womb that needs nourishment and sustenance to grow and develop, so too does the body that is to be recycled. That is why subjects were submerged in the bio-tanks alive. And they were kept that way until the point at which they were biologically incapable of consciousness. But unlike a human that takes nine months to be fully viable, the reverse process was much quicker—it only took a month.

JANN SLOWLY BECAME aware of conscious thought, like awakening from a dream. But she existed only in her mind, and so began to focus and tentatively assess the extent of her physical existence. There was none.

She felt a wave of panic rise up from deep within her core. She had no physical sensation, no sight, no sound, nothing to define the limits of her body. She was pure thought, nothing more. *Jesus, what have they done to me?* Fear graduated to terror. She knew what was happening, she was slowly being biologically dissolved. How was this to end? How long would she be conscious of this horror? Hours, sols, weeks?

Time ceased to have meaning. Her thoughts could have occupied a few seconds or an eternity, she had no way of knowing. She felt like she was floating out in the vacuum of space, except there were no stars to orient her. She simply existed in nothingness. There was no pain, at least that was something. But to endure like this, knowing what was happening to her, was a slow descent into a tortured insanity. In the end, there is no more terrifying a place than your own mind.

A VIBRATION. Was she dreaming? No, she felt it again, slight, but it was there, all around her. How could she feel it? She probed the extremities of her body and began to sense her physical being. It grew in intensity and she forced herself to move some part of her. With every fiber of her being she bent her will to the task, to lift a finger, to open an eye, anything. Then the dam burst and she was released from her viscous sarcophagus in a deluge. She broke through to the other side. Voices. She could hear voices, distant, indistinct. Vague lights swam across her vision and she felt her throat being ripped from the inside. It was the tube being pulled out. She gasped and spat and retched. Her body temperature plummeted and pain bound itself to every nerve. Voices. More voices.

"SHIT, SHE'S GETTING HYPOTHERMIA."

"I told you we should have done it in stages. This could kill her."

"We don't have time, quick get her into the blanket, switch it on, get her warm. Shit, don't let her have a cardiac arrest."

"Christ, she's no good to us like this."

"It will pass, trust me, she's been in the tank for less than an hour. Just keep her warm."

"How the hell are we going to get her into an EVA suit like this?"

Jann felt something warm wrap itself around her, and an oxygen mask was held over her mouth. Her shaking began to subside.

"She's okay."

"Thank god for that."

"Right, let's get moving. We only have a twenty-five minute window and we've already used seven."

. . .

Jann still shook and shivered, but less with each passing minute. She tried to open her eyes and speak. "It's okay, we got you out." Someone placed a hand on her head; she went quiet again. She could feel herself being carried on a stretcher of some kind. It was dim but she began to make out lights here and there as they moved. After a while they stopped and set her down. She was beginning to come around and tried to lift a hand to wipe her forehead but she felt pinned down, and her mouth was like sandpaper. "Water," she croaked. "Some water?"

"She's coming out of it," someone said.

"Water."

"Wait, hold on, let me get you out of this thermal blanket." Jann could feel the heat drain away as the blanket deflated. She could move again. Someone unzipped it a little and placed a bottle of water against her lips. She raised a hand to hold it as she lifted herself up on her elbow. She drank it all.

"Feeling better?" Kayden knelt down beside and took the empty bottle.

Jann sat up and ran her fingers across her face and over her skull. She shook her head and looked at Kayden. "Bastard, you put me in there."

"The Council put you in there. I had no choice but to go along with it, otherwise they would have suspected me. Anyway, you're out now. Time to leave."

"Jesus, I thought I was going to go insane in that tank."

"Think you can stand? We don't have much time." Kayden put a hand under her shoulder." Samir, give me some help here."

Together they lifted her into a standing position. She was shaky, but her body was beginning to recalibrate itself back to normality. She was still wet with slime from the tank. She shivered in horror when she realized, and started to frantically wipe herself down with the blanket that was still partly wrapped around her. "Get this crap off me."

"It's okay, Jann. Just calm down, it's inactive outside of the tank. Just take a deep breath."

She clutched the blanket close to her as the panic began to subside. She let out a deep breath. "Okay, I'm okay." She looked around. They were in a small, dimly lit storeroom. "Where is this place?"

"Near the main entrance to Colony Two."

There were two others with Kayden. Samir, who was speaking to her now, and another woman who looked agitated.

"I don't suppose you have some clothes for me? Or do I go around naked?"

"The best sort, we've got your EVA suit. Think you can handle it?"

"If it means getting out of this place, then, yeah, lead me to it."

"Behind here." Samir started moving storage boxes out of the way.

"Noome, get Jann some more water. I'll help Samir with the suits." Kayden started to move more of the storage boxes.

Hidden in behind them were four EVA suits. Samir started to check them one by one. "Looking good. Fully prepped, should do the job."

"I hope you're right, they all look a bit ragged, save for Dr. Malbec's." Noome was giving Jann a second bottle of water.

"They may look like shit, but they'll get the job done."

"Come on, we're wasting time." Kayden started to get into his suit.

"Shhhh..."

"What?" whispered Noome.

Samir placed a finger over his mouth. "Listen."

They all stopped and looked towards the door. Footsteps —getting closer.

"Shit."

"Shhhh."

The sound of footsteps stopped outside. Jann looked around for a weapon to arm herself with as they all waited for the door to open. A moment passed, then another, and another, but the door stayed closed. Voices, hybrids—even Jann could recognize their deep resonant tone. Then the sound of movement, more footsteps, this time heading away from the door, back down the corridor, disappearing into silence.

"Whoa, what was that? Noome was trembling with fear, clutching Samir's arm. He wasn't much better.

"Hybrids. Looks like we had a close encounter," said Kayden.

"That was weird, why didn't they come in? They must have known someone was in here."

"Who knows, who cares. They didn't, that's all that matters. Come on let's get going before they come back."

It took them all a few minutes to get suited up and checked. The plan, as far as Jann understood it, was to enter the main Colony Two airlock. This was where they had stashed her rover. They would commandeer it, open the main airlock door and head for Colony One. As an escape plan, she didn't like it, way too risky, too high a chance of being spotted or setting off some alarm when the main airlock door opened. They had nearly been rumbled once so far, and they might not be so lucky again. But there was no other way of getting to Colony One. They had to risk it.

Kayden slowly opened the door and peered out, looking up and down the corridor. "All clear, let's go." He stepped out and waved to the others to follow. They all had the heavy suits on but carried their helmets, they wouldn't need them just yet. They tried to move quietly but it was difficult. It took them a few minutes to pass through into the main entrance cavern for Colony Two. It was dark but as Samir and Kayden swept the area with a flashlight Jann could see it housed not just one but two pressurized rovers along with a myriad of other small vehicles.

"Samir, go open the inner door. We'll get the rover started." Kayden pointed off to one side of the cavern. The rest of them clambered into the rover and Jann started it up just as the inner door opened. Samir ran back and hopped in. She ran through systems checks to ensure pressure and then drove into the airlock. The door automatically closed behind them and there was a moment or two of nervous waiting before the outer door opened. It was pitch black outside as Jann slowly inched the machine out onto the Martian surface.

IT WAS slow progress at first, and the lights on the rover had little range. But her confidence grew, and the farther they got from Colony Two, the faster she pushed it. There was a collective mood of relief. "We did it, we did it." Noome was ecstatic and slapped Samir on the back. He ventured a smile in return.

Jann pushed the machine as fast as she dared in the darkness. "I saw a bunch of other rovers in that cavern. Did anyone think to disable them?"

"Don't worry, they haven't moved in years. This is the only operational one," said Kayden.

"I hope so, because it's going to take time to get the tanks ready. We don't want them following us." Jann started to slow down a bit.

"Once we get to Colony One, we're home free. They can't get there, not for a while anyway."

"How can you be so sure?"

"Trust me, we have a sol or two head start, that should be enough time."

Jann felt relief ripple through her. She pushed the rover as hard as she dared to get more distance between her and the nightmare of Colony Two. She was running away, yet again. She felt like she had spent a lot of her time on Mars running away from one thing or another. Someday, she would have to stop.

13

COLONY ONE

They had been moving slowly across the Jezero crater for over an hour, Jann reckoned. Assuming Kayden was right and the other vehicles in the cavern were out of commission, they were in no immediate danger of being followed. So she decided to drive with caution. The last thing she wanted now was to run into a gully or get caught up in a sand dune. Nonetheless, they were making progress and getting close to Colony One. The mood in the rover was one of fatigue mixed with excited relief.

"There it is, over there, look." Jann pointed out into the darkness at the lights on the roof of the Colony One biodome. Noome and Samir got up from their seats in the back and leaned into the cockpit to get a better look.

"Cool," said Noome. "I had nearly forgotten what it was like, it seems like so long ago since we left there. Wish I never did."

"Yeah, it doesn't seem so bad after all this time."

During the journey Jann discovered that it was these two that had been tracking the Odyssey craft and intercepting ISA communications. They were original colonists but not on the council, they wanted no part of Vanji's vision of Colony Two. How they hooked up with Kayden, Jann had not yet found out. Not that she cared, she was free of the place and now had a way off Mars, and a return ticket to Earth.

They stood there for a while just watching the lights getting closer until eventually Jann reached down and tapped a few icons on the comms panel.

"Gizmo, this is Jann Malbec, are you still there, over?"

"Gizmo? Who's Gizmo? I thought you were alone in there?" said Kayden.

"I was the only human."

"So who's Gizmo?"

"You'll see soon enough—I hope."

"Gizmo, are you receiving this, over?" Her call was met with static coming over the rover comm as she waited for a reply. Finally, it crackled into life.

"Dr. Malbec, this is a surprise. Do you realize I calculated the probability of your existence being compatible with life at 0.03%?"

"Nice to know you still care, Gizmo."

"I have been tracking a rover crossing the crater for some time now, I assume this is you?"

"It is. I have three other people with me, we're heading for the workshop, can you ensure it's got atmosphere?"

"Certainly, Jann. I am here to assist."

"Okay, we'll be there shortly, we can catch up when we arrive. Over and out."

"Who was that?"

Jann looked over and smiled. "Like I said, that's Gizmo, and you'll meet very soon."

SHE PULLED up outside the main workshop airlock with a jolt. Dust and sand rose up all around as the wheels skidded to a halt. Through the swirling dust they could see the door beginning to rise as a crack of light pushed back the night. They drove in, pressurized and finally came to a stop inside the workshop. Jann got out of the rover first, followed by the others.

Gizmo raced over to her and waved a metal hand. "Welcome back, Jann."

"Thank you, Gizmo."

"At the risk of sounding sentimental, I was beginning to miss your company."

Jann gave the little robot a smile. "Me too, Gizmo." She turned to the others. "Kayden, Noome, Samir, meet Gizmo."

The little robot raised a hand. "Greetings Earthlings."

"Wow, that's a pretty cool droid," said Noome. "Where did it come from? I don't remember there being a robot here."

"The last colonist here built it. Nills Langthorp."

"Nills?" said Kayden. "Well, I'm not surprised. He's an amazing engineer, if his clone is anything to go by."

"Nills has a clone?" Jann stopped and looked at him.

"Yeah, of course. There were two of him, I believe, but one got recycled for some reason, I can't remember."

"Inciting insurrection," said Samir.

"Nills-beta is one of the main engineers in Colony Two. I don't think the place would function without him. I think that's why he gets away with so much." Kayden continued.

"With what?"

"He's a leader amongst the betas, if you're to believe the Colony Two rumor mill. He's well respected, and not someone that can be gotten rid of without very good reason. He's too valuable a resource and he keeps the betas in line," said Samir.

"Nills is alive?" said Gizmo.

"Yes and no, his clone is."

"I would very much like to meet him again."

"Me too," said Jann. "But I don't think that's going to happen as we are leaving this planet as soon as possible."

"Leaving?" replied the little robot.

"Yes, on the MAV, so we need to get the new fuel tanks organized. What's the status on them?"

"Fabrication was complete some time ago, but they need to be filled with fuel, and then a diagnostics run to check integrity."

"How long?"

"Best estimate, thirty-six point seven hours."

"What? We don't have that much time," said Noome. "They'll find us before then."

"Thirty-six hours?" Kayden directed his question to Gizmo.

"Approximately."

"Shit, shit." Noome started jumping around. "This is not good, not good."

"Kayden, you better get a handle on her or I will kill her myself."

"Noome, we still have enough time, they won't find us that quick." Kayden's voice was measured.

"How can you be so sure? You're just talking shit."

Kayden grabbed her by the arm. "Listen, just put a sock in it. This isn't helping us."

Noome settled down—a bit.

Jann turned around to face them. "Okay, it is what it is, so here's what we're going to do. We need to get into the main Colony One facility. That means EVA, there's no way through from here. The propellant processing plant is in dome five. Gizmo can run through the procedures once we're inside. It's going to take a while so if they come for us before we're ready then we can defend ourselves better in there. Also I need to clean up, I feel like shit. Anyone got any problems with that, Noome?"

They all shook their heads, even Noome.

"Sounds good to me," said Kayden.

They started to get their suits ready to EVA. Kayden approached Jann. "I was just thinking, seeing as how you're the only one who knows the launch sequence for the MAV, maybe it would be a good idea to tell me, just in case anything happens to you. You know, otherwise we could all end up stranded."

Jann looked back at the renegade council member. "Well then, you better make sure nothing happens to me."

"Yeah, but..."

"Ready to go?" Jann snapped her helmet on.

THEY MADE their way out of the workshop and along the outside perimeter of the Colony One facility. Gizmo raced ahead and got the main airlock ready. As they walked, Jann noticed that Samir and Noome would look out across the crater in the direction of Colony Two, waiting for any sign that the hybrids were coming for them. Understandable considering the situation, but what interested Jann was the fact the Kayden never once looked, like he wasn't in the least concerned. Perhaps he was made of stronger stuff. *He must have nerves of steel,* she thought.

When Jann finally stepped into Colony One and removed her helmet she took in a long deep breath. There was the familiar smell, a scent of home, fragrant and botanical. It sent her mind back to the very first time she opened her visor in Colony One, all those years ago. So much had happened, so much death, so much destruction. But soon she would be free of it, free of this place, free of Mars. Part of her would miss it, she knew that. Deep down she knew it owned a little bit of her now. How much she wasn't sure, but it was there all the same.

Her body itched and chafed inside the EVA suit and she could feel patches of ooze from the tank dried on to her flesh. She needed a shower, a very long shower to wash away the horror of her time in the recycling tank.

"Gizmo, can you show these guys where they can get some food and rest? I'm heading for the biodome."

"Certainly, Jann. May I say, it is good to have you back."

She smiled at the little droid. "It's good to be back, Gizmo." With that she stepped out of her EVA suit and ran into the garden. As she raced past the hydroponics and the food crops, she could see that Gizmo had been very diligent. All looked well tended to and lush. But it was different, more verdant than she remembered. She dashed across the central dais and dived headfirst into the pond, coming up again just under the waterfall. She felt instantly alive and full of vitality. She would wash the memory of Colony Two from her if it took all night.

IN THE END, it didn't last that long. Just half an hour or so. She had Gizmo bring her some fresh clothes and she sat in her old wicker recliner, drying her hair. It had grown quite a bit since the little robot had cut it off for her at this very spot.

"I have primed the fuel processing plant and it is now in production. I calculate thirty-four point two hours to complete the process. Then a further one point four three hours for filling and calibration."

"Excellent. Did you lock down all the airlocks like I asked?"

"It is done. No one can get in here without the use of heavy tools."

"And the others, what are they up to?"

"I took them into dome five and explained the procedure to them. They are taking it in shifts."

"Okay, good."

DOME FIVE HOUSED THE ARE, the Atmosphere Resource Extractor. This consisted of several units, each one dedicated to processing the thin Martian atmosphere and extracting various gasses from it, such as carbon dioxide, nitrogen, argon and even small amounts of oxygen. The area also housed the fuel processing plant. This took both carbon dioxide from the ARE and hydrogen from the SRE, the Soil Resource Extractor. The SRE was originally in dome five but had been moved by the early colonists down into the cave beneath the facility, the one that Jann entered when Nills had rescued her from the demented Commander Decker. It broke down the Martian soil into many components, one of which was water. This was further split into hydrogen and oxygen. Both units worked in tandem to provide Colony One with the essential resources needed to provide life support.

The dome also housed many other units that further

combined these raw resources to create many more, one of which was methane—rocket fuel. This was manufactured by a chemical reaction between carbon dioxide and hydrogen. The resultant product was not stored inside the dome, but outside in a string of tanks that lined the exterior wall. There were several good reasons for this. One was simply to save space, but more importantly, methane would be highly dangerous stored in the oxygen-rich environment inside the colony, so it was safer to store it outside. As a result the process of filling the MAV tanks needed to be done by EVA, on the planet's surface.

As for the MAV fuel tanks, these were individually fabricated on trolleys, as once filled, they would be heavy, even in the one-third gravity of Mars. Each one needed to be wheeled out from dome five via an airlock, and moved into position to be filled, then a diagnostics routine run to check integrity. Once completed it would be parked out of the way so the next one could be processed. On top of this, there were several smaller oxygen tanks required. The combination of these two gasses created the propellant that would thrust the MAV off the surface and out of the Martian gravity well to rendezvous with the orbiter.

The whole process was slow and tedious, not designed for speed. So they had agreed to take it in shifts.

"Who's taking the first shift?"

"Noome and Samir."

"Where's Kayden?"

"He is in the galley making tea."

"He's very calm, don't you think?"

"I do not think, Jann. I merely extrapolate."

Jann laughed—a long deep laugh. "Oh Gizmo, I've

missed your quirky turn of phrase, and your blunt honesty. I never really appreciated it before now."

"I will take that as a compliment."

Jann sat back in the chair and looked around her. "I'll miss this place, too."

"What did you find in the mining outpost? I am curious to gather more data on it."

Jann sighed. "I found what I was looking for, a way to kill the bacteria."

"So you are no longer a biohazard?"

"No. It was a simple solution in the end. Expose it to a very high oxygen level at low pressure for around twenty-four hours. I don't know why I didn't think of it myself."

"Would you like me to initiate this procedure in the Colony One environment?"

"Oh god, yes. I had forgotten about it, what with everyone trying to kill me. But, yes, yes, absolutely, otherwise we'll be carrying it back with us."

"Should I inform the clones?"

"No, there's no need, and they're not clones, they are original colonists. Alphas, they call them." Jann sat up in the chair. "You know, Gizmo, there are hundreds of clones in Colony Two."

"Do tell me more."

"It's a vast cave system, with power generated from aero-thermal heat exchangers, a near limitless water supply, and a growing population. The whole shebang is run by Dr. Vanji, the original geneticist sent here by COM, and a small council of alphas."

"Sounds intriguing."

"The clones came from the analogues we saw in the research lab. These were the seeds they used to create their society, all in secret. No one outside this planet knows they exist."

"Even more intriguing."

Jann sat back in the chair again. "Well it's all messed up, if you ask me."

"Why is that?"

She leaned forward again and whispered. "Hybrids, Gizmo. They've created a new species of human. Not strictly clones, but an amalgam of enhanced human genetics. They call them Homo Aries."

"I have to admit, I am impressed."

"It's insane, Gizmo. Nobody should have that power. But that's not really the main problem. They are a form of super-human, with very strange behavior. The Council want to suspend the hybrid program, they're simply too scared of them. But Vanji is pursuing it, with ever more complex enhancements. They are his personal guard. They lay down the law in Colony Two, and watch out anyone who crosses him or his hybrids."

"So, who are these people with you?"

"Kayden is, was, on the council. Like a lot of the others, he became disillusioned with the way things were going, and he saw his chance to escape and return to Earth when I showed up."

"Because you know the launch sequence for the ISA MAV."

"As always, Gizmo, you are correct. I do."

"And the other two?"

"I don't really know. I only just met them a few hours ago. They're alphas, I'm pretty sure of that. But they're not on the Council, so they could be just some disgruntled colonists that Kayden recruited for his escape plan. They've been tracking the Odyssey and intercepting ISA comms for quite some time."

"Interesting."

"Look, Gizmo, I would love nothing better that to chat with you all night, but I have to get some sleep. It could get very hairy around here."

"Of course, Jann."

"What's our range on the perimeter scanner?"

"We can track surface movement up to approximately five klicks away."

She sighed. "Okay, alert me when anything shows up."

"Sounds like you're expecting company."

"Listen, Gizmo, I have a feeling they'll show up. Sooner rather than later. I don't care what Kayden says, they will come for us, hybrids most likely, so we need to be ready."

14

THE PURGE

Dr. Ataman Vanji sat at his study table, his face illuminated by a 3D projection of the planet Mars slowly rotating in front of him. It was rendered in high detail and showed the positions of all known satellites in orbit. Vanji zoomed in and examined one in particular. It wasn't a satellite, as such, it was the ISA Mars transit craft, Odyssey. Still faithfully waiting for the return of its crew, all these years later.

His ruminations were interrupted by the entrance of Xenon, his chief of security and the de-facto leader of the hybrids. He was tall, strong and elegant. He was a splendid specimen. Vanji allowed himself a faint smile as he admired his own work.

"Dr. Vanji, we have just received confirmation from Daniel Kayden. He is in situ in Colony One and has given a timeframe of thirty-six hours."

Vanji jumped up from his seat and clapped his hands together. "Excellent. Then we have what we need to proceed."

"Is it time, then?"

Vanji wandered over to the balcony and looked out across the vast cavern. It was dimly lit now as it mirrored the Martin nighttime cycle. In less than an hour, though, dawn would break over the crater rim and a new day would begin.

"It is time, Xenon. Time to put our plan into action. Time to right the wrongs and take back the vision." He spun back. "How long to raise all the hybrids?"

"We are hive-mind, we speak as one, we gather quickly." He stopped, stood stock still and went into a momentary trance. The others on the Council all found this very disconcerting, but Vanji reveled in witnessing a hive-mind communicating.

Xenon returned from the trance and spoke. "We are ready."

"Then you know what to do. One group to round up all the council members and bring them here. The other group to eliminate the self-proclaimed leaders of the betas. Kill any who try to assist them. Is that clear?"

"It is clear." He turned on his heel and left Vanji to contemplate the coup he was now embarking on.

For too long had he compromised his vision, given in to consensus, bowed to the mewling for harmony. But no more. By dawn of this sol he would be master, free to pursue his experiments and all those who had thwarted him in the past would be pushed aside. *Recycling is too good for them,* he thought.

He walked out onto the balcony and looked down at the lush vegetation. A scream cracked the stillness, then another. He could just make out the faint, *phit, phit* of a railgun. "So it begins."

. . .

The first to arrive were his science team, three of them. They were the trusted few. They filed into the chamber in silence and took up positions beside Vanji, looking down over the cavern. "It won't be long now, then we will be free," said Vanji. The others nodded.

The door burst open and an ashen-faced Luka Modric rushed in, followed by two hybrids, who had now added railguns to their array of weapons.

"What is the meaning of this outrage? Have you gone mad?"

"Ahh, Luka, good of you to join us. Please, have a seat." He smiled and pointed at the council table.

Luka made a move towards Vanji, but he didn't get far. One of the guards raised a weapon at him. "Do as Dr. Vanji says and sit."

He stopped and a look of fear registered on his face as the realization of Vanji's ruthless arrogance finally sunk in. He sat down. By now more of the council members had been brought into the chamber, some willingly, some kicking and screaming, literally. Anyone who objected to this outrage or who put up any sort of a fight was cowed into submission by a few thousand volts jabbed into their ribs.

Finally, they were all assembled, meekly awaiting their fate.

"You may be wondering why I called you all here," Vanji began. "Well, the reason is simple, it's time to move on."

"You have finally lost your mind, Vanji. This will not be tolerated. You are out of control." Luka stood up and shook a fist.

Vanji stayed quiet for a moment, then turned to one of the guards. "Would you mind if I borrowed that for a moment?" He pointed at the railgun the hybrid was holding. It used an electromagnet to fire a hard metal spike. It was not very accurate, but at close range it could release a projectile with enough force to penetrate a human skull. Vanji took the gun, aimed it at the hapless councilor—and fired.

A dull red blot appeared in the center of his forehead, his eyes rolled back and he collapsed on the floor, a pool of blood forming where he lay.

"Anyone else have anything to say?" Vanji swept the room with the gun. They were all silent. "I thought so. Good, I will continue then." He handed the railgun back to the hybrid.

"You all want to know what's going on? Well, here it is. It's very simple. I'm taking control of Colony Two. No more compromising my vision, no more pandering to the small-mindedness of the fearful. It is time to fully embrace the future. A future that belongs to the genetically superior. It is the very essence of evolution, it is nature's law and I intend to see it come to pass."

There was a momentary silence as the council members tried to comprehend the exact meaning of Vanji's words. Some were horrified, some were petrified, and some simply tried to understand how they didn't see this coming.

"So, members of the council, you are no longer required." With that he nodded to the hybrid leader and the room was filled, for a brief moment, with gunfire.

Some members died instantly. Some made a mad dash for the door, but never made it. After only a short few moments they were all dead. Vanji and his team of three geneticists were all that remained of the Colony Two council.

"And so it is done." He clapped his hands together and

turned to the leader of the hybrids, Xenon. "The future of your species is now secure. I foresee a bright and productive time ahead for Homo Aries." With that, the light in the main cavern grew brighter. Vanji looked out at it. "Ah, a new dawn. How prophetic."

For a few moments they watched as the light grew brighter until the cavern was filled with a golden illumination.

"Xenon, have this mess cleaned up."

"Yes, Dr. Vanji."

"Now that we have accomplished this part of the plan, where are we with rounding up the beta leaders?"

Xenon entered his trance state as he communicated with the other hybrids. "They are putting up a fight. We have the main cohort corralled in the entrance cavern."

"How long before they are eliminated?"

"Not long. We will break through shortly."

"Good, get it done. We need to prepare the rover for departure as soon as possible."

"Yes, Dr. Vanji."

15

A NEW OLD FRIEND

Jann opened her eyes and had to think for a moment to establish where she was. Soft morning light illuminated her surroundings and she could hear the sound of a waterfall the background. She realized she was in the biodome of Colony One, and had fallen asleep in the wicker recliner after Gizmo had left. Jann breathed a gentle sigh of relief, stood up and looked around as she stretched her body. It was a beautiful morning in the biodome. And, compared to the horrors of Colony Two, it felt like heaven.

The familiar sound of Gizmo's tracked wheels burst through the vegetation, and zipped over to her. "Ah Gizmo, good morning."

"Sleep well, I trust?"

"Eh, no, not really, but it will do. Where are the others? Is it time for my shift?"

"Samir and Noome have just returned to rest. Kayden has been wandering around since first light."

"Really?"

"As far as I can tell. However, there is something that has

come to my attention. I have picked up a rover, traveling this way, about five klicks out."

"Shit, when?"

"Just now."

"Have you told the others?"

"Not yet."

Jann thought about that. "This is not good. How much time before it gets here?"

"Twenty two point seven minutes, approximately."

"Dammit. Tell the others, we had better get ready."

Gizmo whizzed off as Jann raced for the operations room.

SHE STOOD over the holo-table looking at a 3D rendering of the Jezero Crater. At the very edge of its range a small orange icon marked the location and progress of the rover. The others had all gathered around to watch.

"We don't have much time," said Jann.

"This is bad, this is so bad, we're all dead," said Noome.

"I thought you said the rovers were all disabled?" Jann directed her question at Kayden, who had been silent since entering the operations room.

"I said they hadn't worked in years," he replied, without taking his eyes off the slowly moving orange marker. "I genuinely didn't think this would happen."

"What? That they wouldn't try and stop us from leaving Mars?"

He looked over at Jann, and back to the marker, shaking his head. "It doesn't make any sense."

"We're all going to die," offered Noome.

"Noome, for God's sake, would you get a grip," Samir shouted at her.

Jann looked at the marker for a moment. "Seems strange. Not because they're coming after us, but because they haven't deactivated the rover beacon."

"What do you mean?" Samir had now progressed to comforting Noome, as anger didn't seem to work.

"Think about it. If you were planning to go after us, you wouldn't advertise it, would you?"

The others looked at the marker as if this revelation from Jann would somehow transform it into something more benign.

"No, I suppose not. But maybe they don't know about the beacon?"

"What are we going to do?" said Noome.

"We hide, that's what we do."

"Hide, are you kidding me?"

"Trust me, I have the perfect place. We can make them think we've left the facility. That way, when they start to scatter to search, we pick them off, one by one."

"Hide sound goods to me," said Noome.

"They'll find us for sure," said Kayden.

"No, I doubt it. When the ISA crew came here first, Nills Langthorp hid out. We never would have found him until he wanted to be found. It's our best chance."

"Wait," said Gizmo. He raised a metal hand and twisted his head like he was looking off into the distance. "They're transmitting." He raced over to the comms desk and tapped a few times on the control pad. Radio static crackled around the Operations room.

"...two injured, need medical assistance, over."

They stood in silence for a moment, looking at the comms desk.

"Colony One, this is Lars-beta, we have two injured, need medical assistance, over."

Jann moved over to the comms desk and pressed transmit.

"This is Dr. Jann Malbec, Colony One. State your purpose."

"Jann Malbec, am I really talking to you?"

Jann looked around at the others and raised an eyebrow.

"Yes you are, now state your purpose."

"We escaped the colony. There's been a coup, many dead, we have two injured and we need help."

"It's a trap, a trick to get us to let them in," said Samir.

"Well, there's no point in hiding, they know we're here now," said Kayden.

"What do you mean coup?" Jann continued.

"The hybrids started rounding up council members this morning. I think they're all dead. Then they went after the leaders of the betas. We fought back, got trapped in the main entrance cavern... we escaped... the others in there... I don't know."

"Christ, I knew it, I knew this would happen, sooner rather than later. Those bastards, they were getting weirder by the day." Samir was stomping around.

"Kayden, you have any thoughts on this, since you're a council member?"

"Eh... well I'm shocked. If it's true, that is."

"Shocked? Is that it, you're *shocked*?"

Kayden raised his hands. "What do you want me to say? Yes, I'm shocked. And it looks like we got out just in time."

Jann turned back to the comms desk.

"Have you got EVA suits?"

There was a pause, presumably they were checking. This was a good sign as far as Jann was concerned. If they were lying then the response would be instant.

"We've got one, wait..." there were some indistinct snippets of conversation in the background. *"...shit, it's got no*

power..." more background talk, "*We have two injured, one I don't think could EVA, even if we had a suit... and there's another problem... we have less than twenty minutes of air left in the rover.*"

"Hang in there, we'll think of something."

"They could just drive in to the workshop garage, there's air in there." Samir had calmed down a bit.

"There's no way through from there, they would still have to EVA."

"You're not seriously thinking of letting them in?" said Noome.

"Look, this is actually good news for us. Because if they are who they say they are, then that means we have both rovers and no one can come after us, unless they walk."

"Boateng-beta walked here."

"Yeah, and it killed him," said Samir.

"I say we do as Samir suggests and send them to the workshop. We can keep them corralled in there. It would be safer, for all of us," said Kayden.

"There is another option," said Gizmo, as it moved over to the holo-table and brought up a 3D schematic of the Colony One facility and zoomed in on one sector.

"This module has an airlock that connects with the one on the back of the rover. They simply reverse it up close, and we can manipulate the umbilical to connect."

Jann looked at the 3D image. "Does it still work?"

"Well that could be a problem. Nills built a windmill in it, back during the sandstorm, so it is full of dust and debris. It would need to be cleaned out and checked. But my analysis suggests that should take only a few minutes."

"Okay, let's do it."

. . .

JANN SENT a message to the stricken rover and gave them instructions where to go and what to do. Then she, Noome and Samir suited up to EVA. Kayden was left to operate the airlock from inside Colony One.

As they stepped out on to the planet's surface they could already see the rover in the distance. Gizmo raced off to direct it to the airlock. Jann and the others made their way there and started to clear out the sand blocking the outer door. They had disconnected the windmill and had cleared out most of the debris when the rover pulled up. Dust blew up around them as Gizmo directed them in. They backed up slowly and the rover inched its way along the guide rails to within operating distance of the airlock. Jann and Noome stepped into the open door and manually hoisted the connecting umbilical. It clicked into place at the rear of the rover with a satisfying clunk.

"Kayden, you can pressurize it now."

"Okay." His reply echoed in her EVA suit helmet. She waited… and waited.

"Christ, Kayden, what's the problem, these guys are breathing nothing but CO_2 by now."

"I'm trying, I'm trying… it's not working."

"Dammit, we've got to do something." With that Jann could feel a noticeable vibration in the airlock and it began to pressurize."

"Wait, it's just started working… that's weird."

"I did a manual override from the control panel on the outside. That is why it is working," said Gizmo.

The alert flashed green and Jann popped the visor on her helmet. The rear door of the rover cracked open and out came two betas, one supporting another who looked badly injured. She had a blood-drenched bandage around her thigh, her face was ashen.

"Thank you, we were dying in there." The beta's eyes widened, "Are you Dr. Jann Malbec?"

"Yes, come on. Let's get you all to the medlab."

"I am honored." He bowed.

"Quick, Noome, help get them inside."

Finally the last beta came out of the rover, his arm was in a sling and he had blood spatter on his face, but there was no mistaking who he was. Jann recognized him immediately.

"Nills! Is that really you?"

He looked at her and smiled. "Yes, I am Nills-beta."

Jann's face betrayed a look of astonishment. He really did look exactly like the Nills she used to know—the same bright smile, the same raggedy chin, the same unkempt hair.

"You knew my alpha, didn't you?"

"Yes, a long time ago now, he... he was a dear friend to me."

16

MEMORIES

"Are they all dead?" Kayden directed his question at Nills who was now sitting on a bed in the Colony One medlab.

"I don't know, it all happened so fast."

"And what about Vanji and the science team?"

Nills shrugged. "I don't know."

"Christ, this is insane," said Samir.

"Well, it looks like we got out not a moment too soon." Kayden patted Samir on the shoulder.

"So you're the one who helped Dr. Jann Malbec escape."

"Yeah, we all did." Kayden waved a hand over at Noome who was tending to the injured beta.

"Why? You're a council member, you had a lot to lose."

"Not any more, it would seem. If what you're saying is true."

"You'd better believe it. The hybrids control Colony Two now."

"Greetings Nills, glad to have you back." Gizmo raced into the medlab followed by Jann who had divested herself of her EVA suit.

"Eh... this is Gizmo, Nills. You built him."

Nills looked quizzically at the droid. "You mean my alpha did."

"Yes."

Nills scratched his chin. "I have no memory of this machine."

"Gizmo was built after the analogues of the colonists were created. So, assuming that was the source for the cloning, then you would have no knowledge of it."

Nills continued to stare intently at the robot.

"Would you like me to fetch you some tea?"

Nills laughed. "Sure, yes, why not." Gizmo raced off.

"That's an amazing machine. And you say my alpha designed it?"

"Yes. He did have a lot of time on his hands."

Nills shook his head and then looked around the medlab. "I have memories of this place. Dreams. I remember the layout."

"Here, let me have a look at that arm." Jann unclasped his hand from his upper arm and inspected the wound. It was superficial. She went off to get some bandages and saw Lars looking around in awe at the place. "Lars?"

He stood up and bowed. "Dr. Malbec."

"Do you know where the galley is?"

He thought about this for a moment. "I do, I have memories of it."

"Then why don't you go there and help Gizmo prepare some food. We'll have it in the common room. You know where that is too, don't you?"

His eyes went wide. "I do, I know this place, as if I've been here before."

"Good, then you know what to do."

When Jann returned to Nills, he was explaining all of what he knew about the hybrid coup to Samir and Kayden.

"When they had finished with the council members they came after us, the beta leaders. It was very early so most of us were still asleep. But we were down in the main entrance cavern. You see, when you guys escaped we were sent down to check on the readiness of the second rover and to see if any of the other vehicles were operational. That's when we heard the news that the hybrids had gone on the rampage. We barricaded ourselves in, but they were too strong and broke through just as we were making run for the rover. They killed six of us in the first charge. Two were injured, we're all that made it out."

"Those bastards." Samir turned to Kayden. "How come you didn't see this coming? You're on the Council."

"Nobody saw it. Do you think any of those on the council who are now dead saw this coming?"

Noome had finished patching up Anika, who sat up on the edge of the bed looking pale. "Well, it doesn't matter now anyway, we're leaving this godforsaken rock forever."

"Leaving?" Nills stood up.

"Yeah, we have a ticket for the next bus, and I for one, am taking it."

"You mean leave Mars, go back to Earth? How?"

"The old ISA MAV," said Jann. "The one I came here in. It's still operational and the Odyssey transit craft is still in orbit, waiting for it to return. I can go back."

"To Earth?"

"Yes, but not for at least another sol. The fuel tanks aren't ready yet." She turned to the others. "We're safe here for the moment, the hybrids have no way to get to us.

"Jann's right, there's no panic," said Kayden.

"Come on then, let's eat." One by one, they shifted out of the medlab into the common room.

GIZMO AND LARS had been busy. The table was arrayed with standard colony fare. Fruit, fish and, if Jann wasn't mistaken, colony cider. They all sat and picked at the food. No one spoke much, it had the feeling of a last supper. The mood was somber. After a while it was Nills who finally broke the silence. "I was wondering, if you have time before you leave, would you show us the biodome?"

"Sure, we have plenty of time now," said Jann. "You probably have a memory of it."

"We do, but I'd like you to show it to us, if that's okay with you all?" He turned to Kayden who just opened his hands. "Sure, go ahead."

The betas all rose. Lars helped Anika as Jann led them toward the biodome. She felt like she was bringing pilgrims on a tour of some sacred site. *Maybe that's how they see it*, she thought. They stopped just inside the entrance and craned their necks to take it all in.

"Wow, I can't believe I'm really here. It's exactly how I dreamed it would be." Lars could not contain his awe. The experience of standing in the biodome of Colony One was visibly emotional for him. Anika too, seemed mesmerized.

"Come on, let me show you the central dais, it used to be my home. I slept in a tree, can you believe that?"

None of them replied, obviously anything Dr. Jann Malbec did was okay with them. Jann was conscious that Anika was finding walking painful. "Here, why don't you sit down in my recliner and rest that leg."

Anika was open mouthed for a moment. "Are you sure that's okay? I mean, I would be occupying your seat."

"Of course, sit." Anika lowered herself into the wicker recliner and looked decidedly uncomfortable at her sacrilege. A mere mortal desecrating the temple of a deity.

"It's okay, sit, I insist."

"You are too kind, Dr. Malbec."

"Don't be silly, you're injured, you need it more than I do."

"Lars, would you keep Anika company here, while Dr. Malbec and I take a quick tour?"

"Of course."

Nills-beta signaled to Jann to take a walk with him. When they were out of earshot he spoke. "You must forgive them, they see you as a deity. A god, if you will."

"I've noticed it already, in Colony Two, the bowing and deference. I feel somewhat unworthy of such consideration."

"It's just the dreams we betas have, they can do strange things to the mind."

"What are they like, these dreams?"

"They are fragments of retained memory, from our alphas, like snippets of encoded experience. At first they are vague, but as we age they become like memories. Memories of places we have never seen, of things we have never touched, of events we have never experienced."

"Is it not difficult to deal with this... retained memory?"

"It is. For some it can be just too much, too confusing. They go insane. Others manage them by creating myths. Like, of this place. We all have memories if it. I can tell you the exact layout of Colony One even though this is the first time I've set foot in here."

"So why am I so special to them?"

"Colony One has become an Eden, or Nirvana, or Heaven. Betas have developed a near religious perception of this place. Some believe it doesn't really exist, it's just, literally, a figment of the imagination. When you showed up, it was like an angel had descended amongst them. A deity who had journeyed from the mythical Colony One. You can see how this would affect some of them."

"I see. I should never have gone there. None of this would have happened if I had just stayed put."

"Why did you come?"

"Oh it's a long story. I was looking for a way out, a way to go home."

"And did you find it?"

"Yes, I found it. Now I can go, get back to Earth."

"But you're still here."

Jann laughed. "Sorry, but you remind me so much of Nills. It's the sort of thing he would say."

Nills-beta smiled. "I'll take that as a good thing, then."

"Please do, he was a very good friend and... I've missed him... all these years."

THEY WALKED for a bit in silence. Then Jann stopped and looked at him for a moment. "Tell me, Nills, what are you going to do now?"

"I'm going back."

"But why? It's extremely dangerous. God knows what's going on in Colony Two by now."

"They're my people, I'm their leader. Without me they will be turned into slaves for Vanji's hybrid army."

"You think Vanji is still alive? You think he is behind all this?"

"You met him, what do you think?"

"I don't know, it's possible. But those hybrids are a very strange species. It's hard to know what they think. If you go back, you would most likely be captured and killed. It would do no good."

"If I were to return with you, then the betas would fight. They might rally behind me, but they would lay down their lives for you."

Jann stopped for a moment as the realization of what Nills was asking her sunk in. "You're asking me to go back there? Are you crazy?"

"Think about it. We outnumber them, seven or eight to one. All they need is the will to fight. You can give them that will."

"But how?"

"Your mere presence. The fact that you have returned, in their darkest hour. All those myths become real, they would be a formidable fighting force. They can win their freedom, all because you have returned."

"I... I need to think... I can't comprehend this all now... we're leaving, for Earth. Home, Nills, I'm going back home."

17

DECISION TIME

Jann sat in the recliner on the central dais of the Colony One biodome and considered her options. Nills had left her there to think about his request, Lars and Anika had followed him out. So she was alone now, with her thoughts.

She had everything she needed to return home. She was no longer a biohazard, the MAV was waiting, all her ducks were lined up. Kayden and his crew couldn't leave without her as she was the only one who knew the launch sequence, and now that both rovers were at Colony One, the hybrids couldn't journey here that quickly, so she had time to think.

EARTH, to walk in the sunshine, to feel the wind in her hair, to get wet in the rain. It was the simple things she missed. Humans were designed for Earth, it was their planet, home. She had dreamed of it for so long, but now that the time had come, she hesitated. What would await her there? She, along with Kayden, Noome and Samir, would be the only humans ever to have returned from

Mars. Many had gone but none had returned, so far. No doubt she would become a celebrity of sorts. Shunted around from one interview to another. Sell her story, want for nothing. They would be bringing back with them stories of Colony Two and the miraculous advances in genetic engineering that had been made there. Human cloning, genome manipulation, the secret of immortality. They would be returning with tales of Eldorado, the city of gold, of riches beyond your wildest dreams. And like the adventurers of old, there would be no shortage of private funding for return missions. Every mega-corporation the world over would pump money into *Mars stocks*, betting on who would be the one to return this life-saving technology to Earth.

And whose life would it be saving? It wouldn't be the poor, or the downtrodden, or those on the margins. It would be the preserve of the very wealthy. The rich would have eternal youth, a new strata of super-elite would be created.

Then, there was the fact that Earth had left her for dead up here. No funding available for a rescue mission for her, she was expendable. What was the cost of her life? Not that she could blame them, really. After all, she was in no danger of dying and the popular consensus of the general population was there were better things to spend taxpayer's money on than rescuing a foolhardy astronaut. She knew the risks, she would have to live with the consequences.

HER OTHER OPTION was to go with Nills, back to Colony Two. To what? Death, the horror of the recycling tank? His assertion that her presence would galvanize the betas into revolution seemed nothing more than fantasy to her, simply wishful thinking on his part. Jann could not see any way that they would get more than two feet inside Colony Two before they were killed.

As for the plight of the betas, she had no doubt that they revered her in some way, but would that be enough to overcome well-armed hybrids, no matter how much they outnumbered them? They were timid and deferential by nature, or maybe nurture, either way she doubted they had the collective balls to put up a fight.

So what would be their fate then? Subjugation, slavery, genocide? It would be one of them. At best they would be domesticated humans, used as beasts of burden, workhorses for the superior species that was Homo Aries. Did they deserve that? They might be clones but they were still human, and Homo sapiens at that, her species.

And what of Vanji? Was he still alive? And if so, what was his game plan? She had the distinct feeling that somehow, he must be behind all this. He wanted to create his advanced race without hindrance or moral sermons from the council members. But then again he could be dead, along with the others. And why should she care? What were they to her that she should forgo her one chance of returning to Earth?

She also had a third option. Stay here in Colony One and take her chances. She sighed, stood up from the recliner, and walked over to where she kept some of her personal belongings. It was a storage box she had refashioned into a kind of table. She opened it up and pulled out a small holo-tab. It was her ISA mission manual, it had everything she needed to launch the MAV and return to Earth. She shoved it into a pocket on the side of her flight suit and headed out of the biodome, probably for the very last time.

18

READY TO LEAVE

"Where's Nills?" Jann entered the common room to find Kayden sitting at the table. The remains of half-eaten plates of food were scattered around it like the aftermath of a party. Kayden looked up. "The robot is giving him a tour."

Jann relaxed. "Okay."

"Are you ready? We need to start helping with the tanks, time is marching on," he said.

"Not yet. I need to show you this first." She took the holo-tab out of her pocket, cleared some space on the table and switched it on. Icons danced in the air above its surface, she tapped one and a 3D rendering of the MAV was displayed. She tapped again and a schematic of one of the fuel tanks broke off from the main diagram. "As you know, the fuel tanks are built on trolleys. Once they're all filled and checked they can be connected together, like a train, and the rover will pull the whole lot over to the MAV."

Kayden nodded.

"Each trolley has a hydraulic arm to lift them individually into position. They fit in like this." She tapped the 3D rendering of the tank. An animation played showing how it locked into position on the MAV and detailed the connecting points. "Once you've got them all into position you open the valves here, using this exterior control panel."

"Okay, looks straightforward."

"It is, it was designed that way. Nothing too fiddly to operate wearing EVA suit gloves." She tapped the MAV again and this time it zoomed in to the cockpit.

"You enter the MAV through this hatch here. Over on the main console is the switch that activates the MAV power system. Once you flip that on, the flight dash should light up like a Christmas tree. Tap the main screen and it will ask you to enter a code. The code is four zeros."

"Four zeros?" asked Kayden incredulously.

"It doesn't need high security. Let's face it, who the hell is going to steal it out here?"

"Makes sense. Go on," said Kayden.

"The MAV will then run a diagnostic routine on all flight systems. You can override any alerts, unless they are mission critical. Assuming all goes okay, it will then try to contact the Odyssey."

"The orbiter?"

"Yes. The launch is controlled from the Odyssey computer systems. It's all automatic, you don't have to do anything from that point on, just sit back and wait."

"How long?"

"Hard to say, could be a few minutes, could be a few hours."

"Hours?"

"Yes, the Odyssey orbits every five hours, so depending where it is you may have to wait. It will calculate the launch time to intercept."

"That could be a long wait."

"Once the MAV makes contact and the trajectory is worked out, it will start to count down. Then you'll know how long." Jann tapped another icon and the 3D image was replaced with a diagram of the Odyssey in orbit around Mars. "Once you reach the correct altitude the Odyssey will also automate docking. You don't have to do anything."

"I like that bit," said Kayden.

"Lastly. Now that the MAV has docked, the Odyssey knows to prepare for return to Earth." She tapped the rendering of the spaceship and the view zoomed into the flight cockpit. "You'll get confirmation on the main console here. Now, you may feel that nothing is happening, because the EM Drive is pretty slow to get going, but it will be accelerating the craft through a number of orbits until it reaches escape velocity and... well, next stop Earth."

Kayden was silent for a moment, looking at the projection and nodding. Then he sat back and looked at her. "Tell me, why did you never return before now? You could have left any time."

Jann rubbed the top of her head; her hair had grown quite a bit so it no longer had that soft velvety feel to it. "I couldn't. I was a biohazard, remember?"

"Even so, you could have just gone, taken the risk, what could they do once you arrived in Earth orbit?"

"Blow me out of the sky, most likely. Or at best, if they actually let me land, contain me in a hermetically sealed bubble, where I would spend the rest of my days being poked and prodded by scientists. No thank you. I'd rather stay here."

Kayden nodded. "Yeah, I see your point."

"Which reminds me. I need to send a report back, let them know the MAV is returning. I'd like to be a fly on the wall when they hear the news about Colony Two, and all that."

"I would suggest holding off on that for the moment. We can do it from the orbiter. We haven't lifted off yet, so best not to tempt fate."

"Don't tell me you're superstitious."

Kayden laughed. "No, it's not that... just... I think it would be better. After all, we still have to persuade them that we're not carrying back the pathogen."

Jann thought about this. "Well, I'll leave it up to you. It doesn't matter to me now anyway. I'm not coming with you." Jann switched off the holo-tab and handed it to Kayden. "Here, this is all you need."

"Not going? But this is your chance to go home, isn't that what you wanted?" Kayden looked shocked.

"I thought I did, but you know what? I decided I like it here."

"You may never get another chance."

"So be it." She waved a dismissive hand.

Kayden stood up, clutching the holo-tab with both hands. "If you change your mind, you know where we are."

"I won't, but thanks."

He stood for a moment, just looking at her, before nodding and walking out of the common room.

JANN SAT for a while before she noticed Nills-beta standing in the doorway of the galley. "How long have you been there?"

He moved over to her and sat down. "Long enough."

So you heard all that?"

"All that I needed to. You're not going back to Earth, then?"

"No."

"Why?"

"Does it matter?"

"No, I don't suppose it does. So what now?"

"You tell me."

"A little counterrevolution, maybe?"

"Count me in. When do we start?"

"I think we already have."

19

WEAPONS

Nills-beta wandered around the main Colony One workshop, examining the various artifacts scattered over every available surface. Part of him felt like he was intruding on the sacred space of a dead relative, a feeling that held some validity. But part of him also felt like he was home, such was the familiarity he had with this workshop. His alpha had worked here, probably where he built the small robot, Gizmo, that now seemed to have attached itself to him. Feeling perhaps that its creator had at long last returned and, like a faithful dog, was not going to let him out of its sensory range again.

"It's just like old times, Nills," said Gizmo.

Nills cocked an eyebrow at the eccentric machine, marveling at its creator's skill. The very same skill that lay within him. The original Nills had attained legendary statue amongst the betas. It was rumored he was still alive, which made Nills-beta the only clone of a living alpha. This made him someone special within the colony and, in a sense, leadership had been foisted on him rather than acquired by rite. That, and the extraordinary engineering skills that he had inherited all added to his prominence in the community. *'There was just something about him,'* was the oft-used refrain. But how much of this was valid, and how much was simply amplified by the myths and legends that propagated through beta society, was anyone's guess. Nonetheless, without the creation myths they would never have had the spiritual strength to contend with their dreams, their memories, their ethereal past.

It was this same spiritual affinity that he was banking on when they returned to Colony Two. That, and the hope that Dr. Jann Malbec's return would galvanize the betas to foment revolution. If he was the de facto leader, then she was the spiritual leader. But again, this was by dint of myth rather than physical reality. Not that it really mattered. If it worked then... good. If not then... so be it.

JANN HAD GONE off with Lars to prepare the rover and EVA suits, they needed everything to be working at a hundred percent if they were to have a chance. Kayden and the alphas had decamped to dome five to get ready for their own departure back to Earth. He gave them no more thought, good luck to them.

That left himself, Gizmo and the injured Anika. His own injuries were minor and healing fast. Anika, however, had sustained a more serious injury from a railgun dart in her upper right thigh, but that too was healing fast and she was already able to put some weight on the leg. Hopefully she would be able to join the fight.

If they were to have any chance of gaining access into Colony Two then what they needed were weapons. Nills and Anika scanned the area for anything they could use. Simple heavy bars or knives were not going to be enough, they needed to manufacture something more lethal, and quickly.

"So what are we looking for, Nills?"

"Coils, capacitors, anything we can make railguns out of."

"What about explosives? They seem to be very popular in human wars," offered Gizmo.

"Yeah, now you're talking, Gizmo. What have you got in mind?"

"I'm eighty-six point seven percent certain I can concoct something usable from the chemicals we have here in Colony One."

"Excellent, get to it then."

"Which would you prefer? Explosive, incendiary or smoke?"

Nills looked at Gizmo. "I suppose all three might come in handy."

"Aye, aye, captain." And it whizzed off out of the workshop.

"How does it know all that stuff?" Anika was watching the little robot disappear off into the bowels of Colony One.

"I really have no idea."

"But you created it."

"Not me, my alpha."

"But there is a little bit of you in that robot, nonetheless."

"Perhaps. All I can say is, it's a damn handy machine to have around."

They continued their search, picking up parts as they went and dropping them into a handcart that Nills was pulling.

"This looks useful." Anika picked up a bank of electromagnetic coils.

Nills examined it. "Good, see if you can find some more, and capacitors, lots of great big ones."

After a half hour or so they cleared a space on one of the workshop tables and dumped all the components onto it. They were making railguns. Similar to those used by the hybrids but these would be significantly cruder. Railguns are electrically powered from batteries, which charged a bank of capacitors to around 1000v. When the trigger is pulled this activates a row of toroidal electromagnets, each one accelerating a metal projectile along the rail.

Nills and Anika toiled away at their task. Fortunately she was also a talented engineer and had no problem crafting sophisticated machines from a bucket of spare parts. This was how most things in Colony Two were made. Nothing was wasted, everything reused and recycled. Even humans.

AFTER A FEW HOURS of intensive fabrication, Jann and Lars finally returned.

"Rover is fully fueled and supplied, EVA suits are patched up and ready to use. How are you getting on here?"

Nills looked up from the bench where he was soldering a component. "Nearly ready for testing." He waved away the smoke that was corkscrewing up from the joint. He picked up the railgun, flicked a switch to charge it, and inserted a sharp metal spike in the breech. He stood up. "Stand back."

Everyone moved aside as Nills aimed the weapon at a disemboweled refrigeration unit about fifteen meters away and pulled the trigger. It fell over with the impact as a shower of fragments exploded from the entry point.

"I think that should do the trick." Nills examined the weapon and placed it back down on the bench. "We've made two of these, this one and a smaller unit that Anika is finishing."

She appeared from behind a mound of parts. "I also made this." She held up a small crossbow, fitted a short metal arrow in it and fired it at the remains of the refrigeration unit. It buried itself deep in the machine.

"Excellent," said Nills.

"Where's Gizmo?" Jann looked around the workshop.

"He's off conjuring up a batch of explosives." Nills picked up a small spherical container from a mound of similar objects. "We can make some grenades out of these."

"Looks like we're nearly ready," said Lars.

"In that case I'd better go and get my weapon," said Jann.

"You have one?"

"Oh yes, and I'm pretty good with it too." She turned and headed out of the workshop.

They continued to test the weapons for a while before Gizmo finally showed up with several containers. It placed them carefully on the floor, moved back and then extended a metal hand, pointing at them, one at a time.

"This will give you an explosion, this flame, and this one here, smoke." It then carefully opened the last box. "I have also utilized these small glass vials from the medlab." Gizmo held one up to the light. It was a standard sealed glass capsule. "You can use these as fuses. There are somewhat crude, but when this breaks open, the chemical inside will start the reaction in these others. Just be careful you do not do it by accident. Otherwise... boom." It made a sweeping move with its arms, to emphasize the point.

"That's great work, Gizmo. Thank you."

"My pleasure, I am here to assist."

. . .

As they gathered around the workbench and started to fabricate the grenades, Nills was beginning to feel more confident. Now that they had some weapons, they might be able to hold out long enough for the betas to get behind them. But even armed to the teeth, if they didn't, all this would be in vain. No amount of clever engineering would save them then. They were just finishing the last of them when Jann returned carrying a bunch of long metal spikes. Lars looked over at her. "I thought you were getting a weapon."

Jann looked around the workshop wall. It was a large space, maybe fifty meters across. "See that chart pined to the wall down there?"

They all looked up from their work and across to where Jann was pointing. It was a small paper chart of some kind. Something a former colonist stuck there for some long forgotten reason.

"Yeah," said Lars.

Jann placed the spears on the ground, sorted through them and selected one. She hefted it above her head and launched it at the target. It split the air at an impressive speed and buried itself, dead center in the chart. It was a good thirty meter throw.

"Wow," said Nills.

"That's amazing," said Anika. "Where did you learn to do that?"

Jann was walking back down the workshop to retrieve the projectile. "Oh, I had a lot on time on my hands here."

She returned with the spear. "Want to see something else?"

"Sure," said Lars.

"Gizmo, would you be so kind?"

"You are not going to do this. I thought we were friends again."

"We are, Gizmo. I just want them to see."

"Oh, all right then." Gizmo whizzed a few meters away from Jann.

"Ready?" said Jann.

"Gizmo is always ready."

She launched the spear directly at the little robot's head. Before any of them had time to think, Gizmo simply grabbed it out of the air.

"Wow, how can it do that?" said Anika.

"Ultra-fast reflexes," said Jann. "Pretty impressive, don't you think?"

"Incredible," said Nills.

"I have a request," said Gizmo.

"Sure, what is it?"

"I would like to join you on your adventure."

Nills and Jann exchanged glances. "It will be dangerous, Gizmo."

"You are forgetting I am a robot, that is meaningless to me. I have extrapolated that being alone is less simulating than being in the company of friends." It moved its head and looked from Nills to Jann. "And you are my friends."

Nills walked over to the robot and put his hand on its metal shoulder. "I, for one, would be glad to have you along."

"I would consider it an honor," said Jann.

Gizmo looked up at its friends and if it could smile it would have had the broadest grin ever seen on a robot.

When the moment had passed Nills turned back to them. "Okay, I think we're ready."

"So what's the plan?" Jann was taking the spear back from Gizmo's metal hand. The others all looked at Nills.

"Let's get some food and we can discuss it."

THE PLAN, such as it was, revolved around the assumption that Jann's return to Colony Two would rouse the betas. Since they outnumbered the hybrids and the few remaining alphas, they could, in theory, take control. But it was evident to Jann that there were a number of gaps in this plan. First and foremost, would the betas be inspired into action, as Nills had asserted? He was convinced, but Jann was not so sure. Second, did they have the strength of arms, the weapons? And third, it assumed that the situation hadn't changed since their escape. In truth, they didn't really know what was going on. What was the end game? Was it being instigated solely by the hybrids, and if so, what was their motivation? Or was there more to it? Was Vanji involved, was he behind it? All these questions they could not answer.

Into this mix were the three alphas in Colony One who were now diligently working away in dome five, preparing the fuel and oxygen tanks for the ISA MAV. Getting ready to leave the planet for good. This struck Jann as somewhat of a coincidence. Was there some relationship between these two events? Was there something else going on that none of them could yet see?

Then there was the very practical issue, how did they get in? And once inside, then what?

They had gathered themselves around the table back in the common room, and were all eating. It might be a while before they ate again so they might as well do it now while they still had the opportunity.

"So Nills, like I said, what's the plan?" Jann looked at him. He sat in the same battered armchair that the old Nills did. He had the same mannerisms and, if she didn't know better, she would think he was the same person.

"How about we drive up to the main entrance, blow it open with some explosives, charge in and start shooting any hybrids we see? Then, we just wing it from there."

"You're kidding me," said Anika.

Nills looked up from his food. "Of course I am, that's a really stupid idea."

Anika laughed. "For a minute there, I thought you were serious."

Nills set his bowl down on the table and sat back in his chair, like he always did. "For this to work, the betas need to know Jann Malbec has returned to free them, and call on all of them to raise up against the hybrids. So we need to get the word to them as soon as possible. Now, assuming life goes on in Colony Two, then the vast bulk of them will be working in the garden. So we need to get in there and hold it long enough for them to rally around."

"Okay, so how do we get in there?" Jann leaned in across the table.

"Yeah, that's not so easy, Nills. They're going to see us coming," said Lars.

"We need to give them the slip somehow, trick them into thinking we're entering by some other route."

"Would I be correct in assuming that their perimeter scanner is the same as the one in Colony One?" said Gizmo.

"I think so. I could check, as I'm very familiar with it. I used to fix it all the time," said Anika.

"Well if it is, then I may be of service."

"How so?" said Jann

"My systems are integrated with Colony One, so if they are the same, I may be able to access it and manipulate it."

"You mean, like hack into their systems."

"Partly. The downside, of course, is once I'm out of range of Colony One I will not be able to access any of the systems here, so my data and processing capabilities will be dramatically reduced. I estimate by a factor of ten point seven two."

"Is that a lot?" said Lars.

"For me yes, but not so much that you would notice unless I had to do a complex extrapolation. In which case it would be glacially slow."

"But you could access the Colony Two systems?"

"Only some, the perimeter scanner would be one. If it is the same as here."

"Okay, then. Sounds like we have a way in. We take the rover up close to the main entrance, park it there, and head on foot to the higher level escape airlock. Gizmo, can block their scanner until we're in."

"Is that the same airlock I used to get in?" said Jann.

"No, higher up. It's a bit of a climb, but it's never guarded and little known. We could get quite a way inside before encountering any hybrids."

"Sounds like we have a plan then," said Jann

They all nodded in agreement.

20

RETURN

By early the next morning, they had assembled in the workshop and organized themselves into teams, Jann and Gizmo, Nills and Lars. Anika was still injured so she kept the weight off her leg while she had the chance. It didn't take them long to get everything ready. Finally they assembled at the entrance to the airlock and got into their EVA suits.

"Should we say goodbye to the others?" said Jann

"Who?" said Lars.

"Kayden, Noome and Samir. After all, they were your colleagues."

"Screw them," said Anika. "If they want to run away, then let them."

"Well, they got me out of there, out of the tank. I can't go without thanking them, it's the least I can do."

"Hey, you've just given them the launch codes to the only ship off this planet, so I'm sure they're pretty happy with you about that," said Lars.

"Go, be quick." Nills waved a hand. "Hurry."

Jann raced off.

"Gizmo, go with her, make sure she's okay."

DOME FIVE WAS CRAMMED with a myriad of flotsam and jetsam from the inventory of Colony One. At the far end Jann could see the crew busying themselves preparing to bring the last fuel tank out onto the surface. Samir and Noome were in EVA suits with their helmets off, while Kayden sat examining the data on the holo-tab that Jann had given him. She could see a 3D schematic of the landing site balloon out across the table from its surface.

"Change your mind?" Noome spotted her first.

"No, I just came to say goodbye. I'm going back with Nills and the others, back to Colony Two. We're ready to leave."

"Colony Two? Are you mad?" Noome looked at her, wide-eyed.

"Maybe." Jann shrugged. "I came to say thanks... for getting me out of that tank."

Kayden switched off the holo-tab, picked it up and waved it at Jann. "Thank you for this, it's our ticket off this godforsaken rock."

"I hope is works out for you," Jann replied.

"Tell me," Kayden put the holo-tab down and. "Are you really going back there?"

"Yeah, we're all tooled up, ready to go."

"It's probably a suicide mission, you know that."

"We'll see."

"They'll see you coming. How do you propose getting in? "

Jann thought about this question. Why was Kayden so interested? He was leaving, so what did it matter to him?

"We're not sure. I think we're going to drive up to the

main entrance, blow a hole in it, charge in and start shooting… as far as I know."

"Sounds totally crazy to me." Samir started fiddling with a fuel valve.

"Yeah, does to me too. But anyway, thanks for getting me out… and, good luck." She turned.

"Good luck to you, too. I think you're the one who's really going to need it," said Kayden as Jann walked out of the dome.

NILLS and the other betas craned their necks to look out of the rover's window at the brooding Martian landscape. Jann realized that since they had lived their entire lives inside a cave, the outside world must be a wondrous spectacle to them. She looked out across the plateau towards the western rim of the crater. A thin haze of Martian dust clung to the atmosphere and colored the entire sky with a dark crimson wash. "Storm coming."

"How do you know?" said Nills.

She pointed out to the far horizon. "Dust darkens the sky when there's a sandstorm approaching." She looked back at him. "But don't worry, it won't hit here for a while yet."

She glanced at her navigation screen. "Coming up on six klicks. What's their scanner range?"

"Five, at most," said Anika.

"Okay, once we cross that boundary they can spot us. I sure hope you can hack that system, Gizmo."

"Hope does not enter into any of my calculations."

"Five point five klicks. We'll be in range in a minute or two. Are you ready, Gizmo?"

"I am always ready Jann."

She eased back on the throttle and the rover slowed to a crawl. They continued like this for a few more minutes. "Four point nine... eight... seven. How are we doing Gizmo?"

"Working on it."

"Four point five... should I stop?"

"Got it. Interesting... it appears to be an exact replica of Colony One's systems. Okay, there you go, disabled."

They looked at each other. "Are you sure? That seemed very easy."

"I am always sure, and yes, it was easy—when you know how," said Gizmo.

Jann pushed the throttle forward and the rover picked up speed. In the distance they could see the crater wall rise up from the horizon. Dust and sand billowed around them as they pushed on. She was driving the rover at the very edge of control. They were all bumped and jostled as the machine rumbled over the rugged terrain. Finally they came to a skidding halt, behind the same rocky outcrop that Jann had parked up at the first time she came here. It seemed like such a long time ago now, so much had happened to her since then. It was a very different Jann that entered Colony Two the first time. And here she was, doing it again.

She powered down the machine and turned around to look back at the others. They were getting their equipment ready. Nills prepared his railgun and checked the satchel containing the grenades Gizmo had fashioned. He had a determined look, and Jann realized this was a very different Nills. Not the carefree bohemian that tended plants and slept in a hammock. This Nills had had a different life, and it was beginning to show.

"Okay, listen up." Nills stood and held the railgun across his chest. "Show these bastards no mercy. They've killed the Council, probably most of the beta leaders and they are hell bent on the subjugation of our kin. They will not hesitate to kill us on sight. So don't mess around, you see one you kill them. Got it?"

Lars and Anika stood wide-eyed and looked a little sheepish. Even Jann had to admit, this was a whole new side of Nills she had never imagined. But in a way, he was being the person he needed to be, at this point in time.

"Got it," Jann replied.

"Pardon me, Nills. But who exactly are we killing? I am loath to admit it, but I am a bit confused," said Gizmo.

"You don't kill anyone, okay Gizmo? You're a robot, leave any killing to us."

"Okay. No killing."

"Right, everyone ready?"

They checked their weapons, flipped down their helmet visors and moved out of the rover.

They kept low behind the rocky outcrop and followed the same path that Jann had taken previously. After a while they started to work their way up the side of the crater rim. They went in single file, Nills leading, picking a path up to the airlock that Jann had used. They stopped for a moment. Nills seemed to be studying the terrain.

"The path should lead to another airlock, farther up." He pointed towards a gentle rising slope strewn with rocks and boulders. "Stay close, keep each other in sight. If anyone falls behind, just shout out." He moved off, the others followed. They picked up the pace, all the time climbing higher until finally they came to a clear, level ledge. Just ahead, built into the cliff face, was the airlock. They approached it slowly, with caution.

"So far so good." Anika's voice echoed in Jann's helmet.

"Let's hope there isn't an army of hybrids waiting for us on the other side." Lars shuffled in behind Anika.

"There may be a few, so be ready." Nills checked his railgun. "Okay then, let's go."

He tapped on the airlock control panel and the outer door opened. They piled in, the door closed. "Well this is it," whispered Lars as they faced the inner door, weapons ready. The airlock pressurized and the door slid open to reveal an empty, dimly lit tunnel. They breathed a collective sigh of relief.

"There should be a storage room up to the right. We can get out of these suits in there. We'll be able to move better. Follow me." Nills led the way along the tunnel. It was little used. Jann noticed their footsteps leaving prints in the thick layer of dust along the floor.

"Here it is." Nills used the barrel of his gun to poke the door open. It was pitch black inside. Gizmo activated its headlight and spread the beam wide it to give 360 degree illumination. It was empty save for some low bench seating along the walls. Above these were tall empty racks.

"What is this place?" said Jann.

"Originally it would have contained EVA suits, to be used in an emergency by the miners working here. Anyway, it's a good place to dump these. Come on, let's hurry. Lars, keep an eye on the door while we get sorted, then we'll cover you."

They wasted no time in divesting themselves of the heavy suits and, when ready, Nills explained their options.

"This tunnel leads to the upper gallery around the top of the main cavern. Mostly this will be deserted save for the atmosphere recycling plant on the far side. That will have at least two, maybe three, betas working in it. If we can get there without being spotted, then we can alert them and get them to spread the word that Dr. Jann Malbec has returned. I suggest we get the betas to assemble in the garden in the main cavern, that's where we'll have the most numbers. We'll need to get down there somehow and rally them, even if it means fighting our way there."

No one spoke. "Anybody got a better idea?" No one did. "Okay, then, let's go."

Nills led the way and they moved out in silence. Gizmo took up the rear.

After a short distance the tunnel opened onto a wider gallery. Nills and Jann took up positions on either side of the tunnel's end and peered around each corner. It was dark so it was hard to make anything out farther than a few meters. "Can't see shit." Jann whispered. Nills nodded to his right and stepped out in to the gallery, keeping his back to the wall. Anika and Lars followed, Jann and Gizmo brought up the rear.

Jann peered behind her into the darkness and thought she saw some movement. Then she heard a *thut.* Lars screamed and collapsed on the ground, grabbing his leg as blood oozed from the wound. Another *thut* and the rock wall beside Jann's head exploded into a hundred fragments. She loosed a spear into the blackness, aiming at nothing. Anika fired off a bolt before she too was hit. She spun around and went sprawling across the dirt floor.

"Shit, get down, down," Nills shouted at Jann as he tossed a grenade into the gloom and hit the deck. There was a blinding flash as the explosion shook the cavern. The shockwave lifted Jann off her feet and sent her tumbling down the gallery. Rock and debris rained down all around her. Dust billowed out, filling the space. *Christ*, thought Jann, *We're being buried alive.*

After a few stunned moments she felt Nills' hand on her shoulder. "You okay?"

She spat and coughed. "Yeah. What the hell did Gizmo put in that?"

"I don't know, but any hope of stealth is gone, it must have taken down half the roof."

Jann spluttered, and spat again, trying to get the grit out of her mouth.

The dust began to clear a little and Jann could see a huge mound of rock blocking both the tunnel entrance and the galley walkway. "Christ, they're going to be all over us in a minute. We've got to move." She stood up and turned to see Nills kneeling over Lars. He was flat on his back, a pair of cold dead eyes staring up. He looked up at Jann and shook his head. He then turned to where Anika was lying. Her hand twitched, then moved, then she sat up slowly, feeling her chest as she rose. She dug a hand into a top pocket and pulled out a battery pack with a two inch long metal spike from a railgun embedded in it. "Shit, that was close. She threw it on the ground and stood up. "Lars?"

"Dead," said Nills.

"Lars, no, no..."

"Come on, there's no time. We've got to get out of here." Jann grabbed her arm and began to pull her along, then she stopped. "Shit, where's Gizmo?" She looked around and scanned the mound of rock that used to be the gallery roof.

"He must have gotten buried when the roof caved in," said Anika.

"No, Gizmo!"

"Forget it Jann. Let's get to the processing plant." Nills shouted.

Jann looked back at the last resting place of the eccentric robot. She had had a love hate relationship with it for more than three years. But now that it was gone, she felt like she had lost another true friend.

"Jann, for God's sake, let's move."

21

REVOLUTION

Dust filled the air along the gallery. Every few meters light from the main cavern penetrated through long slits cut in the wall. Each slit had an extractor fan attached, making it one big air recycling duct, running most of the way around the upper level. The light flickered and danced off the walls and floor as the blades rotated.

Nills stopped suddenly and put his fingers to his lips. "Wait, hold up, I hear something," he whispered.

Jann could hear it too. Footsteps, running, coming toward them fast. Out of the gloom two figures burst into view, Anika fired off a shot, but missed, her bolt clanging off an extractor blade. The two figures stopped dead in their tracks. She was about to fire again when Nills shouted.

"Wait!" He ran forward. "Alban, sorry, are you okay?"

The figures stood wide-eyed. "Nills?"

"Yes, it's me."

"Nills, oh my god, we thought you were dead. What's going on? What are you doing here?"

"We can't talk here, hybrids will be coming."

"Those bastards, they've killed at least ten of us so far."

"Can we get to the recycling plant without being seen?"

They didn't reply. Instead they just stood there dumbly.

"Alban, can we get to the plant?"

"Dr. Malbec. You have returned." Alban stepped back and bowed, as did the other.

Jann came forward. "Yes, I have. Now, we must get try to the main cavern without being seen."

"I know a way. Come, quick... follow me, hurry."

THE RECYCLING PLANT was one of two situated on the upper gallery of the vast main cavern of Colony Two. Their purpose was to regulate CO2 and expel any excess out into the Martian atmosphere. It also maintained the level of moisture and humidity in its local area. There were two of these plants, working independently, to create different microclimates depending on the vegetation it was supporting. Dust and particulate matter was also extracted. The main difference between these air recycling systems and those used back on Earth was these used genetically engineered bacteria to get the job done, instead of a chemical process. The room was sizable but tightly packed with tanks and ducting, like the bowels of an oil refinery.

"This way." Alban led them through the maze to the far end of the room. He stopped in front of a large vertical duct and started to unbolt an inspection panel. "This leads down to the main cavern level. It's a tight fit but you should be able to shimmy down. We'll take the stairs, we can start to spread the word."

Jann stuck her head in through the gaping hole in the front of the duct and looked down. It was dark and the sides were lined with a thick layer of fine black dust. “It’s a long way down. Got any rope?”

“No, sorry. You’ll have to brace your back against one side, feet on the other and step down that way.”

Nills was now poking his head into the duct and looking down.

“How many betas can we count on to join the fight?” said Jann as she shouldered the small crossbow.

“I’m not the only one in the colony that’s sick of Vanji, and his experiments to create a master race of hybrids. But a lot will be frightened, some are emotionally fragile. You know this Nills, you don’t need me to tell you.”

“So, Vanji is behind all this?”

“You better believe it. Him and those weird hybrids of his.”

“So, how many can we count on?” Nills had brought his head out from the duct opening.

“Hard to say. There’s at least thirty that I know of who would definitely take the opportunity to get rid of him. Others would follow if Dr. Malbec is in the mix, maybe sixty would fight.”

“That’s more than enough. Do you know where everyone is located?”

“At this time, the bulk will be in the main cavern. Vanji and the remains of the council are up in the chamber, big meeting.”

“And the hybrids?”

“They’re all over the place. Although, I know a cohort were heading for the entrance cavern a while ago.”

“The entrance?” said Jann. “Any idea why?”

“Nope.”

“Is that unusual?”

“Very, I’ve never seen them do that.”

"We need to get moving before this place is overrun." Nills clambered into the duct. "It's a bit tight in here."

"That's probably a good thing, it will stop you falling too far when you slip," said Anika.

JANN WAS last to enter the duct. Nills went first, then Anika. As soon as she was sure of her footing, Alban closed up the inspection panel and the space became pitch-black, save for a very distant light, far below.

They moved slowly, feeling their way. Every three meters or so, the ducting was clamped together, affording a little ledge to place the edge of a foot. In other places it was joined by more ducts heading off at right angles. These junctions gave them a little respite from the long slow descent. Jann could hear Anika wince as they moved, her injured leg was taking a lot of strain. In the distance they could hear the muffled sounds of running and clamoring voices. The hybrids were racing up to the gallery where the explosion took place. So far no one had opened the inspection panel above Jann's head. They kept moving.

After a while, Jann's back and thigh muscles ached from the constant pressure being put on them. She didn't know how much longer she could keep this up before starting to cramp. The descent was torturous. Finally Anika stopped moving, and whispered back at Jann, "I think we're here."

They waited.

The plan was that Alban and his colleague would go down to the main cavern via the stairs and spread the word. Then they would make their way to the access panel and open it. But it was still sealed shut. Down below, Jann could see Nills checking all around him, looking up and down. Maybe he had missed the opening.

He froze, then looked back at them and put his finger to his lips. He unshouldered the railgun and faced it towards the access panel. Jann could hear movement outside, then scraping on the duct walls. Finally light flooded in. Nills clambered out.

A FEW MINUTES later Jann was sitting on the floor beside a side wall of the main Colony Two cavern. It was an out of the way place, concealed at the front by a waist-high row of hydroponics. She rubbed some feeling back into her legs.

Alban had now been joined by several other betas. Fewer than Jann had hoped for, and with nothing useful as weapons. "Trouble," he said as they all crouched down.

"Define *trouble*," said Jann.

"Apparently they were expecting you... they thought you would arrive by the main entrance, so a heavily armed hybrid group are over there."

"Shit," said Nills. "How did they know we were coming? I thought Gizmo jammed the perimeter scanner?"

"Kayden," said Jann.

"Kayden?" Nills looked at her.

"Yes. Before we left Colony One, when I went off to say my goodbyes, he asked me how we were going to get in. I told him your crazy plan, you know... charge into the main entrance and start shooting."

Nills thought about this. "Why would Kayden tip off the hybrids? I mean, he's planning his exit off this rock."

"How else would they know?"

"But, say even if he wanted to, how would he make contact?"

"There must have been comms between the two facilities in the past. Maybe he got it working?"

"It doesn't make any sense."

"There's obviously something more going on than we can see yet, Nills."

A few more betas arrived. One knelt down and whispered to them. "Armed hybrids are moving out from the entrance."

"Shit, we don't have much time then." Nills poked his head over the row of vegetation, looked around and sat back down. "Okay, here's the plan. Over at the far end of the cavern is a wide stair leading up to the council chamber. We need to take that, and fast. Once we have, it Jann can rally the rest of the betas from the balcony overlooking the whole cavern. We'll go first, those with weapons directly behind, the rest of you spread the word. Any questions?"

They all looked petrified.

"Ready?"

"Let's do it," said Jann as she hefted a spear.

They crouched down and moved off, using the vegetation for cover. They zigzagged their way through the central cavern, extracting astonishment and shock from the betas they happened upon en route. Some simply stood back, but others merged in with the mob that was forming behind them.

Then it all went to rat shit.

From both left and right two pairs of hybrids appeared and started firing. Jann, Nills and Anika hit the deck, but the betas behind were not so fast. Three went down in the first volley, two more with the second, by the third they had all scattered into the dense vegetation.

Jann was pinned down behind a low grow-bed. Nills and Anika were a good five meters away, also unable to move. "Nills, cover me," she shouted. He nodded and started firing.

Anika joined in. It was blind, no accuracy, it was just to draw fire the hybrids' fire.

She peeped out and gauged the distance to the nearest pair. She hefted her spear, stood up and threw it at them. It arrowed through the intervening space, skewered the left arm of the first one and embedded itself in the chest of the one directly behind. Jann dropped down again and looked over at Nills. He gave her the thumbs up, and started firing again. She joined in with the crossbow. Another hybrid was hit and went down. The fourth one decided not to hang around and backed off.

Behind her, the fallen were being dragged back to relative safety by their comrades. Some screamed in agony, others were dead. It was a mess. If she didn't do something now, they would lose all momentum. She stood up and raced over to them.

"Listen, you all know who I am. I've come back to help you find your way." Heads moved out from the undergrowth, she was connecting. "For too long you have lived in the dream world of your past, locked inside the memories of your alphas." She opened her arms to them. "But you are more than that, you are your own people, the first true Martians. This is your place, your home, your paradise. A heaven on Mars that you alone have built." More moved out from the undergrowth to listen. She continued, "There is no greater place here on this planet, not the surface dunes, not the great canyons, not even Colony One. This is your Eden, your birthright. It's time for you to take it back and claim it as your own."

By now a crowd had gathered and Jann could feel the mood changing. Their fear was subsiding, she could feel desire growing in them. She pressed on.

"We will storm the council chamber and hold Vanji to

account for his actions. We take back what is yours, we do it now, and we do it quick." She raised a spear high above her head. "So who's with me?"

But before the crowd could react, two small canisters clanked and rolled across the floor, smoke hissing out from their sides. *Shit,* thought Jann, *Gas*. She reacted instantly and ran. But the betas weren't so fast. They began to cough and splutter and hold their throats as they scattered.

"Dammit." She had lost the moment. It was going against them. If she could not rouse them to action then there was no hope. She looked back up to the council chamber balcony. A hybrid was holding another gas canister, pulling a pin from the side, getting ready to throw it into the dispersing betas.

"Screw this." Jann judged the distance. It was a good forty meters; it was literally a long shot. She hefted a spear above her head and just when the hybrid was distracted with the pin mechanism, she fired. It shot through the space with impressive speed, arching slightly as it traversed the cavern. The hybrid looked up just in time to feel it bury itself in his skull, straight through his right eye. He tottered, one hand reached up as the other dropped the canister on the balcony floor. It rolled back into the council chamber as he fell.

A cheer went up from the betas. Jann seized her moment, turned around and raised another spear high in the air and shouted, "Who's with me?"

There was no mistaking the answer this time, a roar went up from the assembled crowd. She had them. A wild, enraged mob ready to do her bidding. She caught sight of Nills. He gave her the thumbs up again. "To the council chamber," she shouted and raced off across the cavern, the mob charging behind.

. . .

Jann, Nills and Anika led the way up the main stairway and into a broad hallway leading up to the council chamber. Already the effects of the gas were emptying the room. Hybrids staggered out, coughing and spluttering. But they were not going down without a fight. As Jann and Nills came out onto the central corridor they were met with a hail of fire. Nills yelled and clutched his right shoulder. He staggered backwards and fell back down the first few steps. They were forced back, behind the cover of the stairwell.

Nills grimaced in pain. "Bastards."

Jann grabbed the satchel of explosives that Nills was carrying. She knelt down and rummaged through it. "Which are the flash bombs?" She held two up with different markings. He nodded to her left hand. "Are you sure?"

"No, I'm too busy dying here."

"Fuck it." Jann pulled the pin out and lobbed it down the hallway. A second or two later the whole space lit up with an incandescent flash. Smoke filled the corridor, screams echoed from the walls.

She turned back to the eager mob of betas crushing up the stairs behind them and raised her arms. "Quiet. Everybody. Stop where you are, wait." The mob murmured and muttered as they settled down. Jann shouted back down the hallway, "The next one's explosive. You saw what it did to the upper gallery, so don't make me throw one down on you."

The hallway was silent.

"The show is over, there's no way out, except through us. So lay down your weapons and surrender. You have ten seconds."

From far down the hallway Jann could hear voices arguing and debating. "Seven... six... five..."

"Okay, okay, we surrender."

A cheer rose up from the mob.

"Send the hybrid leader out first. Hold your weapon in the air, high above your head." Jann ventured a peek around the corner. Smoke and dust clouded the corridor and obscured her view, she could see very little.

Then, from out of the fog, a figure emerged. It was Xenon, the hybrid leader, arms in the air, weapon over his head. Jann held up a grenade, pulled the pin, but held the lever tight. She moved towards him.

"Any sudden move and this gets lobbed into the council chamber."

Xenon moved slowly forward.

"That's close enough." A knot of betas had come up behind her. "Put the weapon on the ground slowly and step back. He did as she asked and she signaled to Anika to pick it up. Jann moved over to the entrance of the council chamber and shouted into the room.

"Everyone out of there now, weapons in the air."

The guards filed out first, then the three geneticists. They lined them up along the wall, kneeling on the floor. The room was emptied, save for Vanji. He was still inside.

NILLS HAD DECIDED he wasn't dying. He stood behind Jann, his right shoulder a bloody mess. "Vanji, Vanji." The mob had started chanting, baying for blood. It would be a lynching and Jann could do nothing to stop it.

"You've got to get them under control, Nills."

"Jann, you're the one they want to follow now. It's up to you."

"Listen, gather up a few betas you trust and put these guys under house arrest. Then we go in together and deal with Vanji. Okay?"

Nills went off and talked to Anika. As they were putting a team together, Jann approached the hybrid leader. "The others, where are they?"

He did that same weird staring into space for a brief moment. "They have put down their weapons, they want an guarantee of safety."

"I can't guarantee that, but I will do my best." She turned to the betas and spoke in a loud, commanding voice.

"Listen up. The hybrids have surrendered along with the remains of the council. We have won, this colony is yours now. The fighting is over, I ask that no more blood be spilled."

"Vanji, we want Vanji."

Jann raised her hand. "Nills and I will deal with Vanji. Then we will let a new council of betas decide what to do." This seemed to placate the mob somewhat. She turned back to Anika. "Get a group down to the entrance cavern and disarm the rest of the hybrids. Put them under house arrest and let them stew for a while. No more killing... if you can manage it."

She nodded, and started to organize the mob into group. They seemed to respond well to her directions. Perhaps it was a symptom of the life they knew here. The safest option was to follow rather than lead.

Jann turned to Nills. "Okay, let's drag him out."

They entered the council chamber. It was empty.

"Dammit, he's not here?" Nills scanned the room.

Jann ran back out and grabbed Xenon by the shoulder. "Where is he? Where's he gone?"

"You're too late."

“What do you mean, too late?”

“He’s left the planet.”

For a moment Jann’s world stood still as her brain tried to fathom this revelation. Slowly the wheels turned and she realized—she had been played all along.

“Kayden,” she said.

The hybrid leader smiled. “Yes, Kayden.”

“Shit,” said Jann.

22

THE MAV

Jann stood over the hybrid leader in stunned silence. How could she have been so dumb as to give the launch codes to Kayden? She had never trusted him, she should have listened to her instincts. Too late now.

Nills slumped on the floor, gripping his badly injured arm. He was losing a lot of blood.

"Nills, shit. You need medical help." She called to some of the other betas, "Get him up, quick."

"I'm okay, there are others that need help more than me."

"You're not okay. You've got a three inch metal spike sticking out of your shoulder."

Two betas came over and helped him stand up. "Come on Nills, let's get to sickbay and get you patched up."

Nills groaned as he was lifted. "That bastard Vanji. How did we not see this coming? He's going to get away with it."

"Maybe not," said Jann

"What do you mean?"

"What other vehicles are there in the entrance cavern? Anything working?"

"Possibly some quad-bikes. Why?"

"Because there may still be time. Depending on the orientation of the Odyssey in orbit, it can take several hours before launch."

"You mean they could still be on the surface?"

"Possibly. Listen, have someone bring my EVA suit to the entrance and get a mechanic to help me start one of those quad-bikes."

She started to move but Nills grabbed her arm. "You're not thinking of stopping them? That's crazy."

"Nills, do you really want him to get away with what he did here, all the recycling, all the torture?"

"No... but..."

"But nothing. Don't imagine for one minute that he's going back to Earth to put his feet up and retire. The knowledge he possesses has the potential to completely alter human society—and not for the better."

Nills' face melted into resignation.

"This was all planned, Nills. He's been working on this for a long time. Someone, or some group on Earth is helping him. That's the scary part. So he has to be stopped."

Nills nodded and then embraced her with his good arm, in a tight grip. "I know. I just don't want you to go and die on us now."

Jann held his face in her hands and touched his forehead with her own. "It's not about us anymore. It's about humanity. It's about all that is right. You once said that to me... a long time ago."

She pulled away. "Just remember me." She ran off.

. . .

By the time she got to the entrance cavern two betas were already working on one of the quad-bikes. Jann assumed it was one of these machines that Vanji must have used to make his escape. “Will it start?”

One poked his head out from the side of the bike. “Should do, give us some time.” He stuck his head back into the guts of the machine. Two more betas rushed in carrying Jann’s EVA suit and helmet. “We checked it over and it looks good for another three or so hours. After that you’re out of power.”

Jann nodded and stepped into the suit. *Well, here I go again,* she thought. *Back to saving the world. Not really what I had signed up to with the ISA.* She remembered her first few tentative steps on Mars after they landed. They weren’t really steps, more like falling flat on her face. How things had changed since then.

The quad-bike burst into life, its engine’s roar reverberating off the cavern walls. It cut out. “Crap.” The mechanic poked at its innards and tried it again. It burst back to life. He revved the engine a few times.

“Okay, keep the revs high or it will cut out.”

Jann nodded as she straddled the bike.

“If it does, then this button starts it, but it’s a bit dicky. You’ve got about fifty klicks worth of fuel in it.”

She revved the bike and popped the clutch. It jumped forward and cut out. She hit the start button a few times before it fired again.

“Open the airlock,” she shouted at the mechanic as she released the clutch, slowly this time. The bike moved forward. “Okay,” she said to no one in particular. “Let’s do this.” She closed her helmet visor and drove into the airlock.

. . .

THE QUAD-BIKE WAS FAST. Jann sped across the crater's surface leaving a wake of sand and dust billowing out behind her. It made short work of the distance and before long she could see the tip of the MAV in the distance. She twisted the throttle and the quad-bike picked up speed. She was bumped and jostled. Without the belt holding her on, she would have been tossed off several times already. But the thought of the MAV rising up from the planet's surface at any moment made her throw caution to the wind. She powered on. She was about eight hundred meters from the MAV when the bike cut out. "Shit." She tried to start it again, and again, and again. But no joy. "Shit, shit, shit." She banged on the handlebars. The MAV still stood motionless in the distance. There was nothing for it, she would have to run.

She moved with all the speed she could muster and closed the distance. She felt a sense of deja vu, remembering the last time she was out on the crater's surface trying to figure out how to stop Annis. But she had learned a thing or two since then. She and Gizmo had built the fuel tanks together, so Jann knew this time what to do to stop the MAV from launching. All she had to do was get there.

Gizmo entered her thoughts. Now would be a good time to have the little robot around. But it was buried under several tons of rock. *Poor Gizmo,* she thought. It had been a good friend to her, even when she was treating it like crap. What she wouldn't do to have it here with her now.

As she approached, Jann could see that all the fuel tanks were in position, so the countdown had probably begun. Disabling the MAV meant climbing up one of the landing struts to get access to the electronics that controlled the fuel flow. But if the MAV were to launch while she was attempting to get to it, she would be incinerated instantly.

Nevertheless, she started climbing and quickly located the panel. She popped the latch and exposed a sealed circuit board. She pulled it out and dropped back on to the surface. She had done it, Vanji was going nowhere.

Jann backed away from the base of the MAV, still clutching the circuit board. A little distance out she could see the rover that Kayden and the others had used, so she headed toward it. As she drew near she spotted two bodies on the ground. It was Noome and Samir. They had broken visors and both had a bloody hole in the middle of their forehead. They had been executed. They were not going back to Earth, it was never in the plan.

THE HATCH on the side of the MAV opened and a body emerged. It stopped on the top rung of the ladder when it saw Jann and stood for a moment, just looking at her. Jann's helmet comms crackled into life. "Malbec, eh... so you decided to come with us after all."

"Not exactly."

"So what are you doing here?" It was Kayden, she recognized the voice. He began to descend the ladder. Jann backed off.

"I assume Vanji is in there with you?"

"Why don't you come with us, back to Earth, back home? Think about it. You could see your family again."

"You mean like Noome and Samir. Was that the tale you spun for them?"

Kayden waved an arm. "We had a... dispute, you know how these things can go."

"They were never going home and neither was I. You just wanted the launch codes."

"That's not true, come..." he beckoned with his free arm. "Think about how pleased your family will be to see you."

"I don't have a family. My father died two years ago."

"I'm sorry to hear that, Jann. Really I am. But you have your ticket booked, so why not come with us off this rock?"

"It's over, Kayden. The betas control Colony Two now and they are baying for blood. So, no one's going anywhere. Especially not without this." She held up the circuit board up for him to see.

"Ah... I assume what you are holding is the reason our countdown has stopped?"

"Like I said, it's game over."

"Well, in that case, I too have something to show you." With that, he reached back in through the MAV hatch, and before Jann realized her mistake, it was too late.

Kayden retrieved a railgun and let rip with a long burst of fire. Jann turned to run but she was jolted forward by a blow to the back of the head. She stumbled and fell, grabbing her helmet with both hands. "Shit." How could she have been so stupid? He was playing her—again, keeping her talking, buying time.

She expected a stream of biometric alerts to flash up, but she got lucky, the railgun spike had not penetrated her helmet. She lifted her head up and looked over at the MAV. Kayden was reloading the gun. "Dammit." She had dropped the circuit board; it was still on the ground, undamaged. She needed to get to it before he did. But he was descending the ladder fast. He aimed again and fired another short burst. Several darts buried themselves in the ground just inches from her. She picked herself up and ran for a good distance before chancing a backward look.

. . .

VANJI HAD NOW LEFT the MAV and was standing beside Kayden, examining the control board. Jann had stopped running, now that she was out of range of the railgun, and stood watching them. They seemed to be discussing what to do. Finally Vanji took the gun and Kayden headed off with the board, presumably to reinstall it—and there was nothing Jann could do about it. Vanji reloaded the gun and looked over at her. "I admire your tenacity, Dr. Malbec," his voice broke through on her helmet comms. "But it seems you have made your last play."

She could see Kayden climbing up the landing strut. "So what about the secrecy, the hiding out all these years?"

"You changed all that, Jann. When you showed up in the airlock in Colony Two."

"How so?" He was moving towards her.

"Your arrival allowed me to advance my plans."

"Like giving the colony over to the hybrids? That didn't work out too well."

"No matter, I had done all I could with Colony Two. Too many obstructionists, too many who were starting to get queasy about the direction we were taking."

"Like creating a new biologically reproductive species of human."

"That, and other plans. So it was time to leave. And you were the way home."

"Because I had the launch codes?" Jann was still backing away as Vanji advanced.

"Tell me, did you ever wonder why that clone showed up in the airlock in Colony One?"

She thought about this for a moment, it seemed a long time ago. She wasn't sure if she really cared.

"He was lonely?"

"I sent him. Well, more accurately I engineered it." Kayden was now back down on the surface and moving over to the ladder. The circuit board had been replaced, there was nothing to stop them leaving.

"Kayden discovered that Samir and Noome had been hacking ISA communication over the last few years. They had formulated a crazy plan to use this MAV to escape. But they needed the launch codes. So how to get you to come to us? Simple, Kayden helped them send one of the more demented betas, one who longed to visit the source of their creation."

"So you just played me the whole time."

"Yes, but to be fair, we had to gain your trust first."

"So the recycling, the escape plan, it was all a ruse?"

"Rather an effective one, don't you think?" Vanji glanced back over his shoulder to see Kayden re-enter the MAV.

"How do you know he's not going to leave you behind, Vanji?"

He fired off a burst but they went nowhere. But then he bolted forward and fired again, darts peppered the ground around her. She turned to run but caught her boot on a rock and stumbled forward. Vanji sensed his chance and ran at her, firing as he went.

She felt a searing snap of pain course up her thigh as the first dart buried itself just above her right knee. The second spun her head around as it smashed off the side of her helmet. "No." She grabbed her leg to stop the air escaping. Vanji, seeing he had her now, stopped to reload. He cocked the gun and started towards her.

"Vanji, three minutes to launch, you'd better get back here now."

Vanji stopped for a moment. He was torn between finishing Jann off, and missing his flight to Earth. In the end, he turned on his heel and ran back to the MAV.

Jann watched him go as the air slowly escaped out of her EVA suit.

23

PALE BLUE LIGHT

Dr. Jann Malbec dragged herself up from the dirt and balanced on one leg. Her heads-up display strobed alerts as her EVA suit tried hard to maintain pressure. She clamped a hand over her thigh, trying to slow the rate of evacuating air. A bolt of pain rifled up through her lower body. She could barely move.

There was no way she could make it back to the MAV, never mind try to prevent it from taking off. So she hobbled across the dusty Martian surface, as fast as the pain in her leg would allow, towards the abandoned rover. All the time the heads up display flashed warnings with ever more urgency until she finally crawled into the rover airlock and pressurized it. She popped opened her helmet visor and collapsed onto the cockpit seat.

Through the window she could see the Mars ascent vehicle, ticking down the seconds until lift off—and there was nothing she could do. Rage welled up inside her. They had played her for a fool, strung her along, and she had fallen for it. She willingly handed over the launch codes and doomed humanity to a future of genetic tyranny. As she sat and waited for the inevitable, a new sense of loss began to compound her anger. Now that the time had come for the MAV to perform its function, return its occupants to the orbiter, and ultimately to Earth, she realized that her last hope of going home would be leaving with it. She thought she had reconciled herself to this fate when she agreed to return to Colony Two with Nills, but now that she was face to face with it, the feeling of abandonment cut her deep.

Over the years, she had clung to the fragile hope that someday, she would be able to return to Earth. But that dream would soon be gone, perhaps forever. She was being robbed of her hope, her dream, it was being taken away from her and there wasn't a damn thing she could do about it. She could only watch. The MAV started venting gas, prepping the engines for ignition. Her anger intensified.

"Well, if I can't have it, then nether will you, Vanji." She stood up and hobbled to the EVA suit storage area at the back of the rover. From an overhead locker she frantically pulled out a container of suit repair patches and applied several to her leg, as she sat back in the cockpit seat. She flipped her visor closed. The heads up display showed the patches were holding. She had around twenty minutes of air remaining. *Should be enough,* she thought.

Jann started the engine, it rumbled into life. Then she hit the comms and spoke. "Vanji?" There was a hiss of static before a response broke into to the helmet.

"Dr. Malbec, your power of survival is impressive."

"There's just one last thing before you go."

"What's that?"

"Go screw yourself." With that, Jann pointed the rover at the MAV and rammed the throttle fully forward. She stuck a few patches over it to lock it into position and ran to the rear airlock. With just seconds to spare she jumped out of the back of the speeding rover onto the surface. She hit the ground hard and fast, and rolled several times before finally coming to rest. She had just enough time to look around and see the rover speed toward the MAV.

At first she thought it was going to miss, but it caught the edge of one of the landing struts. Then everything happened all at once. The MAV began to topple just as the engines ignited, and there was split second when she thought it might actually lift off. But it didn't. Instead it exploded in a gigantic fireball.

Even in the thin Martian atmosphere, the force felt like a kick to her chest. Dust billowed out from the epicenter and debris rained down, peppering the ground all around her. She rolled face down and covered her head with her hands. It was a reflex action and would do nothing to protect her if she was hit by any fragment of the MAV. Something struck the ground inches from her head, then something else. She had to move, get out of the zone, fast. She picked herself up and hobbled as best she could. She wasn't sure of the direction as the atmosphere was immersed in sand and dust. New alerts flashed on her heads up, the suit was losing pressure. "Shit." Either the patches weren't holding or she had torn it again. She kept going.

After a few minutes the air began to clear and she sat down for a moment to gather her strength. The pain in her leg came back with a vengeance. She was breathing hard, using up valuable air she didn't have to spare. "Calm down, focus," she said to herself. "You can still do this."

Her plan had been to patch the suit enough to make the walk back to Colony One. It wasn't that far. But now she wasn't so sure. It was losing pressure and worked hard to backfill with nitrogen reserves. Ordinarily this would be fine but she was low on resources. Her display calculated she had around ten minutes left. She had better get going. Jann stood up again and looked back at where the MAV had been. All she could see was an enormous cloud of dust. Probably nothing remained of it but a charred hulk of metal. It was gone, along with Vanji and Kayden, and any chance she ever had of leaving Mars. "Move." She forced herself to start walking.

THE FASTER SHE moved the more oxygen she would use up, the slower she went the less chance she would have to make it to Colony One in time. "Don't think about it, just keep moving." She could see its massive dome off in the distance. *Home,* she thought. It really did feel like that to her. She had spent so many years there it was part of her, it was what defined her. It kept her moving forward, beckoning to her, calling out her name like a loving parent standing in the doorway with open arms, welcoming you back after a long journey away. She kept going.

Her suit was running dangerously low on oxygen, she could feel it, her steps were getting shorter, more labored as her body grew progressively weaker from hypoxia. Her mind was getting fuzzy, her thoughts muddled.

Why had she done it? Killed Vanji. She could have let him go and taken the rover back to Colony One. She would not be in this position now. Was it out of some grand moral outrage she felt for what this technology would do to the socioeconomics of Earth? What did she care what happened to Earth. Or was it simply her rage? Rage for what Vanji did to her, rage for her time in the horror of the recycling tank? But did it go deeper than that? Rage for being abandoned by the ISA, by Earth, by all that she had known and loved. Rage for the loss of Paolio and Nills and all her friends, all gone, all dead. She stopped, and slumped down on to ground on her knees. She looked up at the dome of Colony One, so near, so far.

Yes, she had been abandoned by them all, and now it seemed even Mars was letting her go. It had no more left to give her. Jann sat back on her heels, she too had no more left to give. She had five minutes remaining and for most of that she would probably be unconscious. She might as well make the best of it.

Jann looked up at the sky. It was a beautiful evening. Over the crater rim to the west the sun was sinking below the horizon, bathing the sky in a pale blue and purple light. Out across the crater plateau she could see a dust devil swirl and twist its way towards her. She watched it for a time, mesmerized by its dance. Mars hadn't abandoned her after all. It was showing her its best, giving her a final sendoff.

She collapsed down on her back and stared up at the heavens. It was growing darker as her life was ebbing away. A dust cloud blew up around her as she took a deep breath, exhaled very slowly, and finally closed her eyes.

24

SEARCH

The hybrids had been disarmed and were now corralled in a number of secure areas throughout Colony Two. They had split them up into several smaller groups, the eighteen that were left. But was this secure enough? The species possessed a strange telepathic ability, so even dividing them up was probably pointless in preventing them from communicating. Nills knew they would ultimately have to find some way for them to regain the trust of the betas, and vice-versa. They were still a problem, but for the moment, at least they were not a threat. As for the remaining geneticists, their future looked increasingly tenuous. Now that the betas were in control, some were getting drunk on power and were stoking up the mob to seek revenge. Like all great upheavals, the aftermath can be as chaotic, if not more so, than the event itself.

As Nills sat in sickbay, surrounded by the dead and the dying from the battle, he realized that the situation could get out of control very quickly. There was a distinct possibility that a cohort of the betas could turn into a rage-fueled mob, and start to agitate for retribution for the loss of their friends and loved ones. The geneticists would be first, then the hybrids, then... where would it go? Anyone who stood in their way?

It was at that very moment Nills realized that they were indeed, truly human. They might be clones, they might have been subservient, but scratch the surface and, underneath it all, they still possessed the same violent instincts. All it needed was the spark, and the ugly side of humanity would ignite.

It didn't help that Jann had gone. If she were here she could have exerted a level of control. None of them would go against her wishes, seeing her as almost divine. But she had left, and as the hours passed, Nills wondered if she would ever return.

"I SAY RECYCLE THEM, they deserve it." Alban was agitating.

"Yeah, a quick death's too good for them." Others were shouting out now.

"Let's take them down to the tanks and throw them in."

"No. We will do nothing until Dr. Malbec returns." Nills raised his voice so that all the betas that had assembled around him in sickbay could hear. They mumbled and grumbled. He might be injured but he was still their leader and the mere mention of Jann's name still held some authority. "They're no threat to us at the moment, so keep them locked up, and keep a close eye on them."

They grumbled some more but it seemed to have quelled the dissent—for the moment. Nills knew he had very little time to try and keep a lid on things. He surveyed the group around him; he knew them all by name. They looked at him intently waiting for leadership. A great weight of responsibility had been thrust upon him, made even greater by the fact that Vanji had killed most of the natural leaders in the colony. There was really only him now, and Jann, but she might well be dead. All he had was the authority to use her name. Would that be enough?

He was no politician either, he was an engineer, he thought in straight lines, in cause and effect, action and reaction, working the problem. So, the first thing he needed to do was to get them busy and get them distracted.

"Before we do anything, we need a full assessment of the damage. I want each of you responsible for your sectors to give me a full report on the state of our resources. You all know the importance of life support. We don't need some system going off the rails now or we all die, and that will be the end of everything. So get to it and I want shift supervisors to report back to me in… three hours. Got it?"

They grumbled a little more but when you spend your entire life depending on the maintenance of artificial life support you learn to respect it. It becomes top priority. Nills knew this would focus their minds. Any thought of a systems failure would kick them into action. So they dispersed, one by one, to their appointed sectors.

ANIKA AND ALBAN REMAINED.

"Why don't you just let them have their way with the goddamn geneticists?" Alban kept his voice low so the others in sickbay would not hear.

"Do you know what would happen to us if they were to die?"

"We would be rid of them, that's what."

"Yes, we would. And we would all die because of it."

Alban didn't reply, he just gave a quizzical look. He didn't understand.

Nills stood up from the edge of the bed and tested his arm. It hurt like hell but he felt a little better. The shock had worn off and his body was coming to terms with the new normal. He moved it around to test the extent of the pain; it was manageable.

"Genetic engineering is the reason that this colony can exist. If it wasn't for all the synthetic microbes in here there would be no clean air, no soil to grow food, no way to recycle waste, no resource processing... do you want me to go on?"

Alban sighed. "Yeah, I know. Just saying, that's all."

"Much as I hate the bastards, we really need them. Without them we will all die. Maybe not right away, it would take time, but as soon as some problem occurred we would not have the knowledge to solve it. It would be like a spaceship without a pilot, a reactor without an engineer."

"We need to keep them safe," said Anika. "Not let them be recycled."

"What about throwing them a hybrid or two?"

"Alban, no one is getting recycled, okay?"

"Just a thought."

"Look I really need you guys with me on this. Justice will be done, but only when things settle down and we have some control of the situation. If we start now then where does it end? Will they then want to recycle Rachel and Becky?"

"Wait a minute. Has anybody seen them?" said Anika.

They looked at each other. Nobody had. They were now the last two original colonists, excluding the geneticists. They were like Noome and Samir, always kept a low profile, avoided the attentions of the council. They wanted no part of Vanji's world. They just wanted a quiet life. But they were alphas, and as such could be a potential target for mob.

"Shit, no. You don't think they're in trouble?"

"Alban, pull some of your people off guard duty and go find them. They have no part in this, I don't want to see them hurt."

"Okay." But he didn't seem too enthusiastic.

"And don't forget they were an endangered species, too. Vanji had it in for any alpha that didn't see things his way. He rid himself of most of them over the years, so don't let anything happen to them on our watch. Find them."

"I'll try." Alban headed out of the sickbay.

"Anika, how are you with EVA?" It seemed like a simple question but betas did not go outside and had no experience in an EVA suit. It was a dangerous business without training, as you never knew how someone would react. They could quite easily freak out. Putting someone in an EVA suit with no training, and shoving them out an airlock could be disastrous. Even Nills had a tough time when they were all entering Colony Two from the rover. And he knew Lars was barely keeping it together. But, Anika... she seemed like a natural, very composed. It was her nature.

"What have you got in mind?"

He looked around, held her gently by the elbow and led her out of sickbay into the empty corridor beyond. "I may have made a mistake."

"Mistake? What do you mean?"

"Because I said we do nothing until Jann returns. I've just bought us some time, nothing more. The longer she stays away, the harder it will be to keep control. Then things might come to a head."

"You mean if she doesn't return?"

"Exactly. And, let's face it, that doesn't look likely to happen. She should be back by now, there was only around three hours life support in her suit."

Anika didn't reply; the reality of the situation was only just dawning on her.

"We need to find her, even if it's just bringing back the body," whispered Nills.

"Shit, you really think she is dead?"

"I really don't know."

"So, what do you want me to do?"

"Go and get the rover back into the colony. Have them check it over and refuel it. Then we go searching for her."

"Okay."

"Come on, I'll walk with you down to the main entrance cavern. I need the betas to see me up and moving, I need to look like I know what I'm doing."

OVER THE NEXT hour Nills set up command in the entrance cavern. Anika had retrieved the rover and it was now being given the once over by the mechanics, by betas that Nills knew well, engineers like himself. Alban had also managed to find the last of the alphas, Rachel and Becky. They had been hiding out where they always hid out. They were not the brightest pair in the colony, but to be fair, they were smart enough to be two of the few original colonists left alive, Nills gave them that. They sat now in the cavern, under Nills' protection. They looked shit scared. Part of him felt sorry for them.

"Do either of you guys remember how to use an EVA suit?"

Neither of them answered, they just looked even more scared. They really didn't know what was happening. Maybe they thought Nills was about to do a *lockout* on them. It was a phrase used to describe when someone was shoved into an airlock with no suit, and the outer door opened.

"Look," Nills stood up and came over to them. "We need some help. Betas don't EVA, at least not very well, and most of them have never seen the planet's surface up close. But you guys have."

Becky nodded. "It's been a while, you know... a few years."

"That's better than never. We need to find Dr. Malbec. That means taking the rover and looking. We may need to EVA and search around. You think you could help me?"

Rachel's eyes were like saucers. "You mean actually go outside?"

"Yes, out there." Nills pointed at the airlock.

They looked at one another, then Becky said, "I would do anything to get back out onto the surface, see the sky again, anything."

"I'll take that as a *yes* then?"

"I'm with her, make that two."

"Good." Nills turned around to one of the maintenance crew. "Check through those suits and get me two more fully resourced."

"I'll see what I can do."

"How much longer before the rover is ready?"

"Half an hour, give or take."

"Okay." Nills shouted across the cavern to Anika. She was helping with the rover servicing so had her head buried in its engine bay. "Anika." She popped her head out. He signaled to her to follow him and walked over to a quiet spot out of earshot of the others. She followed him over, wiping her hands on an oily rag as she went.

"Anika, I want you to stay here, help Alban keep things under control."

"What? No, you can't do this on your own, Nills."

"I'm taking the two alphas, they can EVA, they've been outside, they have the experience."

"Those two," she nodded over to where the two alphas were sitting. "You can't be serious."

"Listen, they may look like a pair of dopes but they have way more experience out on the surface than anyone else here. And if I leave them here, god knows what will happen to them. End up in a tank, maybe."

Anika screwed her mouth up. "Hmmm, I suppose."

"Anyway, I need you here to help keep the betas from doing something stupid."

"You stay, Nills. They respect you more. Let me go and find Dr. Malbec."

"No, this is something I've got to do. I need to know for sure."

"Okay, but be careful. If we lose you as well..." she placed a gentle hand on his elbow. "We'll really be up shit creek."

The sound of the rover engine starting up reverberated in the cavern and they looked over. The mechanic gave them the thumbs up. Nills nodded back, then looked over to where Rachel and Becky were getting ready. One was holding an EVA suit, looking it up and down like she was trying to work out how to get in to it. *This is not filling me with a lot of confidence*, thought Nills.

So it was that when the rover finally rumbled out of the airlock, Nills felt a deep uneasiness about what he was doing. How much was he putting the stability of Colony Two and all that they had fought for in jeopardy by leaving? The situation was still volatile. Now that blood had been tasted, there was a faction within the betas that wanted more.

He didn't have to do this. Anika could have done the search. What's more, Jann knew the risks when she charged off to stop Vanji, it was reckless of her. What did she have to gain? If it had been up to Nills, he would have let him go. Good riddance to him—and to Earth. But with Jann he suspected it was personal, perhaps she had a deeper connection to the planet they had all left. In truth, none of the betas had ever seen Earth and they were more a part of this planet, this was their home. What did they care for a long forgotten world?

It didn't take long before they could see a tall plume of dust rising high into the atmosphere. Rachel checked the map on the rover main navigation screen. "Looks like that's coming up from the ISA MAV location."

"You think they launched, is that a vapor trail?"

"I'm not sure, we never got to see a takeoff. Remember we came here to stay. There was no going back for any of us."

IT SEEMED to Nills to take forever to close the distance to the location. But as the rover drew closer, they began to make out the charred remains of the MAV revealing itself from within the cloud of dust that shrouded the site. All around lay a thick carpet of crumpled metal and debris.

"It must have been some explosion. What a mess," said Rachel as she brought the rover to stop, several meters away from the charred hulk.

"I think it's safe to say they didn't take off."

"No one could have survived that." Becky looked at Nills.

He surveyed the devastation. "If Jann was caught up in

that explosion then I think we're looking for a body. Okay, let's get out and take a look."

Rachel and Becky flipped down their visors and checked each other's EVA suits with a practiced, confident efficiency. Perhaps Nills had figured them wrong. In Colony Two they had come across as a pair of slackers, avoiding anything that looked like work. But now he was beginning to realize that this might have been just an act. The best way for them to stay alive was to not be noticed by Vanji. Maybe they were a lot smarter than he had initially given them credit for.

They cleared the airlock and started scouring the site for bodies, and it wasn't long before Nills found one. His heart skipped a beat when he spotted a pair of legs sticking out from under a mound of wreckage. He tapped his helmet comms. "Over here, give me a hand."

They lifted off a blackened wedge of fuel tank casing to reveal two bodies. "Samir." Nills said as he knelt down to inspect the broken visor. "And Noome," said Becky. "Looks like they were killed. See the wounds on their foreheads? They were never going to leave, were they?"

"No. They were just pawns, a means to an end, nothing more." Nills stood up, saddened at all the carnage that had taken place, but relieved it wasn't Jann that they had found. They widened their search.

"Nills, over here. What do you make of this?" Rachel's voice broke in to Nills' helmet, he looked up so see her bending down examining a patch of ground, far away from the epicenter of the explosion.

There was a lot of disturbance. The sand had been trampled and shifted from its natural state. A set of parallel caterpillar tracks led into the spot where the three of them now stood.

"What sort of machine would make tracks like that?"

Rachel pointed off along the lines. “Looks like they came from the direction of the colony.” She bent down to examine them more closely.

“It’s not a rover or a quad-bike.”

“I know of only one thing on this planet that could make tracks like that,” said Nills.

“What’s that?”

“Gizmo.”

25

DUST DEVIL

When the initial shock wave from the detonation hit Gizmo's sensors, it did exactly the same thing that any human would have done—it ran like hell. The difference, of course, was the little droid's ability to analyze and compute at speeds a human could not even comprehend. In a fraction of a nanosecond it had calculated speed, force and acceleration of the impending shockwave. It then extrapolated, from the multitude of possible options it had, the best direction to run. Or, in this case, the least worst direction to take. So as the first rocks were being torn from the gallery roof Gizmo had decided to move back down the entrance tunnel—at full speed. This was still not enough for it to escape the impact completely. The explosion hit the little robot with sufficient force to knock it over and send it tumbling down the tunnel for at least twenty-five meters. Gizmo's systems went into the robotic equivalent of a nervous breakdown. Energy spiked, sensors overloaded, circuits fused and data corrupted.

It finally came to rest halfway down the tunnel, flat on its back. Even for Gizmo's speed of thought it took quite a while to reassemble its brain function and figure out the extent of the damage. The first thing it did was assess the state of its systems. Several sensor inputs were gone: infrared, ultra-violet, radiation. It still had ultrasonics so it could still determine range and proximity. Its radio antennas were history so no comms, and no way to connect with the broader data environment of Colony Two, or anywhere else for that matter. But its tracks were intact so it could move. Its power source was also intact. However, one of its arms had suffered severe damage and was not responding to any signals, it was still attached, but totally dead. After it made a full inventory of its remaining capabilities Gizmo turned its attention to—what to do?

The little droid analyzed the situation. Jann, Nills and the betas were on the other side of several tons of rock, assuming they were still alive. Gizmo put that at an approximate 56.4% probability. It could try and dig its way out. But it did not have enough power to complete the task. So it eliminated that as an option. Another option was to simply put itself into sleep mode and wait it out. Someone would find it eventually. It seemed like a reasonable choice but it was the least productive.

However, it could still get back out on to the surface, through the entrance airlock at the far end of the tunnel. And then what? Try and get back into Colony Two by some other route? Or, it could simply return to Colony One. It was a long journey for the little robot, and it would take a few hours, but it would have just enough power to complete it. There was much to do back in the colony, and it was being left unattended and maintenance tasks would only increase the longer it was left idle. Gizmo made its decision. Of the three options open to it, returning to Colony One was the most productive. It powered up its tracks and sped off down the tunnel.

Once out on the surface of the crater basin Gizmo adjusted its speed to maximize power consumption. If it went too fast it would use too much power and not make it, too slow and its other systems would consume more energy than necessary. So it moved across the crater at a leisurely pace—for a robot. But even at this speed, its tracked wheels kicked up a tall tail of dust high into the Martian sky. It looked like a dust devil dancing across the plateau.

It had taken well over an hour to traverse most of the area, and it was nearing Colony One when its ultrasonics detected an atmospheric disturbance. A waveform of an amplitude compatible with an explosion entered its silicon consciousness. Gizmo searched its internal map of the crater to ascertain where it might have emanated from. The only thing it had was the location of the ISA ascent vehicle. Gizmo stopped. This new data required further analysis. It had estimated it would still have approximately 7.63% power remaining when it finally entered the airlock at Colony One. To detour via the source of the explosion would use up a further 2.7%. This was within limits, so the little robot altered direction and headed for the site of the MAV.

From a distance Gizmo could detect the dust cloud surrounding the site. And even with its limited sensory input it ascertained that not much was left of the launch craft. As it moved closer Gizmo bounced ultrasonics off the burnt out husk. It determined that the rover was the most likely initiator of the destruction. Someone must have crashed it into the MAV. Gizmo scanned the area looking for more data to work with, its power was running low so it hadn't much time to waste. It found nothing to warrant any further investigation. Whatever happened was over, time to move on, nothing to see here. So it turned and made for Colony One.

At around seven hundred meters from epicenter, Gizmo's sensors picked up a new object, a body shaped form, lying on the ground. The robot moved as fast as its power mode would allow and stopped at the site of the prostrate form. It would have liked to access the Colony One systems and get some data from the EVA suit's bio-monitor. But Gizmo's antenna array was long gone so it couldn't tell if the person was still alive or not. With its one functioning camera it scanned the face behind the visor. It was Dr. Jann Malbec.

"Well now, Jann," it said to itself. "You do seem to be in a spot of bother."

Gizmo could not lift her with just one arm, but it could drag her. But there were two problems with this. One, it would be risking damaging her suit, and killing her for certain if it ripped it enough to lose pressure. And two, it would be draining power fast with the added energy requirements of hauling a body.

But, it was here to assist, that was the little robot's motto, so assist it would. Gizmo reached down, clamped a metal hand onto the shoulder strap of Jann's EVA suit and started dragging her towards the airlock.

Power drained at an alarming rate. Worse, it was slowing down, too much torque was needed. It realigned its circuits and shut down all but its most essential systems. It kept moving, inching its way slowly to the airlock door.

The final power requirements needed to drag Dr. Jann

Malbec up the ramp and into the airlock were virtually all that Gizmo had to give. The outer door closed and it sensed the airlock pressurizing. Then, with the very last few milliamps of its resources it reached down and popped open her helmet visor. It was all the little robot was able to do. It had done what it could, it had no more left to give.

26

SCHISM

"Gizmo?"

Nills looked up and smiled. "Yeah, it's a robot, it must have survived the rock fall."

"A robot?"

Nills waved a hand. "It's a long story, I'll explain it to you some other time." He stood up and examined the site. "See here," he pointed. "It came to this area, moved around quite a bit, and then headed off in that direction." He stood up and pointed off in the distance.

"The tracks look very different though, like it was dragging something behind it." He bent down again. "See the way there's a deep trough gouged out of the sand? Must have been something heavy."

"A body?"

Nills stood. "Maybe. Let's take the rover and follow it. Come on."

It didn't take Nills long before he realized the tracks were heading for Colony One. When they arrived at the facility, they parked the rover and followed the tracks on foot, right up to the main entrance airlock. As Nills pushed the button to open the outer door, he did so with a deep sense of trepidation. Was it Jann's body that Gizmo was dragging?

It took a few moments for the airlock to pressurize and the inner door to open. Gizmo was standing in the airlock. It waved a metal hand. "Greetings, Earthlings."

"Gizmo, you're alive," said Nills as he popped open his visor.

"Technically no, since I am a robot. But I am operational. Well mostly." It tried to move its damaged arm, which just made a low grinding noise.

"Where's Jann?" Nills had his helmet off.

"You will be glad to hear that she is alive and well, and in the biodome." It raised its good arm towards the connecting entrance.

Nills got the EVA suit off in seconds and ran through the tunnel, past the rows of hydroponics and out on to the central dais, just as Jann was stepping out of the pond.

"Jann."

She looked up and smiled. "Nills, what took you so long?"

THEY SAT for a while on the central dais and talked. The little robot had saved her skin, for the second time. It was becoming a habit. Jann had woken to find herself in the Colony One airlock. She crawled her way to the medlab, patched herself up, and, when she managed to regain some strength, dragged Gizmo off to its recharging station. But she had no way to communicate with Colony Two, to let Nills know she was still alive. Even though Kayden had had some way to do it, she couldn't find it. Also, she had no transport. One rover was in Colony Two and the other was a charred metal husk. She had considered trying to drag back the quad-bike but now that was not necessary. Nills had come.

He filled her in on all that had happened as Rachel and Becky spent their time wandering around the facility, simply remembering things. Looking at this and that and sharing stories of times past. Nills had forgotten that they had lived here for quite some time. Perhaps they thought they would never see it again.

After a time Nills decided he needed to report back to Anika and let her know they were all okay. He took his leave, donned his EVA suit again and headed out to the rover to use the comms. As he sat down in the rover cockpit Nills gave a satisfied sigh, things had worked out. Jann was alive and some sense of control could now be established. He flipped the comms unit on. "Colony Two, this is Nills, over."

Static filled the rover. He tried again. "Colony Two, this is Nills, are you hearing me?"

"Nills, where are you?" It was a voice Nills didn't recognize.

"At Colony One, We found Jann, she's fine."

"That's great, but you better get your ass back here as quick as you can."

"Why, what's going on?"

"It's Alban. He and a few others have taken the geneticists and Xenon down to the tanks. I think they're going to recycle them. We can't do anything to stop it, you need to get back here... like now."

"Oh shit," said Nills.

JANN COULD TELL something was wrong by the look on Nills' face when he returned.

"We've got to get back, now... this minute."

"Why, what's going on?"

"Alban. I warned him not to do it, explained all the reasons, I thought he understood."

"What, Nills... do what?"

Nills stopped for a moment. "They're going to tank the geneticists... and the hybrid leader. If they do, then all that knowledge will be lost to us. I explained to him the reasons why we need them, but he is just blinded by hate and revenge."

"Shit."

NILLS WANTED the alphas to come back with him but Jann intervened. A leader he might be but the subtleties of politics were lost on him.

"They have to stay here," she argued.

"But why? They're on the same side as us, they could be useful."

"No offense, guys," she turned to them, and opened her hands out for emphasis, "But you're alphas. Your presence with us will only confuse the loyalties of those we need to rally."

They both gave a look of relieved acceptance.

"Also, I doubt you'd be much good in a fight."

They stood silent, like two school kids being chastised. But they were no fools either, they had not survived this long by sticking their necks out.

"That's settled, you stay here and try not to break anything. Gizmo, keep an eye on them."

"Certainly, Dr. Malbec."

27

XENON

Jann pushed the rover hard. It bounced and rocked as it sped across the expanse of the Jezero Crater basin. Nills had managed to contact Anika. The situation was delicate, but had not deteriorated—yet.

Alban and a small group of betas, those who had argued most for retribution, had seized their chance while Nills had gone to look for Jann. With her presumed dead, a momentary power vacuum had opened up and they rushed in to fill it. It was a wild sort of counter rebellion, it was mob rule.

They had argued with the betas holding the captives and demanded they be handed over. Anika had tried to talk them down but she wasn't getting any support. So, rather than see beta fighting beta, she had to back down.

Then followed a period of confusion as they debated what they would do to them, now that they had the upper hand. In the end they had taken all of the remaining geneticists and Xenon, the hybrid leader, down to the tanks. They would be made to pay the price. Justice would be served.

But they had not thought it through. It was not a quick death, not a hanging or death by firing squad. The counterrevolutionaries had barricaded themselves in the birthing room hoping to wait it out. Waiting for the point after which the body may be technically alive, but incapable of sustaining life outside the tank. How long was this? No one was really sure, but it was several hours at least. Although it would still take a few weeks to fully dissolve a live human in the tank.

WHEN THE ROVER finally lumbered into the main entrance airlock in Colony Two, quite a few betas had assembled there to greet them. Word of their return had spread. As Jann stepped out and removed her helmet she could sense the feeling of adulation that emanated from the group. It was something that didn't sit easy with her, too much responsibility, perhaps. It was a dangerous thing, one false word, or some casual action on her part could have unintended repercussions.

"What's the situation now?" Nills directed his question at Anika who had been trying to hold the line in his absence.

"They have them down in the birthing room, the doors are all locked and barricaded from the inside, there's no way in."

"Well, they're not going anywhere soon. It takes a long time to die in the tank, so we've got some time." Jann had removed her EVA suit.

Nills walked over to a workbench and stood up on it so he could see over the assembled betas. "Listen up. We're going to break our way in to the birthing room and we are going to rescue those people."

"Let them die," someone shouted.

"Okay. And when they're finished with them, they'll come for the rest of the hybrids. After that, they'll come for the last of the alphas. And after that, they come for you." Nills jabbed a finger at the crowd. "So tell me, who will be left to save you when that happens?"

There was muted chorus of mumbling from the crowd.

"That's right—no one. Because you will have stood by and let them all be killed. This is not what we fought for, this is not who we are. So let's get these people out of there." He jumped down from the workbench. It had done the trick. The mood had shifted, their confidence was returning. Jann had to hand it to him. The old Nills would have been proud.

THE PLAN WAS SIMPLE. Break open the main door into the labs with a laser cutter, then start removing the barricade. After that it was talk. If that failed, then they would figure something out. Anika had organized a cutting crew, Nills was busy recruiting and arming some of the more levelheaded betas. Jann chose instead to visit the remaining hybrids, to assure them they were safe and that attempts were being made to rescue their leader, unharmed.

She made her way to the operations room next to the council chamber, on the upper level of the main cavern. Unlike the chamber itself this had not sustained any damage from the earlier fight to overthrow Vanji. It was from this room the council kept an eye on all activity within the colony. Around the walls were mounted dozens of monitors, all made with the same organic material as the ceiling illumination. They had a strange eerie look to them as they had no discernible edge, just patches of video here and there. She studied the feeds from the holding rooms for a few minutes.

"What are they doing?"

"I don't know," said one of the technicians. "They were fine up until thirty minutes ago… you know, walking, talking, that sort of thing. Now this." He waved a hand at the screen.

The hybrids were all huddled on the floor in groups, groaning and moaning. Holding their heads, eyes filled with sheer terror.

"Christ." Jann stepped back in horror. "It's their hive-mind. What one feels they all feel."

The technician looked intently at the screen. "I still don't get what's wrong with them."

"Alban has just tanked Xenon. They are feeling what he's feeling. What it's like to slowly dissolve to death."

The technician stood speechless, his mouth wide open.

"Do you have a feed from the labs?"

"No, all cameras are cut. But that one there is from the corridor." He pointed to a feed of the crew that was trying to cut open the main lab door. *Shit,* thought Jann, *they're going too slow*. She raced out of the operations room and headed to the labs. She found Nills resting against the wall of the corridor, just down from where the crew was working. He was armed to the teeth, along with Anika and two others. He wasn't taking any chances. The crew had finished opening the door and were now removing the equipment used to block the entrance.

"Nills," Jann shouted. He smiled when he saw her coming. "Xenon has already been tanked."

"How do you know?"

She explained what she had seen. "So we have to get

him out of the tank quick, before he's passed the point of no return. The point where his body cannot sustain life outside the tank. If we don't hurry then we'll doom the remaining hybrids to weeks of writhing agony—it may even kill them all."

"Dammit," was the best reply Nills could manage.

"Nills," one of the crew shouted up to him. "We're nearly through."

"Okay." Nills signaled to his team and they moved up to the lab entrance, taking up positions either side of the doorway. It had been fully cleared. Nills stuck his head around the doorjamb.

"Alban, this is Nills here. Killing those captives will do us no good. We need them to survive. Nobody else has the knowledge."

There was a moment of silence. Nills moved in through the door. The others followed, keeping low. Once inside they spread out across the space of the vast lab cavern. They could see Alban and a few others at the far end, standing beside one of the birthing tanks.

"Alban." Nills held his hand up in the air. "Give it up. This is pointless."

Alban swung around, reached for a railgun and pointed it at him. Nills kept his hands high and moved forward, slowly.

"That's far enough. Come any closer and I will shoot you." He looked like he meant it.

"Where are the geneticists?" Nills stopped. Jann had slipped off to the side and was moving closer, using the tanks as cover.

"They're getting what they deserve. Except now that you've showed up we'll need to speed up the process." He shouted back to the others who were now all pointing weapons. "Bring them out, we'll do it here."

Two geneticists were dragged out from behind one of the tanks. Their hands were tied behind their backs and they both had defeated looks on their faces. They were forced down on their knees in front of Alban.

"This is for our friends." He pointed the railgun at one of the forlorn figures and fired. A spray of blood exploded from the back of his skull, he collapsed backwards, and everyone lost it—fire erupted from both sides.

Nills dove for cover, metal barbs bouncing off the floor as he ran. One of Alban's crew went down. There was a scream from one of the betas. Jann hit the deck just as the tank behind her got hit and exploded into a thousand glass shards. The contents spilled out in a deluge, and with it came a body with tubes and wires still connected— it was Xenon, the Hybrid leader.

The ooze spread out across the floor in all directions and sloshed around Jann's feet as she peered around the edge of a tank she was using as cover. The hybrid kicked and squirmed. Several other bodies lay on the floor, dead. But there was no sign of Alban. So Jann crawled out from behind the tank toward the writhing body of the hybrid. Nills appeared on the other side.

"Nills," she called. "We need to get those tubes out of him quick."

Nills nodded and looked behind him to see Anika and a few others moving forward. He signaled for them to take up covering positions.

Jann rushed over to Xenon. "Nills, hold him down, stop him moving."

Nills grappled with the squirming body. "Dammit, he's really slippery."

Jann cut away the wires that had entangled him and pulled out the long tube running down his throat. He coughed, and spluttered, and spat. Then he started to shiver violently. Nills released his grip. "Shit, he's going into shock."

"He'll be okay. Remember I've been here, I survived. But we do need to get him to sickbay."

Nills called over to the betas that were now coming into the lab. They had been drawn in by the unfolding drama, but were keeping their distance all the same.

"Hey, over here. Get him to sickbay." A few ran forward, gathered him up and carried him back out of the lab. Jann stood up and surveyed the devastation. The bodies of two geneticists lay dead along with one of Alban's cohort. "Two dead. That means there's only one still alive. We need to find him."

"Over here, have a look at this." Anika pointed to drops of blood on the ground. "Looks like one of them is injured. We just need to follow."

The trail led off towards the back of the cavern. "What's back there?" Jann whispered.

"The main research lab, where they did all the experimental work."

"Any way out?"

"There are metal stairs leading back up to the main colony area. It comes out near Vanji's living quarters."

THEY PASSED along by the experimentation rooms. Long tubular tanks filled with strange aquatic species. Flat rows of experimental flora, new strains of genetically modified plants for the colony gardens.

"Shhhh." Nills held a finger to his lips.

Jann listened to the silence, then she heard a clang of metal on metal.

"He's making for the stairs. Come, let's finish this."

But before they could move, the forlorn figure of the last geneticist moved out from behind a tall equipment rack. Behind him, Alban gripped his neck with one hand. In the other he held a grenade high in the air. The pin was removed. The only thing stopping it from detonating was his grip on the lever.

"Lower your weapons or I let go of this and take us all down."

"Alban, this is crazy. There's no way out."

"Oh yes there is. So just do it and step aside."

Nills was first to drop his weapon, then Jann, followed by Anika. Alban pushed the geneticist forward as he moved, and they let him pass, back into the research lab, turning around as he went.

"Back, move right back, as far as the wall."

They stepped back slowly until they were against the cave wall.

When Alban reached the center of the research lab he kicked the back of his captive's legs, and the geneticist collapsed to his knees on the floor. They could see him now taking off a shoulder bag and laying it down on a workbench.

"Oh shit," said Nills. "That's the bag with all the grenades Gizmo made."

"You know, Nills, I never really liked what happened to us up here. It's not what I had imagined when I signed up."

"You mean, when your alpha signed up."

"You see, that's what I'm talking about. Where does my alpha stop and me begin?" Ever think about that, Nills?"

"All the time, Alban. But we are what we are, we just need to get past it."

"Well I'm sorry, Nills. But I finally realized that I can't." Alban let go of the spring and dropped the live grenade into the bag. "I told you there was a way out."

"OH SHIT," was the last thing Jann heard before she was slammed against the cave wall and lost consciousness.

28

A NEW SOL

Nills moved through the Colony Two entrance cavern to the waiting rover. The mechanics working in the area waved to him as he passed. He nodded his acknowledgment. The colony was beginning to settle down in the weeks after the revolt. The seeds of a fragile peace were beginning to grow. Life would go on.

He stepped inside the machine and sat down in the cockpit. Xenon was already there, waiting.

"Ready to go, Nills?"

"Yeah, let's take it out, I hear it's a nice day outside."

Xenon took the controls and moved the rover through the main airlock and out onto the Martian surface. Nills was right, it was a nice day. A pale orb hung high in the sky, the air was clear, no wind to whip up the dust. Xenon looked up through the windscreen at the clear sky. "You think they're up there, watching us?"

Nills took a glance up, as if it was actually possible for him to spot a satellite flying past. "You better believe it. After all the coming and going, not to mention explosions on the planet's surface, they will have everything they can called into service. All trained on this very spot. NASA's deep space communications network is probably working overtime."

Xenon looked up again and gave the sky the one fingered salute. Nills laughed.

The hybrid leader had changed since his experience in the tank. All the hybrids had. Their uncanny ability to communicate by thought, far from being an evolutionary advantage, was in reality their Achilles heel. It had traumatized them to the point of despair. After the events of the recycling it took some time to get them out of their collective shell. Xenon was the one to do it. He was a different person now, with a different perspective. It was like some door had opened in his mind and he realized that the hybrids were a very fragile species. Their survival relied on the support and social cooperation of the betas. It took time for him to bring everybody around to this new reality. Some of the hybrids were still scarred, they would take longer. For a few, it would be never at all. But they would all help them as best they could.

"Do you have many memories of Earth?" Xenon asked.

"Yeah, sure. Although, technically I've never been there."

"It must be strange to walk out in the open, feel rain on your face, swim in an ocean of water."

"We all have memories of times on Earth, even you, Xenon. Anyway, our home is here. We need to make it our very own paradise."

They traveled in silence for a while and Nills reflected on the events that had brought them to this point.

The geneticists were all dead and the explosion in the labs had destroyed much of what they had created. It was certain that a considerable amount of their knowledge died with them, or was lost in the chaos. Still, they weren't without hope that what they needed could be salvaged, and at least the cave wall held the blast. A breach would have meant catastrophe, the end of human life on Mars.

Xenon broke his ruminations. "So what do think they're up to?

"Who?"

Xenon pointed skyward.

"We'll know soon enough, once we get to Colony One." They could already see its outline, and the massive biodome sparkled in the mid-sol sun. They rolled up to the facility and Xenon deftly reversed the rover up to the umbilical airlock. There was a satisfying clunk as the connection was made secure. Using this airlock meant that they had no need for bulky EVA suits, and made the trip a little easier.

When they stepped out, Becky and Gizmo were there to greet them. Gizmo's arm had been repaired and the little robot was back to being 97.65% operational, as it put it. Quite what the remaining 2.35% was, nobody could fully understand. They walked through the connecting tunnel and into the main common room.

"Rachel's in the operations room, reviewing the facility schematics, if you're ready to have a look?"

The plan was to survey the derelict areas of Colony One to assess what would be required to repair those sections and bring them back online. Rachel and Becky had taken charge of the project and were eager to get started.

"Xenon, you go ahead. I'm just going to visit the biodome for a while."

"Sure." He nodded.

Nills walked through the short connecting tunnel, past the hydroponics, under the hanging vines and eventually found his way out onto the central dais. Sitting in a wicker recliner was Dr. Jann Malbec. She jumped up when she saw him come.

"Nills, you finally got here. Come, sit down." She walked over to the pond and pulled out a bottle of colony cider. "I've been saving this." She sat down and poured some glasses. "Here you go." They clinked. "To..." Jann thought for a second. "To Mars."

Nills raised his glass. "To Mars."

Jann had escaped the carnage in the labs with a gash on her head and a very sore body. Other than that she was okay. By the time order had been restored, and the population in Colony Two had come to terms with the new normal, she had decided to make the trip back. Nills stayed behind, promising to follow later when he was sure things had settled down. That was three weeks ago.

He sipped his drink. "So, any news from the ISA... from Earth?"

"We're front page news, have been for the last month. It's all out in the open."

"What do they know?"

"That's not really the problem, it's what people are speculating that's the problem."

"Is always is."

"What about Xenon, did you get any more of the story out of him?"

"A bit. From what he's told me, Vanji grot frustrated with being consistently blocked by the council over his ambitions. So when he realized that you held the key to getting back to Earth, he did a deal with COM."

"VanHoff?"

"Yes. He had been communicating with them for a

while, hatching a deal. They were going to give him anything he wanted, if he would come back. Xenon didn't know the details, just that they would take control of Colony Two and start a breeding program."

"Well, Earth thinks we hold the key to immortality, that we possess the elixir of life and they all want it now. The ISA are being sued to open up communications control with us. They're freaking out, they can't handle it."

"Well, that's their problem. We don't have to talk to anybody if we don't want to."

"Yes and no. Sure, we can switch off comms but that's not going to stop them coming here. I imagine that right now there are corporate boards meeting back on Earth, talking about how to raise money for a Mars mission. They are going to come, not just COM, but every space company and reckless adventurer."

"I don't suppose it would do any good to tell them we don't know anything."

"I already did. They don't believe me. They just think we're keeping it for ourselves." Jann sighed and sipped her drink.

"Nills, this could get very messy. The people that come will be non-state, well funded and probably well armed. Any so-called Outer Space Treaty laws that exist will be torn up and burned. They will fight each other for this knowledge, they will fight us for it and if we don't, or can't, give it to them they will simply experiment on us until they find it—or we're all dead. Make no mistake, Nills, a battle is coming. A battle for control of Mars."

They sat in silence for some time. Eventually Jann stood up. "But hey, it's not going to happen anytime soon, so let's enjoy the peace while we've got it." She stripped out of her jumpsuit, ran naked to the pond and dived in. Her head broke back up through the surface and she shook the water from her hair.

"So what are you waiting for?"

Nills gave a broad grin, stripped out of his own clothes and dived in beside her.

COLONY THREE MARS

1

SECRET

Dr. Jann Malbec delicately removed the cover on the petri dish inside the biolab's hermetically sealed isolation chamber. She could now see the profusion of bacterial blooms that radiated out across the surface of the agar gel. This was the last living sample of the bacteria that had caused so much death and destruction to the original colony and the later ISA mission.

Yet, for those lucky enough to be immune to its devastating psychotic dementia, it bestowed a biological reinvigoration and rejuvenation. It was a two-faced Janus. It could be both a beginning or an end. On the one hand, it was the very elixir of life. On the other, it was insanity and death.

Fortunately, it posed no threat to the current colony population, as they had all evolved, one way or another, to be immune to its darker attributes. But there were those, currently en route to Mars, that would not be so lucky should they be exposed to it—even though this was the very thing that they sought. One of these missions was already imminent, with others not far behind—all of them hell bent on acquiring this duplicitous mutation.

Jann removed her hand from the joystick controlling the mechanical manipulator within the sealed chamber. She flexed her fingers for a moment, then reached up to the control panel above the unit and flicked open the protective cover on a switch marked *IRRADIATE*. Her finger hovered over the exposed red button—pressing this would send a stream of accelerated electrons directly through the sample, killing all bacteria within and eradicating it forever. She hesitated.

In the aftermath of the upheavals that had traumatized Colony Two, Jann realized, that if they were to survive, she would need to have a better understanding of the complex, genetically engineered, biology of the colony's ecosystem. This technology was, after all, the very reason that a human outpost on Mars could ever hope to function. But much of this knowhow was lost in the mayhem wrought by the events of the revolt, specifically the destruction of the Colony Two labs. So, Jann set about building a new research facility in the hope of regaining this lost knowledge. To this end, the medlab in Colony One had been repurposed and extended. New modules were added, and much of the lab equipment that was salvageable had been moved here from Colony Two. It was during this period of rebuilding that she realized the cave where Nills and Gizmo had hid out, during the first wave of infection by the bacteria, was still there, and that only she and the eccentric droid knew of its existence. So she decided to keep it that way, and had sworn the robot to secrecy. Although, quite what that meant for a droid was hard to know. That said, it did seem to be very attached to her and followed her around everywhere. Nills tried to explain its behavior to her many times.

It learns. That's how it's programmed. And like most intelligent beings it learns from experience, by doing things. The more data it has to work with the more it will change and modify its behavior. It has spent a long time with you, Jann. And Gizmo has also saved your ass more than once. So, it has moved you up its hierarchy of priorities. You have become important to it. Basically, it likes you, you are its friend.

Jann also realized, that when they had purged the Colony One environment of the malignant bacteria, they had neglected to consider this hidden space. It was sealed off and environmentally isolated from the main facility. But, if the bacteria still existed down there then it would pose a fundamental threat to any new arrivals. So, shortly after the medlab's reconstruction as a research facility, she and the droid secretly entered the cave and went on the hunt—and it didn't take her long to find it. But rather than eradicate it she took a sample for investigation, isolated in this sealed enclosure and then purged the cave environment. This was now the only living sample in existence.

Since then, she had spent long hours down here, testing, probing, exploring the bacteria. All the time hoping to gain some better understanding of its extraordinary properties. But time was running out. Missions were already on their way to Mars. New people coming—all seeking this very biology.

She could give it to them. Let them have it. It could spare the colony from the pressure to reveal its secrets. If the bacteria were here, then why not just hand it over? But could they be trusted with it? Not be tempted to return it to Earth where it had the potential to cause havoc on a truly global scale? No, it was simply too dangerous. It must be eradicated for good. *Do it!* She commanded herself to press the button—but still she hesitated.

A LIGHT BLINKED on her comms earpiece lying on the workbench beside her. Jann sighed, removed her finger from the button and picked up the comms unit.

"Yes?"

"Jann, where are you? I've been trying to find you for, like, half an hour."

"I'm... eh... doing something. What is it?"

"Operations just picked up a craft entering Mars orbit."

"So soon?"

"Yes, they're here. Nills has called for an emergency council meeting over at Colony Two. He's on his way here to pick you up."

"OK. Tell him I'll meet him in the common room in twenty."

"Will do."

Jann pulled the comms unit out of her ear and put it in her pocket. She looked in at the sample again for a moment as her hand reached for the button on the control panel. She hesitated again, then finally flicked the protective cover closed. She grabbed the joystick and manipulated the cover back on the petri dish, and returned it to its compartment. It would live for another while longer. Maybe after the council meeting she could bring herself to eradicate it—once and for all.

2

CLONE

The clone known as Nills Langthorp exited the main airlock of Colony Two into a bright Martian morning and looked out across the vast expanse of the Jezero Crater. A flat, unbroken landscape stretched before him all the way to the horizon, around three and a half kilometers distant. Out there, far beyond his field of vision, lay Colony One, where Dr. Jann Malbec had chosen to set up home. He had hoped she would stay with him, here in Colony Two, but she had been adamant in her desire to establish a new research facility. Since most of the labs had been destroyed in Colony Two, they had moved all that was salvageable to a new home in the now extended medlab of Colony One.

Gizmo had also gone with her. Nills missed the company of the little droid, missed its eccentric ways and quirky turn of phrase. But it had formed a strong attachment to Dr. Malbec, and seemed to want to be in her orbit all the time. He didn't mind, really. In fact he was glad that the robot was with her, keeping an eye on her, keeping her safe.

Nevertheless, Nills had started building a second *Gizmo* some time back. But he simply could not spare the components needed for its construction. Things were becoming scarce, some would even argue critical. Yes, they had food a plenty, and air and water. But it was the electronics that kept all the control systems functioning, and those they could not fabricate. So as components failed, less critical systems would be scavenged for parts.

This was a situation made worse by the destruction of the labs during the upheavals surrounding the ousting of Dr. Vanji. And it was further exacerbated by a disaster in the resource processing sector some time later. That catastrophe had nearly tipped the viability of the colony over the edge. A hydrogen leak in the lower cavern led to a devastating explosion. Twenty-six colonists died, including all of the Hybrids, except for Xenon—he was now the last of his species. And, as if that wasn't bad enough, most of the machinery used to fabricate basic components was also destroyed.

In the aftermath of this fiasco, the council had argued that the resources of the two colonies should be consolidated into one, it would give them a better chance of survival. But in the end it was felt that retaining both locations would provide them with a better defense against potential subjugation by any of the new forces now heading their way from Earth.

So, Gizmo II was parked as a half-built project and Nills' mind turned to finding a way in which the two facilities could be more efficiently managed and maintained. The big problem was distance, they were over thirty kilometers apart, too far to EVA on foot. So the only way to go from one to the other was by rover, and that could take up to two hours, particularly with a full load on board. So for some time Nills bent his mind to the conundrum of affecting a speedier and more efficient, cross crater, transit. But he also had his own, more selfish, motivation for solving this problem. If he wanted to spend more time with Jann, then he was going to have to come up with a better transport solution. One that could take minutes rather than hours to cross the crater.

The solution, of course, was flight. But not winged flight, as the Martian atmosphere was too thin to make this practical. Nills also ruled out an airship type design for similar reasons. His idea—one which he'd had for some time—was to repurpose one of the landers the original colonists arrived in. Since they used retro-thrusters to affect a landing on the surface, they all came with methlox engines, tanks and a control system for stabilization.

However, it would need a considerable amount of re-engineering to transform it into a true flying machine—one that could traverse the crater. Since it only had the ability to move up or down, not sideways to any significant degree, he would need to add on a forward thruster, as well as lateral and rotational control. The fuel tanks were also too small, affording only a few minutes of burn time. So his first task was to dramatically reduce the weight by stripping it of everything that wasn't directly required for flight, including the outer shell. Since he could operate it while wearing an EVA suit, there was no need to have it enclosed. By the time he was finished it had been reduced down to a bare chassis, just enough to support the four retro-thrusters, tanks and a rudimentary pilot seat of Nills' own construction. The landing gear was permanently extended and the entire contraption looked like some experimental craft from the mind of a 50's NASA engineer. It was nicknamed *the flying bed* or simply *the bed*, for short.

Fortunately, the retro-thrusters were not powerful enough to reach Martian escape velocity, so Nills had no fear of accidentally sending himself into orbit with it. But they were more than sufficient to lift the entire craft off the surface and then some—that took care of going up. For forward motion, Nills added a simple gas powered thruster on the stern of the craft. One of the advantages of a thin atmosphere was very little friction so this unit did not need to be that powerful to get a decent amount of momentum going, and once moving, it pretty much kept on going. He also added lateral thrusters to port and starboard to give him rotational control.

It used methlox—methane and liquid oxygen, as the propellant, and they still possessed the infrastructure to manufacture plenty of this, in both facilities. So Nills only needed to add enough additional tanks to travel the distance between the two colonies. After each trip it would be refueled and made ready for the return.

From Nills' perspective, it was a thing of beauty. However, it was a view not necessarily shared by Jann, who, while she appreciated the speed at which it could traverse the crater, was not as convinced as Nills was of its mechanical integrity.

Nills walked over to where the bed now sat, its spindly structure silhouetted against the Martian sky, like some giant metal arachnid warming itself up with the rise of the morning sun. He clambered up the superstructure onto the wide, flat platform that served as the passenger area and sat in the pilot's seat. He flicked on the power and pre-ignition check routines started to scroll down a central screen. It would take a few minutes for this process to complete so, as he waited, Nills looked up at the sky above him. Somewhere overhead a Chinese mission, Xaing Zu Industries, had just entered orbit. They would spend the next few sols slowing the craft down by using their main engines and the atmosphere as a braking system, going lower and lower as they slowed, until they had burned off enough energy to enter a stable orbit and prepare for landing.

For a long time now, the colonists had known this would happen, new missions, and new people arriving—all anxious to investigate the strange and exotic world of the colony. But he had mixed feelings about this intrusion, as did the other colonists. On the one hand these new missions would bring badly needed supplies and components that could not be manufactured in situ. And these supplies could ultimately make the difference between survival or death. Not that it was a quick death that faced the colony, but a slow death by a thousand cuts as each component failure would stress the life support a little further each time, until finally, it could no longer sustain its dependents. So Nills had welcomed these new missions, he was, on balance, looking forward to them.

However, Jann was not of the same opinion. In fact, she had an almost visceral paranoia as to the intentions of these new arrivals. It was not a view that Nills subscribed to, although he was not so naive to assume, for one minute, that their motives were truly honorable. No, he knew damn well what they were after—the so-called Janus bacteria. But, since it no longer existed, then what was the problem?

His ruminations were broken by a message flashing on the control screen. *Ready!* It had run through all the checks, time to lift off. Nills settled himself deeper in the pilot's seat, strapped himself in and hit the ignition button. He could feel the vibrations of the pumps kicking in up through his spinal column. It increased in intensity until the control screen flashed *Ready to rock!*

On either side of the pilot's seat, mounted onto the rudimentary armrests, were two simple joysticks. One on the left was simply up/down. This was really the business end of the machine. It was also the moment that Nills loved the most, so he hesitated slightly so as to savor the moment, then he gently pushed the joystick forward.

A massive cloud of sand billowed up and around the craft, completely obscuring his view. The vibrations increased dramatically and, if he had not been strapped in, he would have been bounced off the platform. The dust cloud thickened as he nudged the joystick further, delivering more propellant to the engines. So dense was the dust cloud, that he was never quite sure when he was airborne until the craft exited out through the top of the plume.

He was now fifteen meters or so up from the surface and still rising. When he reached around thirty, he throttled back to hover the craft at this altitude and took a moment to survey the area. It was a clear morning and he now had a commanding view across the Jezero Crater. He nudged the joystick on his right side to rotate the craft in the direction of Colony One, then pushed forward on the same stick. The machine moved off, slowly at first, but all the time picking up speed as it flew over the crater's surface. It would take him less than fifteen minutes to make the trip.

His heart gladdened at the thought of being with Jann again. They had been apart for quite a while, as she spent most of her time holed up in the medlab of Colony One, while he saw to the engineering and maintenance demands of Colony Two. He looked skyward again, as if to catch a glimpse of what was to come. For better or for worse, things were about to change. A new era was now unfolding, one where the humanity of the colony, and all those who called it home, would be truly tested.

3

COUNCIL

After Nills had picked her up, the trip back across the crater for Jann had been uneventful. That is to say, the bed didn't blow up en route. She even began to enjoy the ride, as some moments were truly exhilarating. And it was in those moments that Jann felt more alive than she had for a very long time. Perhaps she had spent too many hours cooped up in her lab, staring down the barrel of a microscope, so to speak. All the time looking inward—seldom outward.

Now though, she was glad in a way that the first of the new missions had finally made it into orbit. At least it gave her an excuse to leave her darkened room and engage with the world, with Nills—she had missed him too. But before any intimacy could pass between them there was a council meeting to undertake. One that required her full attention, because what was decided now could dictate their very survival as a self-governing human colony.

. . .

The post revolution colonists had initially established a kind of governance by general consensus, where everybody's voice was heard. This had the advantage of minimizing arguments and fostering an inclusive and harmonious environment. In a sense, it kept everybody in the loop. But as time passed, and decisions on strategy and resource allocation became more important, a new council of sorts began to manifest itself. First to rise to prominence were those who had the knowledge and expertise in the functioning of various sectors of the colony infrastructure: biotech, agriculture, engineering, medical, communications, et cetera. Then there were those that the colonists simply held in high regard, such as Dr. Malbec. The Hybrid, Xenon, was also one such. He was viewed by all as a considered thinker, never rash, one who carefully analyzed the various options and possible outcomes. So, when a final decision needed to be made on some tricky issue, it was generally he they would turn to.

They had now gathered in the same council chamber, overlooking the vast central cavern in Colony Two, that the original council of Dr. Vanji had occupied. But this council was markedly different. For one, all were welcome regardless of perceived status in the colony. Secondly, there really was no official hierarchy, save for Xenon sitting at the head of the long stone table. He had taken to donning a dark robe for these sessions, like a Victorian judge. He sat now, as mediator and final arbiter—should that be needed.

In the center of the table, a 3D rendering of the planet Mars rotated, and around this, the current estimated orbital position of the Chinese Xaing Zu Industries spacecraft. Holburn, who knew most about these things, hence his elevation to the role of systems tech, was currently explaining the orbital mechanics that the Chinese crew was undertaking.

"They have to execute several elliptical orbits, using both their main engine and the atmosphere to help slow them down." They all watched as the spacecraft's planetary transit was drawn out in ever decreasing ellipses.

"It will be a few more sols before they're in a position to contemplate landing."

"So, how long is *a few more sols*?" Anika pitched in with the question.

"They estimate three sols to reach optimal orbit. Another one for systems checks and prep."

"Four sols," she replied, and left the words to hang in the air.

The council were all silent for a moment. Their collective gaze fixed on the slowly rotating orb.

"And how long before COM gets here?" It was Jann who finally broke this moment of communal contemplation.

Holburn consulted a tablet he was holding. "Around fourteen."

"COM are the people we need to worry about the most. Now that they've won the court case to regain ownership of the Colony, all they have to do is set foot in either facility, and it all reverts to them." Anika made a wide sweeping gesture with her hands. "Including everything that's ever been developed here."

Her fears focused on the fact that the Colony One Mars consortium had taken the International Space Agency through the Court of Arbitration to regain ownership of the Colony. And they had won. But there was one caveat, they physically needed to set foot inside either of the facilities before it would all legally revert to them.

"And what happens then? Where does that leave us? Are we all just products of COM's bioengineering division? I mean, will COM own us—physically?"

"That's why we should keep these bastards out. I'm not going to end up as a lab rat." It was a voice from the crowd of colonists that had packed themselves in to the council chamber and taken up standing positions around the walls.

"What choice do we really have? We can't survive, long-term, without critical component supplies from Earth. And once they land, how long could we realistically keep them all out, even if we wanted to?" Nills gestured at the mass of colonists.

"We have no choice but to let this play out." Jann's voice was calm and measured. "I for one, have no love of COM. After all, it was me who prevented Dr. Vanji from leaving, and I also scuppered their original plan. So they'll have it in for me, first and foremost. But there's no point in hiding from it. Nills is right, we have no future in isolation, we'll all end up dead anyway."

Before anyone else could reply, Xenon rose, extended his arms slightly, palms facing out, and spoke.

"It seems, on balance, we have no choice. We must embrace this challenge and try as best we can to assimilate the newcomers. Only then do we have a future."

There was another moment's contemplation by the ad-hoc colony council while they all considered the words spoken by the Hybrid.

"However, that doesn't mean we should make it easy for them," he finally said before sitting down.

Jann now took up the baton again. "Our immediate issue is how best to prepare for the imminent arrival of Xaing Zu Industries. And let's face it, their intentions are clear, they're after the exact same thing as COM. Acquire the genetic knowledge that extends human lifespan and return to Earth with the prize—and achieve this before COM land and reclaim ownership of the facility."

Holburn deactivated the 3D holograph of the planet and sat down. "And what if they don't?"

"Don't what? Find what they're looking for or leave when COM arrive?" said Anika.

"Both, I suppose." He gave a vague shrug.

"The knowledge that they, and COM, seek resides in all of us, it's now part of our DNA. How they plan to divine its properties is not clear. But my fear is that it will involve invasive examination on... selected subjects."

"I'm not going to be a goddamn lab rat," came a voice from the assembled mass of colonists.

Jann raised her hand to silence the outburst. "Even with this, the likelihood of Xaing Zu discovering anything substantive in the time they have available is minimal."

"Meaning they will not be inclined to depart when COM arrive," said Holburn.

"Precisely. So at that point I would envision a face-off between the two parties." Jann replied.

"And therein lies our opportunity," said Nills. "If we can pit one against the other, then..." He made a gesture. "Divide and conquer, as they say."

Again there was a moment's contemplation by the council before Xenon leaned forward and spoke.

"It would seem then, that this is the point where outcomes become uncertain, and thus open to considered manipulation for our benefit." The council all nodded at this summation of the situation.

"So, what do we know of their respective numbers and resources?" Anika pitched her question at Holburn.

He stood up, tapped an icon on his tablet and a 3D

rendering of the Chinese landing craft materialized in the center of the long table. "There are eight crew," he began, "generally referred to as *taikonauts*. The commander is Jing Tzu. A highly regarded individual. Two are flight and systems, two are scientists, presumably geneticists. That leaves three that are, well, probably military."

"Weapons?" said Anika

"Unknown. But we should assume they're packing something. Also, and this is curious, they have no transport with them. So they'll be relying on us to move them between facilities."

"Why do you think that is?" Said Anika.

"My guess is that they'll have full fuel tanks, ready to take off again at a moment's notice. So they're trimming as much weight as they can elsewhere. Not having a rover would be a considerable saving."

"And COM?"

Holburn tapped a few more icons on his tablet and the Chinese craft was replaced by the COM lander. It was enormous by comparison, and there was an almost audible moment of awe from around the table when it rendered.

"As you can see, this is a much larger mission. Twelve crew. We have little information on who or what they are bringing with them. But it's safe to assume, judging by the size of the craft, they've brought everything and the kitchen sink."

"Weapons, rovers?" said Anika.

Holburn shrugged. "I would guess, all of the above."

"Okay," said Jann. "Let's focus on Xaing Zu first. The plan is to meet at the landing site and bring them all to Colony One. That's where the research lab is, that's where they want to start."

"Then we should put on a show of force. We'll bring

both rovers and the bed, and have some of us visibly armed, just to let them know we won't be a pushover," said Nills.

"I will endeavor to be as open and transparent with them as possible regarding access to the research lab. Let them see that the knowledge they seek no longer exists. Maybe then they'll be satisfied."

"And if not?"

"Then there is still a population of around twenty-five over there, it won't be that easy for them to try and coerce us."

"Maybe for Xaing Zu, but COM will be a different matter."

"True, but there's not much we can do at the moment. We'll just have to wait and see what transpires. Then seize our opportunity, if one should present itself."

"And if it doesn't?" said Anika

Xenon once again rose and spoke. "If such a moment escapes us, then we fail. And if that is the case, then so be it."

4

EMBRACE

Jann sat in the dim light of the balcony, looking out across the expanse of the main Colony Two cavern. Here and there she could glimpse the night shift going about the business of maintenance, their presence evidenced only by the sweep of a torchlight. The ceiling illumination was many hours into its nocturnal cycle, painting the cavern roof with the illusion of stars. She felt a cool breeze across her face from the array of large air recyclers overhead. It felt like a summer's night back on Earth.

"Can't sleep?" Nills' voice drifted out from within the darkened room.

Jann turned her head, trying to penetrate the inner gloom to where she and Nills had been sleeping.

"No, my mind is like a racetrack, it won't let me sleep."

She heard a rustle of sheets and Nills materialized from the dim interior and sat down opposite her on the balcony. He was naked save for a sheet gathered around his waist.

"Want to talk about it?"

Jann looked back across the cavern. "I wonder if we're doing the right thing."

"Letting these guys in?"

"Yeah. Maybe the others are right. We should batten down the hatches and throw boiling oil over them at the gates."

"And how long would that go on for? We agreed the best way forward is to face it head on."

"I know... and you're right, but I just have a bad feeling about it all."

"Well, there's nothing we can do. We don't have what they're looking for so we're going to have to convince them of that one way or the other."

Jann looked over at Nills and studied him for a while. He was silhouetted against the dim light of the cavern, his face obscured save for his bright smile and a faint glint from his eyes.

"Actually, Nills, that's not entirely true."

Nills froze for a moment and Jann could sense his mind was coming to terms with the implications of what she just said.

"Go on," he finally managed.

Jann shifted in her seat, and pulled the sheet around her.

"I went looking for it, in the cave under the medlab in Colony One, the place where I first met you and Gizmo."

"You mean my Alpha."

"Yes, sorry... I didn't mean to..."

"It's okay, I shouldn't have said that... go on."

"Anyway, that was months ago, when we were extending the research facilities."

"And you found it."

"Yes. I isolated a test sample and then purged the cave."

Nills leaned forward. "When were you going to tell me this? Who else knows?"

"Just Gizmo. I was planning to kill it before they got here. I didn't want to burden you with it."

Nills sighed. "Do you still have it?"

"Yes. I was about to irradiate it this morning, before the meeting, but..."

"But what?"

Jann took a moment before replying, then sat forward. "If it's what they want, what they've come here for, then we could simply hand it over, be done with it. It could spare the colony a world of grief."

"And what if they take it back to Earth?"

Jann sighed and sat back again. "Therein lies the dilemma. The irony is if we deny them this then we are doing it for the good of Earth, not Mars, not for us."

Nills thought about this for some time, scratching his chin in a slow absent-minded manner. "Tell no one else," he finally said. "Keep it between us. We've time yet to decide. Maybe it's good... you know, to have an ace in the hole."

They sat in silence for a while before Nills finally spoke.

"Do you ever miss Earth? I mean, it is your home."

"I'm not sure if I know where home is anymore, Nills."

"I'd like to think it's here, Jann. But I know, in my heart, you will want to go back to Earth at some point."

Jann hesitated. "I don't know. There's nothing there for me anymore. My father's dead now and... well, I don't have any other family alive."

"You don't talk about him much, what was he like?"

"He was like any alcoholic, tormented by his demons. But don't get me wrong, he wasn't a bad man. My mother died when I was still a baby. So my father was left to his grief, to the demands of a small farm and to the needs of an infant. It must have been hard."

"Well, from where I'm sitting, he did a good job." Nills smiled.

"It came at a cost, Nills. If I were to sum up his legacy, it's that he instilled in me an almost primal need to run away and hide. And I've come to realize it's probably what defines me. Run and hide, that's all I ever do."

"You're being too hard on yourself, there's more to you than that."

"I grew up on a rural farm, no family, few friends, just myself and my father. Every now and then, when things got too much, he would drink himself into a rage. All the anger, the grief, the frustration would come out in a torrent of violence. Not directed at me, thankfully, but at anything that wasn't nailed down in the house, and some things that were. So, at those times, I would run and hide. Out into the fields to my secret place. I would stay out all night sometimes, staring up at the night sky and wish some alien spacecraft would beam me up and take me on an adventure through the stars. Then, in the morning I would go back. My father would be crashed out on the sofa, or sometimes he would make it to his bed. When he woke up later, he would say nothing, just clean up the mess and be extra nice to me for a few days."

"That must have been scary, for a kid."

"In a way, it's what gave me a love of nature, of biology. My friends were the plants and the animals, and the stars were my dreams." Jann shrugged. "Ahh... I'm getting soppy. I'm sure you're not really interested in hearing about my screwed up childhood."

Nills didn't reply and remained quiet for a time. Finally he shifted in his seat, leaned in closer to Jann and, in a low voice, said. "The family of Nills Langthorp has tried to contact me."

Jann felt a wave of emotion wash over her and she gathered him up in her arms and held him tight. She had always feared this might happen. In truth, she knew it was only a matter of time.

THE COLONY HAD, for some time, adopted a policy of open and transparent communications with the public back on Earth. It had been envisaged as a first-line defense strategy —open themselves up to the world, be accessible and get the people on their side. It helped that Rachel and Xenon were masters at picking the right stories to focus on. The message was controlled, managed and massaged to present the colony, and its colonists, as people you could relate to. They no longer referred to the inhabitants as clones or Betas or Hybrids. They were all simply colonists. The stories were about everyday life in the colony: the trials and tribulations, the ups and downs, the hope and fears. In reality, it was a kind of propaganda.

They broadcast as much as they could over X-band so anyone on Earth with a big enough dish could receive it. This resulted in a number of enthusiastic amateurs relaying all this information via the Internet out to the broader world. By now there were thousands of media channels back on Earth dedicated to dissecting and discussing everything that the Colony transmitted.

Recently, they had been putting out more and more stories about their fears for the colony with the arrival of Xaing Zu Industries, COM, and other planned missions. As a strategy, it worked. People started to question the motives of these corporations, and how they would treat the colonists. So the propaganda war that they now waged mattered. If communications stopped when COM arrived then at least Earth would know that something was not right. How much all of this effort helped in the fight for the colonists to keep control was debatable. In reality it probably didn't matter to the likes of COM one way or the other. They were going to do whatever they wanted and the colonists were powerless to stop them.

But this openness also had some unexpected repercussions. Now that they were open for all to communicate with, the families of original colonists, who they assumed were dead, found that clones existed of their loved ones. Identical in every way to the person they had lost. It raised hitherto unknown emotional and ethical issues for both parties. This communication had to be handled very delicately. Some embraced it, some retreated from it, and some on Earth simply reviled it as being the devil's work, advocating that the entire colony on Mars should be razed to the ground, with everybody in it.

JANN DETACHED herself from Nills and looked at him. "What are you going to do?"

"I don't know. To be honest, I'm a little confused. I mean, I'm not who they think I am. I'm not here to satisfy someone's morbid curiosity."

"You don't have to engage if you don't want to, Nills."

"I know, but... I have memories of them... I really don't know who I am."

Jann moved closer again and held his hand in hers. "For what it's worth, I know who you are. Someone I'm very glad I found."

Nills gave a wide grin. "Now, you *are* getting soppy." He

stood up. "Come on, let's try and get some sleep. There's nothing to gain from dwelling on things that have no clear answer. We're here now, so we may as well get on with it."

"You go, I'm going to sit here for a while longer."

He kissed her on the forehead. "Okay, but don't try and work it all out tonight. There's much we don't know yet. Too many uncertainties lie ahead."

5

XAING ZU

Over the next few sols, as they counted down to the arrival of the Chinese expedition, messages began to flow back and forth between the colony and the orbiting craft as arrangements were being made for the landing. Much was already known to the colonists about the history and scale of Xaing Zu Industries. They were a global industrial conglomerate, with interests in space exploration, biotech, mining and more. They had a long-standing helium 3 lunar extraction operation, and also controlled over ninety percent of the global stockpile of many rare-earth resources. Their decision to land near Colony One had been made long before they had lifted off from Earth. And all communication, hitherto, had been polite and efficient, if somewhat clandestine. They gave nothing away about their mission, other than on a need to know basis.

JANN, Nills and Xenon, along with a few other colonists that constituted the reception party, were in full EVA suits standing out on the planet's surface, well back from the proposed landing site. They had assembled there around an hour ago, and were now all craning their necks to try and spot the telltale streak in the sky that would be the Chinese Mars Descent Vehicle. It should be currently ploughing its way through the upper atmosphere, hurtling towards the surface. All going well, it would land in a few minutes.

"There." Xenon pointed over across the horizon.

They all watched as the speck in the distance grew in size and formed into the recognizable shape of a Mars lander. Finally, its descent slowed as retro-thrusters kicked in, then it was lost in an enormous cloud of dust and sand. They had landed successfully. The first craft to do so since the ill-fated ISA mission. The one that brought Dr. Jann Malbec to this place, many Earth years ago.

"Okay, let's saddle up and go say hello," said Nills. They clambered onboard one of the colony rovers and Jann took the controls. She started up the machine, and headed in the direction of the slowly dissipating dust cloud. As she drew closer, Jann could see just how big it was, maybe three times the size of the now destroyed ISA lander.

"That's a sizable bit of machinery," she said to no one in particular.

"Well there are eight of them. And fully fueled to lift off again in a hurry," said Nills.

"They're not taking any chances, are they?" she said, as she slowed the rover down.

"Would you? To be fair, they don't know what to expect on the ground. We could turn out to be a ravenous horde of cannibals," said Nills.

Jann pulled up around twenty meters from the base of the craft. A thin cloud of dust still shrouded the enormous lander, giving it a ghostly aura. On her left she could see the second colony rover, driven by Anika, pull up close by. On Jann's right another enormous plume of dust kicked up from the planet's surface as Xenon brought the flying bed in to land. They were all in position. Nothing to do now but wait.

"THEY'RE TAKING THEIR TIME. No sign of any activity." Nills began to fiddle with the comms unit on the rover. "Gizmo, are you sure this is the correct frequency for two-way with the lander?"

"Are you seriously asking me that question?" The robot had made its own way out from Colony One to meet up with the reception party, at Jann's request. She felt safer having it around.

"Wait... look."

On the side of the gleaming white craft a hatch cracked open. It was low and wide, and pushed out from the main structure as it gently rose upward revealing a low, wide gap. From this, a platform extended slowly, giving the impression of a balcony on the side of the craft. From within the shadows of the ship six taikonauts stepped out. They wore gleaming white EVA suits, all identical. The platform slowly started to descend.

"I have to admit that's pretty slick. I feel like we're being visited by a technologically superior race," said Nills. "Okay, well it's time to get our game faces on, let's go"

They clambered out on to the surface and stood for a while watching the taikonauts slowly descend. One waved at them. They all waved back. Jann wondered what they must look like to these clean sleek spacefarers. A band of rag-tag colonists, with their battered and dirty EVA suits, and strange space-trash transport. Like a Mad Max on Mars, probably.

GIZMO MOVED UP BESIDE JANN. "If I am not mistaken, and let us face it, I never am—they have brought a robot with them."

"Where? I just see six crew and some equipment on the platform."

Before Gizmo had time to answer, the elevator came to a rest on the surface, a small plume of dust kicking up from its base. The taikonauts stepped off and waited, while what looked like a stack of equipment unfolded itself and perambulated out on the dusty Martian soil. It was a quadruped, about waist high, with a small head that seemed to be scanning all around it.

"I see it," Jann said as she watched the machine advance.

"It is scanning us, multiple spectrum analysis. Hmmm... that is interesting."

"What is?"

"It just said hello to me. Its name is Yutu, which means *jade rabbit* in Mandarin."

"I don't know which is the most surprising, the fact that they have a robot with them or the fact that you know Mandarin."

"I have been studying many of the Chinese dialects, of which there are hundreds, in anticipation of this very event."

"I'm switching to broadcast, Gizmo." Jann tapped her wrist pad to change comms frequencies. In preparing for this they had agreed a common VHF channel to use for communications. It was old school but worked just as well on Mars as it did on Earth. Jann looked over at Nills and nodded. The three of them then walked forward to greet the new arrivals. Gizmo followed behind.

"Welcome to Mars," said Jann.

One of the taikonauts waved. "It is an honor to be here. I am Jing Tzu, commander of the Xaing Zu Industries Mars Exploration Mission, and on behalf of our crew we are humbled to be among you on this momentous day."

Nills stepped forward and extended a hand. "I am Nills Langthorp, pleased to meet you." They shook hands. "And this is Dr. Jann Malbec."

"Ah... Dr. Malbec, we have heard so much about you."

Jann simply shook his hand and nodded. The other taikonauts all hung back and said nothing. Jann noticed that they were distracted by the Martian vista, preferring instead to look all around them rather than focus on the colonists. Yet she felt they had a distinctly military air about them.

The robot, Yutu, sat down on its hind legs, like a big cat, beside the commander. Gizmo was studying it intently, its head twitching as it probed. Yutu looked to be doing the same thing. It reminded Jann of two dogs meeting for the first time. She half expected them to start sniffing each others' butts.

"We can assist carrying your equipment and supplies on to the transport," Nills waved an arm behind him at the two colony rovers and the bed.

"Thank you for your kindness and consideration but we can manage it on our own."

"No, I insist, it's no problem." Nills nodded to the other colonists and they moved forward to help carry the boxes that were now being emptied onto the surface by the crew. This provoked an immediate reaction from the Chinese. They stood together, blocking the way, one held his hand out signaling for them to stop. The broadcast channel broke into a chorus of excited Mandarin chatter. The colonists halted, and looked over at Nills. Jing Tzu turned back to his crew and jabbered in a sharp authoritative manner. This seemed to calm them all down a bit. He returned to face Nills and the colonists with his hands in the air. "Please accept my apologies, we are all a bit anxious from our journey."

Nills nodded. "That's okay, we'll leave you to carry your own equipment, then."

Jing Tzu bowed. "You are most gracious." He returned to his crew and started gesticulating wildly.

Jann flipped her comms to private. "They're a bit jumpy."

"Understandable," said Nills.

"I wonder what's in the boxes that's so important?"

"Who knows? Maybe it's a year's supply of fine whiskey."

"How do we know they're not full of weapons?"

"We don't."

"Well, we can't risk them bringing in concealed weapons." Jann stepped forward towards Jing Tzu, and flipped her comms to broadcast. "Commander, it was agreed that we cannot allow weapons inside the colony. Once we are there you will allow us to conduct a thorough and complete search of your equipment. Is this acceptable to you?"

Jing Tzu nodded. "Yes of course, we understand."

"Very well. When you're ready we can move out."

Jing Tzu turned back to his crew and looked to be explaining this new procedure to them. It was met with confusion by the others, like they were trying to decide something. Then they removed two boxes from the stack and returned them to the craft. Jann and the other colonists watched all this unfold. When the cart was repacked, Jing

Tzu signaled that they were ready. Nills climbed up to the cockpit of the bed and fired it up. He waved to Jann.

"I'll see you all back there." With that, the thrusters fired up a great plume of dust as it rose into the air and flew off across the crater. Jann stood beside Xenon as they watched the Chinese board the waiting rovers.

She turned to Xenon, her back to the rovers. "Did you see them putting those boxes back in the craft?"

"Yes, I did."

"Weapons. And lots of them."

"It would seem so."

Gizmo whizzed by them, with the Chinese robot Yutu following close behind. Jann was not sure what they were doing, racing? Seeing how fast each other could go? Or was Gizmo being chased? It was hard to know what went on in the mind of a robot.

Yutu broke away and joined the Chinese contingent. Gizmo looped around and headed over to where Jann and Xenon were.

"I see you've found a new friend. Gizmo."

"That machine is not my friend, Jann. It is a feebleminded conglomeration of spare parts. I do not like that robot."

6

ASTERX

Xaing Zu Industries and the Colony One Mars consortium were not the only corporations planning missions to the red planet. But of the others, only one stood any real hope of achieving such an enormous undertaking, and that was the asteroid mining company, AsterX. It was headed up by the charismatic tech billionaire, Lane Zebos, who was currently looking out a window in the giant rotating torus of the AsterX space station. From this vantage point, he could see the central axle of the mining facility stretch out above him, and the dark brooding form of the kilometer wide asteroid that was grafted onto its terminus. All across the surface of this primeval rock was dotted robotic mining installations, like spiky metallic carbuncles.

Some years ago, his company had conceived of an audacious plan to capture a near-earth asteroid (NEA) and park it in orbit around the planet where it could then be mined for all it was worth—which turned out to be a considerable amount, as it had a core rich in platinum.

But that was then, and soon Lane Zebos was looking

around for the next challenge. His searches kept returning him to that great swath of rubble that spread itself out between the orbits of Mars and Jupiter—the asteroid belt. But this would be a mammoth undertaking, a bridge too far, even for an asteroid mining company with the skill and experience of AsterX. It was only when the colony on Mars popped back onto everyone's radar, revealing itself to be very much alive, that a mission strategy began to formulate in his mind. One which might just be possible. And the first leg of that strategy was get to the red planet.

Lane looked up at the central truss of the mining station. Attached to it, and now coming into full view as the torus rotated, was the AsterX Mars transit craft, ready to embark. All they needed was the official mission authorization from the State Department, so that they would be in compliance with the Outer Space Treaty. Lane glanced at his watch, *this is cutting it very fine*, he thought. To take his mind off the waiting, he pulled a cigar canister from the top pocket of his shirt, unscrewed the cap, and slid a thick Cuban Cohiba out into the palm of his hand. But he didn't light it. That would be later. Instead he brought it up to his nose and inhaled the deep redolent aroma.

"You're not planning on lighting that up?"

Lane looked over at Chuck Goldswater, his chief technical officer, and gave him a wink. He slid the fat smoke back into its metal sarcophagus and returned it to his top pocket.

"Well now, that depends."

"You think the scrubbers will handle the heart attack they're going to get if you kick that thing off in here?"

Lane smiled. "When I actually get to light this bad boy

up then I couldn't give a damn about what the systems think of air quality." He raised an extended finger at Chuck. "That's one of the great things about being the boss. I get to do what I like."

Chuck laughed. "Ha, maybe so, but it's still a filthy habit."

"And you're a philistine, with no understanding of the deep pleasures of smoking tobacco. Granted, it's a dying art form, practiced now only by the true connoisseur." He made a kind of a flourish with his hand.

"You're full of shit, Lane."

"Anyway, you know I only partake when something truly worthy merits it." Lane sat back down into a well upholstered white leather seat, and swung it around a few degrees to get a better view of the universe gently rotating outside.

"You think we'll get the oversight we need?" Chuck slumped back into his chair.

"We'll know soon enough."

"It's ridiculously antiquated when you think about it, the Outer Space Treaty and the need for private operators to get some government rubber stamp before we can do any mission."

"Yeah, I know. It frustrating. As far as I can see, it just gives them an opportunity to meddle and look important."

"Life was easier before COM went and sued the ISA. Back then this would just have been a formality. Now everybody is running scared."

"Yeah, Mars has turned into a political and legal minefield."

Chuck looked at this watch. "What's keeping them? How long do they need?"

"Patience. We've waited this long, a half hour more isn't

going to make any difference." Lane stood up, walked over to the window, and looked out at the massive asteroid that they had tamed. He considered the problems with the Outer Space Treaty, of which there were many. Under its current guise, there was nothing to stop another company just attaching itself to the far side of the AsterX asteroid and mining it. Not that anybody would, they were an exclusive club and had all, more or less, agreed on a set of unwritten rules. Nevertheless, everyone conceded that the treaty was grossly out of date. Formulated back in the late 60s, before Armstrong even put a boot print on the moon, it served, at least, to establish some international rules for the exploration of space and, more importantly, for the exploitation of its resources. But back when it was signed, the concept of a private company making it into space was laughable. But, to their credit, they had to consider that the possibility could exist sometime in the future, even if it was fanciful.

In short, no country could lay claim to any object in space. So when the US flag was hammered into the surface of the Moon, it wasn't to proclaim it as the fifty-first state. However, under the terms, you could dig a hole in it, and whatever you dug up you could keep. This was the basis that AsterX, and a bunch of other companies like them, operated under. The problem for private companies, though, was they needed oversight from a national government before they could do anything in space. So politics entered the arena. In Lane's mind it was almost medieval. To venture forth and explore needed the equivalent of a royal seal.

Of course private corporations were lobbying hard to remove the need for national oversight, but after all the shenanigans up on Mars, and the subsequent high-profile court case by COM, there were those who argued that national oversight was needed now more than ever. Others countered that what was really needed was a truly independent body to be set up to oversee and arbitrate all space exploration. With the rush to Mars now in full swing, the need to get clarity was even more urgent. To this end, a revision to the original 1967 Outer Space Treaty was to be discussed, and hopefully ratified, at a special UN session due to take place in a few months time.

But this was of no use to Lane Zebos and AsterX. They had to do it the old fashioned way, and that meant greasing the palms of a select number of gray and anonymous mandarins in the key positions in government. A slow and frustratingly tedious process whose ultimate climax was, this very moment, being played out behind closed doors in the State Department.

So all Lane could do was wait until the session ended and the fate of the AsterX Mars mission would be revealed, but he wasn't expecting any surprises. The right moves had been made, so it should be a simple rubber stamping. Yet, you never truly knew for sure. Something might yet upset the fall of the dominoes that AsterX had so carefully set up.

So, for now the cigar was staying firmly in his top pocket.

LANE GLANCED over to the far side of the room to see Dr. Jane Foster, the chief medical officer, step onto the floor from the ceiling tunnel connecting this section of the torus with the central body of the mining station. It was a tricky transition from zero gravity at the center to one third G at the outer edge of the torus. The connecting tube was one of four spokes, with a ladder running inside its length. The trick was to enter it feet first at the start so you were oriented correctly when the centrifugal force began to kick in. Some people would make the mistake of entering head first, like climbing a ladder, only to realize they were effectively upside down when it was time to exit. It was a mistake you only made once.

Lane nodded to her as a greeting. She nodded back, then moved over and began to fix herself a coffee from the small galley. Finally she sat down beside them in one of the luxurious leather seats, tucked her feet up under her and sipped her drink. "Any word?"

The both looked at her in silence.

"I'll take that as a no, then."

Lane simply nodded.

"Oh, a bit of news for you. Xaing Zu Industries just landed on Mars."

"When?" said Chuck.

"About six hours ago. The news just came in, direct from Colony One. It's on their feed."

"How is that going down with them?" said Lane.

"Hard to say, it was just a one line announcement."

Chuck jotted down a quick calculation on the tablet he was holding. "If that's the case then COM will be... let's see... fourteen days behind, give or take."

"Should that not be sols?" Lane gave him a sideways grin.

"Sols, days, who cares. It just means we're going to be very late to the party."

"Well, that might be a good thing. Plenty of time for the other guests to get acquainted."

Chuck laughed. "Ha, that's one way of putting it. I would say, at this rate there may be nothing for us to visit, even if we do get the go ahead."

Lane said nothing, just extracted the cigar canister from

his top pocket again and repeated the same examination procedure as before.

"You're not thinking of lighting that up in here?" said Dr. Foster.

Lane just gave her a sideways smile.

"As the medical doctor assigned to this mission I would be negligent in my duties if I didn't inform you that inhaling tobacco smoke is a serious health risk." She sipped her coffee.

"I would say that going to Mars is a serious health risk." Lane held up the cigar. "This, on the other hand, is an art form."

Before the merits of cigar smoking could be discussed any further, an alert flashed on the main lounge monitor. They all stopped talking and focused on the screen. A head and shoulders materialized. It was Jake Lester, from the legal team, sitting at his desk back on Earth.

"Good news, the mission to salvage the ISA Odyssey Mars transit craft is a go."

The executive lounge on the AsterX mining station erupted into cheers, and high-fives, and hugs.

"Do we get to land?" Lane broke away from the celebrations and directed his question to Jake. There was a slight time delay as the message wound its way back to Earth.

"Yes."

More cheers and air punches ensued.

"There's just one caveat."

They stopped, and looked at the screen.

"You must do everything you can to bring home the ISA crewmember, Dr. Jann Malbec."

7

SEARCH

After a brief period of stilted pleasantries, the Xaing Zu expedition was assigned to an accommodation pod and left to themselves. Nevertheless, the pod was monitored by hidden cameras that fed back to the workstations in the central dais of the biodome. Gizmo had been charged with the task of monitoring their activity. So far, it all looked to be innocuous, at least on the surface. During the sols that followed, the Chinese settled in to a routine of survey and analysis of the colony's biology and infrastructure.

They had initially left two of their crew still onboard the landing craft, and from Jann's discussions with their commander, Jing Tzu, she ascertained that this was to ensure the craft was manned and ready to take off at any time. Of the six that now resided in the colony Jann had reckoned that two were geneticists/biologists and the rest seemed to be more military. This latter group spent their time surveying the facility, checking layouts, airlocks, power, operations, life support and a host of other inventory tasks. The biologists had taken up residence in the medlab where

Jann had given them some space to work in. She had also gone into great detail with them about the various genetically engineered biomes that populated the colony and made it function. But it was clear to all that what they were truly looking for was the genetic understanding of what gave Jann and all the other colonists their remarkable healing abilities and youthful demeanor.

The Chinese, to their credit, had tried to work within the restrictions placed on them by the colonists, but with each passing sol they pushed at the boundaries. There had been a lot of friction and even a punch up or two, but for the most part they tried to do what they came here to do without killing anyone, at least so far. Nonetheless, time was running out for them. No doubt there were powerful people behind this enterprise applying pressure on Jing Tzu to come up with the goods. And the situation was going to get increasingly more difficult for all concerned once COM set foot in the colony. Because as soon as that happened, they would legally own it, and everything belonging to it. Jing Tzu and Xaing Zu Industries would be booted out and their mission would fail. All this Jann knew, but she also knew that a cornered rat was a dangerous animal, ready to strike out. And Jing Tzu was being backed into an impossible corner.

JANN WAS CURRENTLY in the medlab, checking on a new data set she had recently received, when Jing Tzu entered. He looked over at one of the Chinese techs and said something in Mandarin that Jann could not understand.

"You're wasting your time, you know." Jann directed her comment at the commander. He looked at her with an air of disdain.

"I keep telling you," Jann continued, "the knowledge you're looking for no longer exists."

"So you keep saying." Jing Tzu finally managed.

"Yet you keep looking. And now time is running out, isn't it?" Jann was baiting him.

Jing Tzu stood for a moment and considered her, then sat down on the other side of the bench where Jann was working.

"You could help us. You could let us conduct some tests on the colonists here."

"That's not going to happen. You know that. If you were to start that, then all hell would break loose. Remember these colonists have already been through one tough fight to get their freedom so they don't take kindly to being pushed around. As it is there are those who are itching to kick you all out onto the planet's surface and leave you there."

Jing Tzu sighed. "They must understand that we are here to help you. We are not the enemy."

Jann laughed. "Bullshit. You're here for one thing and one thing only. We all know that."

"Then help us."

"By letting you experiment on the colony population?"

"Just tests, to get an understanding of the underlying physiological changes that have occurred here."

"You just don't get it, do you? This will not help you find what you are looking for. The Janus bacterium that causes this... physical transformation was eradicated a long time ago." Jann waved her hand in the air. "Which is lucky for you because if it did then some of your crew would be raging psychopaths, out to kill everyone in their path."

Jing Tzu abruptly stood up and pointed a finger at Jann. "You are a fool if you think this is all there is to it. COM are landing in less than a week, don't think they will be as accommodating as we are. You are going to need some friends when they get here, because *they* are going to find it with or without your help. So I suggest you go and think about that for a while." He walked out of the medlab leaving Jann to contemplate the shit storm that was coming down the track.

THIS ENCOUNTER with Jing Tzu had left Jann feeling distracted, but she tried to put it out of her mind and focus on her work. For a long time she had been cataloging the many GM bacteria that were utilized within the colony environment, everything from soil processing to fuel manufacture. A good deal of this work had been done already, with the help of scientists back on Earth. Jann had built up an extensive network of academics interested in the development of the Mars colony. She had just received a theoretical analysis on how a particular bacterium could be modified to improve CO_2 breakdown. She tried to reread the paper but could not keep her concentration for long.

It didn't help that Nills had had to return to Colony Two. Some technical emergency with one of the thermal heat exchangers that only he could fix. Perhaps that's what made her so tetchy, made her bait Jing Tzu like that. Nills had left that morning, on the bed, flying off across the crater in a cloud of dust, leaving Jann to contend with the ever invasive investigations of the Chinese crew. He vowed to return before COM landed, as that would be a pivotal moment. In accordance with the ruling from the International Court of Arbitration, once they set foot in the colony it would automatically return to their ownership. Since the Chinese were currently operating under the public domain legality that had been established by the ISA, they were going to get booted out by COM—first item on the agenda. How would they react to this, considering the pressure they were under to source the Janus bacteria? This was a question that greatly troubled the entire colony. Would they go quietly? Would they try and negotiate with COM? Or would a fight begin? And where would the colonists fall in all of this? What would happen to them?

HER THOUGHTS WERE INTERRUPTED by Gizmo whizzing into the medlab.

"Jann, could you possibly spare me a moment of your time?" Jann looked at the quirky robot. She understood what it was really saying to her. *I have something important to reveal, in private, away from prying eyes.*

"Sure. Let's take a walk." She rose from her workbench and they headed out of the medlab towards the biodome. They zigzagged their way though the rows of hydroponics and finally entered one of the food processing rooms. These were small landers attached to the main biodome used for sorting and packing of harvested produce. They had chosen this place because of its isolation and also because the processing machines made quite a racket when switched on. Jann closed the door behind them and looked over at Gizmo.

A light flickered on from Gizmo's breastplate and a video image was projected on the wall. It was an aerial view of the surface of Mars.

"When Nills was making his trip to Colony Two this morning he detoured over the Chinese lander. This is what he saw."

Jann watched as the craft came into view. The video was taken from quite high up, Nills had obviously decided to be as unobtrusive as possible. Then it zoomed in on the base of the craft. On the surface two small mobile units could be seen parked close to the foot of the craft. Mounted on these were what looked to Jann to be artillery weapons.

"Nills reckons that these are PEP's. Pulsed Energy Projectile weapons, with considerable range. He asked me to contact him as soon as you have seen this video. I will try and make the connection now."

A new picture-in-picture image was projected on the wall. It was Nills facing the camera.

"Jann, you saw that, did you?"

"Yeah, what do you make of it?"

"It looks like you were right. They're carrying a lot of very sophisticated weaponry."

"Jesus, they're armed to the teeth."

"Yeah, so I'd say they're here for the long haul. They're not leaving without a fight."

Jann looked at the grainy image for a moment, digesting the implications of this discovery. Xaing Zu Industries had come prepared to battle it out if necessary. And it was safe to assume they had even more weapons, probably handheld.

"Nills, you'd better get back here as soon as you can."

"Yeah, once I can get this heat exchanger sorted out."

"Okay, but don't leave it too long. We need to formulate a plan on how best to deal with the possibility of a firefight between COM and the Chinese."

"I know." Nills signed off and Gizmo stopped the projection.

"Have you had any luck hacking into their comms, Gizmo?"

"None. Other than I established that their systems are encrypted using quantum entanglement."

"What does that mean?"

"It is impossible to crack."

Jann considered this for a moment. "We have grossly underestimated them, Gizmo."

"It would seem so."

"It now looks like a war is about to start."

8

FIRE

Lieutenant Dan Ma of the Xaing Zu Mars mission scanned the row of EVA suits that hung from makeshift hangers along one wall of the accommodation pod that the colonists had assigned them. Having located his suit, he reached into the side section and released the clip on the concealed compartment. He withdrew a small electronic unit and flicked the switch. All cameras and audio devices within this general area would now be jammed. It was a precaution, but one worth taking. Next he withdrew a bulkier unit, examined it, and placed it carefully inside the pocket of his flight suit. With COM due to land very soon, and their own mission no further along in accomplishing their primary objective, it was time to take assertive action.

It was mid-afternoon and the colonists were busy with their various tasks. Mostly they would be in the biodome tending to food production. It seemed to be their primary job, that and the maintenance of life support. In many ways, he admired them. Particularly considering what they had already been through. To survive up here, on this godforsaken rock, took a special kind of person. One who understood the fragility of life, who tended to its needs with diligence and dedication. Nothing was ever taken for granted. You survived by the sweat of your brow. It was life on the edge, one false move and it could be extinguished in a heartbeat. But time was running out, and there was no more room for sentimentality.

Some of the colonists eyed him with suspicion as he passed. They did not like them being here. He couldn't blame them, if they only knew what was in store they would have never let them inside in the first place. He ignored their looks and continued deeper into the biodome. Over the last few sols he and his team had planned for this moment to have the maximum effect. They had poured over the facilities schematics, probing, testing, finding the perfect spot to install the device where it would give them the best chance of success. They had ascertained that the optimum location was at the very far end of the biodome, beside a number of the food-processing pods, where a lot of storage crates had been stacked.

He had to circle around a few times so as to ensure the area was empty of colonists when he arrived. On the third approach he got his chance. He ducked in behind the crates and withdrew the device from his pocket. He set the timer and then carefully placed it near the center of the stack. Job done, time to leave. He absolutely did not want to be here when this thing went off.

~

NILLS HAD BEEN AWAY for several sols, and still not returned. So, with the imminent arrival of COM, Jann was getting anxious. She sat at the workstation in the medlab trying to concentrate on her work, something to take her mind off the uncertainty that lay ahead. She was alone in the lab, save for Gizmo, who was preparing DNA samples for her. A tediously repetitive task that the robot was ideally suited for. The Chinese had brought a DNA sequencer with them and Jann had decided to put it to good use. She had struggled with much of her analysis through lack of this type of equipment. Now that it was here she would make good use of it. The Chinese lab techs were not around, the place was hers. Xenon had observed them leaving Colony One early that morning, ostensibly to retrieve more supplies from their craft. They would need to be checked and searched on return, before anything was allowed into the facility. Xenon had been designated to this responsibility, one in which he was admirably suited due to his imposing physique. He would ensure that no weapons were brought on site.

But, there was still no definitive answer from COM as to their expected landing time. They were already in orbit, and had been for some time now. But they were being very circumspect in their communication. The colonists had planned to meet them on the surface, a welcoming party of sorts, like they did with the Xaing Zu mission. But, COM were not interested in this, in fact they seemed openly hostile to it. This irked Jann no end. Who did they think they were? They had an arrogance that implied that the colonists were not important in the Colony One Mars consortium's worldview. Jann reckoned that this was probably true. It angered her, and the more she thought about it the angrier she got. Who the hell did they think they were? How were they even allowed to set foot on this planet after all they had done? The destruction of the original ISA mission was due, in no small part, to the treachery of COM and its agent Annis Romanov. Not to mention the horror of the cloning tanks in Colony Two being a result of their vision for genetic research. Although, one could argue, that COM was not in direct control of the insane Dr. Vanji. Nevertheless, once they were aware of what was going on up here, they openly embraced it.

But what angered Jann the most was the fact that the courts on Earth saw fit to hand it all back to them. It was a morally repugnant concept to Jann, which reinforced in her the feeling that Earth had abandoned them, once again.

"Jann... Jann."

"Uh... Gizmo, sorry, I was just... somewhere else."

"Your hand, it is bleeding."

"What?" Jann looked down. She had been so distracted by her thoughts that she had accidentally cut herself with the scalpel. She opened her fingers and let the blood drop on to the workbench. She wrapped a bandage around the hand to staunch the bleeding. "Any word from Nills?"

"None. Would you like me to open a communications channel with Colony Two?"

"No. It's okay. Leave him be. He'll contact us when he's ready. Although he's cutting it fine. COM are due to land soon."

"Very well."

Jann was just finished tending to her hand when an ear-splitting klaxon blasted out from all corners of the colony facility.

"What the hell is that?"

"Fire alarm. Emanating in the biodome, far end, near the food processing pods."

"Shit, fire... come on, let's go."

They raced out of the medlab heading for the biodome. Fire in an enclosed environment such as Colony One could be disastrous if not extinguished quickly. If left to grow, it would suck in all the oxygen, and had the potential to seriously compromise life support. Every colonist and astronaut's worst fear was fire. You died, not from burning, but suffocation.

Others were also racing towards the source of the fire, having been trained to drop everything and focus on putting out any fire that started as quickly as humanly possible. By the time Jann and Gizmo had reached the food processing pods, it looked like the entire population of the colony was already there. The storage crates stacked along the inner wall of the biodome were completely ablaze. Flame blossomed out from the center of the stack and the air was filled with the oddly sweet smell of burning bio-plastic. Jann could see Xenon marshaling a group of colonists with water hoses. He shouted and waved as they wrestled with the apparatus. Finally a jet of frothy H2O burst out and the colonists began to douse the flames. It didn't take long to get it under control, and within a few minutes the drama was over. As the colonists began to gather up the firefighting equipment Jann and Xenon tentatively approached the smoldering pile.

"How the hell did that happen?"

"I don't know." Xenon picked up a lump of melted plastic. "This stuff takes a lot to burn. You would need a sustained flame to get it going like that."

Jann toed something on the ground, hidden in a mound of debris. She reached down, and with the help of a pen she had pulled from her pocket, she prodded the unit free from the pile, all the time covering her mouth and nose to try and lessen the effects of the smoke, and the sickly sweet smell of burnt bio-plastic. She poked the pen through a loop of charred wire that protruded from the unit and held it up. Xenon looked over at her. "What have you got there?"

Jann shuffled through the group of colonists that were busy cleaning up the mess, holding the unit out in front of her like she had discovered a dead rat and was disposing of it. She laid it down at the edge of the path just as Xenon came over. They both knelt down and Jann started knocking the dust and ash from the unit.

"I could be mistaken, Xenon, but this does *not* look like food to me." She picked it up and examined it. It was small, about the size of a pack of cigarettes, on one side a charred circuit board was attached to a rectangular container which was split and broken.

"You think this is an incendiary device, you think somebody started this fire deliberately?" Xenon was now inspecting the device.

"Sure looks that way. But why would anyone want to do that?"

Xenon just looked at her blankly.

"We need to contact Nills, maybe he can shed some light on who might have built this." She handed the device to Gizmo who took it gently in its metal hand. "Can you get some images off to Nills and explain to him what happened."

"Will do," said Gizmo.

By now some of the other colonists had spotted them and came over. "Is someone trying to burn the place down? Have we got some crazy pyromaniac on our hands now? Jesus, that's all we need."

Xenon looked around. "It's okay, let's just get this place sorted."

He started getting the colonists busy again, issuing directions and organizing them into cleanup groups.

"Jann, may I have a word with you?" said Gizmo

She looked at the quirky droid. Generally when Gizmo said may I have a word with you, it was never good.

"Sure, Gizmo. Let's go over here a bit and we can talk."

They moved off away from the throng of colonists who were now busy sweeping, picking and sorting through the mess that was left after the fire. "What is it, Gizmo?"

"I cannot seem to raise a communication channel with Colony Two."

"Has the fire damaged comms?"

"No. That would be highly improbable."

"Then what?"

"I am being prevented from accessing it."

"Prevented?"

"Yes, blocked. I cannot access a comms channel and what's more, I cannot access any of the Colony One systems."

"Are you serious?"

"I assure you Jann, this is not one of my attempts at humor."

Before Jann could interrogate Gizmo any further, a colonist came rushing into the crowd. "Can someone give me a hand? The entrance door is jammed and I can't get open, I need some help."

Ever since Jann had been in Colony One, and that was several years, she had never seen the tunnel door to the biodome closed, save for one time when she herself had forced it closed, to prevent the demented Decker from beating her head in. So, if the door was closed then someone had to have closed it—deliberately.

"We'll give you a hand. Gizmo come with us." They dashed through the biodome to the far side and Jann could see the door shut tight. She threw her weight behind the locking wheel but it was stuck even with Gizmo and the other colonist helping her, there was no moving the wheel. *What the hell is going on?* she thought.

By now others had gathered around, and a sense of entrapment was beginning to build. They took turns to try and open it, but it refused to budge no matter how much muscle power was brought to bear on the locking mechanism.

Xenon arrived with a party of colonists. "What's going on"?

"The door's jammed, we're locked in, there's no other way out of here," said one of the colonists.

"I think Xaing Zu have locked us in here deliberately," said another.

"What? Why would they do that?" The colonists were confused.

"Gizmo can't raise a comm channel or get access to any Colony One systems. The droid has been blocked."

"Oh shit, they're going to kill us all, gas us while we're all trapped in here." A sense of panic was beginning to build, as a number of them started to bang on the steel door.

"This is your fault." A colonist pointed an accusatory finger at Jann. "It was you who convinced us to allow them in. We should have never listened to you. Now we're all going to die."

Xenon moved in front of Jann and raised a hand. "This is not the time to lose your cool. That isn't helping anyone."

The colonists were panicking, banging the door, shouting. Things were becoming ugly.

"Attention." A disembodied voice echoed out from the overhead speakers and reverberated around the biodome. *"Please be calm. We have secured you in the biodome for your own protection. Do not be alarmed. You are safe in here while we negotiate this transition."*

"Screw you," a colonist shook her fist at the speaker. "Let us out of here, you bastards."

Xenon signaled to Jann and they took a short walk, out of earshot of the other colonists. "COM must have landed and Xaing Zu knew about it. My guess is the fire was a way to get us all in here. They knew our emergency fire protocols, knew we would all drop everything and run in to the biodome."

"But why?" Said Jann.

"To get us all out of the way while they prepare to defend the facility."

"They're not going to let COM have access, are they?"

"Unlikely."

"This is not good, Xenon."

"No. I fear we are trapped. They have tricked us, and now we are powerless to intervene."

9

COM

Of the three heat exchangers that provided power for Colony Two, only one now functioned, and that had broken down twice in the last month. Nills used the other units that were offline to scavenge parts, just so he could keep this one going. Systems were breaking down all the time. Already they had shut down significant areas within Colony Two, they simply did not have the resources to keep everything maintained. Worse, this technological disintegration was also being mirrored in the slow physical and mental degradation of the colonists.

Nills had hoped that the arrival of Xaing Zu and COM would bring with them sufficient supplies and spare parts to enable, at least, a partial rejuvenation of the colony. But what the Chinese brought with them was merely a drop in the bucket. Nills felt that they were just paying lip service to the requirements of the colonists, as if in reality, they were not that important. Perhaps he had been naive, as Jann had often said to him. *You're too nice. Nills. You believe that humans are genuinely good. But in my experience, everybody wants something, and it's generally not your well being.* He found it hard to be that cynical, even if there was a grain of truth in it. Yet, soon COM would land, if they hadn't already. It was hard to know as the communication was as sparse as it was terse. They had offered to bring supplies and badly needed spare parts. Hopefully they would be true to their word and Nills could get his hands on these, before everything went to rat-shit.

Nills checked the seals on the replacement pump one last time, and then nodded to Anika, who was monitoring the starters for the heat exchanger on the control panel.

"Can you try it again now?"

With that, Anika set the controls to activate the newly replaced pump and reroute pressure back into the turbine.

"Okay, here goes." She hit the switch, and slowly the turbine started spinning up. She gave Nills the thumbs up. He gathered up his tools and joined her over at the control board, checking stats on the readouts.

"Okay, it's back up again, but for how long, who knows. Anyway, let's close up shop here, and head back up to operations. We'll see if there's been any news on COM."

With the colony being low on power for the last while, the temperature inside had dropped noticeably. It didn't help that a sandstorm had been building outside, reducing the efficiency of the solar array field. If Nills and Anika hadn't managed to fix the heat exchanger they would be in real trouble. It seemed to Nills that the threat of these life-and-death scenarios were being overlooked in the climate of uncertainty that had enveloped the colony ever since the arrival of Xaing Zu. When Nills finally arrived in the operations room, he had wrapped himself up in a long brown coat that he had become very attached to. It was old and worn and how it came to be here, in the colony, or even how it came into his possession he had long forgotten.

Holburn looked up from his console when he spotted Nills entering. "Good work on that heat exchanger, not a moment too soon either. Storm is getting pretty bad out there. Any longer and we'd be running on fumes."

"Any word on COM?"

"Yes and no. They dropped out of orbit about two hours ago, but I've had no comms and no confirmation of touchdown."

"You think the sandstorm is affecting comms?"

"Possibly. It can do that, if it gets bad enough."

Nills sat down at the table and shoved his hands into his coat pockets to get some warmth back into them. "Did you try to contact Colony One and see if they've heard anything?"

"I can't get through to them either."

"This is not really going to plan, is it?"

Holburn looked over at Nills and shrugged. "Could be worse, maybe COM crash landed and everyone is dead."

Nills gave him back a sideways grin. "Problem solved, then."

"Oh, nearly forgot." Holburn passed a holo-tab over to Nills. "One message did come through, about an hour ago, from your friend, Lane Zebos, AsterX."

Nills picked up the tab and tapped an icon. It was a video message. Nills tapped again to bring it up on the main screen. It was a head and shoulders shot of the AsterX CEO inside their cramped spacecraft. Of all the expeditions en route to Mars these guys were definitely the poor cousins. But, they were also the least threatening, concerning themselves more with the mineralogy and the technical capabilities of Mars, and Colony Two in particular. Understandable, considering that they were a mining company. Where Jann, Xenon and the rest of the council had concerned themselves with countering the machinations of Xaing Zu and COM, Nills had found Lane Zebos to be more like himself. Interested in the technicalities of the colony: its functioning, its resources. They were also the only one of the three that took a deep interest in bringing what Nills had wanted in terms of equipment, supplies and spare parts. But since they were not seen as a direct threat, the council had spent very little time communicating with them, leaving it to Nills to deal with their queries. As a result Nills had built up a reasonably friendly relationship with Zebos, who was now on screen.

The good news is we have embarked with all of the items you have requested. Some are bit hard to come by, but where we couldn't source the exact item we have endeavored to acquire a substitute. I've also added in a little gift for you. You'll see it on the manifest attached. Nills started reading down through the list.

That's the good news. The bad news is we won't be in Mars orbit for another eight weeks, give or take. It took us a long time to secure the necessary oversight. But we're on our way now, so see you all in two months. That's it for now. Will keep you posted. The message ended.

Anika had entered the operations room as the Zebos message was on screen, and had taken a seat beside Nills. "So what's the *little gift,* then?"

Nills pushed the tab over to her and pointed to the last two lines on the manifest.

"Ten kilos of Blue Mountain coffee and a case of twenty-five year old Scotch." Anika read it aloud.

Nills smiled. "I, for one, cannot wait. I count the days until they land."

"What, nothing for the girls? You know, silk stockings, a few ounces of Coco Chanel, perhaps."

Nills took the tab back, looked at the list again, and spun it back to Anika, and pointed at an entry higher up in the manifest. It read, *5lbs Belgian Chocolates*. "Your favorite, if I'm not mistaken."

"Oooh..." said Anika.

"Hey guys, you'd better take a look at this." Holburn's fingers danced across the face of his control pad and a new image materialized on screen. A ghostly cloud of dust filled the monitor and from its center an image of a rover emerged, moving slowly towards them. The trio watched in silence for a few moments.

"That's outside the main airlock here in Colony Two."

"Yep, but that's not one of our rovers, too big."

"COM?" Said Nills.

They looked from one to the other. Then comms burst into life.

Colony Two, this is Commander Willem Kruger, of the Colony One Mars consortium, seeking permission to enter.

"Holy crap," said Anika. "What do we do?"

Nills stood up. "Goddammit, this was not part of the plan. This was not supposed to happen."

"What are they doing? Why didn't they contact us and let us know they were landing?" said Holburn.

"Because we would be better prepared. They want us off balance."

"So what do we do? Tell them the store is closed, come back tomorrow?" said Anika.

"No, it makes no difference whether it's now, tomorrow, next week. We have to face this sometime, may as well be now." Nills was on his feet now. "Holburn, tell them we're opening the airlock. Anika, you come with me. We'll gather up the reception party and meet them in the main entrance. Make sure everyone is armed."

Nills realized they had been thrown a curveball. What everyone thought COM would do, they had just gone and done the opposite.. He should have known not to trust them. They were trying to gain the upper hand and they knew that leaving them outside on the surface was not an option. At least not a very good one.

"Are you expecting trouble?" said Anika.

"You need to understand that as far as the people in that rover are concerned, they own this place, and everything in it. That includes us—you, me and everyone in here. So yeah, I'm expecting trouble if we don't do what they want."

By the time they got to the entrance cavern other colonists were beginning to gather. The COM rover had been left waiting outside the entrance airlock, as the colonists got themselves organized. Anika was now distributing weapons from one of the storage rooms at the back entrance cavern. These were mainly railguns, kept primed and ready for action.

"I want two up there, high on the gantry, one on each side. And two more at the back of the cavern, high up on those storage crates over there. Keep your weapons visible, let them see we're armed."

As the colonists left to take up their positions, others gathered round Nills and Anika who had taken up a central position facing the airlock entrance.

"Okay, let's do this." Nills tapped his earpiece to talk to Holburn, who was monitoring the situation from the operations room. "You can open the airlock now."

From inside the cavern they could hear the rumble of the exterior door opening to expose the inner airlock to the maelstrom outside. A few moments later they heard the rumble again to signify that the COM rover had now entered. A few tense moments passed as the volume within was repressurized and the dust and sand purged through the scrubbers.

Nills tapped his earpiece again. "Tell them to exit the rover inside the airlock before we open the door."

Nills looked up and around at the people he had positioned on high ground within the cavern.

"Okay, everyone ready?"

A chorus of *ready* echoed around the space. Nills turned back to face the door and tapped his earpiece again. "Okay Holburn, ready when you are."

Anxious moments passed as they waited, and waited. Finally they heard motors kick in as the inner airlock door started to rise to reveal six COM crew members in full EVA suits—all armed to the teeth.

"Holy crap," said Anika.

Nills raised his hand and stepped forward. Then one of the COM crew popped open his visor, and stepped forward.

"Welcome to Mars," said Nills. Then he pointed at them. "Now I would ask you to put down your weapons as they are not allowed inside the colony."

"I am commander Willem Kruger, and you are?"

"Nills Langthorp."

Kruger looked around the entrance cavern, spotting the elevated positions of the weapons that were trained on them.

"Ahh... The famous Nills Langthorp, in the flesh. Do you realize that you're a legend back on Earth?"

Nills took another step forward. "I would appreciate if you would put away those weapons."

Kruger smiled. "Let's not start off on the wrong foot. We were expecting a better welcome than this." He looked around at the assembled colonists, who were becoming decidedly twitchy.

"I think perhaps a little demonstration might be in order." With that he lifted a small handheld weapon and fired at one of the colonists high up in the gantry. A burst of incandescent brilliance strobed the cavern as the colonist was encased in a mesh of flashing light. He shook violently and then fell from his position down onto a plastic crate with a thump. This resulted in the colonists directing a hail of fire at the six COM crewmembers, who were also returning fire. All around Nills and Anika colonists were engulfed in flashing balls of plasma. The cavern reverberated with the sounds of shrieking and whoomp, whoomp from the weapons of the COM crew.

Nills shouted, "Stop, stop, cease fire."

The six COM crew stood exactly where they were, as if nothing had happened, the colonists' railguns having had absolutely no effect against the amour of their EVA suits. They stood and faced off against each other as the realization slowly sank in to the colonists that they were completely defenseless.

"Like I said, let's not start off on the wrong foot. There is nothing you have that can threaten us. So why don't you all just drop your weapons and behave. You'll find your fallen comrades to be just temporarily paralyzed, they'll come to —eventually."

Nills knew there was no point in fighting. They were totally outclassed. So he turned around to the colonists still standing. "Put down the weapons. Nothing will be gained by any more fighting." And he threw his own weapon on the ground in front of the commander. One by one the colonists followed suit. The battle was over. They had lost.

The COM mercenaries began to split them up into

groups and then started herding them back in to the main cavern in Colony Two, carrying their fallen comrades as they went. It was clear to Nills that COM had detailed knowledge of its layout. They knew where to go, how to get there and what to do to keep complete control of the situation. He was about to fall into line with the others when the commander came over and tapped his shoulder. Nills spun around.

"Mr. Langthorp. If you would be so kind as to follow me."

"Where to?"

"This way, into the rover. We're going on a little journey. There is someone who very much wants to meet you."

10

VANHOFF

Nills sat in the back of the rover as it bounced over the surface. Outside, the Martian world was obscured by a thick cloud of dust. The driver navigated through this impenetrable fog by virtue of a heads-up display overlaid across the entire front windscreen. The oncoming topography rendered itself in grainy detail like seeing the world through a old fashioned video game. To Nills, the machine had a distinct military design about it: sparse, utilitarian, and crammed with technical wizardry. Facing him, on the opposite side of the rover, Commander Kruger sat clutching a short but bulky weapon across his lap.

"Pulsed Energy Projectile, if I'm not mistaken." Nills nodded at the weapon. Kruger gave a sideways grin and gripped the weapon closer.

"Very good, right on the money. How did you know that?"

"I read about them. Interesting technology. Although, the ones I looked at needed a truck to carry them around."

Kruger held up the weapon and examined it like it was a

treasured possession. "Things have moved on a bit since then."

The problem with ballistic weapons in any space environment is similar to that in an aircraft with a pressurized cabin. There is a strong likelihood of puncturing the delicate fabric of the hull and suffering a catastrophic loss of internal pressure. The problem of course, is far greater in space because, at least with the aircraft you could technically still be alive while you plummeted to your death from 10,000 ft. In space however, you died almost instantly just from the decompression, not to mention lack of oxygen and sub-zero temperatures.

So when it became apparent to the powers that be that a different type of weapon would be required by any future spacefaring law enforcement agency, the task fell to DARPA to come up with a solution. Some argued that there should be no need for this sort of thing at all. Others said just keep it simple, and go back to using bows and arrows. But this didn't fit very well with the high-tech space exploration image.

As luck would have it, DARPA happened to have something that might fit the bill, something they had been working on for quite some time. It came about from the desire of terrestrial agencies for a non-lethal weapon. Something they could use in riots and general public disorder situations where killing the actual protagonists would be... well, overkill.

It was called a Pulsed Energy Projectile Weapon, or simple PEP. It utilized a high-energy laser pulse that created a small plasma explosion on impact. This explosion created an electromagnetic shock wave that stunned the target.

Because it relied on electrical energy rather than a projectile to get the job done, it could be used with relative safety in the enclosed confines of a space station, with little risk of puncturing a hole in the outer skin. Although, it would do a good job of frying any electronics that happened to be in the way.

So far so good. The only downside was it weighed in at a hefty 250kg, about the weight of three men, and needed a truck to carry it around. Nevertheless, their early developments were dusted off and over time it became lighter and deadlier. The variants that the COM mercenaries used were still a good deal heavier than even a fully tooled up Browning M2, but in one-third G, that really didn't matter. They also could be lethal, although they did come with a very handy knob allowing you to adjust the level of deadliness, dialing it down from *lethal* to *paralyze* to *stun*.

It was a revolutionary weapon, particularly for crowd control. No longer did security personnel need to be hesitant, they could take out large numbers of aggressors with impunity. It made it viable for a small number of well armed individuals to safely deal with a much larger number of subjects. In Commander Kruger's mind, it was the weapon that made this mission possible.

"SO WHERE ARE WE GOING?" Nills already knew the answer to this. Let's face it, there were not many places on Mars you could go. But he had Kruger talking, so decided to keep probing.

"Back to the ship. Somebody wants to meet you."

"Somebody too important to risk entering the colony facility."

"Yeah, something like that." It was a hesitant reply.

"So you haven't entered Colony One then?"

Kruger stayed silent for a minute, sizing Nills up. "I'm sure he'll fill you in when you meet."

The driver cocked his head around. "Commander, ETA in one minute."

Nills looked at the heads up display. A new shape was beginning to format itself in the gloom, it was big. And since it was still one minute away, it must be very big indeed.

By the time they arrived Nills realized that big was too small a word for it. The only thing he saw outside through the windshield was a gigantic landing strut as they passed on the right hand side of it. Ahead of them a gantry had been lowered, presumably from the underside of the ship. Yellow lights flashed and illuminated the clouds of dust that had been whipped up in the storm. The rover drove straight onto the gantry platform, came to a halt, and then started to slowly ascend—into the belly of the whale.

A few moments later, Nills stepped out of the rover and into a compact utilitarian loading bay. It was crammed full of equipment and machines, they were anticipating a long stay. As he looked around the ship he considered just how far things had progressed since the early days of the first colonist landings. They had all been packed like sardines into tiny craft. *How long ago was that now,* he wondered. *Over a decade?*

"This way." Kruger ushered him across the loading bay to a ladder leading up into the interior of the craft.

"Follow me." He started climbing up. Nills followed. They passed up through a number of levels until finally they stepped off into an operations area. Several crewmembers occupied various workstations around the perimeter of the space. They all stopped what they were doing and turned around to look at Nills. In the middle of the room, sitting at a circular holo-table was a gaunt looking old man.

"Nills Langthorp, a pleasure to meet you. Please have a seat." The old man signaled to an empty chair on the opposite side of the holo-table. Nills obliged.

He leaned in and studied Nills for a moment. "Incredible. To know of your existence is one thing, but to see you in the flesh is another thing entirely."

"Let me guess," said Nills. "Peter VanHoff, head honcho of the Colony One Mars consortium."

VanHoff gave a thin smile. "Very good, you are correct. How did you guess?"

"To know of your existence is one thing, but to see you in the flesh, well..."

VanHoff stopped smiling.

"So what do you want with me?" Nills continued.

VanHoff waved a dismissive hand. "Later. In the meantime I just want you where I can see you, out of harm's way."

"Why, is there going to be some harm?"

VanHoff shifted in his seat. "It seems our Oriental friends are being somewhat obstinate. Things could get a little... fractious, shall we say. They have battened down the hatches in Colony One and are refusing to cede authority."

"So they've given you the middle finger, then."

"Mere petulance on their part. I assure you we will regain control of what is rightfully ours."

"And what about the colonists?"

"That's what we would like to know. Whose side are they on?"

"They're on nobody's side. They just want to live in peace."

"Don't we all, Mr. Langthorp."

Nills stood up. "Well, it was nice talking to you, Peter. Let's do it again sometime. Now, if you don't mind I could do with a lift back."

VanHoff laughed. "Fascinating. You are a character, I'll give you that." His face stiffened. "Now sit down, you're not going anywhere."

Nills surveyed the room, several of the crew were gathered around, ready for action. Nills sighed, and sat down again. "Maybe I could stay a bit longer, then."

"Very good. Now, to answer your question. You are here for two reasons. Firstly, if the Chinese don't cooperate, and accept the ruling of the courts, then we will simply take over Colony One through force of arms. What I need you to do is settle the clones down, and make sure they don't do anything foolish."

"You mean the colonists."

"You know what I mean. Let's not make this any more difficult that it needs to be."

"What about Dr. Malbec? How are you planning to get her on your side?"

VanHoff's lips tightened. "Leave Malbec to me. She is the primary cause of all this mayhem—and she needs to pay for it."

Nills jumped up, leaned across the holo-table and gripped VanHoff by the lapels. "Over my dead body, you twisted little shit."

The crew scrambled to drag Nills off. He let go of VanHoff, just as a few thousand volts from a cattle prod shot through his body. He collapsed back down on the seat, his arm was twisted back and held tight by one of the crew. VanHoff dusted himself off and regained his composure. "I see you are a little upset. I appreciate that change can be disconcerting for all concerned. But you'll get used to it, eventually."

The pain that had engulfed Nills' body was subsiding and he too had regained some composure. "So what's the second one? You said there were two reasons I was here?"

VanHoff smiled. "Ah... yes. Indeed I did. You see, Nills. You are rather special. You are the reason we are all here fighting on this godforsaken rock. You are the key—and you always were."

"And what if I were to tell you to go shove it up your ass?"

VanHoff scowled and turned to Kruger. "Take him below and keep him secure."

THEY TOOK Nills and locked him in a small accommodation compartment on one of the lower levels of the craft. The room was compact, with a bed and not much else. He reckoned that it must have been regarded as first class digs on this ship, so he should feel privileged. The first half hour of his incarceration Nills spent examining every possible nook and cranny, looking for anything that he could find and use to his advantage. He didn't find anything. Eventually he sat down on the bed and considered what his next course of action should be. That was assuming that he even had a choice in the matter.

So VanHoff had made the trip himself, that much was evident. *But why would he do that?* Nills wondered. Maybe it was simply a case of, *if you want to do something right, then you just gotta do it yourself.* Every effort VanHoff had made so far to acquire the Janus bacteria had been thwarted by Dr. Jann Malbec. So she was number one on his hit list, he even said so himself. On top of that he expressed a clear disdain for the *clones* in Colony One. Whether they lived or died seemed to be of little interest to VanHoff. As for Xaing Zu? They really had no idea how outclassed they were by the resources that COM had brought to the planet. VanHoff just didn't care a damn for the lives in Colony One. Nills had to find a way to warn them. This was his number one task. Find a way to get a message to them—somehow.

GATHERED around the holo-table in the operations room of the COM craft sat VanHoff, Commander Willem Kruger and several others of the crew. Kruger cleared his throat and spoke. "Phase one of the operation is now complete. Colony Two is in our control and the clone specimen Langthorp has been acquired. Time now to move on to phase two. Are we ready?"

"Please proceed." VanHoff waved a hand.

"Raising a channel now, sir." One of the operatives tapped several icons on the holo-table. A 3D rendering of the COM logo materialized and rotated. *Channel open... waiting for connection... connection established.* The rotating logo was replaced with a video feed from inside the operations room in Colony One. Several Chinese sat around a similar holo-table.

Kruger cleared his throat again and spoke. "This is Commander Willem Kruger, of the Colony One Mars consortium mission. Please be advised that we have entered and secured the mining outpost, known as Colony Two, located at the northern edge of the Jezero Crater. In doing so we have now fulfilled the obligations required by the International Court of Arbitration for full ownership of the Colony One facilities to revert to COM ownership.

Therefore, you are now trespassing on our property and we would be obliged if you would vacate the facility immediately. If you fail to do so within the next twelve hours then we will remove you by force. Do you understand this message?"

The figures around the corresponding holo-table in Colony One sat unmoved. There was a moment of tense silence before they replied. "*This is Commander Jing Tzu, of Xaing Zu Industries Mars mission. We understand your claim is issued by a terrestrial court which we do not recognize. Therefore we see your request as invalid and furthermore your threats to use force are taken as an act of aggression against a peaceful enterprise. We have claimed this facility under salvage and, as such, are legally entitled to remain. Any attempt by your people to gain access will be seen as trespassing on Xaing Zu property and will be repelled, with force if necessary. Do you understand this message?*"

Commander Kruger clasped his hands together and slowly leaned in across the holo-table. "You have twelve hours to leave." The video feed went dead and they all took a moment before VanHoff finally spoke.

"What's your assessment, Commander—are they bluffing?"

"We have to assume that they are not bluffing and have convinced themselves that they can hold it. Which means we need to reassess their capability and recalibrate our strategy to take control of Colony One."

"We need to keep damage to the facility to a minimum. Rebuilding it is not something we have the resources for."

"What about the clones?" said Kruger.

VanHoff waved a dismissive hand, "They're expendable. We already have what we need."

"Very well, then."

"Just one request, Commander Kruger. I would like, if at all possible, that Dr. Jann Malbec be taken alive. I have a bone to pick with her, and it would bring me no end of pleasure to do it face-to-face."

"Understood, sir."

11

SUBTERRANEAN

The colonists trapped in the biodome made several futile attempts to get the door open, ignoring the broadcasts by the Chinese that persistence in their attempts would be met with violence. After a time though, it became increasingly evident to them that it was just not going to happen. They were trapped, held captive inside their own biodome, with no way to access the larger facility save through the door to the connecting tunnel. So one by one they wandered away.

Jann contented herself by retiring to her old wicker chair on the central dais. Some of the other colonists had also gathered around, but their mood was somber and resigned.

"I am really getting sick of this shit," said Rachel, one of the few remaining original colonists. And who could blame her? Since landing on the planet, over a decade ago now, she had seen nothing but hardship and the constant attempts by others to manipulate and interfere with the very serious business of surviving in a hostile environment.

"You know, I had this naive idea once that things might get better," she continued.

"Yeah, I know how you feel. It would be real nice if they all just left us alone," said Steven, another long-suffering colonist.

"Isn't gonna happen. We're just too valuable to them," Rachel replied with a resigned sigh. "We're just a group of lab monkeys as far as they're concerned. They want us for what's inside us."

They went silent for a while before Steven spoke again. "So, what now? What have they got planned? What's going to happen to us?"

JANN COULDN'T TAKE this conversation anymore. It seemed to her that the colonists had resigned themselves to their fates and nothing she could say was going to change that. She rose from the wicker chair and went for a walk around the outer rim of the biodome. Gizmo followed beside her. After a short period of aimless meandering, Jann arrived at the place in the biodome wall where it opened out into a long tunnel. This was the fish farm. Next to it was another, similar tunnel, but this one was derelict, the roof structure had collapsed in on itself many years ago. There was still a door into it but it had been sealed up for a long time. This tunnel had originally been used for soil processing and had an airlock entrance out onto the planet's surface. But this process had long been relocated to the cave system that Nills had discovered beneath the colony itself. Jann stopped and stared at the sealed door for some time.

"Gizmo, can you access Colony One schematics or do you need to be connected to the main systems?"

"I have them stored locally so, yes, I can access them."

"Show me what you've got on this old tunnel."

Gizmo projected various schematics onto the wall beside Jann.

"Wait, this one here—can you zoom in a bit more on this?"

Jann looked at the exploded diagram of the soil processing tunnel as it would have been when it was in operation.

"Do you have any schematics of the cave system beneath the biodome?"

"Not as such, Jann. These are hidden places. There were no maps or drawings created of them. Remember, it was only discovered during the collapse of the original colony. Nills never made any schematic of it. However, I could replicate a reasonably accurate rendering from my own accumulated sensory data."

"Really, you can do that?"

"Of course. Let me show you."

With that the droid began to sketch out the cave system. It took it less than a few seconds to complete it. "There, that is as much detail as I can access."

Jann looked at it for a moment, examining the curved organic structure that the droid had rendered. "Can you overlay the derelict tunnel onto this drawing, in the exact location it would be?"

"Sure."

Jann studied the resultant schematic at the point where the two intersected with each other for quite some time. "Can you zoom in on this section here, Gizmo?"

Jann pointed to an area on the diagram. "Wait. What's that?"

"That is an access point."

"You mean, there is a way down into the cave system from this tunnel?"

"Correct. I remember Nills discussing this access route. There is a 72.3% probability of it still functioning, assuming the tunnel has sufficient integrity to hold one atmosphere of pressure."

Jann looked at Gizmo. "Well, there's only one way to find out. I need you to go find Xenon. Don't tell anyone else what we're planning here. Just say I need him, and bring him here, okay?"

"Sure." Gizmo sped off through the dense vegetation of the biodome to seek out Xenon.

It didn't take long for them to return, and Jann had Gizmo project the schematics again for Xenon, so she could explain to him what her plan was.

"I think there may be a way to get out of here and make contact with Colony Two. There's an access route from this old derelict tunnel into the subterranean cave system that is now used for soil processing."

"I see." Xenon scratched his chin. "But I don't understand how that can help us. There's nothing down there except some autonomous machines and an airlock out onto the surface that the soil harvesters use. There are sections that don't even have an atmosphere."

"Yes, I know." Jann lowered her voice. "But there is an area down there, a secret area, an area that the original Nills used to hide out when the colony was going to hell, during the first wave of infection. If I can get in there, it has the systems that will enable me to see what's going on in Colony One, and possibly contact Colony Two."

"A secret place?"

"It's a long story, Xenon. But trust me, it's there."

"I see. So how can I help?"

"Well, we need to open this door. Gizmo has run the numbers and calculated a high probability that the access point still functions. However, there may not be an atmosphere behind this door. So we'll need to edge it open slowly until it sucks in enough air from the biodome to equalize the pressure."

"It's worth a shot. But you're forgetting one thing." He looked up at the roof of the biodome and pointed. "This place is covered with cameras, see there's one over there." He pointed to a small opaque hemisphere attached to the superstructure of the roof. "They'll see everything we're trying to do."

"Then we need to take them out."

"How? They're too high up to reach."

"Leave it to me." With that Jann disappeared off through the vegetation. Over to where the hydroponics were arrayed in neat symmetrical rows. From one of the beds she pulled out half a dozen long, thin aluminum bars that had been used to support the growing plants. She brought them back to where Xenon and Gizmo were waiting.

Jann hefted one of the thin bars over her shoulder, took a step back, and launched it straight at the camera. It buried itself dead center, plastic shards falling onto the floor all around.

"Okay, that's one. Let's go find the others."

AFTER ABOUT HALF AN HOUR, Jann had managed to take out four cameras at different locations around the biodome. She also managed to acquire a number of other colonists who were keen to know what she was up to. She brought them back with her to the sealed door to the soil processing tunnel and outlined the plan. They also acquired a number of steel bars that they could use to help lever the door open against the one atmosphere of pressure inside the biodome.

Word spread around the captive colonists that Jann Malbec had a plan—hope had returned. But for some, it was not hope they saw, but recklessness. Exposing the biodome to the exterior environment could mean disaster. As a consequence, a crowd had gathered and far from acting as a cohesive unit, in their own best interest, they squabbled and bickered. Jann was now concerned that this would achieve nothing other that to attract the attention of their Asian overlords.

It was Xenon who finally managed to establish some rational thinking amongst the group. "We must try. Otherwise we are at the mercy of those who regard us as laboratory experiments. That future is not one that I wish to contemplate."

It was through this line of dialogue that order in the biodome was restored, even if it was somewhat reluctant. It was agreed that the bulk of the colonists would disperse and act as normal, whatever that meant within the constraints of the current situation. This left Jann, Xenon, Gizmo and around a half dozen others to wrestle with the door into the derelict tunnel. Gizmo, for its part, had calculated the probability of the area behind the door having integrity compatible with sustaining one atmosphere at approximately 67.54%. But, as the little robot was no longer connected to the main Colony One systems, this had been derived with greatly reduced computational power. Nonetheless, it was good enough for Jann.

She spun the locking wheel on the door. Xenon and a few others rammed a number of the steel bars into the doorjamb to act as levers.

"Okay, see if it will move." Jann stepped back.

A gap appeared as the colonists applied leverage, it hissed with the sound of air escaping into the space behind.

"Keep it open, let it fill." Jann had now thrown her weight into the mix.

The hissing increased and the gap became larger. It grew in intensity as they applied more pressure. The colonists all groaned with the physical exertion expended to keep the door from slamming shut.

"How long do we need to keep this up?"

"Just keep it open."

"What if it doesn't stop?"

"Just shut up, and keep the pressure on."

After what seemed like an eternity of physical endurance, the hissing slowed. Jann smiled. "Listen, it's holding. Come on, push harder."

When it came, it was almost instant. The pressure equalized and the door swung open in one swift movement. Two of the colonists lost their balance and went sprawling across the floor. Gizmo switched on its floodlight and illuminated the long forgotten tunnel. Ahead they could see where the roof had collapsed. It was only around ten meters in. There was nothing else in the space save for dust and crumpled metal roof structure. But it held the pressure, the tons of Martin dirt overhead creating an effective seal.

"Gizmo, how far in is the access point?"

The little robot was already moving in through the tunnel. "Approximately two meters past that point." It pointed to where the collapsed roof structure met the floor.

"Dammit, we'll have to dig."

Fortunately the biodome was well stocked with tools for moving soil and before long Xenon had organized a team. They quickly worked their way forward through the tunnel. A spade clanged off the floor. "I think this is it." Xenon tapped the floor again as a hollow sound revealed the location of the long forgotten access point. Jann knew it would be similar to one in the module attached to the medlab. A flat, hinged, plate lying flush with the floor. They swept the dirt off it, and Xenon jammed the edge of the spade into the gap, and leaned on it. It cracked open enough for the others to grab it with their fingers and lift it up to reveal a dark hole descending into the Martian sub-surface. Gizmo shone its light down. They could see a ladder extending a short distance to the floor of a narrow tunnel.

"Do you think you can climb down there to check it out, Gizmo?"

With that the little droid grabbed the sides of the opening and lowered itself down, telescoping its arms as it went, then finally dropping onto the floor below. It moved its light slowly around the space and then disappeared off down a tunnel. They could hear it move around and, after a few minutes, it returned.

"There's another airlock up ahead that leads into the soil processing cave."

"Does it have an atmosphere?"

"Yes, it should."

"Okay, let's try it." Jann descended the ladder and looked down along the dark passage.

"I see it," she shouted up to Xenon and the others.

A trickle of dirt started to fall down into the opening and Jann looked up. "What's that?"

"The tunnel roof, it's becoming unstable. Quick you better get out of there now." Xenon was shouting down to her.

"No, we've come this far, I'm not going back."

More dirt fell in as the roof shifted, its enormous weight too much for the flimsy support the colonists had rigged up.

"Go..." Jann shouted at Xenon. "Get out... get out now."

The trickle of dirt turned into a cascade, then into a

torrent and the space began to fill up at an alarming rate, forcing Jann and Gizmo to move farther along the passageway.

"Quick, Gizmo. Let's get this airlock open." Jann moved just as the tunnel roof finally collapsed in a tsunami of dust, and dirt, and darkness.

12

SANCTUM

Jann spat and coughed as grit filled her mouth. Darkness enveloped her. "Gizmo?"

She stood up and felt for the wall, or anything that would orient her. She heard Gizmo's motors whirr and turned to see a light emanating from the little robot's head, as it extracted itself from a mound of soil.

"Gizmo, are you okay?"

"I'm 98.6% operational, excluding that fact that I have no external systems access."

Jann coughed again. "We need to get this airlock open, the air in here will run out soon." She spun the locking wheel and opened the door as a waft of stale air overpowered her nostrils.

"Ahh... what's that smell?"

"I am sorry, I can not offer any assistance in that regard as my olfactory sensors pale in comparison to the performance of the human apparatus."

"Count yourself lucky you can't smell this." She held her nose.

They moved into the airlock and Jann spun the locking wheel on the outer door. A green light flashed on an alert panel.

"Okay, here goes." She tugged at the door.

"It's not moving." She put her foot against the wall and pulled. It refused to budge.

"Help me Gizmo, if we don't get this open I'll run out of breathable air."

"I estimate you have forty-two hours before you die."

"I really don't need to know that, Gizmo."

"My pleasure, I am here to assist."

Jann looked at the eccentric robot as it grabbed the door handle.

"Are you sure a rock didn't fall on your head and readjust your brain?"

"Quite sure, Jann. My brain is not in my head."

"Never mind. Let's push... one, two, three..."

The door moved a little. Buoyed by this achievement Jann redoubled her efforts and they finally created an opening wide enough for both Jann and Gizmo to pass through.

They entered a long narrow passageway. The air was fresher here, gone was the foul smell from the airlock. After around ten meters or so, it opened out into the main soil processing cave. This was where the colony extracted its water. Robotic harvesters fed the processing plant with soil acquired from outside. At the far end of the cave, automatic airlocks facilitated the coming and going of these robots. Some fed the plant and some removed the spent soil back out onto the surface. None were moving when Jann and Gizmo entered. This was not unusual, as the reclamation and recycling system in Colony One was highly efficient.

The plant only needed to top up the reservoir every so often, and since Martian soil contained a lot of H_2O, the process required only brief periods of activity for the harvesters.

They moved through the cave illuminated only by the light from the droid. Jann caught glimpses in the shadows of the slumbering harvesters, waiting patiently to be called into action by the colony systems. They passed by the main access route, a stairway leading up to a concourse near the operations area above. Jann could take this route but it would only lead her right slap bang in to the hornet's nest. If the Chinese were planning the defense of the colony then that area would be busy. Instead she was heading for the cave beneath the medlab. The same one that Nills had taken her when he had rescued her and Paolio from the demented Decker, where she had first met Gizmo. This cave had been utilized by Nills and the other colonists as a refuge from the mayhem that raged through the original colony population. It was in there that he had carved out an operations center for clandestine surveillance. *It's the perfect place to... do what?* thought Jann. *What exactly am I going to do, even If I manage to get there?*

She put it out of her mind and concentrated on finding the location of the access point. This was not an easy task, as it had been sealed up long ago. What was the point of having a secret place if anyone could find it and enter? And since the soil processing area was frequently visited by technicians maintaining the equipment, the access point would be well hidden.

"Gizmo, where are we?"

The little robot projected a 3D schematic into the space directly in front of them. It zoomed and rotated as Gizmo calculated the correct orientation. "This is us here," a red dot illuminated their position on the diagram, "...and that should be where the entrance is."

"Okay, let's keep going."

Gizmo led the way, as its sensors derived their position in space from a combination of ultrasonic and microwave frequencies. It was like a bat. It did not require light to know where it was or what surrounded it. It might not be able to smell as well as a human but it had many more useful tricks up its metallic sleeve.

"Here it is." The droid stopped and shone its light onto a bare cave wall.

"Where? I don't see anything."

"It is here, behind approximately one meter of regolith."

"Great, more digging." Jann started looking around for something to use as a tool.

"Wait," said Gizmo, "I have a better idea."

The droid went quiet for a moment, not moving, not saying anything. Jann began to wonder if it had shut itself down. "Gizmo?"

Before it replied she heard the whirr of an electric motor starting up, and she spun around to locate its direction. Across the cave the sound grew louder, moving toward them. She stepped back, "Gizmo?"

Out of the gloom a harvester bot trundled across the floor.

"I thought one of these would be useful. After all this is what they are designed to do— dig."

"Gizmo, you are a genius."

"Yes, I know."

"But how did you do that? I thought you were denied access to the colony mainframe?"

"These are on a sub-system, low level stuff. I am able to access those sectors."

The harvester moved over to the cave wall and started to literally eat it. It began to churn up the hard compacted regolith and fill its hopper. Dust filled the air as it chewed into the wall, loose dirt piled up around it like crumbs from a mechanical feast. It worked at a furious pace, devouring everything in its path, both soil and rock fell equally to its mechanical jaws. It stopped with a loud wheeze, dust billowing up from its base, then reversed out of the gaping hole. Gizmo shone its light inside.

"There it is, just as I calculated."

"The only problem now is, how can we hide this? If someone were to come down here they would see it?"

"I can set the harvester to clear away the debris into the processing plant."

"We'll still need something to conceal the entrance. Even if it's just cosmetic. I don't think there's anything we can do that will pass a close examination."

Gizmo slowly swept the area with light, coming to a halt on a stack of storage containers.

"We could move these in front of the entrance, and pull them in closer once we are inside."

"Okay, let's get going then."

They moved fast to drag everything into position. Jann's main concern now was of being discovered. Any moment the door to the concourse area above could open and the game would be up. As it was, they were making one hell of a racket.

"Hurry, Gizmo." They squeezed in behind the container camouflage they had just assembled. Jann grabbed the locking wheel on the door and put all her weight behind it. It was stiff from the dirt that had penetrated the mechanism it had been entombed in for so long. But it moved. And after much grunting from Jann they finally entered the hidden space that she had repurposed for her experiments beneath the medlab.

"Quick, Gizmo, get the door shut. I'll see what's going on." She sat down at the monitors and flipped a number of switches to bring them online. Screens flickered to life as Jann tapped icons to display camera feeds from inside the colony. It was the same setup that Nills had used to monitor the whereabouts of the unfortunate ISA Commander Decker.

"Jann, my sensors have picked up activity in the soil processing area."

"What? They must have heard us, dammit." She tapped an icon to bring up a video feed. It was dark and grainy, but some illumination had entered the space from the direction of the stairs to the operations area.

"Look." Jann pointed to movement on the monitor. "It's the robot, Yutu. They must have sent it down to investigate."

The quadruped moved silently into the camera's field of view, then stopped, and its head slowly rotated.

"I do not like that robot," said Gizmo.

"What's it doing?"

"It is scanning the area for anomalies."

"Define anomaly—wait, it's stopped." The robot's head was pointing directly at the storage containers that Jann and Gizmo had just moved. It rose up on its four legs and started to move again. This time straight for the containers.

"Shit, it's coming over."

The robot moved slowly and purposefully, like a big cat stalking prey. It arrived at the location of the containers and started to move around the stack.

"Godamit." Jann jumped up. "Quick find something we can jam into the door handle, anything."

Gizmo picked up a long steel rod. "This might do."

Jann grabbed it and raced for the door. But before she could reach it the ground shook with the force of an explosion somewhere up above and the cave was plunged into total darkness.

"What the hell?"

13

BATTLE

Emergency lighting flickered on inside the cave as Jann's brain tried to make sense of what had just happened. It took her a moment to reorient herself.

"The main power source has shut down. The facility is now operating on backup power." Gizmo was at the console, seemingly trying to reconnect with the broader colony systems. Jann stood motionless, her senses on high alert. She realized she was still holding the steel bar. "The robot, Yutu, is it still there?" she said as she moved to wedge it into the door's locking mechanism.

"I have no feed, minimal systems operational."

"Life support? Do we still have life support?"

"Affirmative... backup systems coming online now."

The monitors started to flicker back to life as Jann returned to the desk. "What the hell is going on?"

"The facility still has full structural integrity. No loss of pressure."

"That explosion came from outside."

Jann's fingers danced across the screens, tapping icons,

bringing up video feeds. "Biodome looks intact." She could make out groups of startled colonists looking around, clutching each other, they were frightened. She scanned the faces and spotted Xenon. *At least he got out before the tunnel roof collapsed,* she thought.

Another feed flickered to life, showing the operations room above; several of the Xaing Zu crew worked the systems at a frenetic pace. They too were trying to figure out what was going on. "Look." Jann pointed at the screen. "It's Yutu. The robot must have been ordered back."

"I do not like that robot," said Gizmo again.

"Gizmo, snap out of it... talk to me... comms, anything on comms?"

"Nothing. But my calculations put the explosion at fifty meters due south of the facility. Near the location of the main reactor. They probably targeted the main power line."

Jann sat back and watched the monitors for a few minutes, trying to divine some meaning from the images. She located two of the Chinese in the operations room, along with Yutu. Two more were outside the biodome door, and armed. That left... how many? She wasn't sure if all of them were in the facility or if some had been sequestered back on their ship.

"I am picking up a transmit," said Gizmo, as radio static hissed out from the comm speaker. Jann could see that the Chinese in the operations room were also getting it, their body language changed suddenly.

"This is Commander Kruger, of the Colony One Mars Consortium. You have failed to comply with our request to vacate our facility." The metallic voice broke through the hiss of static, the sandstorm raging outside causing the signal to break up. *"...last chance... leave now..."* Then it went dead.

"Xaing Zu are up to something. Look." Jann pointed at

the monitor of the operations room. The Chinese were putting on their EVA suits. "Are they planning to go outside, in this storm?"

"It could also be that COM are coming in."

"But why EVA suits, then?"

"Because they fear a loss of pressure."

Jann looked over at Gizmo. "You mean, if they don't leave then COM are going to open a hole in the facility—oh shit."

"Indeed," said Gizmo. "For what it is worth you are relatively safe here, as this section is sealed and isolated from the main structure."

"But what about the biodome, the colonists? This will be a disaster—the end of Colony One—we have to do something." Jann jumped up from her seat and started pacing. "This is nuts, they'll destroy everything that's taken over a decade to establish—and for what? So they can simply repossess it?"

"Activity on the surface around the perimeter." Gizmo jolted Jann back to the immediate situation by projecting a holographic image of the Colony One facility onto a small holo-table. It stuttered and fizzed as it rendered.

"The storm is interfering with the sensors."

Nonetheless, they could clearly see two dots approaching the colony from the northern side.

"There, look, what's that?" Jann pointed at the dots.

"COM rovers approaching, judging by the speed."

"Do we have any cameras working on the outside?"

The monitors flickered through a series of blurry images of dust and sand. They failed to penetrate the swirling maelstrom, serving only to show a few meters of visibility and rendering a vague outline of the exterior of the colony. But it was enough to make out a new addition to the infrastructure. On the roof of one of the airlocks, a bulky pulsed energy weapon had been mounted. It was squat, not unlike a standard artillery piece. As Jann studied the structure she could see a suited figure operating it, moving the weapon, aiming it at something.

"Are they're preparing to fire that weapon?"

But before Gizmo could reply another explosion rocked the cave, dust rained down on Jann, the power flickered off, and all went dark again.

"Shit. What was that?" Jann tried to orient herself in the pitch black of the cave before Gizmo flicked on its lights. The little robot moved back to the operations desk and started to investigate, interrogating and probing what colony systems still remained operational. A few seconds later auxiliary power came back online.

"The airlock in sector two has been compromised... loss of atmosphere in sector one... extensive damage."

"Shit, COM must have taken out that weapon before Xaing Zu could fire it."

"Still losing atmosphere in that sector... rate slowing..."

"The biodome?"

"Integrity at one hundred percent, still one atmosphere."

The monitors flicked back on again and the holograph of the facility ballooned back to life. They could see the advancing dots had reached within a few meters of the facility. From the exterior cameras that still worked, several COM mercenaries disgorged themselves from the vehicles —all heavily armed.

"Good god, it's a full scale invasion." Jann pointed at the armed figures entering via a damaged airlock. They now had access to a section of the facility with no atmosphere. Jann wondered how this was going to help them take over but then she realized they were sealing it up behind them. Once finished they would be able to enter the rest of the colony, without any loss of integrity. She struggled with her desire to do something—anything. Maybe she could get the colonists out of the biodome, hide them all down here. But that was pointless, the access route had caved in and even if she did manage to get them all in here, then what?

Another blast rocked the cave. This time it was an internal door being blown open. From the monitors Jann could see a firefight starting. COM had entered, the Chinese were firing weapons to try and repel the invasion. She could see two already down, injured or dead. The air was thick with dust from the blast and it bloomed with incandescent flashes from the pulse weapons. All she could do was stand and watch as the fate of Colony One was decided, once again, by violence.

14

CONTROL

Peter VanHoff watched the battle for Colony One unfold from the relative comfort of the COM Mars lander. In the end it had gone exactly to plan, although it would have been better had Xaing Zu just vacated the facility. But, they had decided to make a stand. He admired them for that, even if it was a futile exercise. He assumed it had more to do with saving face than any real consideration of military superiority.

It had taken less than twenty minutes from the moment Commander Kruger had given the command until the facility was secured, and his people in control. Kruger had sent him the *all clear* so now it was time for VanHoff to finally set foot in the very facility where the Janus bacteria had been created. His hope, his wish, his deepest desire, was that it still existed either in the facility or within the biology of the clone subject Langthorp. Time to find out. He rose from operations and signaled to the two remaining COM crew. "The facility is secure and a rover is on its way to pick us up. Bring the clone to the airlock, I will meet you down there. And make sure he's sedated for the trip."

. . .

THEY ENCASED Nills in an ill-fitting EVA suit so that he could be transported over to the medlab in Colony One. VanHoff and his genetics team needed him alive, at least for the moment. Nills was now strapped into a seat in the rover, his head bobbing and rocking as the rover bounced along the planet's surface. Outside, dust and sand whipped up all around, visibility was poor and the driver operated by means of a heads-up display rendered on the rover windshield. The journey was mercifully short and soon VanHoff could make out the lights atop of the Colony One biodome penetrating the dust. The rover came to a halt outside the main airlock, time to EVA. This was not a procedure that VanHoff relished. Far from it. Being cocooned inside bulky life support brought on a rising panic inside him. He fought to control it. It was only a few meters to the colony entrance, surely he could make that. Yet, what this situation did highlight in his mind was just how much Malbec had corrupted his ambition. He could be back home, in the warm and comforting environment of Earth, free from the debilitating curse of accelerated aging, enjoying life. But no, here he was, having to travel 200 million kilometers to this hellhole of a planet. He steeled himself and stepped out of the rover onto the surface of Mars.

From just inside the airlock Commander Kruger beckoned to him with a free arm, gesturing encouragement to move. VanHoff focused on the figure of the commander, and excluded all other exterior stimuli. It worked, he inched his way forward and into the airlock. A few moments later he removed his helmet and tried to calm his breathing.

"Are you okay?" The commander gave him a concerned look.

"I'm fine... fine." He composed himself for a moment before removing the bulky EVA suit.

By the time he arrived at the operations room in Colony One, the commander had brought him up to speed on the current status. He found it hard to focus on what Kruger was saying, as he kept looking around. It was hard to believe he was actually here, in the very place that had occupied his every waking moment for years. He sat down at the central table and surveyed the subdued figure of Jing Tzu, Xaing Zu Industries commander. His hands were bound behind his back, his head bowed in defeat.

"You should have left when you had the chance."

Jing Tzu lifted his head up slowly and glared at VanHoff.

"It seems two of your crew are dead. A high price to pay for naught."

VanHoff then turned to the commander. "What is your plan for them?"

"Fortunately, our Asian friends had the bright idea of incarcerating the current colonist population in the biodome. So I think we'll just throw them inside and see how they get on."

"Excellent. I trust you'll keep their hands tied before you cast them to the lions, it should make for good entertainment."

Jing Tzu was lifted out of his seat by two COM mercenaries, and dragged off to face an uncertain fate inside the biodome.

VanHoff now surveyed the monitors arrayed around the operations room. He was particularly interested in the video feed from the biodome, and could see clusters of colonists gathered together in various sectors. But there was one member of the colony population he was most interested in.

"Commander Kruger."

"Yes, sir."

"Before you deal with the Chinese, I want you to take a team, enter the biodome and find me Dr. Jann Malbec. Bring her to me—alive, if possible. I'll be in the medlab getting things set up."

"Yes sir."

By the time VanHoff reached the medlab he was beginning to feel an increasing sense of confidence in the mission. They had successfully taken back control of both facilities, and the situation was now completely under COM control. What's more, they had not sustained a single casualty. Now he was finally ready to get started on the main phase of the operation—to find the source of the Janus bacteria.

Already his team had moved the clone subject, Langthorp, onto the operating table in the medlab, where he lay sedated until they were ready. His genetics team were also in the process of moving in the new equipment that they had brought with them. VanHoff cast an eye around the medlab space. It was well set up, much better that he had anticipated. He did a cursory audit of its equipment as he moved from area to area. Finally he came to a sealed door. It was currently locked, access was via a keypad on the side. He peered in through the small window at its interior. It had been fashioned from one of the original landers, its circular interior was lined with units not unlike rows of safety deposit boxes in a bank vault. He looked back at the keypad and made a mental note to have his team get this door open.

It was some time later when his work in the medlab was disrupted by Kruger entering. He bore a concerned look, not something VanHoff wanted to see. The commander signaled to him to follow him outside. VanHoff obliged.

When they were out of earshot of the other crewmembers Kruger spoke. "We have not located Dr. Malbec yet. She's not in the biodome and the colonists either don't know where she is or are not saying."

VanHoff stood silent for a moment. "This is a finite space. There are few places for someone to hide, she has to be here somewhere. And I want that woman found—now."

"Yes sir, she will be found."

"Wait a minute." VanHoff stroked his chin again. "I have a better idea. Come, follow me. We're going to talk to these colonists again. They know where she is, so let's not waste any more time pussyfooting around."

VANHOFF and the commander were flanked by four well-armed COM mercenaries as the inner door to the biodome swung open. Inside, a knot of colonists were backing away as they advanced.

"You," shouted VanHoff at a frightened looking colonist. "Over here."

One of the mercenaries marched over, and grabbed her by the arm. "You heard the man." He dragged her over to where VanHoff and the others were standing, and kicked her in the back of the knees. She dropped down on the floor, frightened and shaking.

VanHoff turned to Kruger and pointed to a stubby pulsed weapon he had tucked inside a holster around his shoulder.

"Mind if I borrow that for a moment?"

Kruger unclipped the weapon and handed it to him. VanHoff then moved to the kneeling colonist and placed a gentle hand on her head. "What's your name?"

"M... Ma... Maria."

"Well, Maria. Here's how you can help us. I want to know where Dr. Jann Malbec is." He stepped back and pointed the gun directly at her forehead.

"You've got ten seconds. Nine... eight... seven..."

15

ROCK

Jann watched the events in the biodome unfold with a deep sense of dread, mixed with an equal measure of helplessness. The very fabric of the colony was being eviscerated before her eyes, and what was she doing? Hiding. She was doing what she always did—run and hide. Like when she was a child. At the first sign of trouble she would take off across the fields and disappear into her secret place, where the world couldn't touch her, where her dreams were still tinged with hope. And here she was again, but this time there was no way out. Like a dystopian deja vu. The same, but worse.

The video feed showed Nills, unconscious on the medlab operating table. His chest rose and fell with each breath. Her hand reached out to touch the monitor, as if the action would make the reality... less painful. She had failed him. As she had failed the other colonists. They had placed their trust in her and now she had deserted them—run away. Now they knew the true Dr. Jann Malbec.

Her eyes moved from the prostrate form of Nills to the man standing over him. She knew that face. It was not one that you could easily forget. Old and haggard, limp fragile skin hung on brittle bones. It was Peter VanHoff. She could feel the cruelty radiate out from his being, even down here, under all this rock. His head moved, and for a brief second he looked straight at the camera. Jann recoiled and drew in a sharp breath.

"Holy crap, can he see us?"

"No, this is not possible," replied Gizmo.

She stood up, walked away from the monitors and sat down again on a low seat against the cave wall. Jann put her head in her hands.

"I hate this place. I hate the dust, and the sand. I hate the constant fight for survival. I hate the naiveté of these clones. I hate the need to run and hide all the time. I just want to go home. Back to Earth. Away from this madness."

"The probability of you returning to Earth is slim to none."

"I know, I know. I am destined to be trapped here... in this cave. Watching Nills die slowly on the monitor—and there's not a damn thing I can do about it. This is what it has come to... this is my fate."

"These events you speak of are yet to happen. And they are just one path of many possible outcomes. For it to come to pass a great many possibilities must line up in the correct sequence. Any disruption to that path, any deviation, no matter how small, will bring a different outcome."

Jann took her head out of her hands and looked over at Gizmo. "What the hell... does any of that mean?"

"It means there are a great many ways that this can play out. Your premonition of Nills' demise is just one possibility."

"I think you have finally lost it, Gizmo. I'm pretty sure

something hard must have fallen on your head. You're not making any sense to me"

"What I am saying is, one rock can change the course of a river, if that rock is carefully placed. It will gather to it silt and sand and over time the river is moved."

"Where are you getting all this... philosophy from? What happened to *probabilities* and *analysis*?"

"I have been researching the writings of Confucius, to gain a better understanding of our Chinese guests."

Jann stood up. "I think I prefer Gizmo the analyst to Gizmo the philosopher. Finding a rock is not going to help us much." She looked over at the video feed from the medlab, and the unconscious figure of Nills. "What are they doing to him?"

"It is the Janus bacteria that they ultimately seek. Nills must be important in that search."

"We need to do something, we can't leave him there, at the mercy of these bastards."

"What do you suggest?"

"We can access the medlab from here so we wait until it's vacated, then sneak in and take him down here."

"Deja vu." said Gizmo. "I have been here before, with Nills, at this same operations desk as he discussed rescuing you from the psychotic Commander Decker."

Jann sat down and sighed. "But what would be the point of moving him? As soon as he was discovered missing they would rip the place apart and find us. We would only be buying time at best, giving ourselves away at worst." She sighed again, stood up and walked back across the cave.

"This is hopeless. There's no way out. They have us completely under their control and it's only a matter of time before they find us down here." She sat down and put her head in her hands again. "I've failed everyone, Nills, the colonists—there's no escaping it." She sat there in silence for quite some time, considering the hopelessness of her situation.

"JANN, you might want to see this."

She looked over at the robot, "What is it?"

"Activity in the biodome."

On the feed Jann could see Peter VanHoff holding a weapon to the head of one of the colonists. She was shaking uncontrollably, all the time pleading with them.

"Can we hear what's going on?"

"No, we have no audio feed."

"Damn, what's she saying?"

"She is telling them... that you are hiding out."

"Are you sure? How do you know that?"

"I can lip read, obviously."

Jann spun around, her hand over her mouth. "Shit, shit, shit. They'll find us."

"Wait... she is saying... you are in Colony Two." Gizmo looked over at Jann.

Jann stood silent for a while. "Are they buying it?"

They watched as VanHoff lowered the weapon, and handed it back to one of the mercenaries.

"Yes, he is not shooting the colonist Maria in the head."

"Well, we've bought some time, nothing more. They'll soon find out I'm not there and VanHoff won't give up trying to find me. I'm a loose end, and he doesn't strike me as a person who likes loose ends."

The mercenaries started to move out of the biodome, but before the door shut, the four remaining Chinese taikonauts were unceremoniously shoved inside. They stood with their backs to the door, hands bound behind them. The colonists gathered around, closing in on them.

"This could get nasty," said Jann, leaning her hand on the table as she peered closer at the monitor. "What are they saying, Gizmo?"

"Bastards... scumbags... let's tear them a new asshole..." Gizmo looked over at Jann.

She pointed back at the monitor. "Xenon, what's he saying?" He had stepped between and was appealing to the angry mob.

"Not enemy now... COM are the fight... don't waste energy on these scum..." His appeals seemed to be having the desired effect. Their body language changed, the moment passed, but not before the taikonauts were pelted with rotten fruit. Xenon raised a hand, the rain of fruit stopped. After some time the colonists dispersed. The Chinese simply sat down on the floor and nursed their bruised and battered egos.

Jann sat and watched until it was clear the mood in the biodome had settled down. She sighed and looked around at the cave as if it might prompt some solution to her dilemma. She had time, but not much else, and even that was limited. Nills was incarcerated in the medlab, soon to be under the scalpel, no doubt. She could do nothing for him, just watch as he was slowly dissected by the COM geneticists, probing his biology in their quest to unlock the secrets of the Janus bacteria.

Jann looked across the cave and her eyes came to rest on the incubator where the last remaining sample of that bacteria still existed. She walked over to it and peered in through the observation window as she placed a hand on its glass. She stood there motionless, just looking at it for some time.

"Gizmo," she finally said.

"Yes, Jann."

She looked back at the robot. "I think we may have found our *rock*."

"What do you mean?"

Jann looked back through the window at the petri dish. "This is what they came here for."

"Are you going to destroy it? You still have some time."

"No, Gizmo. I'm going to give it to them."

The droid moved over to where Jann stood and looked in through the window. "Is that wise?"

"It depends on the manner in which it is given."

"Now it is you that sounds like an ancient philosopher. I hate to admit it but I am confused."

Jann stood back from the incubator and turned to Gizmo. "I'm not going to hand it to them, Gizmo. I'm going to release it to the environment."

The robot was silent for a moment as it analyzed the ramifications of this strategy. "That would be more that just throwing a *rock* in the river. That would be a very large boulder."

Jann turned back to the incubator. "The colonists are all immune to it, but the others..." Her sentence trailed off.

"It may give us an edge."

"The repercussions of its release into the general environment are difficult to predict, Jann. Too much random chaos in the equation to enable any reliable analysis."

"Chaos is our ally. If past performance is anything to go by, then by morning, they should all be fighting each other. My only concern is the taikonauts in the biodome. They could put the colonists at risk."

"Their hands are bound, that would reduce the risk somewhat."

Jann's hand moved to the console on the incubator, her finger hovered over the button marked *open*.

She hesitated.

"Why have you stopped?"

"Before I do this, there is a greater concern that needs to be considered."

"What is that?"

"None of them can ever be allowed to return to Earth." She looked at Gizmo for a moment, then hit the button.

There was a faint hiss as the front of the incubator cracked open and slowly rose up. Jann reached in and took the petri dish in her hand. "Well, here goes." She opened the lid, exposing the bacteria to the environment.

For a moment, she stood still, looking at the splattered agar gel. Perhaps she expected more to happen, a more dramatic moment to herald the enormity of what she had just done. But there was none. Just silence.

"What would be the most efficient way to have the bacteria permeate the facility, Gizmo?"

"I would suggest waiting until the colony is asleep. Then access the medlab and place the dish in there, into an air recycling vent."

"Then let's do that." Jann checked the time. "Another hour or so and we should be ready to go."

Darkness falls quickly on Mars. The transition from day to night is abrupt. As the sun sinks below the horizon so too does the light. Mars possesses insufficient atmosphere to soften the blow with a dusky prelude. So, Jann and Gizmo had not long to wait for the inhabitants of Colony One to settle into the nighttime ritual of preparing for sleep. She had worried that some of the COM mercenaries, and maybe even VanHoff, would go back to their ship for the night. But that was not the case. Jann watched as VanHoff made preparation to retire to one of the bigger accommodation pods. She gave it a few more hours before she and Gizmo took the short tunnel to the medlab access point. It was the same tunnel that Gizmo had carried the stricken ISA medical doctor Paolio, when Nills had rescued her. Now, it seemed it was almost time to return the favor.

Gizmo slipped out of the airlock and up the ramp, its tracked wheels making barely a sound. Jann followed and entered the code into the keypad to open the door into the medlab proper. It was dim, with just spots of localized light around some of the workbenches. She walked over the where Nills lay and checked the monitor. His vitals were good, if somewhat elevated. She could just make out his face in the dull reflected green light from the screens. He looked pained. While Jann checked Nills, Gizmo unscrewed a grill from an air vent on the back wall of the medlab. It then placed the petri dish with the exposed bacteria inside and replaced the panel. It would be sucked through the recyclers and then redistributed to all areas of Colony One. Gizmo had estimated approximately 1.34 hours for full environmental contamination.

Jann breathed a sigh of relief as they moved back down through the connecting tunnel, although it pained her terribly to leave Nills behind. But by morning, the bacteria would be starting to work on the physiology of those who had no immunity to it. Some would go the way of Commander Decker, turning into deranged killers. Others would end up being the victims. Jann was counting on it.

16

TAIKONAUT DOWN

Xenon shifted his position, for possibly the hundredth time, on the bed of leaves he had fashioned in the hope that he might find a more comfortable arrangement. It was a futile exercise, made bearable only by the onset of extreme fatigue. But now that the Martian dawn was starting to filter through the semi-transparent biodome membrane, his body clock was no longer cooperating with his need for sleep. He was contemplating returning to his back as he began to feel the hard floor of the biodome dig into his pelvis, when a sharp, loud shriek reverberated around the cavernous space. He sat up and listened. Others had also heard it. Heads and bodies popped up through the vegetation all around him, like prairie dogs on alert.

"Did you hear that?" Rachel asked in a whisper from her position wedged between the bases of two banana trees.

Before Xenon had a chance to utter a response another shriek pierced the dawn silence. It was louder this time and was followed by the sound of running—getting closer and louder, until finally a frenzied Xaing Zu taikonaut burst through the vegetation heading straight for Xenon. Fortunately, his hands were still tied behind his back so his gait was ragged and unbalanced. Xenon dived for his legs as he passed and took him down swiftly. The other colonists, observing this spectacle, emerged from the surrounding foliage and pounced on the hapless runner.

Even though he was pinned down beneath several colonists he still put up a frenzied fight, kicking and screaming in Mandarin, a language none of them understood. Not that they needed to. It was clearly evident that he was totally demented. Two other Chinese crew came panting onto the scene, both had their hands still bound. They stopped and bent over as they tried to catch a breath, now that their crazy runaway friend had been halted and contained.

"What the hell is up with him?" Xenon looked over at the Chinese as they slowly regained the ability to breathe enough to speak.

"Crazy bastard... started bashing his head on the floor, then ran off."

Xenon stood up, once he was sure that the others had a good grip on the distraught captive. He still kicked and bucked with demonic strength. "Rachel, go find something to tie him up with. He'll just injure himself more if we don't."

Xenon reached down to where he had been lying earlier, picked up his knife and unsheathed it. He turned to the Chinese commander, Jing Tzu, who backed off as Xenon approached.

"You came here thinking we are all just lab rats, to be experimented on, to be disposed of, as a means to an end."

"Some did, yes, this is true, I will not lie."

"It was your mission."

"Not mine. You have my word on that, not mine."

"Then what was your mission?"

"As commander... to keep everybody safe... as best I can."

Xenon looked down at the still struggling crewmember, then back at the commander. "Well, you failed, didn't you?"

The commander lowered his head.

"Yes, I failed."

Xenon hefted the knife in his hand, grabbed the commander by the arm—and cut his bonds.

"We are not animals."

Jing Tzu nodded his thanks as Xenon freed the others. They rubbed their wrists and arms as they tried to get some feeling back. Jing Tzu knelt down beside his stricken colleague and snapped at him in Mandarin. But the response was muted as the deranged crewmember had finally run out of steam. His eyes rolled in his head and he stopped fighting.

"I don't understand what happened to him. Dan Ma is one of our most competent taikonauts. That's why he was chosen for this mission."

"He needs medical help," said Xenon.

"Do you have any idea what caused him to go crazy like that?" Jing Tzu gestured down at his comrade.

"It's just Mars. It can send some people demented. Too much for them, I suppose." Xenon looked at him and shook his head. "Pick him up and follow me."

They took him into one of the food processing pods, off the main biodome, and laid him out on a bench. "You all stay locked up in here and keep an eye on him. That's the deal. Otherwise we tie you up again."

Jing Tzu gave a reluctant nod. What choice did he have?

Xenon retreated with Rachel and the other colonists to

the central dais of the biodome. They were all clearly agitated by the morning's events.

"Could it be happening again, you know, like the stories about how the first colony went crazy?"

Xenon scratched his chin. "That was a long time ago, Rachel. All in the past."

"He needs medical help," she said. "And we need to get out of here. What are these COM guys playing at, they can't keep us in here forever."

"No, they can't. Soon things will start needing maintenance. The colony can't run unless they let us out." Xenon lifted his head up. "I have an idea. Maybe this is an opportunity to get COM in here."

"How?"

"I'm going to write them a message."

"I can't see how that's going to work."

"It all depends on what you say. So let's find something to make a sign with."

Ten minutes later Xenon was standing in front of one of the working cameras monitoring the biodome. He held a sign aloft, cobbled together from the side of a food storage crate.

~

KRUGER SIPPED on a coffee and surveyed his surroundings. He was sitting in an old battered armchair in an area the colonists referred to as *the common room*. What struck him most was the shabbiness of it all. The walls were scuffed and yellowing. The furniture, if you could call it that, was made from materials scavenged from a scrapheap, albeit a space age one. It was in deep contrast to the elegant gleam of their own spacecraft. He had seen this sort of place before. It reminded him of asteroid mines where there seemed to be this visceral need for the miners to deconstruct anything resembling a clean modern environment into a post apocalyptic interior. He hated those places. To him they stank of discord and disorder. As if the natural order of the universe towards entropy had been allowed free reign. The descent into chaos aided by humanity rather than met head on and overcome. His job was to see order maintained at all times. Now that the primary mission objectives of securing control of both colony facilities had been achieved, he needed to get control of the colonists. The hardware was secure, time to deal with the wetware.

VanHoff and his team of geneticists were now free to pursue their mission. That left him to manage the transition to COM control as he saw fit. That was his job, and he was damn good at it. He was helped, of course, by the fact that he enjoyed it. He relished the thought of returning this place to the gleaming white modern citadel that it ought to be. In fact, he couldn't wait to get started. But first it was time to take stock. He refilled his coffee cup and started on a mental inventory.

First was an assessment of human resources. One crewmember was stationed on the landing craft. There she would stay. In the event that they needed to run away fast, the ship would be ready to take off. Three others were stationed in Colony Two along with one of the geneticists. Kruger considered that this was a little under resourced, he would have preferred twice that for comfort. But making do with limited resources was the hallmark of space travel. These would be sufficient, as long as the colonists remained subdued. That left five in Colony One, excluding VanHoff and the other geneticist, Dr. Molotov. A totally inadequate number. There was no question in Kruger's mind, he would need to get the colonists on board with the reality of the new hegemony—the sooner the better. Things needed to be maintained, managed, processed. The great engine that was Colony One needed care and attention to support the survival of all it contained. The colonists would come around. They would move on and accept the realities given time. And the best way to do that was to deal with the leaders first. Cut off the head, so to speak.

Before leaving Earth, Kruger had done his research. In military terms the colonists had already proved their mettle by dispensing with Dr. Vanji and his collaborators. Then they had to deal with internal insurrection. No mean feat for a ragtag bunch of subhumans. It took leadership to achieve these victories. And if the transition back to COM control was to go smoothly then this very same leadership needed to be quashed. Nills Langthorp, the clone, had already been subdued. VanHoff had him locked down and ready to go under the knife in his quest to discover the biological voodoo that Dr. Vanji had engineered here. Kruger felt a twinge of sorrow for the clone. *Poor bastard,* he thought. To die in battle was one thing, but to be dissected to death was a gruesome end to such a leader. But this was not Kruger's department. VanHoff, and COM, wrote his paycheck, so they got to call the shots. His job was to execute the mission, secure the facilities and ensure a smooth transition of power.

So the clone was ticked off Kruger's mental list. Next was Xenon, the weird Hybrid, the last of his species. A shiver ran up Kruger's spine as he thought of what this person represented. VanHoff and his crew regarded him as a very precious individual, not because of any great intellectual prowess but because he represented, in their eyes, the very pinnacle of their craft. To Kruger, though, he was just another weird biological product from the genetic horror show that was Colony Mars. But still, he would be easy to deal with. As it was, he was securely incarcerated along with the others in the biodome. But this was a situation that could not be sustained for much longer. It was a fortunate stroke of luck that the Chinese had herded them all in there, for their own safety. It made his task of taking the facility much more of a direct military confrontation, without the risk of civilian casualties. The Chinese had paid the price for their concern, now they too were locked up tight.

So Xenon was also accounted for. He would be the one that Kruger would need to get on board and show the reality of the new situation. They would have a chat and the colonists would be released from the biodome, back to work —and life would go on. But time enough for that, he would let them stew for a while longer. Then their freedom would taste so much sweeter. Less incentive for agitation, lest their freedoms be taken away again.

That left Dr. Jann Malbec, a loose end in his plan, a box that Kruger could not yet tick. He refilled his coffee cup one more time and considered this enigma. *Where the hell is she?* There were only so many places that you could hide out on Mars. It's not like she could head for the hills, hole up in some cave, living off the land. She had to be in one of the colonies. His crew in Colony Two had not reported back yet, which suggested they had nothing to report, which suggested they had not found her. But the longer this went on the more of an enigma it posed for him. What's more, VanHoff was getting increasingly agitated by the lack of closure. It seemed to Kruger that VanHoff had a deep systemic hatred of her. In his mind she was the single individual responsible for the destruction of his dream. Kruger could see his point. If he was locked inside the disintegrating body that VanHoff possessed then he too would be pretty pissed off, if the cure he had spent so much time and resources on was taken from him. Particularly by a rookie astronaut with a moral conscience. Seriously pissed off.

Yet she was not to be underestimated. She had proved herself thus far. The only surviving member of the ill-fated ISA mission. And she had elevated herself to an almost spiritual reverence within the colonist psyche. Those sorts of leaders were always the most formidable. They had a way of really screwing up the plan. She needed to be found and fast.

His earpiece chimed. "Commander, you'd better come in to operations and take a look at this."

"What is it?"

"Best you just take a look."

Kruger downed the dregs of his now cold coffee with a grimace and stood up. He picked up the PEP weapon that he had laid on the table while having breakfast, looped it over his shoulders and headed out.

"HOW LONG HAS this been going on?" Kruger was looking at a video feed from the biodome.

"Just started, sir. Five minutes, tops."

The main monitor showed a number of colonists gathered around Xenon. He was holding a makeshift sign. It said, *URGENT. Medical assistance needed!*

"Hmmm." Kruger rubbed the corners of his mouth with the thumb and index finger of his right hand, as if this gesture would somehow coax his brain into a better understanding of what the problem might be. Nothing came to mind. But it did present an opportunity to start talking turkey with the Hybrid.

"Come on, follow me. Let's go find what the hell they're up to."

COMMANDER KRUGER, flanked by two other COM crew stood inside the short biodome entrance tunnel. Their weapons were drawn, taking no chances. At the far end stood Xenon. Beside him some colonists were carrying what looked to be an unconscious Xaing Zu taikonaut.

"He needs help." Xenon gestured at the comatose figure. "Medical help."

"Yeah? What's his problem?"

"He went crazy, started bashing his head on the floor, then we tied him up, for his own safety."

Kruger sighed and turned to his team. "You two get ahold of him and drag him in to the medlab."

"Yes sir."

"And you," he pointed the business end of a PEP weapon at Xenon. "You're coming with me. We need to talk."

17

HAPPENING AGAIN

Peter VanHoff awoke with a headache. Not a bad one, as such. But he felt it had the potential to develop into something far more debilitating, given time. It was still roaming around the foothills of his frontal lobes an hour later when he finally made it to the medlab. He was anxious to get started on a series of experiments he and his team of geneticists had planned for the clone. So he was not amused when two COM mercenaries barged in carrying a comatose Xaing Zu taikonaut.

"The commander said we were to bring him in here. He needs some medical attention."

VanHoff looked up from his notes. "I would suggest putting him in an airlock without an EVA suit, and opening the outer door."

"The mercenaries looked from one to the other as they seriously considered this option.

"Wait." Dr. Alexi Molotov, geneticist and chief medical officer assigned to the mission, looked up from his microscope. "What's the matter with him?"

"I think he bashed his head on something."

Dr. Molotov came over and shone a light in the taikonaut's eyes. "Looks like concussion all right. Put him on that bed. I'll take a look at him."

The mercenaries did as ordered.

"Don't waste your time with him, Alexi." VanHoff's headache was getting worse.

"I'll just give him a quick scan. Make sure he hasn't fractured his skull."

"That makes you responsible for him."

"Understood."

"Just make sure you strap him down. We don't want him waking up and going kamikaze on us."

"He's Chinese, not Japanese."

"You know what I mean." VanHoff went back to his notes as the doctor started his tests on the taikonaut.

Playing nursemaid to the very people that tried to prevent him from taking over what was rightfully his was not what he wanted his team to be doing. But Dr. Molotov was not the type of individual he could just order around. He was one of the best geneticist money could buy. Sure, there were better ones. But VanHoff needed someone who was prepared to travel to Mars. Such a commute to work narrowed down the pool of available candidates considerably. But Dr. Molotov was not simply taking the job just for the money. He was also trying to make his name and saw this mission as a way of doing just that. Nevertheless, he would not be pushed into doing something he didn't want to. So VanHoff gritted his teeth and let the doctor indulge his Hippocratic conscience. For VanHoff the end always justified the means. And if Dr. Molotov's desire to provide humanitarian aid to the vanquished kept him content then so be it. He let him get on with it.

But there were more pressing matters. The ultimate

objective of the mission was to piece together, from the scattered fragments of the genetically engineered biology of the colonists, the secret that enabled them to regenerate and repair their physiology. This was the end goal. Since the original source bacteria was now all but destroyed, as far as VanHoff was aware, then the only way left was for him and his team to forensically piece it together from whatever clues they could uncover. This needed to be planned and Dr. Molotov was getting himself sidetracked. Not a good start.

Yet VanHoff was glad of this distraction in a way, as his rumbling headache was not conducive to doing the complex cognitive gymnastics required for genetic reverse engineering. He rubbed his temples, popped another painkiller and sighed. There wasn't much he could do here at present so he decided to find commander Kruger and get an update on the search for the elusive Dr. Jann Malbec. Although the mere thought of her made his head throb even more. He headed out of the medlab as Dr. Molotov was applying a bandage to the injured taikonaut. He left him to it.

VanHoff had assumed that Malbec would be located by now. In fact he assumed she would be dead at this stage. But, as always, she seemed to posses an innate ability to throw a spanner in the works, and ruin his plans. *Not this time,* he thought.

KRUGER SAT in the operations room, his feet up on the edge of the holo-table. He was cleaning his nails with a long knife. It had a serrated blade and looked like a tool more suited to gutting shark than to giving a manicure. Across from him sat Xenon. He was still and silent and exuded a

Zen-like calm. VanHoff caught his eye momentarily as he entered the room. He found it hard to break away from his gaze, he felt sucked in, like his soul was laid bare for Xenon to see. He had to drag his eyes away by sheer force of will.

"Ahh... Peter. Excellent timing. I was just discussing with our colonist friend here the need for cooperation and harmony in the colony as we progress to COM governance."

"And how's that going?" said VanHoff as he sat down at the table.

"Very well. We have agreed on a plan to release a small contingent of colonists so that important maintenance tasks can be performed. Assuming full cooperation, and a positive mental attitude, then we can proceed over time to release all colonists into productive duties. Isn't that so?" He directed his question at Xenon.

He simply nodded in reply.

"And what about Malbec?" VanHoff rubbed his temples again.

"I'm glad you asked that." The commander sheathed the knife into a leather scabbard strapped to his belt, with a quick reflex action.

"No sign of her in Colony Two, which leads me to believe that someone is leading us on a merry dance." He fixed his gaze on the Hybrid.

Xenon remained totally unfazed, it seemed to VanHoff that there was very little that could crack his aura of serenity. He almost envied him.

"So," the commander slapped the table. "Tell me, where is she?"

"In Colony Two." Xenon's voice was smooth and calm, so much so that VanHoff had no trouble believing him.

"Bollocks." Kruger leaned across the table. The tenor

and amplitude of his reply startled VanHoff, and broke the spell that the Hybrid had conjured.

The commander stood up straight. "If she was there, we would have found her by now. So she isn't, is she?"

Xenon remained silent.

"Okay, let's see if we can realign your memory." He tapped his earpiece and spoke. "Ready? Excellent. It's show time." He turned around to the main monitor. "You may want to have a look at this, Xenon."

An aerial view of the biodome central dais materialized on screen. Two mercenaries pointed weapons at a group of colonists, who were all on their knees, hands on heads.

He turned back to Xenon. "Now, here's what's going to happen. I'm going to ask you again, and if I don't like what I hear..." his arm moved to point back at the monitor. "One of your friends is going to fry. Got that"

Xenon remained silent.

"So, where is she?"

VanHoff liked this man. Brutal but efficient, a kindred spirit. As for Xenon, VanHoff perceived a note of tension ripple across his calm serene shell. Like a pebble being dropped into a still pool. The commander was not bluffing, everyone knew that.

"I don't hear anything." Kruger cocked a hand behind his ear as if to catch the sound of some distant echo.

"Fine," he said at last. "If that's the way you want to play it, so be it." He turned back to the monitor and tapped his earpiece. "Pick one, and waste them."

On screen a mercenary moved forward and aimed his weapon at the head of a hapless colonist. VanHoff could see the look of sheer terror etch itself on her face. Her body trembled and she mouthed a plea the he couldn't quite make out.

The Commander turned back. “Last chance—no? Okay then.”

“No, wait.” Xenon finally broke, he lowered his head.

A faint smile cracked across VanHoff’s face. *Finally, some results,* he thought.

“I’m listening.”

Xenon slowly raised his head and looked at Kruger. His lips parted, ready to utter the truth—then he seemed to hesitate. A strange look came over his face, then VanHoff realized he was not looking at the commander, he was looking past him, at the feed from the biodome. VanHoff followed his gaze.

On screen, one of the mercenaries had doubled over and was on his knees, clawing at his head. His comrade looked unsure of what to do. He was keeping his weapon trained on the colonists, at the same time as shouting down to the distressed mercenary. In the operations room Kruger finally realized that both Xenon and VanHoff had their eyes fixed on the screen, he turned around to see what was happening.

“What the...” He tapped his earpiece. “Talk to me.”

Currently none of the weapons in the biodome were set to stun. A thought that ran through the Commander’s mind as he watched the demented mercenary raise his PEP and fire it at his comrade. Fortunately, he missed.

“Shit... take him out—now!” the commander screamed into his earpiece. But the mercenary bolted off into the undergrowth of the biodome before his comrade had a chance to return fire.”

“Benson, go after him... find him, and take him down!”

The colonists were beginning to panic and, seeing their chance, they ran for the now open tunnel exit. VanHoff watched all this with a sense of rising trepidation. A phrase that one of his old board members keep using, back when they first discovered that Colony One was still functioning, came into his head. *What if it's happening again?* But before he could finish this particular line of thought a scream echoed around the main colony facility. It sounded to VanHoff like it came from the medlab. The commander was already on the move, barking orders to the COM mercenaries in the operations room with them. "You, stay here and keep an eye on the hybrid. And you, Slade, come with me." VanHoff followed after them, racing through the facility to the medlab. They stopped and took up positions either side of the medlab door. The commander shouted in. "Dr. Molotov!" No answer. He signaled for Slade to enter, then followed in behind him.

The doctor was lying on the floor, blood oozing from a head wound. Standing over him, holding a long steel bar, was the taikonaut they had brought in earlier. The commander raised his weapon to shoot.

"Don't kill him," VanHoff shouted.

"What? He's a homicidal maniac."

"No, don't kill him, I need him."

The commander gave VanHoff a wary look, then tilted his weapon to set it on stun, and fired. The taikonaut did a kind of chicken dance for a second as his nerve endings spasmed from the electrical overload. Then he dropped on top of the doctor.

"I hope to hell you know what you're doing. Next time I take him out—permanently." The commander nodded to Slade. "You go and help Benson in the biodome. I'll deal with this."

KRUGER LIFTED up the unconscious taikonaut and strapped him down to one of the operating tables. VanHoff checked on the status of the clone Nills. All good, vitals looked stable. Only then did he turn his attention to the doctor. He was still alive, the wound on his head looked worse than it actually was. He sat him up and after a minute he began to come around.

"What the hell happened?" Kruger leaned over him like a storm cloud about to burst.

The doctor lifted a feeble hand as if to wave off the impending threat. "He just suddenly woke up. Started saying something about his head, something like *he couldn't get them out*. I went over to talk to him and he just whacked me on the skull."

"What do you mean, *he couldn't get them out*?"

The doctor said nothing, just shrugged his shoulders.

"Well it all sounds pretty goddamn weird to me." Kruger stood upright and took a few steps back from the doctor.

VanHoff turned around to him. "I think it's all under control now, Commander. I can take it from here."

The commander leaned in, his face close to VanHoff. "In case you haven't noticed, there is a crazy on the loose in the biodome and a population of panicked colonists trying to get out. So I would say things are far from being under control."

VanHoff raised himself up as best he could and answered the commander's stare. "You are here to do a job, now I suggest you go do it."

There was a momentary silence, as taut as a fully wound spring. Kruger backed off, unclipped a small PEP weapon from his waistband and set it down on the workbench. "Part of my job is to keep people alive. So use this if you have to."

VanHoff nodded reluctantly.

"I've set it to stun. Don't want you killing any of us by mistake." He spun around and headed out of the medlab.

~

If there was one thing that Kruger enjoyed more than having everything under control, it was when everything was totally out of control. He was in his element in these situations, it was an addictive adrenaline rush that made life worth living. When things were just on the edge, ready to spiral into chaos, that's when Willem Kruger felt most alive. Now, as he raced across the common room to the biodome door, he felt a wave of excitement ripple through him as he reviewed the current situation.

There was no doubt in his mind that his crew were exposed to the same infection that he had feared might happen. The COM mission hierarchy had gone to great pains to dismiss this scenario as highly unlikely, but Kruger was not paid to live in the *unlikely*. His worth lay in situations where the shit had hit the fan.

So far one of the Xaing Zu crew had gone over to the dark side. He should have killed him when he had the chance. But at least he was incapacitated, and now out of the fight. The colonists had also seen fit to corral the rest of the Chinese in one of the food processing pods, so they too were rendered inactive. His thoughts now turned to his own COM crew. Already one had gone feral in the biodome. But his major concern was how many more would succumb to this psychotic malaise. A horrific thought struck him—*could he too become infected?* And how would he even know? He put these thoughts out of his mind and concentrated on the current active threats, and how best to contain them. He checked his weapon.

As Kruger approached the tunnel entrance to the biodome he could hear screaming and yelling emanating from within. He pressed his hand to his earpiece. "Slade,

Benson, talk to me. I'm approaching the entrance to the biodome, what's the situation?"

Stay frosty, he's heading your way, commander.

With that a number of colonists ran out through the tunnel, they didn't even skip a beat when they saw him. This was not a good sign, as the threat that he posed to them obviously paled in comparison to what they were running from.

A blast from a PEP weapon split the air ahead of him and a colonist collapsed in a writhing heap of flashing light. It snaked and swirled around his body before finally extinguishing itself. The colonist's forward momentum kept him sliding along the floor right up to Kruger's feet. He resisted the temptation to look down and check on the immobilized colonist, his ingrained training instead keeping him focused on the threat, fortunately for Kruger, as the crazed mercenary now came into view.

He was moving at speed towards the commander, but his gait was awkward and he seemed to be rolling his head as he ran. Kruger raised his weapon to take a shot, but he was too slow, a bolt of incandescent light burst out from the mercenary's weapon. Kruger threw himself sideways as the flash passed him by. He hit the floor, rolled and came around for a shot, but something was wrong. His left side was not responding. His arm was paralyzed, he must have been hit. All he could do was watch as the crazed mercenary sped past him, knocking over panicked colonists like ninepins as he barreled forward.

"Guys, talk to me, I'm down, he's getting past me. Where the hell are you?"

"Here, Commander." Kruger looked up and saw lieutenants Benson and Slade standing over him. Benson offered him a hand up. "You okay, sir?"

"Bastard winged me. My left arm is non-operational for a while." He stood up and gripped the weapon tight in his good arm and looked down through the biodome entrance tunnel. The flow of panicking colonists had stopped. Those still inside, which was the bulk of them, had chosen to stay there, assuming it to be the safer option, which from where Kruger was standing made perfect sense.

"Listen to me, Benson. I want you to get VanHoff and the doctor out of the medlab, get them into EVA suits and bring them to the safe zone we identified. You know where that is?"

"Yes sir. What about the biodome door, and the escaped colonists?"

"Screw them. They're too scared to do anything but hide. The ones still in the biodome aren't going anywhere. We can round up the stragglers later. First *you* need to get VanHoff to the safe zone. We will track down this crazy bastard. Got it?"

"Got it, sir." Lieutenant Benson ran off to the medlab.

Kruger watched him go as he took a moment to rub some feeling back in to his arm, then he took a look around. The colonists that had escaped from the biodome were nowhere to be seen, save for the one lying on the ground in front of him. He wondered if he was dead and then he saw the gentle rise and fall of his chest. *He's okay, he'll live—probably.* Kruger checked his weapon again, gripped it tight, and moved off in the direction of the operations room. This was also the access route to the other sectors of the facility. The situation was still volatile, but he was back in the saddle and on the hunt for live game. God, he loved this job.

It took VanHoff a few moments to regain his composure after facing off with the commander. He ignored the weapon Kruger had left on the workbench and instead focused his attentions on Dr. Molotov, who was now strapping his head with a bandage and checking himself in the mirror. "Going to need a few stitches I should think," he said as he gingerly touched the wound above his temple. VanHoff, seeing Molotov was okay, turned back to look over the unconscious Xaing Zu taikonaut. Now that the mayhem had been brought under control, a slow realization had been building in his mind since observing the incident in the biodome. This realization was now becoming fully formed as he stared down at the face of this crazed individual. "Could be happening again?" he said to no one in particular.

"What was that you said?" Dr. Molotov was applying an adhesive bandage to close his wound.

"There's only one thing that could make this guy and the COM mercenary in the biodome go crazy like that."

Dr. Molotov spun around and stared at VanHoff for a moment. "You mean there's another one?"

"Yes. In the biodome. A while ago, one of our own crew went crazy, started shooting up the place."

The doctor walked over and looked down at the taikonaut. "We'd better get an IV into him, keep him sedated. We don't want him going nuts again." He pulled out a cannula from a drawer beside the operating table and cracked open the seal.

While Dr. Molotov set about ensuring the unfortunate Chinese crewmember was well out of harm's way, VanHoff's mind began to race with the implications of these chaotic events. If his suspicions were true then there was only one sure way to find out. So, it was with shaking fingers that

VanHoff drew a vial of blood from the patient's arm. If it was truly happening again then he wouldn't need much blood to confirm it.

He prepared a slide and slid it under the microscope. He leaned in to look through the eyepiece, and slowly nudged the focus. His point of view moved around the sample, nothing looked out of the ordinary. But then he stopped and froze. There it was, a clump of dark elongated bacteria. There was no mistaking it. His heart skipped a beat and he snapped his head away from the microscope eyepiece.

"What is it?" Dr. Molotov looked over at him.

VanHoff waved a hand to silence him. This was a seminal moment. The thing that he had been searching for, the thing that had been denied him so many times—here it was at last. He peered in through the microscope eyepiece again. He was afraid that he might have been imagining it, that it wasn't really there. He scanned the sample for a few more moments before saying, "I've found it."

Then a thought came to him like a hammer blow, the genetic miracle that he had been searching for his whole life was probably already inside him, infecting him, changing his biology. He wondered if that was the reason for the headache that had been rumbling around the folds of his brain since morning. Yet, he had not gone mad like the others. He felt the skin on the back of his hand as if to find some physical evidence that the bacteria was working its magic on him. But this was ludicrous, his excitement was dulling his scientific mind, there was a better way to be certain. A few moments later, Peter VanHoff again peered into the microscope at the dark elongated shapes of the Janus bacteria. Except this time he was looking at a sample of his own blood. He sat back. A broad smile broke across aged face. He had done it. He had found it at last.

But he didn't get time to revel in his triumph, as a wave of screaming and yelling emanated from somewhere outside the medlab. He stopped and listened as the mayhem slowly died down. He was just about to relax again when Lieutenant Benson burst through the door.

"Dr. VanHoff, Dr. Molotov. You'd better come with me. Right now!"

18

CHAOS

So far her plan was having the desired effect, causing chaos and mayhem to run riot in the colony. COM was off balance, losing control of the colonists now running out of the biodome in panic. The medlab had also been evacuated. The battle had begun, but Jann had to act now if the momentum were to stay in her favor. She turned around to Gizmo. "Time to go, come on."

They raced over to the airlock door that gave them access through the short tunnel to the medlab. Within minutes they had ascended to the ancillary medlab module. Jann peered through the small window in the door and scanned the room. It was empty save for Nills lying on one of the operating tables and one of the Chinese crew strapped down to another.

"Okay," she whispered to Gizmo. "Once we're inside you need to get that main door closed."

"Will do."

She cracked open the door and stepped inside. Gizmo whizzed, as silently as possible for a robot on tracks, over to the entrance door and closed it gently. Jann moved to where

Nills lay. His face was pale, and from his body ran a profusion of wires and tubes. But his vitals looked good as they drew themselves out on the monitors. Her first reaction was to start pulling out the invasive tubes but that might not be such a bright idea. She needed to calm herself down and figure out what each one was doing. Only then could she start to bring him back to the real world.

Outside she could hear the colony descending into chaos. Yelling and screeching interspersed with the telltale whoomp of a PEP weapon being discharged. Gizmo had explained the operation of these weapons to her, so she dearly hoped that they had set them to stun. The last thing she wanted was the death of a colonist because of her high-stakes gamble. An alarm shrieked on the monitor as she withdrew a tube from Nills' upper arm. She jumped, then tapped the screen to switch it off. The noise from outside was getting louder. After a few more anxious minutes she finally extracted the last of the IVs, the one that kept him sedated. She pulled it gently from his neck and held her finger over the insertion point to stem the blood. She looked up at the monitor, all was okay, his vital signs were holding steady.

The medlab door burst open and in rushed two colonists, dragging a third along the floor between them. They stopped in surprise when they saw her and Gizmo.

"Dr. Malbec... we thought you were dead... how did you survive the tunnel collapse?"

Jann looked down at the body of the colonist that they had deposited on the floor. "Is he dead?"

"Eh... I don't think so... I'm not sure."

"Gizmo, go check on him." Jann was in the process of applying bandages to the numerous punctures on Nills' body.

"Low but steady pulse, some pupil dilation, some scorching of the cervical epidermis." The droid looked up at Jann. "Not dead. Injuries symptomatic of plasma energy pulse weapon set on *paralyze*."

This was good news to Jann. At least the COM mercenaries had seen fit to show some restraint, having presumably established that killing them all would not be in their best interests. After all they were not the enemy—yet. They were simply running in panic from the infected. That said, non-lethal weaponry had the advantage of enabling the user to disable anyone with impunity. So they could, if they wanted to, turn the tables very quickly. Jann knew she didn't have much time. If she hoped to regain control she would have to act fast. She eyed the PEP weapon that VanHoff had forgotten to take with him when he was unceremoniously whisked out of the medlab. She had spotted it earlier, but now Jann reached over and picked it up. It was small and stubby, but surprisingly heavy.

"What's going on out there?" she said to the others.

They all stopped and listened. It had gone very quiet. No one spoke for a moment. Jann inched her way to the main door and opened it a crack. What she could see of the outside area seemed empty of people. She turned back to the colonists. "How many people got out of the biodome?"

"I don't know... the door was open so we just ran. One of the COM mercenaries went totally crazy in there... shooting up the place."

"Gizmo, can you get any location data on the COM mercenaries?"

"I'm picking up readings from multiple sectors."

"Your best guess for where they are now?"

"There is a cohort heading for dome five. Their

signature shows patterns symptomatic of multiple high energy sources."

"PEP weapons?"

"Precisely."

"And the operations room?"

"I estimate one, maybe two lifeforms."

"Okay, well it looks as if Xenon is still in there, so here's the plan. You guys stay here and keep an eye on Nills and your colleague. Myself and Gizmo will go and find Xenon."

"What about him?" The colonist pointed over to the unconscious taikonaut.

"He isn't going anywhere."

The colonist wasn't convinced. "Are you sure?"

"Trust me. He's strapped down good and tight." She moved back to the door, opened it a bit wider and scanned the area. It was deserted.

"Okay Gizmo, let's go."

PETER VANHOFF FOLLOWED close behind Lieutenant Benson as they navigated their way to the safe zone. Dr. Molotov took up the rear. This was an area within the facility that the commander had deemed the safest place to hole up should the situation become volatile. As a precaution, EVA suits had been stashed there along with other necessary supplies.

VanHoff had followed along in a kind of daze, not really paying attention to where they were going. His mind was still trying to fathom the enormity of his discovery. Not how it came to be that the Janus bacteria had suddenly materialized after so much time lying dormant, but more about how it was multiplying in his bloodstream and what that meant for his own flawed biology. He had sought this moment for so very long that now it had arrived, he felt like he was in a dream.

"You need to get into this EVA suit, sir."

"What?" He was snapped back to the here and now by the mention of the words, *EVA suit*.

"The suit, sir. You need to put it on." Benson motioned at it with his a nod of his head.

Under normal circumstances VanHoff would have balked at the thought of encasing himself in an EVA suit unless it was absolutely necessary, such was his fear of being enclosed in one. He had barely kept it together for the few short steps it took to get from the rover to the entrance airlock when they arrived. But now his fear was virtually nonexistent, it had evaporated. The claustrophobic environment held no threat for him. With the bacteria now working its miracle within, he felt invulnerable, invincible, even superhuman. Yet, he knew all this was purely psychological, any improvement in his physiology would take time to be evidenced. Nevertheless, it was a fundamentally different VanHoff that now inspected the EVA suit, than the VanHoff that landed on Mars, not so long ago.

"It's just a precaution, sir. In case we need to get you out of here in a hurry."

Dr. Molotov was already suiting himself up, so VanHoff nodded. "Sure, no problem, I understand." He moved over to where the EVA suit was hanging and started to get it ready to put on. He was opening up the front and just in the process of performing the initial checks on the suit system when he noticed that Benson had a vacant, distracted look. "Are you okay?"

Benson looked back at him with a kind of confused expression. Like he couldn't quite remember where he was.

VanHoff felt an anxious twinge ripple through him as he considered that Benson might be succumbing to the infection, and not in a good way.

Benson seemed to snap out of it. "Sorry, sir. Just kind of... zoned out for a moment." He shook his head and touched his earpiece, listening to some message from the commander, no doubt. "Gotta go. Will you be okay here, sir?"

"Yeah, we'll be fine. Go. You need to get this facility back under control."

Benson nodded and headed off. VanHoff watched him go. He wondered if he should inform Kruger of his suspicions about the mental health of the mercenary. Maybe not, perhaps he was just being a bit paranoid. Best leave the commander do his job.

~

As Jann and Gizmo entered the common room, they startled a group of colonists that had hidden out in there. They were armed with hastily constructed weapons such as spears, clubs, and knives from the galley that were now repurposed and brought into emergency service.

"It's me... it's me." She held her hands up and moved into the light so they could see her better. One by one they moved out from alcoves and the dark corners of the space. "Dr. Malbec, you're alive!"

"Yes, it's me, still here. Where are the others?"

They looked from one to the other. "Scattered... I think. One of the mercenaries went nuclear in the biodome, everyone ran."

"It's that crazy bug, isn't it? It's starting to happen again... oh god we're all going to go insane."

"No, you're not. And yes, it is that *crazy bug*, but colonists are immune to it, we all are. So it's just COM and the Chinese that have to worry." Jann's words had a visible calming effect on the ragtag group. It was only then that she noticed the colonists had kept quite a distance from each other, fearing that at any moment a friend might flip and drive a stake though their heart.

"How can you be so sure that's what it is? I thought it had died out, long ago."

"No. A small sample remained. I released it into the colony environment last night."

"Holy crap, so it's true?

Jann smiled. "Yes, and we now have them on the run. So we need to pull together and take back control."

"What should we do?"

"Xenon is being held in the operations room, we need to get him out. But we need to be careful, there may be a COM mercenary in there with him."

The colonists all gripped their makeshift weapons tighter and moved closer to Jann and Gizmo. They were ready for the fight.

The operations room was the nerve center for Colony One. All systems could be monitored and managed from there. It had one main door, with a long window along the wall facing out onto the concourse that connected several different sectors of the facility. One side led to domes four, five and accommodation. Another side had a short connecting tunnel which led to the common room and farther on to the biodome, medlab and a raft of other sectors. They were all now moving through this connecting tunnel but stopped once they reached the concourse intersection. Jann looked across at the operations room window. It was blacked out, no way to see in.

"Gizmo, any movement around here?"

"Data indicates lifeforms located in various sectors, none in close proximity, save for two in the operations room. But this is only an estimate based on ambient temperature readings and sundry data."

Jann hefted the PEP weapon, looking it over to get a feel for how it worked. Maybe it had an *on* switch. She didn't want to be in a situation, needing to pull the trigger, only for nothing to happen. A small screen on the side displayed *ready*. She took this to be a good sign. Below it were a series of bars, which she reckoned must be charge or perhaps shots. It displayed 9. Other than that she couldn't figure much more about it. Whether it was set to stun or lethal she couldn't tell. Maybe it didn't have such a setting. The only real way she could test it would be when she fired off a shot. But if she were to enter a fight she needed to trust her weapon and this was not good enough. She thought about giving it to Gizmo, and instead using a spear one of the colonists was carrying. But it looked too bent and twisted, no good for straight flight. There was nothing else to do, she would have to chance it.

Jann nodded to the others and they followed her quietly across the concourse, lining themselves up on either side of the operations room door. Surprise was the only way this was going to work. But the mercenary inside might already be on high alert, with an itchy trigger finger, waiting for some crazed comrade to come bursting through the door and attack. But then she thought, *that might help us.* She whispered her instruction to the others, then counted silently down from three—and kicked the door in.

She dropped down to the floor as a blast of plasma energy screamed over her head out though the open door and dissipated in a cackling wave across the far wall of the concourse. She knew her direction now, rolled over, sighted her target, and fired.

A ball of flashing brilliance enveloped the mercenary. It burst out across his body encasing it in a fiery mesh of flashing light. He shook and jerked as his coordination broke down under the massive surge in electrical signals now overloading his nervous system. Sparks exploded from various electronic equipment he had strapped to his person. No longer able to stand upright he collapsed across a control desk. It too began to pop and spark, as monitors flickered on and off. Finally he slumped to the floor as the last of the plasma burst fizzled out. His eyes were wide, his body still and a thin filament of smoke rose from his skull.

"Holy crap."

"Go check on him." Jann waved to one of the colonists now coming through the door. She ran over to where Xenon was crouched down. One arm covered his head, the other was zip tied to the bar that ran around the edge of the comms desk. He poked his head out and looked up.

"Jann. I thought you were dead." A look of surprise burst on his face.

"Yeah, I'm still alive. It's hard to get rid of me. Gizmo, can you get these zip ties off?"

The little droid selected a suitable tool from its inventory and snapped off the nylon cuffs. Xenon stood up. "How did you survive the tunnel collapse?" He was rubbing his wrist.

"That doesn't matter. What matters is getting control back. We have an opportunity now, so we need to grab it."

"What's going on? Everyone is running around, going crazy."

"You remember the Janus bacteria?"

"Yes. It decimated the original colony. But that was destroyed a long time ago."

"Not exactly. There was one sample remaining—and I released in to the colony environment last night."

Xenon eyes went wide. "I see. Well that would explain a lot."

"But don't worry, all colonists are immune to it. It will only affect COM... and the Chinese."

"Very clever. So they're all going insane."

"Not all, just some. But enough to throw a very crazy cat or two among some very scared pigeons."

Xenon smiled. "So we have a chance to get rid of them?"

"No." Jann grabbed his arm and looked hard at him. "We cannot let them leave the planet. That would be a disaster. We can't let them bring this back to Earth."

"Ah... I see. No, that would not be good."

Gizmo's head twitched.

"What is it?"

"Movement... multiple sectors."

"Can we see from here?"

Gizmo tapped at the control desk. "The network is down. The electrified COM mercenary shorted out a lot of circuits. It will take time to get them repaired." A few sparks exploded from the desk as Gizmo tested it. "This could take a while."

~

DR. PETER VANHOFF had finally encased himself in his EVA suit, but left the helmet off for the moment. It would only take a few seconds to attach it, should the need arise. And he was hoping that was not going to happen. He had briefly contacted Kruger on his comms but got no information from him other than, *sit tight and wait until you get the all clear*. So he and Dr. Molotov sat on an old storage container. VanHoff occupied himself with his thoughts as he waited.

The reason he had come to Mars in the first place was to find the very thing that was now inside him, working to restore his flawed genetics. He had so far escaped the negative side effect, insanity. So he felt a deep calm wash over him, something that he had not felt for as long as he could remember. It bathed him in a warm glow of peace and contentment, mixed with a dash of anticipation—the future looked good, very good for Peter VanHoff.

It struck him then that he did not need to be here anymore. Not in this safe zone, not in Colony One, not even on this planet. Now that he had found it, what need was there for him to remain? He could return to Earth. Sure, there were a few practical issues to deal with. But to all intents and purposes it was *job done*, time to go home.

Yet there was always a possibility that the Janus bacteria would not work to counter the effects of his genetic disease, as it did with those who were not so afflicted. So more scientific investigation might be needed to divine its function. But this could be better realized in a fully resourced genetics lab back on Earth, than in the rudimentary facilities here on Mars.

He thought about contacting Kruger again but decided it might be best not to bother him. He was probably busy trying to contain the various members of the crew that had gone psychotic. Assuming, of course, that the commander himself had not succumbed. And if he had, then how would VanHoff get out? He looked around the space that they had been sequestered in. It was subterranean, that much he knew. But was there a way out from here on to the Martian surface? And even if he could find a way there was still the long walk back to the COM ship. Could he handle that? He was more confident now in undertaking such an arduous journey. Physically he should be able to manage it. It would be controlling his debilitating claustrophobia that would be the challenge. However, he felt sure he could overcome it. With the flight officer ready and waiting, and everything prepped, he could, in theory, leave the planet and return to Earth.

The only problem with this plan was he could not see a way out of here, save for going back into the facility and exiting via one of the usable airlocks. It was doable. But it would mean exposing himself to more danger than was necessary. So he decided to wait. Well, he would give it another thirty minutes. Then, if there was no resolution, he and Dr. Molotov would attempt to leave this place and make their way back to the MAV, and ultimately off this hellhole of a planet.

19

JING TZU

It had gotten quiet, too quiet. Jing Tzu stood with his ear pressed against the locked door of the food processing pod, where he and the two other Xaing Zu crew had been imprisoned. Outside in the biodome nothing could be heard. Something was going on, and he didn't like it.

A short while after Xenon and the other colonists had unceremoniously dumped them in here, the biodome descended into chaos. Shouting, yelling, the sound of a PEP weapon, then running. Now there was a deathly silence. Yet it could be an opportunity.

He and his crew needed to get out of here somehow. Better still, would be to get off the planet and return to Earth. They would have to leave sometime, COM couldn't hold them here forever. But he didn't trust them either. He wouldn't put it past that maniacal VanHoff to just blow them out of an airlock.

He pressed his ear against the door again—silence.

"Anything?" His first officer, Chen Deng, called over from the back of the pod. He had finished tying up their mission geneticist, who had started to get that same strange look in his eyes that Dan Ma had just before he went psychotic. So they decided to tie him up, much to his consternation, before he started killing them all. He protested for quite a while before finally zoning out, or maybe he was unconscious, Chang couldn't tell. Commander Jing Tzu moved away from the door and shook his head. "Nothing." He looked down at the geneticist. "How is he?"

"Well, if he wakes up and goes ballistic, like Dan Ma, at least we've got him contained."

"We need to get out of here, back to the lander if possible. There's something going on out there, and I have a bad feeling about it. However, it might just give us an opportunity."

"Back to the lander? How? We'd need our EVA suits."

"Well you can stay here and go insane if you want."

Chen looked down at the unconscious geneticist. "What's happening to them?"

"It's this place, it's possessed by a corrupt biology. One that eats away at the mind. They warned us about it, remember?"

"But it was supposed to be eradicated."

"Well, you can stay here and think about it if you like, or you can help get us out of this place."

Chen stood up. "So we just leave him here... and Dan Ma as well?"

"Screw him. He's a geneticist, the very people who create these abominations." Jing Tzu moved closer to Chen and calmed his voice. "Two of our crew are dead, killed by COM. Dan Ma is probably dead too or may as well be." He looked down at the geneticist. "And we can guess what's going to happen to him. So the mission is over. There is nothing to be gained by staying here. We need to grab this chance and try to escape."

Chen looked at him for a moment and eventually nodded. "You're right, let's get the hell out of here."

It took them less than five minutes to break open the pod door. They stepped out into the biodome and looked around. It was still and silent. "Where are they all?" Chen whispered.

Jing Tzu didn't answer, instead he was looking high up to the biodome roof trying to spot cameras. "Come." He moved into where the undergrowth would hide them from any prying eyes. Chen followed. When Jing Tzu was sure they were well hidden he broke a small twig from a bush, hunkered down and started drawing in the dirt.

"We're here. Over here is the airlock with our spare EVA suits. The only problem is that was damaged by COM in the attack. So the suits may also be damaged."

"They might not even be there," said Chen.

"True. Also, there is a distinct possibility that the colony is in lockdown. If that's the case then none of the airlocks will be operational."

"Great."

"However, there is another option." He started scratching again with the twig. "This is the operations room, over here. Beside it is the storage pod where we put some of the additional equipment we brought. There should be some more spare EVA suits in there somewhere."

"That sounds like a better plan to me. But, assuming we find the suits, how do we get out?"

"There is an access route, around here, that goes down into the soil processing area."

"But that's subterranean, how's that going to help us?"

"There is an automatic airlock system for the soil harvesting robots." He looked up at Chen. "It doesn't go into lockdown."

Chen looked at the commander's scratchings for a moment. "Okay, let's do it."

THEY MOVED THROUGH THE BIODOME, sticking to the areas where the vegetation was thickest, hoping it would keep them concealed from view. They passed along the dense rows of hydroponics and finally to where the main entrance door stood, wide open. "Come on, let's keep going." They hurried to the side of the door, keeping low and quiet. Jing Tzu looked down the length of the short tunnel. "Clear, let's go."

They hugged the tunnel wall as they moved along and out into the main common room. "This way," Jing Tzu signaled and they moved off in the direction of the operations room. They had only taken a few steps when they heard the telltale *whoomp* of a PEP weapon, followed by a scream, followed by footsteps—running their way.

Jing Tzu dived out of sight behind a low counter, Chen followed behind. They waited as the footsteps grew louder. It sounded like multiple people, running fast. As they charged past they could see they were colonists, carrying two others, all heading in the direction of the medlab. As soon as they were out of sight Jing Tzu rose from his hiding place and nodded to Chen to follow him. They moved with caution, keeping their ears alert to any danger.

When they arrived at the concourse it was deserted, but they could see shadows moving behind the smoked glass window of the operations room. Somewhere far off in the depths of the facility they could hear shouts.

Jing Tzu put his finger to his lips and pointed in the direction of the storage pod. Chen nodded his understanding and they tiptoed across the concourse, all the time keeping an eye on the movements within the operations room. They reached the door to the storage pod, as the racket emanating from deep within the facility was getting louder and more frenetic.

The door was locked. “Shit. I don’t suppose you know the code?” Jing Tzu was pushing his shoulder to it trying to break it open.

“Here, let me try.” Chen pushed Jing Tzu out of the way and tapped at the keypad a few times. The door clicked open. He looked over at Jing Tzu and winked. “Its good to pay attention to the details sometimes.” They bundled themselves inside.

Automatic lights flickered on, illuminating a chaotic scene of equipment and storage strewn all around the space. They stood with their backs to the door looking out across the tumbled landscape.

“We’re never going to find anything in here.” Chen scanned the jumble of crates and boxes.

“There should be at least three spare EVA suits in here somewhere, and the sooner we find them the sooner we can get off this rock.” Jing Tzu started sorting through the detritus, reading labels, righting boxes.

“Commander Jing.” Chen was on the other side of a mound of equipment.

“Did you find them?”

“No, but I found something else.”

Jing Tzu moved over to look at where Chen was pointing. Sitting on the floor, partially covered by a tarpaulin was Yutu. He looked over at his First Officer and smiled. "This is good fortune indeed. Maybe even auspicious." He reached down and ripped the cover off. The robot looked undamaged, but inactive, no power lights. Jing Tzu slid open a metal panel on the robot's back, revealing a small flat screen, with several switches arrayed on either side. He flicked a number of them and the screen lit up, then placed his palm momentarily on the screen so it could be scanned. The robot twitched and the screen filled with scrolling code as the boot-up sequence began to reanimate the machine.

The robot rose up from its haunches and moved several of its limbs as if testing their function. Jing Tzu and Chen stood back as it performed its systems checks. When it finished it raised its head and spoke. "Commander Jing Tzu, First Officer Chen Deng. I am at your service."

"Debrief, show last visual." Jing Tzu instructed.

Yutu's eyes flickered and a 3D image was projected into the space in front of the robot. It showed the main airlock exploding inward as the COM assault began. COM had set up an outer umbilical so the facility would not lose atmospheric integrity when it blew. Smoke and dust filled the scene, punctuated by streaks of bright blue plasma bursts from the PEP weapons. Then a COM mercenary came into view and aimed something at the robot. The visual ended abruptly.

"Replay—data only," said Jing Tzu.

This time Yutu projected a stream of stylized data for the time period. It was part environmental: what existed in the space around the robot at the time, and part internal: what was happening to its own systems.

"There, stop." Jing Tzu pointed into space. "A massive electromagnetic spike. That's what disabled Yutu."

"I thought it was hardened against EMP from a PEP weapon."

"It is, this is different, maybe a direct hit from something designed to overload electronic circuitry."

"Well, at least it didn't damage it. Yutu is designed to shut down immediately to protect its systems. But, I have a better idea."

"What's that?"

"Something that will give them a shock if they try it again." The commander turned back to Yutu. "Access."

The robot stood up on all four limbs as the panel on its back slid open again. Jing Tzu proceeded to tap commands into the interface.

"What are you doing?"

Jing Tzu didn't answer for a few more minutes until he was finished. "Self-destruct." He winked at Chen. "If Yutu senses another attack like that it will give them all a very big surprise."

Chen looked concerned. "Is that wise?"

Jing Tzu spun around, visibly angry at his subordinate questioning his authority. "This place is an abomination. As soon as we are safely on the planet's surface away from here I will instruct Yutu to return—and self-destruct. It will take this place with it. Destroy it, hopefully for good."

The first officer simply nodded. Jing Tzu turned back to the machine. "Yutu, locate spare EVA suits."

The robot moved off, shifting its head this way and that, scanning the area. Like a metal sniffer dog, it poked and prodded with its sensors. It stopped beside three elongated storage containers with the Xaing Zu Industries logo on the side. "Located." It pointed with one of its forelimbs.

They cracked them open and spent the next few minutes checking the suits' resources. None were fully charged but they were reasonably well resourced otherwise. With the help of the robot they calculated they had enough to make it to the Xaing Zu ship and still have 32.5% resources in reserve, more than enough. A few more minutes and they were back at the entrance door, suited and booted, carrying their helmets.

Jing Tzu stuck his ear to the inside of the door and listened. He could hear muffled sounds far off in the depths of the colony. Whatever was going on was still in play. He opened the door a crack and peered out. Two colonists passed right by, but didn't see him—a moment earlier and they would have. He watched them move along the concourse and finally out of sight, he thought one of them might be Jann Malbec. When he was sure they were gone, he stepped out and looked around, then he signaled to Chen to follow. They moved out of the storage pod as silently as a bulky EVA suit would allow. Yutu followed, hunkered low to the floor. Fortunately they didn't have far to go, just a few meters to the soil processing access door. Jing Tzu opened it while Chen kept watch. They finally slipped inside, unseen.

THE SPACE WAS NARROW, and short. Only a few feet of floor before they started to descend down a steep ramp into the subterranean cave system beneath Colony One. It was designed as an access route for maintenance crews who needed to service the soil processing machinery and harvester robots. The walls and floor of this cave were not sealed and hence the air within had a high concentration of perchlorates. Not something you want to spend much time breathing, as it could cause thyroid problems. But that was the least of their worries, they weren't planning on staying here too long.

It was dark. The hum of machinery grew more intense as they descended. Yutu went ahead, a beam of light flicked on from its head. It slowed down as it probed the area by bouncing a multitude of frequencies around the volume. It stopped, forcing Jing Tzu and Chen to halt.

"What's it doing?"

"Shhh." Jing Tzu held a finger to his lips.

The robot's head tilted this way and that, and just when the commander considered it had stopped completely, it shot off across the cave with impressive speed. A figure darted out from a hiding place and ran. But it didn't get far. By the time Jing Tzu and Chen had caught up with the robot it had both of its forelimbs resting on the shoulders of its victim, pinning him to the floor. The figure held an arm across his face and shouted. "Get this goddamn thing off me."

Jing Tzu looked down at him. It was Peter VanHoff.

20

DOME FIVE

As Gizmo worked to repair the operation room console, Jann had a moment to consider their next move. With the limited data that the droid could provide, she began to get a picture of where people were located. The bulk of the *lifeforms*, as Gizmo put it, were in the biodome. This made sense as Jann considered the colonists were too scared to move from whatever hiding places they had found for themselves in there, and if you were of the mindset to lay low and keep out of trouble, then the biodome was the perfect place for it. She also discovered from Xenon that the remains of the Xaing Zu crew were locked up in one of the food processing pods, so at least she didn't have to consider them as an immediate threat.

Of the colonists that had run out of the biodome, some were in the medlab looking after Nills and the injured. The rest were here in the operations room with her. She looked around. Some were tending to the COM mercenary she had just blasted. Surprisingly, he was still alive, lying on the floor unconscious. How long the effects of a blast from a PEP weapon lasted, she had no idea. So he could potentially wake up at any minute and start causing trouble. Although, he was bound to be in considerable pain from all the burns inflicted on him by the exploding electronics. Nevertheless, it would be a good idea to restrain him now, before he came to.

But her main consideration was COM, and how to immobilize them as a threat. Yet, to do this they needed to know where they all were—and where was VanHoff?

"Gizmo, any joy with that console?"

"That depends on how you define joy. There is the joy of fixing, and then there is the joy of having fixed."

Jann looked over at Xenon and sighed. He was in the process of tying up the mercenary. He just nodded at the quirky robot and smiled as if he had read her mind.

"Gizmo, I just want to know where the bulk of the COM crew are located." Jann tried again.

"Well why didn't you say so?" Gizmo spun around to face Jann. "The console is too badly damaged for me to effect repairs in any immediate time frame, and I have no visual or audio feeds. So, from the limited amount of data available to me, and extrapolating two-dimensional direction vectors over time, my best guess is the main COM cohort are somewhere in the connecting tunnel between domes four and five, and accommodation."

"And VanHoff?"

"Much as I hate to admit it, but I do not know with any certainty where he is."

"Well, we know he was in the medlab until a short time ago. I would imagine that COM are keeping him close, keeping him safe," said Xenon. He was now examining the PEP weapon belonging to the fallen mercenary.

"Gizmo, can we lockdown the facility so no one can get out?"

The little robot moved to an undamaged section of the operations room and tapped some icons. “It is already locked down.”

“Good,” said Jann. “Now we just need to isolate COM. Can we close off that sector?”

“Yes, but unfortunately I can not do this remotely.” Gizmo swiveled his head back to look at Jann. “Come, let me show you.” It moved over to the holo-table and brought up a 3D schematic of the colony. “This door here will close off the entire sector from the rest of the colony. No way out for COM. But you must do this manually.”

Jann considered this for a moment, then stood back from the holo-table and faced the others. “Okay, so here’s what we do...” But before she had time to explain her plan a COM mercenary appeared in the doorway to the operations room. He just stood there, not moving, and his eyes possessed a very long distance stare.

“Shit.” Jann grabbed her weapon and pointed it at him as the others dove for cover. “Drop the weapon!”

The mercenary looked confused. His head tilted to the side for a moment then looked down at his weapon. He lifted it up and examined it as if its function and purpose had escaped his memory.

“Just drop it!” Jann moved closer, her weapon held with both hands, arms outstretched. Xenon also raised his weapon and pointed at the confused mercenary.

Something suddenly snapped into place in the mercenary’s confused mind and several things happened all at once. He let out a long blood-curdling scream that physically stunned them. At the same time he raised his weapon, having somehow remembered its function, and fired a blast before running off.

Jann took a moment to react, and fired. But the

mercenary had gone and her shot dissipated off the far wall of the concourse. She ran out the door, followed by Xenon. Jann looked around but he was nowhere to be seen. "Dammit. Where did he come from?"

"It is unlikely he's the same mercenary that went psycho in the biodome. Which means we have a second one to deal with," said Xenon.

Jann was still looking down the concourse in the direction of dome five. "This could work in our favor. It looks like he's headed for the main COM cohort. So if we can get that door closed then they can fight it out between themselves in there." She lowered her weapon and turned back to Xenon. Some of the other colonists had come out of the operations room holding various rudimentary weapons.

"Anyone hit?"

"Yes, Melva. She's alive, but unconscious."

Jann walked back into the operations room. Melva was lying on the floor, flat on her back. A large burn mark, the size of a dinner plate, bloomed out across her chest.

"You'd better get her to the medlab, and take that COM mercenary as well," Jann instructed.

The colonists started to gather up the fallen.

Gizmo, you stay here and get that console back up and running."

"I shall do my best, Jann."

"Xenon. You and I will go and get the door to that sector sealed. If we can do that, then we have a chance at finishing this. Come on, let's go."

~

COMMANDER WILLEM KRUGER had tracked the psychotic crewmember that had gone ballistic inside the biodome to a cluster of domes on the far side of the facility. These were connected via a short tunnel to a concourse that acted as a kind of backbone for the Colony One infrastructure. Several sectors were linked to this concourse. The area that he and the rest of his crew were now searching consisted of two small domes, collectively named *accommodation,* and two larger ones, each with the unimaginative titles of dome four and dome five. His crew had already conducted a thorough search of all these sectors except for dome five. All were clear. Kruger checked his PEP weapon for the umpteenth time and then signaled for his crew to gather around.

"Okay, listen up. I want this guy taken down quick. I don't care if he's your best buddy, he's now a homicidal maniac ready to gut you on sight. So take him down at the first opportunity. Got it?"

Both Slade and Jones nodded.

"Second thing, and this is very important so pay attention," Kruger paused for a moment and looked over at the entrance to dome five. "There is a methane processing reactor in there, highly volatile."

"Well that's just great."

"Put a sock in it, Jones. It is what it is, so let's just be careful what we're shooting at. The storage tanks are on the outside of the dome so that's something. But do me a favor and try not to shoot the processing unit."

"Why not, sir?" said Slade

Kruger and Jones each gave an exasperated sigh. "Ka-boom. That's why." The commander did an exploding gesture with his hands to emphasize the point. But as he was about to lead them in, a scream echoed from back along the concourse.

"Shit, what the hell was that?" Jones swiveled in its direction, weapon at the ready.

Kruger snapped his fingers. "You stay here. If anyone shows up at that door not looking real friendly, you take them out, no questions."

"Yes sir."

"Slade, you come with me."

They stepped in through the half open door of dome five. It was a large space that was part manufacturing plant, part storage space and part workshop. Strewn here and there were stacks of crates, machine parts and even the skeleton of an old lander module that someone had stripped of all useful components. Kruger moved silently and gave a hand signal that instructed Slade to move out and start searching. It didn't take them long. The deranged mercenary shot out from behind a mountain of crates and fired off two blasts in quick succession. Kruger and Slade dived for cover. A moment later, the commander stuck his head up from behind a crate and scanned the area. The mercenary was nowhere to be seen. He signaled to Slade again to move out. This time Kruger kept his weapon high and ready to fire at the first opportunity.

The whoop of a PEP weapon being fired, back where Kruger had left Jones, stopped them dead in their tracks. "Sounds like Jones has met someone who wasn't real friendly," Slade whispered.

But before Kruger could answer, the mercenary burst out from cover again. This time he didn't get a chance to discharge his weapon. He was encased in a ball of electrical craziness that hit him from two different directions at the same time. He shook and jerked and bounced around like a pinball before collapsing to the floor, incandescent flashes still arcing around his body.

When the light show had finally stopped Kruger and Slade approached the body with caution. He was dead, no question about that. It was job done as far as the commander was concerned so he shouldered his weapon. "Okay, let's get out of here. It's time to start herding the colonists back into the biodome."

They walked off slowly, there was no rush. The thorn in Kruger's side had finally been taken care of. From here on in it would be just a mop up operation.

A scream reverberated around the dome as another deranged COM crewmember came bursting through the door. It was Benson, his weapon aimed in their direction. Before either Kruger or Slade could unshoulder their weapons he fired. It was at that instant that Willem Kruger, commander of the Colony One Mars mission, realized they were both standing right in front of the methane reactor.

"Oh shit," was all he could manage.

~

JANN AND XENON slowly inched their way down along the concourse, moving on opposite sides, keeping close to the walls. Up ahead on the left was the entrance tunnel to where they assumed the COM mercenaries were. It was set at right angles to the concourse, so Jann crept along and peered carefully around the corner. She signaled to Xenon who darted across and took up a position beside her.

"All clear, as far as I can tell." She ventured another look around the corner. "Come on, let's get that door closed."

They entered the tunnel, and could now see the door, about halfway along. This was a large circular bulkhead, hinged on one side and opened back against the tunnel wall on their side. Closing this would isolate everything on the far side and lock the COM mercenaries in. Jann hurried forward, but as she came close to the door she thought she could see a body farther in, on the far side, close to the junction for the domes.

"There's someone on the floor down there."

Xenon looked down the tunnel, moving his head around trying to see. "I can just make out a foot."

Jann looked back at Xenon. "Could it be a colonist?"

Xenon said nothing for a moment as he considered this. Then he stuck his head around the side of the door. "Hard to know from here."

Jann stepped out from the wall and started forward. "I'll take a closer look."

Xenon seemed unsure of this decision but didn't protest as Jann moved quietly down the tunnel. She passed the bulkhead door. The foot turned into a leg which eventually turned into the body of a COM mercenary. Jann checked his nametag, *Jones*. He was still alive but had obviously been hit by a PEP weapon. He lay unconscious with a thin trail of smoke rising up from the blast mark. Jann couldn't tell if he had been one of the infected. *Was he the same one that attacked them in the operations room?* She wasn't sure but he seemed shorter, with different color hair, more blond. She looked back at Xenon. "Come on, give me a hand with him."

Xenon stalled for a moment before stepping over the threshold of the bulkhead door. He ran down to her. "Jann, this is very risky."

"Quick, we'll grab one leg each and drag him back."

He did so reluctantly. "I don't see why you're going out of your way for this guy."

"Call it my maternal instinct."

Xenon smiled and nodded.

Jann suddenly lost her balance as the tunnel physically shook with the force of a massive explosion. She dropped the leg she had been dragging and braced herself against the wall. Xenon was doing the same, and staring into her eyes as if to say. *I told you this was a stupid idea.*

She began to feel the atmosphere being sucked out. Not so much that it would knock her over but enough to know that this was serious, and getting more so. A klaxon blared and red strobe lights kicked on overhead.

"What the hell was that?" Jann was getting herself upright again.

"We'd better get out of here." They ran for the door but it was automatically closing. Having detected the drop in pressure the bulkhead was sealing itself to protect the integrity of the main colony facility. It was sacrificing this sector, and all who were in it.

"Hurry!" Xenon dived through the door to the other side, grabbed the edge with both hands and planted his feet against the wall trying to stop it from closing. Jann squeezed in through the gap and just managed to bring her feet in as the door slammed shut. They sat there for a few moments, gasping and calming themselves down. "That was close." Xenon gave a wry smile.

Jann smiled back and looked at the bulkhead door. "Well, I think that solves our COM infestation problem."

After a few moments the alarms stopped just as Gizmo came racing down the tunnel.

"What the hell just happened back there, Gizmo?"

"An explosion in dome five, most probably the methane processing unit. It has caused a significant loss of integrity in that sector."

"Is the rest of the facility safe?"

"Yes, quite safe, now that this bulkhead door is sealed."

"Okay, but we need to get back to operations and check out all the systems. Let's make sure there are no other disasters waiting to jump up and bite us."

. . .

By the time they returned to the operations room, Jann was beginning to sense that it was all over, they had won. Her crazy scheme had paid off. The COM mercenaries in dome five were most likely all dead, including, she surmised, Peter VanHoff. She collapsed into a chair and let out a long, exhausted sigh.

Gizmo started scanning systems, checking integrity, adjusting levels, establishing that the colony would survive the amputation of one of its limbs.

"Atmosphere nominal, pressure has stabilized."

"Thank god for that."

"Wait a minute."

"What?"

"Oh, nothing major, Jann. I am picking up some infrared readings from the subterranean soil processing area."

"Meaning?"

"Meaning I think there is somebody down there."

Jann sighed. "Oh it's probably just some colonists hiding out." She stood. "Come on, let's go take a look."

21

RUN

Jann held the PEP weapon tight as she and Gizmo traversed the narrow passage down into the soil processing area. She had brought it with her just in case and, as they entered the cave, she held the weapon up in front of her and shouted in, “Hello? Anyone there?”

A vague shuffling sound emanated from the back of the cave. “It’s okay, you can come out, it’s safe now.”

The shuffling stopped. Jann looked back at Gizmo. “Stay close.” They moved off into the cave and worked their way around a number of storage crates. She stopped short when she finally realized who it was that had been hiding down here.

Two of the Chinese crew, in full EVA suits were standing there, holding up a bloodied and battered Peter VanHoff. On the ground farther back looked to be the unconscious body of another COM crewmember. Jann recognized him as Dr. Molotov. In front of this unlikely quartet stood Yutu. It was staring directly at her, looking like it was ready to pounce. She instinctively pointed the weapon at it. For a moment no one moved, no one said anything. Jann felt like a schoolteacher that had caught two boys beating up on another in the school locker room.

"I see you guys are getting to know one another."

VanHoff seemed to perk up a bit. He looked at her, and a vague scowl grew across his face.

"It's time to pack it in, show's over. Commander Kruger is dead. Colony One is back in our control now." She waved the weapon to signal them to move out.

"I think not." Jing Tzu let go of VanHoff, who collapsed on the ground. "We're getting off this planet, so I suggest you just let us part company. No need for more violence."

"I'd love to, but you can't leave now. You're infected. If you leave you'll be bringing the Janus bacteria back to Earth."

VanHoff seemed to regain some life. He raised himself up. "Don't listen to her, don't listen to anything that comes out of her mouth. She's the cause of all this chaos."

"It's okay, we can eradicate it, we have a way. It'll take a while, but after that I see no reason why you can't go back then. Come on, let's move." She waved the weapon again.

"Don't listen to..." VanHoff tried to speak again but he was cut off.

"You shut up." Chen Deng punched him in the stomach.

"I'm sorry, but we've had enough of this place."

With that Jing Tzu stepped forward and said something in Mandarin to Yutu. The robot shifted slightly then sprang at Jann. She fired the weapon but she was too slow. The robot rammed her in the chest at full force as her shot hit the ceiling and fizzled out. She tumbled backward with the impact, slammed up against a tall stack of storage containers and collapsed on the ground.

The Chinese crew were now running for the automatic

airlocks that the harvesters used, putting their helmets on as they went. VanHoff was tottering behind them. Yutu remained, moving slowly towards the fallen Jann.

"Shit, Gizmo… they're getting away."

Gizmo shifted around, reorienting itself in the space, as if it was unsure of what to do. Jann began to pick herself up from the dusty cave floor when she saw the stack of containers lean in towards her; they were falling. She raised her arms up to protect herself, but they all came crashing down on top of her. Her leg was caught under something, she was trapped. Jann tried to pull it free but it held fast. Yutu circled.

"Gizmo, I'm stuck."

The little robot twitched and shifted, extrapolating the probabilities, calculating the odds, and realizing they were not good. It turned its head to Jann. "I do not like that robot." Then it shot off across the floor at high speed and slammed straight into Yutu. The quadruped reacted instantly and was also propelling it self forward when they connected. The two robots tumbled down along the floor, entangled together. Jann could only look on in horror as both machines pulled bits off each other. And it was happening fast, their reaction speed being so much quicker than a human.

They broke apart as Gizmo was flung across the cave. It skidded along the floor, gouging out a deep rut before it came to a halt. But the same instant it was back up on its tracks heading for Yutu at top speed. They slammed into one another again.

Jann pushed and pulled at the container to get it off her leg with all the strength she could muster. It shifted a little, she pushed harder. Time was running out. VanHoff and the

Chinese were already at the airlock, trying to hack it open. She had to stop them.

She looked back to see Gizmo and Yutu circling each other. The little droid had sustained considerable damage. Its left arm hung loose at an odd angle, a number of its sensors and antennae were gone completely. The quadruped on the other hand looked to be virtually undamaged. Jann knew that it was only a matter of time before it destroyed Gizmo completely. She searched around for a bar or something she could use as a lever to try and shift the weight pinning her down.

The robots slammed into one another again with a deafening screech of metal on metal. Again Gizmo was flung into the air and skidded to a halt farther up the cave. Jann arched her head to see. It had righted itself, but one of its tracks was broken. It lay on the cave floor like a flattened snake. Gizmo tried to move forward but it fell over.

"No, Gizmo!" she yelled.

Yutu moved in closer, like a jackal stalking its prey, ready to strike the killing blow. Gizmo managed to get itself upright again, and seemed to have calculated a new method of perambulation based on its remaining articulations. It moved using its one functioning arm like a crutch. Then it simply stopped.

Has it just died? she thought. "Gizmo, Gizmo," she shouted.

Yutu crouched low and crept forward, inch by stealthy inch. It sprang high into the air, aiming to land the final blow on Gizmo.

But the little droid had one last trick up its metallic sleeve. As the quadruped reached the apex of its arc, Gizmo fired its taser. Two metal prongs shot out of the little droid, trailing thin spools of wire and buried themselves deep in

Yutu's underbelly. The quadruped sparked and shook as 10,000 volts fried its electronics and traumatized its systems. It landed hard on Gizmo, sending the two tumbling across the floor again. When the dust settled, neither moved.

Jann pushed with all her might. The crate shifted a fraction, enough for her to get free. She looked over to where Gizmo lay, there was no movement. "Gizmo."

She looked past the robot down to the airlocks at the far end. VanHoff and the Chinese were gone, out on the surface. She would have to get back up top and alert everyone. Maybe they still had time to stop them reaching their landers. She dragged herself up to a standing position and tested her legs. They were battered and bruised, but nothing broken. She tottered over to where Gizmo lay and knelt down beside her friend. "Gizmo... Gizmo?"

The little robot twitched and tried to move, but it couldn't seem to manage it. "Oh Gizmo, you're all banged up."

It slowly raised a battered arm and pointed at Yutu, and the little robot spoke just one word, "Run."

"What?" Jann stood up and looked over at Yutu. Its back panel had retracted and a screen flashed a bright red warning. *Self-destruct sequence initiated... Detonation in T-3 seconds.*

"Oh shit." She ran—not fast enough.

The shockwave rammed into Jann's back, lifting her off her feet and she went sailing through the air for what seemed like an eternity, until she finally slammed into the cave wall. She collapsed on the ground like a wet towel. Her eyes were wide and blood oozed from her ears, pooling out across the dusty cave floor.

22

ASTERX LAND

Nills cocked his head up and scanned the sky northward of his position at the edge of the landing site. The atmosphere was clear and bright, there had been no storms recently to kick up dust and create a haze.

"There." Anika's voice echoed in his helmet. He looked to where she was pointing. A long trail streaked across the firmament, growing longer and longer with each passing second. They all watched it as it came closer and the dark smudge at its tip began to resolve. They could now see the chutes trailing out from the top of the craft, swinging and twisting as they fought back against the downward acceleration. Something then detached itself from the base of the craft and plummeted to the planet's surface far off across the horizon.

"Is that the heat shield falling?" Xenon's question seemed to be for no one in particular.

"Yeah, chutes will go soon," Nills replied as he adjusted the anti-glare setting on his visor. Even before he finished his sentence they could see the craft was now in free fall, having slowed itself down as much as it could using primitive fabric. It dropped down towards them with impressive speed. If Nills could cross his fingers in thick EVA suit gloves, he would have done so. The retro-thrusters should fire soon to bring the craft down for a safe landing. Yet it was still plummeting down to the planet with extreme velocity. Just when he thought something must have gone wrong the engines fired and the craft slowed dramatically.

"They're cutting it a bit tight, that's a lot of G to take."

The others didn't reply. They were too transfixed by the unfolding drama.

The craft spun slightly as it descended. Its landing gear started to extend and finally it touched down gently around two kilometers from where Nills, Anika and Xenon were standing.

"Okay, let's go get them." Anika and Xenon clambered onboard the rover, while Nills walked back to the flying bed.

It had taken Nills and the others quite some time to convince AsterX that it was safe to land on Mars and enter Colony One. They had rendezvoused with the old ISA Odyssey orbiter some weeks earlier. They were already well versed in the chaotic events of the combined COM and Xaing Zu Industries attempts at takeover. Even though that was some months previous, they were still extremely paranoid about the stories of the Janus bacteria that seemed to curse any mission to Mars. So the general feeling of the AsterX team was to keep well clear, forgo any attempt at landing on the planet and instead focus their energies on the main task of the mission. That being to salvage the stranded ISA Odyssey and bring it back into Earth orbit.

However, the situation in Colony One was borderline critical. The explosion in the soil processing area had severely damaged a lot of equipment, not to mention the loss of all processing facilities in dome five. That meant limited water and oxygen production. Not enough to sustain the entire colony. So the council had all agreed that the only option was to move most of the resources and people back to Colony Two. Colony One would be stripped of anything useful, most sectors shut down completely and only a very basic life support left operational to maintain the medlab and a greatly reduced biodome. Everything else would have to be closed up and brought offline. That was about as much as the systems could maintain. Any existing reserves of oxygen would now be used to purge the remaining environment of the Janus bacteria. It took over a month to make the transition before Colony One was finally purged and made safe again.

All this activity was relayed to AsterX until Lane Zebos was finally convinced to take the risk and land. After all, Nills had communicated over many months with Zebos; on supplies needed, life on Mars, and a myriad of other topics that had fascinated the AsterX CEO. Nills knew he really wanted to land. All he had to do was convince Zebos it was safe, or at least, safe enough.

Nills hit the ignition and each of the four thrusters on the flying bed belched into life. He increased the flow of fuel and the bed began to rise slowly. He nudged the joystick and it gently moved forward, gaining speed as he passed over the slower rover. Far out into the Jezero crater the AsterX landing craft was already disgorging its occupants. He could see two on the surface and one climbing down the exterior ladder.

It was a much smaller craft than the behemoths of COM

and Xaing Zu Industries. Reminiscent of the early landers the original colonists had arrived in, but somewhat bigger. It was utilitarian, nothing fancy. Built to do one job and do it well.

The crew had spotted him and were now looking up at this strange craft, this flying bed. Nills nudged the joystick again and the craft slowed to a hover. He reduced the fuel flow and the bed lowered itself back on the surface in a billowing cloud of dust. He clambered down from the open cockpit and started towards the AsterX craft on foot. One of the crew broke away from the main group and headed out to meet him. Nills waved, he waved back and Nills' comms crackled to life.

Nills Langthorp, I presume.

"Yes." By now the crewmember was only a few paces away, he closed the gap and extended a hand.

"Lane Zebos, it's a pleasure to finally meet you." They shook hands like old friends meeting after many years apart.

"So glad you could come," said Nills.

"That's one hell of an entrance you made." Lane was looking over at the flying contraption.

"Yours was pretty spectacular, too. You had us all worried, waiting for those retro-thrusters to fire."

Lane laughed. "You and me both. I was praying to every god I know. Fortunately one of them was listening." He looked over again at the bed. "You must take me for a spin in that sometime."

"You can have a spin in it now, if you like."

Lane hesitated. Nills continued, "Here's the rover." He pointed to a cloud of dust charging across the crater towards them. "They can take your crew and supplies. We can travel on the bed."

"The bed. Is that what you call it?"

Nills laughed. "Yeah, the flying bed."

It took a while for the AsterX crew to organize themselves. They spent most of the time simply looking around or picking up handfuls of Martian dust and letting it fall through their hands as if this simple act could verify, in some way, the truth of their arrival on the planet. Neither Nills nor Anika hurried them, it was a simple pleasure watching the joy they exuded at being here.

But, eventually the rover was packed with initial supplies and the bed also had some equipment strapped on. Nills and Lane clambered on to the open cockpit while the two other AsterX crew got into the rover.

Nills tapped his comms. "See you at Colony One."

"First one there buys the beers," replied Anika.

Nills kept the machine low, not too low that it kicked up dust, yet low enough to experience the ground moving fast beneath it.

"Wow, this is an incredible machine, the only way to travel. When I get back to Earth I want one of these."

"That would be difficult. It's the one-third gravity that makes it possible. On Earth you would need much bigger thrusters and, as you know, a massive fuel tank."

"Gravity's a bitch."

They laughed.

Nills banked the machine to circle back and increased in altitude. He came swooping over the rover as it trundled across the crater. Then he went higher and pointed. "There it is, Colony One."

"Ahh, the fabled El Dorado of the solar system."

"What was that?"

"It's what some people on Earth call it, El Dorado. The legendary cursed city of gold."

"Yeah, I can see how that story would get around. But it's not cursed anymore, we've made sure of that, so you don't need to worry about it. As for the gold, well, I'm afraid it's well past its former glory. Only around twenty percent of it is online."

"Well it still looks incredible."

"If you think this is cool, wait until you see Colony Two."

"Just so you know, Nills, from my perspective, I have died and gone to heaven."

They laughed again.

By the time Nills had finished his scenic route to Colony One, and finally brought the bed in to land, the rover had caught up and was just reversing to the umbilical airlock. This was kept maintained as it was the most efficient way to get people and goods in and out of the rovers. Once connected the rover's interior was now directly connected to the Colony One environment. Nills and Lane entered via the main airlock. The only sections that remained functioning were the common room, operations, a few accommodation pods and the medlab. The biodome was technically still online but it had been stripped of seventy percent of its biomass and was simply put into maintenance mode. All other sectors were closed up and offline.

But it wasn't just physical resources that they had lost, it was also personnel. After all that had happened they now found themselves bereft of any general medical expertise. The COM doctor, Molotov, had died trying to follow VanHoff out of the airlock in the soil processing area. Their second geneticist in Colony Two evacuated with the others when the COM craft departed for Earth. That left one of the

Chinese scientists, stranded now, but purged of the bacteria, so at least he was sane. But, he lacked general medical experience and was totally at sea in dealing with their situation. What Nills really needed was someone with knowledge to help them understand the condition of the patient and give advice on what to do. Fortunately, AsterX had a medical doctor with them, Dr. Jane Foster. And since the communication time between them and the AsterX crew in orbit, was virtually instant, they were able to establish the best treatment that could be provided, given the available resources. But that was some time ago now.

When they had finally divested themselves of their EVA suits, Nills was introduced to Chuck Goldswater and lastly to Dr. Jane Foster.

"I suppose you want me to see the patient straight away?" she said.

"That would be great. Follow me, this way." Nills led her across the common room, through the connecting tunnel and into the medlab. He gestured in the direction of the bed. Lying there was Dr. Jann Malbec, her life charted out in waves and graphs on a myriad of different monitors. All about her body, a profusion of tubes and wires sprouted. Her chest rose and fell in a steady rhythm.

After the explosion in the soil processing cave, they had found her barely alive and with severe brain damage. With the help of Dr. Foster's advice they put her into a coma, and she had been in it ever since.

The AsterX doctor now checked the stats on the monitors, then started on a series of seemingly simple tests: shining a light to check pupil dilation, running a pen along the sole of the foot. After a while she stepped back and looked at Nills.

"I'll be straight with you. It's unlikely she'll ever come out of it. Her brain is too badly damaged, I'm sorry, but there's nothing anyone can do for her now."

23

WHILE YOU WERE ASLEEP

Sounds and shadows drifted in and out of Jann's subconscious. Tendrils of reality coalescing into fragments of cognition. Bubbles of coherence percolated in her brain as it tried to reassemble its shattered matrix. At first these inputs were lost along damaged pathways, fizzling out at dead-ends, extinguished by misfiring synapses. But as time progressed fragmented connections reestablished themselves, laid down new conduit and reformed their structures. Yet, in the confused carnage that was Jann Malbec's brain tissue, alternative undamaged areas had stepped up to the plate to provide interpretation and analysis of exterior stimuli.

Even with all this cellular and synaptic reconstruction going on inside her cranium it took a long time before she had what most people would consider a thought. It came after her receptor infrastructure gained sufficient bandwidth to process incoming data and assign it labels: sound, light, heat. It was these inbound stimuli that she was first aware of. And, as time passed, she began to make some sense of them, voices, shadows, movements.

So it was that three months and twenty-seven sols after the explosion in the soil processing cave, Dr. Jann Malbec opened her eyes and looked up at the world.

Over the next few sols Jann opened her eyes more and more. Each time, her understanding of what she was experiencing deepened. Across her field of vision shapes moved, blurred and indistinct. Sounds. *Were they voices? Saying what?* Finally, after around a week, she recognized a shape. It was a face, it was Nills, and the face said, "Jann, can you hear me?"

She tried to reply, but her brain had difficulty in establishing the correct procedure. So she simply blinked.

"I think she's come back to us," the voice said.

JANN'S MIND swam in a sea of dissonance, sometimes ethereal and dreamlike, sometimes reconnecting with the exterior world. At its most focused she could respond, just a word or two at first, *yes, no.* These lucid moments became more frequent, and over time she began to reconnect with reality. It was during this latter period that she began to have questions, lots of questions about why she and Gizmo were in the soil processing cave. These thoughts grew, with ever increasing urgency in her mind until her eyes snapped open. For the first time in what felt like an eternity, she felt truly awake and hyper-aware, like all the switches in her brain flicked on—all at once.

IT WAS MORNING. She wasn't sure how she knew this, but somehow she did. Jann instinctively tried to sit up in bed. Her body felt like clay and she was not certain of the position or location of her limbs. Her extremities seemed slow to respond to the signals her brain was sending. There was an urgency welling up inside her, forcing her body to respond. She swiveled her torso and slid her legs over the side of the bed. Then with one herculean effort, she slapped her feet on the floor.

Dr. Foster came rushing in, followed by Nills, then Anika. *How did they know she was awake and moving?*

"Holy crap, she's moving." Dr. Foster stopped dead in her tracks before rushing over to her again when she realized Jann was trying to stand.

"Jann, wait up, you need to take it slow." Dr. Foster grabbed her under one arm. "Nills, grab her other arm, will you? Help her back up on the bed."

Jann tried to fight them off. "I need to... stop them."

"Stop who. Jann?" Dr. Foster's voice was soft and patient, like a parent putting a child back to bed after a nightmare.

"VanHoff... Xaing Zu. I need to stop them, they can't leave, it would be disastrous."

"It's okay, Jann." Nills rowed in with the platitudes.

Jann stopped and looked at the doctor. "Who are you?"

"That's Doctor Foster. One of the AsterX crew. She's here to help you."

"AsterX... but?" Jann's question trailed off and her obvious confused state allowed Nills and Foster a window of opportunity to get her back in the bed. Finally she looked across at Nills. "What the hell is going on?"

Nills shifted and looked down at the floor, he began to scratch his chin.

"Tell me."

"Okay. What's the last thing you remember?"

Jann thought about this. Vague, fragmentary memories

drifted up from deep within her subconscious, or were they dreams? "The soil processing cave... with Gizmo... and... and..." She shook her head slightly, trying to give shape to some deeper fragments. "VanHoff... and the others, they were leaving... I... I can't remember anything more." Her shoulders slumped. The strain of remembering extracting a physical toll.

Nills looked over at the doctor and Anika for a moment and then back at Jann. "You've been in a coma for over four months."

Jann remained silent as shock began to register on her face.

"There was an explosion in the cave. You were very badly injured, barely alive."

"Your recovery is remarkable. Under normal circumstances someone with your brain injury would be... well, a vegetable. It's extraordinary that you're sitting up talking to us." Dr. Foster circled the bed as she spoke.

"What happened to VanHoff... and Jing Tzu?"

Nills looked down again and gave a deep sigh. "I'm not sure if you're ready to hear all this."

"Tell me. What happened?"

Nills sighed again. Then sat down on a chair and started.

"WHAT I'M GOING to tell you are only some of the events, as they were explained to me. When the explosion took place in the cave, I was still unconscious on that very bed that you're in now. It was a few sols later that I finally came around. So I tell you some of this third-hand."

He sat forward in the seat. "It was the Chinese robot, Yutu, that detonated. It had a self-destruct mode, I believe. Gizmo. I'm afraid... was destroyed."

"Gizmo? No!" Jann was visibly shocked, as if she had taken a punch to the gut.

"Yes, I'm afraid so. Fortunately the cave contained the force of the blast and retained its integrity. You were found near the airlocks. Your body was smashed to a pulp. Broken bones, damage to internal organs, and severe brain damage." Nills shook his head a few times. "I honestly thought there was nothing left of you to put back together. But... well, here you are." He gestured to her with open hands.

"VanHoff and the remains of the Xaing Zu crew both took off from the planet within a few hours of each other. COM evacuated their people from Colony Two, but the rest of their respective crews were stranded here."

"Did they get back to Earth?"

"Yes, I'm getting to that. Anyway, we sorted out the mess, purged the colony environment of the bacteria and brought the infected back to reality. But we almost had to abandon this place." He waved an arm around. "Too much damage to sustain a full environment. So we moved most people over to Colony Two. The stranded COM crew are over there. We kept the stranded Chinese here. One was a biologist, so we thought he might help with putting you back together, Jann."

"Was Earth alerted to what went on, I mean, did they know what COM and Xaing Zu were bringing back with them?"

"Oh, yes, yes. We were in constant communication with them. They knew all right."

"And?"

Nills scratched his chin again and sneaked a glance at the others. They were staying silent, preferring to let Nills break the news. "Well COM were first to return. You have to understand that VanHoff and the crew were the first humans ever to have traveled to Mars and returned. There was a media shit storm. On top of that, rumors began to spread that he had returned with the secret to immortality, you know how these things get blown out of proportion."

"But the Janus bacteria, they did purge the spacecraft environment before they landed?"

"Yes, but..."

"Don't tell me it got out?"

Nills said nothing, just looked over at Jann. "It got out."

It was Jann's turn to be silent and the realization sunk in.

"They think it was the rover. Its internal environment was not part of the COM craft's main systems. So they simply overlooked it. And that's where they think it started."

"What's the situation now?"

"Not good."

"Not good?"

"At first they had a strict quarantine in place, but... I don't know, someone opened something they shouldn't have. I don't know all the details because they tried to hush it up at first, not cause a panic. But after a few weeks it was infecting the local population around Cape Canaveral."

"No." Jann put her head in her hands and began to rock back and forth. "No, no, no."

"I think maybe that's enough for the moment, Nills." Dr. Foster was getting concerned. "Let me give you something to help you rest."

Jann jabbed an index finger in the doctor's direction. "Don't even think about it. I've been out of it for too long."

Nills stood up. "It's okay. She needs to hear this."

The doctor backed down with a shrug of her shoulders.

"What about the Chinese? Were they okay?"

Nills sat down again, this time on the edge of the bed

beside her. “No, they didn’t escape either.” He shook his head again. “I’m not sure of the full story there. They’re very secretive. But again a week or so after they landed people started to go crazy.”

“Jesus Christ, this is a mess. What have I done, Nills, what have I done?”

“It wasn’t you that created this thing, Jann.”

“But it was me that released it.”

“Well, I for one, am damn glad you did, otherwise I would still be a lab rat... at best. At worst I’d be dead. So don’t beat yourself up over it. How many times have you tried to stop them?”

Jann rubbed her face with the back of her hand. “They just wouldn’t stop, would they? Not until they screwed everything up.” She shook her head and looked up at Nills. “So what’s the situation now? Did they get it under control?”

“Eh... no. Not as such.”

“What... tell me, what?”

“They knew how to kill it, you know, saturated oxygen at low pressure. That may be easy to do up here, inside a sealed environment. But on Earth... not so easy. No sooner had they brought the infected in and cured them, they would get reinfected as soon as they went outside. It’s in the open... can’t stop it. All they can do is slow the spread. But eventually it will be everywhere.”

“How long?”

“The World Health Organization just sent us their latest report.” Dr. Foster finally had something to add. “The current infection sites are localized to the area around Florida in the US and Wenchang in southern China. But new outbreaks are happening in Europe, Russia and South America. These outbreaks will start to rise exponentially over time. They estimate the entire planet will be infected within six to eight months."

Jann looked at her and shook her head again. "Why did you leave me in this state for so long?"

"We had no choice. We had to get the brain swelling down, and that meant induced coma."

"But for so long..."

"Your physiology is... unusual. I'm not an anesthesiologist, I had to be sure you would get the best chance of healing before taking you out of it. My duty is to the patient."

"You should have done it sooner. Earth would not be in the dire situation that's unfolding now."

"Well, I don't see how that would have changed anything."

Jann looked over at her. "Using a saturated oxygen medium is one way to expunge the bacteria from the environment—but there's another way to kill it."

There was silence for a moment as they digested this new information.

"Another way?"

"Yes, Nills. What do you think I've been working on, holed up in my secret lab? I've been studying it, testing, probing. But mostly trying to find a way to control it. Ultimately I stumbled on another way to kill it without killing the patient in the process."

"We need to get this information back to Earth. This is great news." Dr. Foster was now visibly animated. "I need to tell the others." And she ran out of the medlab.

NILLS SAT on the edge of the bed and a craggy smile broke across his face. "I can't believe you're back—just like that.

You are an extraordinary human, Jann." He reached in and gave her a hug. "You really don't give up, do you?"

Jann sighed. "It's this cursed bacteria, Nills. It's defined me. The life that I had has been wrenched from me because of it. It mutated my biology and gave me... superpowers, I suppose. But look what it's taken from me—from you, and all who live up here. Trapped us all in a never ending cycle of fear and conflict."

"It's gone from here now. We purged the colony. It doesn't exist anymore. Unless you have another secret stash somewhere."

"No, I don't. No more experimenting. We need to make sure it's gone from here forever. But even with that, we're back to where we started. COM and Xaing Zu may be gone, but there will be others. Don't you see, nothing changes?"

Nills shoulders slumped a bit. "That's a very pessimistic view, Jann."

"It's the truth, Nills." She reached and placed a weak hand on his arm. "You know it is."

Nills lowered his head a little. "They're not all like that. AsterX aren't interested in... genetics."

Jann sighed, "Oh Nills, you may be a technical genius, but you can be very naive sometimes. You trust people too much."

"Perhaps you're right, but then again, you can be a bit paranoid. No offense."

Jann laughed. "Yeah, but it's hard not to be when everyone is trying to kill you."

"Well they haven't managed to do that just yet, and the good news is you know how to kill this thing. Looks like you get to save the world—again."

"Maybe."

"What do you mean *maybe*?"

"I'm still... confused." She shifted in the bed, trying to move. "My body feels like lead."

"But you're cognizant... it's amazing."

"Yes, yes, a bit disoriented, that's all. Listen, Nills, before I do or say anything, we need a council meeting. And before that you need to tell me everything that's happened."

24

PANDEMIC

Nills wasted no time in bringing Jann up to speed on all that had happened, not just in the colony but also on the spread of the bacteria back on Earth. It was during his enthusiastic explanation of the intricacies of the asteroid mining exploits of AsterX that Jann began to lose focus. She was finding it increasingly difficult to keep track of the information. Perhaps it was merely a symptom of the dry subject matter, or more likely a manifestation of her own physical frailty. She could only keep her concentration for a relatively short period of time before losing track. She needed to rest. So Nills left her in peace, with strict instructions from Dr. Foster not to let anyone disturb her.

Now that Jann was left to her own thoughts she slowly began to realize that, ultimately, she had failed. All her efforts to protect Earth, her home, from the ravages of the Janus bacteria had come to nothing. It was now raging across the planet, doing exactly as she had predicted. Sending the people into panic. It was not just that it would turn one third of the population into homicidal psychotics, they in turn would probably kill at least another third. Whoever survived this holocaust would be living in a world devoid of utilities as industry and institutions ground to a halt. Law and order would break down for a while before any sort of equilibrium was reached—if at all.

But Nills was right. She didn't create this thing. This was the product of humanity playing god, of technology without bounds. And what were the colonists but guinea pigs for their creators' experiments? They had been used and grossly abused. *Goddammit, she shouldn't even be here*. If it wasn't for McAllister getting sick, well... she would be sitting happily back on Earth instead of trying to fight for the right of a handful of humans, on a far off planet, to live in peace.

She thought of home, of her father's farm. How she longed to walk the hills again, in the fresh clean air, with no need for EVA suits and life support. All the things the Earthlings took for granted. They didn't know how good they had it, always wanting to go one step beyond. How she would love to swim in a lake again, like when she was a kid. Those were happier times. How she missed them, the simple things: air, water, grass—and family. All gone now, no one left but her. Her father's ashes sat in an urn on some dusty shelf in the Green Mountain Crematorium, the funeral directors in the local town. She knew the son, Freddy Turlock, she went to college with him. *I wonder if he's still there, in the family business, or has he moved on, like me*? She laughed to herself at the thought of meeting him. *So what have you been up to, Jann?*

Oh, I've been up on Mars for a while. Trying to save a colony of clones from enslavement.

Really, and how did that go?

It was not right that his ashes be stored in some dusty

drawer and forgotten, she would claim them and bring them back to the farm when she got home. That's what she would do. But, that was just a dream, a fantasy. She was here on Mars, no getting around that fact. If this place was going to be her home then she would make Earth respect it and its people. If all they wanted was to battle for control of Mars, well that wasn't going too well for them right now.

Jann could sense a window of opportunity opening in the midst of the carnage that now infected planet Earth. *Was it crazy for her to even contemplate this? But they might just be desperate enough to do it*, she thought. It's not hard to imagine what people will sacrifice to save themselves from the abyss. Time was of the essence. She needed to act quickly. And above all, what she needed to do was convince.

SHE AWOKE to find Xenon sitting beside her bed. His thin aquiline face broke into an elegant smile when he realized she was awake. "Jann, nice to have you back."

"Xenon, I thought... you were in Colony Two?"

"I was. But since you have requested a council meeting, and are in not any position to travel yet, we decided to come here."

"Oh... yes, meeting... that's right. Sorry... I'm still trying to get... my head together," she looked over at him. "Literally."

Nills arrived, followed by Dr. Foster. They must be monitoring her remotely, keeping an eye out for when she awoke. She sat up as the doctor fussed. Jann swung her legs off one side of the bed.

"No, you're not ready to move yet, you need to rest." Dr. Foster was trying to gently push Jann back in.

"I'm getting out of this bed, even if I fall flat on my face and have to crawl on the floor."

"Wait a minute," Nills stalled the protest. "I have an idea. Just stay there until I get back."

Jann decided to wait, but she still had her legs over the side. A minute or two later Nills returned—with a scrapyard wheelchair.

"I recognize that," said Jann. "Paolio's old chair."

"That's right, it still works. Come on I'll help you in."

By now Dr. Foster had conceded defeat, so she helped Nills guide the determined Jann onto the seat. Jann fiddled with the joystick, the wheelchair jumped back and forth as she gained a feel for it. Finally she looked up at Nills. "I'm starving. What's there to eat?"

Nills laughed. "Come on then, let's go find something."

Jann moved herself to the table in the common room, while Nills organized some food for her. It was only when she started to eat that Jann realized how hungry she was, it seemed she couldn't get the food in fast enough. Dr. Foster was also at the table, she looked on at this ravenous exhibition with a visible air of concern. Jann considered starting to cough and splutter and clutch her chest, just for a laugh, just to see how Dr. Foster would react. But, in the end she was too hungry to sidestep into amateur dramatics.

THE COUNCIL MEETING could not be held until all members had arrived. Xenon had already left in the rover to ferry across the remainder, which would take a few hours. Jann planned to use the intervening time to get a better understanding of the intentions of the asteroid mining company, AsterX, and its charismatic CEO, Lane Zebos. Her concern, apart from her natural state of distrusting anyone until proven otherwise, was the fact that Nills seemed to be besotted by them, particularly Zebos. They were thick as thieves, always talking, discussing, debating. Perhaps it was just a natural maternal instinct within her to feel a need to protect those she loved. Not to see them hurt by false promises and duplicity. After all, AsterX, like COM and Xaing Zu Industries were not here for the scenery.

She pushed the empty plate away, lifted up the coffee with both hands and sat back in the chair. She took a sip of the astringent brew, and raised it up towards Lane Zebos, who had been sitting quietly across from her. "Nice coffee, thanks for bringing it."

"No problem, it's Blue Mountain. I thought Nills would really like it."

"Indeed. So tell me, Lane. Why are you all here?"

There was a sudden silence around the common room, everyone stopped talking and readied themselves in anticipation of the bout that was about to take place. Jann Malbec was back, and she was now going to haul Lane Zebos and AsterX over the coals. No more mister nice guy, the free ride was over.

"Our mission is to salvage the Odyssey on behalf of the ISA." It was Lane's sidekick, Chuck Goldswater who answered. Lane raised a hand to silence him.

"That's just one element of it. The real reason we managed to get the governmental oversight we needed for this mission was to bring you back home."

"Well, that's very kind of you to come all this way just for me. But it looks like Mars is a much safer place to be right at this moment, what with Earth undergoing the zombie apocalypse."

"You said you knew how to kill it. We should get that information back as soon as possible, the longer we wait the more people will be affected." Dr. Foster saw her opportunity to push Jann.

Jann sipped her coffee. "So you're just helping the ISA out, is that it?"

"We're a mining company. Our business is the extraction of physical resources for profit, it's very simple."

"So you want to mine on Mars?"

"No, not exactly." Lane leaned in and pointed vaguely skyward. "Out there, in the asteroid belt, lies the greatest untapped wealth in the solar system. We're an asteroid mining company, so our mission is to investigate whether Mars can be a waypoint for the exploration of the belt. Our objective is establishing a base on Ceres. From there we can investigate suitable asteroids for mining."

"So why cozy up to the ISA, surely they're no longer viable as a space exploration entity?"

"As far as they're concerned, you're still an ISA astronaut, on a mission." Chuck blurted.

Nills had joined the group around the table, but had remained silent until now. He burst out laughing. "Ha... you obviously haven't been reading the newspapers lately."

Lane gave his sidekick another look, to imply he should let him do the talking from now on. "Perhaps it was a naive dream to imagine that cooperation between international space agencies was the way forward for space exploration. That dream ended when COM landed the first settlers on Mars. I remember watching those landings. I was a kid then, it was what inspired me to pursue a career in space engineering. Even then I could see the future, and it belonged to corporations, not governments. But it is still a fallacy to assume that the privateer has it all their own way. There are laws governing what we do and how we do it, namely the Outer

Space Treaty. And where there are laws there are politics. So in a sense, government still controls the exploration of the solar system. Those corporations who have the ear of government are those who will be the chosen few. Like a royal seal or a blessing from the Pope. It's almost medieval." He waved a dismissive hand. "It's very frustrating."

"So you needed to get into bed with the ISA so you could get oversight?"

"Correct. You see, AsterX are small fry. China is so powerful it can do whatever the hell it likes. COM too has become a monster, taking up a lot of political bandwidth. Their involvement with the ISA was the worst thing that the international space agencies could have done. It fractured them technologically. But they still have significant political clout, with tendrils leading right in to the heart of the UN itself. They can, and do, effect changes to the Outer Space Treaty."

"So the deal is you get to land on Mars and they get their spacecraft back?" said Jann.

"That, and they get to bring their astronaut home."

"And what makes you think I want to go back?"

Lane shrugged. "That's up to you."

Jann placed the now cold coffee back down on the table. She was a bit uncoordinated, it spilled when she set it down too hard. "I'm tired... I need to rest again." She moved the wheelchair back. "Nills, can you help me?"

Dr. Foster stood up to help as well. "I'm okay." Jann raised a hand to her. "Just Nills."

He lifted her into the bed in the medlab. "We should move you into an accommodation pod and out of here."

"It's fine for the moment." She was propped up with a multitude of pillows. "Do you trust this guy, Zebos?"

Nills sat down on the edge of the bed. "Insofar as I trust anyone. He is genuinely interested in exploring the asteroid belt. Deep down he's just an engineering nerd. I can relate to that. We've been talking a lot about it. How Mars could work as a waypoint." Jann's eyes closed. "Anyway, enough of my rambling. You need to rest before the council meeting."

Her eyes popped open again. "No, go on, I'm interested to hear it, don't stop."

"Well, we think we can build the craft here, on Mars. They would be robotic, initially. Simple enough engineering, although we would need specialist components from Earth. But it could be done in Colony Two. The one-third gravity here makes it considerably easier. Once a suitable asteroid is identified by one of the robotic scout missions, we send up harvester robots. The ore would be shipped back here for processing in Colony Two, we do a lot of that already. Then the final product would be shipped back to Earth."

"Do you think this is actually possible, I mean, in reality?"

"Absolutely, and it could be very lucrative."

"For AsterX."

"And for us. The main thing, though, is it would give us a future, Jann."

"Yes, I can see it would." Her eyes closed again.

"Jann, I'm sorry but I have to ask."

Her eyes opened again and her hand went to his. "Sure, what is it?"

"Are you really going to go back to Earth?"

She looked at him and squeezed his fingers. Her grip was weak. "I don't know, Nills. I can't say because I really don't know where home is anymore. Anyway, if the WHO is correct then there may not be an Earth to return to, at least not the same one I left."

"But you know how to kill this thing, don't you?"

"Yes, I do. But before I tell them, I want to know what's in it for us, for Mars."

25

ULTIMATUM

Jann emerged several hours later into the common room, now full of colonists. What constituted the governing body on Mars was now assembled. Nills, Xenon, Anika, Rachel, and several others that had been added to the council by merit of their knowledge. The only one that was missing was Gizmo. Not that the little robot was a council member but, it had always been a kind of counselor to Jann. Able to analyze a complex situation and present her with the decision forks and their respective consequences. She missed Gizmo, and felt a deep pang for its loss.

Also at the meeting were the crew of the AsterX mission, at Jann's request. No one was quite sure what was going down but the anticipation was palpable. When everyone was seated Xenon called the meeting to order. He stood. "The colony council session will now commence." He paused. "The only item currently on the agenda is a general discussion of the epidemic that now afflicts Earth. I would ask Rachel to update us on the latest media analysis." He sat down.

"There's a very confused picture evolving. Rumor, counter-rumor, and conspiracy theories abound, reflecting a fragmented message being disseminated by the various governing authorities. Reading between the lines, I would say the situation regarding the spread of the infection is worse than anyone is admitting to. The general population is trending towards panic. I'm monitoring the intensity and frequency of several keywords and using these as a measure of general levels of anarchy. Best guess, I would say ten Earth days, maybe two weeks at most before the start of civil breakdown."

Chuck Goldswater jumped up. "This is crazy, if you know how to stop this pandemic then you must tell us now."

Lane grabbed him by the arm. "Sit down and keep quiet."

"But..."

"Now!"

Chuck sat down and folded his arms.

"Please forgive my associate's emotional outburst. It's a stressful time for all. Please continue."

Jann now took up the baton. "I think you are under the mistaken illusion that any of us here actually give a shit about Earth. Apart from myself and two others no one else has connections to Earth. And to you, they're all just clones." She looked Goldswater straight in the eye. "One could argue they are products of the machine, a machine whose only concern is the acquisition of ever greater wealth, and the self-aggrandizement of the egos that control it. What is happening on Earth, right now, is an unfortunate by-product. It is a self-inflicted wound, not of our making. Yet, by an ironic twist of fate it seems that the tables have turned and it is we who have the power of life and death on those who seek to enslave this place, these people—my people." Jann moved the wheelchair back from the table, and stood up, placing both her hands on the table for a moment as she established her balance. She stood up straight and scanned the council.

"That said, we're not monsters. We will not sit idly by and see Earth destroyed. That would be immoral." She directed this last word at Goldswater. "No, we will do what's right, but first there is something Earth can do for us. In two Earth days time there is a UN meeting in New York. Is this correct?" She directed her question at Lane.

"Yes, you're correct, two days."

"At that meeting I want them to declare Mars and the twin moons of Phobos and Deimos an independent, self-governing planet."

"Have you lost you mind? That's totally crazy!" Goldswater jumped up. He was apoplectic.

"Chuck, sit down, and don't open your mouth again."

"Bullshit, Lane. I can't listen to any more of this crap. It's clear her mind is gone, the brain damage is affecting her thinking."

"Chuck, if you don't stay quiet I will personally eject you. Now put a zip in it."

He reluctantly sat down.

"Much as I hate to say this, but the AsterX dude has a point, Jann," said Anika. "How do you suppose we get them to do that?"

"Thank you." Goldswater nodded at Anika.

"Hey, don't read too much into it, you're still an asshole," Anika hit back.

"Well, it's very simple, really. We withhold all information on how to kill the Janus bacteria until they do." There was a momentary silence around the room.

"Put yourself in their position," she continued, "...they

don't really have any other choice." Jann lowered herself back on to the chair and moved it into the table.

By now the room was abuzz with astonished chatter. All except for Lane Zebos. He remained very quiet, staring intently at Jann.

"Okay, let's assume for a minute that *they*, whoever they are, were in agreement. An independent Mars in return for salvation. I still don't think you fully understand the sheer political complexity of obtaining such a resolution to the treaty. There would be a multitude of parties that might see this as an opportunity to stick it to the superpowers of the US and China. There would have to be unanimous agreement."

"No, there doesn't. You see, Lane, it was you who gave me the idea. And it's you that is going to fast track this for us."

"Ah..." A laugh escaped from him, unintentionally it seemed. "I don't mean to belittle your... proposal, but I think you have grossly overestimated the influence AsterX has in these matters."

"You're a partner with the International Space Agency. And, as you said so yourself, they may no longer be capable of getting people off the ground, but they still have political muscle. Through them we can go direct to the people who matter, the ones who can get this done, quick and painless."

Jann caught Nills' eye. A wry smile broke across the corner of his face.

"Jann's right. You've told me this yourself, many times," said Nills.

Lane argued, "It's just not that simple. I mean, the political and economic machinations of this proposal are labyrinthine. Not even a master analyst could fathom them." He stood up and started to pace. "Okay, let's say by some stroke of magic they agreed to this, and I can't see how they would, but let's say it actually happened. You give them whatever snake oil you've conjured up, they can just turn around and say, it wasn't you after all it was us, and the whole deal is null and void. I mean, there's no way on Earth, or Mars for that matter, that they will agree to this and then actually adhere to it. They'll say, yeah sure, and then find a way to renege at the very first opportunity."

"Yes, I know that. But it will still be law. And if it's law we can defend it. Not ideal but it means we have opened a new front."

Lane sat down again and looked at her.

"Look we're going to do this. You can help us if you want. If not, well, that's fine too, it's your decision. But just think about this for a moment. As a freely independent and self-governing planet, any requests to land on, even orbit, would require our approval. This, of course, would extend to mining rights. Particularly if Mars were to be used as a waypoint for the exploitation of the asteroid belt."

"Lane, you're not seriously going to consider this insanity?" said Goldswater.

Lane raised his hand again to silence his colleague. He stood up. "Let me see if I have this straight. You're offering us landing rights?"

"No, we're offering you *exclusive* rights. With those, AsterX would have a significant commercial advantage, a virtual monopoly on the wealth of the asteroid belt."

Jann could see a change in even Goldswater's body language. The sullenness was evaporating, his arms unfolded and he leaned in a little closer to the table. She had hit the mark.

"For how long?" he said.

"Long enough that it's in your interest to see the treaty is not overturned. There will need to be a review period of some kind, but ultimately our opportunity is now your opportunity."

"I'll agree, this is tempting, but what happens if you fail in this attempt to... blackmail Earth?" Lane rubbed his chin.

"Then mining the asteroid belt isn't going to matter, is it?"

There was a muted silence around the table as the implications of this sank in.

Finally, Dr. Foster spoke. "You're playing a very dangerous game. Billions of lives are at stake here, you seem to forget that."

Jann leaned in to the table. "Did we create this monster that is raging across the planet? No, Earth did. Did we start this war of worlds? No, Earth did. Did we seek to enslave the people of Earth? No, but they want to do that to us. You're right, Dr. Foster, this is a dangerous game. If you want to start a war, then you best be prepared for the consequences if you lose. We didn't start this, but we're sure as hell going to finish it."

Lane rose slowly from the table. "I need to confer with my colleagues for a moment, if I may."

Jann opened her hands. "By all means. But don't take too long."

IT TOOK ONLY six minutes and forty-eight seconds, if any one was counting, for Lane Zebos and his crew to convince themselves that they had just been presented with the opportunity of the century. Complete and exclusive rights to the wealth of the asteroid belt. That was not to say that others couldn't go there. But it was as far, if not farther, away again from Mars, as the red planet was from Earth. A direct journey was an enormous undertaking. Without Mars as a waypoint, it would be commercially unviable for anyone. And, it would take several decades at least before technology would catch up enough to make the figures stack up for a direct mission from Earth. But by then AsterX would be so far advanced, it might not be possible to up with catch them. Perhaps they might even be established on Ceres.

In the common room, the colonists murmured and buzzed with a palpable excitement.

"My only concern," said Anika, "is that we are not going to end up like China giving Hong Kong to the British, or Macau to the Portuguese. We could be stuck with these guys."

"We'll need a review clause, and one that ensures production and processing takes place here," Nills chimed in.

Jann could tell from their body language when they returned AsterX were in.

"Okay, we'll help you, but there are no guarantees that we can pull this off. The main problems we see are twofold. One, we need a mechanism to verify the UN treaty is authentic. And secondly, how do we make it stick?"

"We may not have much clout in terms of political influence. But we can punch well above our weight on media spin. You need to remember that this colony was founded as a reality TV show. We've had our tendrils into Earthbound media for a very long time. We know how to spin a story, how to saturate the chatter, how to influence the masses. And, let's face it, this is one of the most powerful weapons there are. The ability to manipulate and influence.

This was Rachel's territory, so she immediately jumped

in. "We would need a live TV broadcast from the UN chamber of the passing of the resolution. We will get this twenty minutes later. To verify that what we are seeing has not been tampered with we will re-broadcast back to Earth. It will then be picked up by our media associates and we can verify its authenticity."

"What can we do about making the treaty stick?" said Xenon, it was the first time he spoke during the session.

"Stories, Xenon. We need to disseminate the right stories. My gut instinct tells me we should herald this as a new opportunity for the Earthlings. Colonization is back on. *Come to Mars, free and equal, land of opportunity*... and all that. Make it like this treaty has made it possible for people to start a new life. That way any attempts to renege on it will be met with howls of protest."

"Very good, can you come work for us?" said Lane.

She laughed. "Well, it's just a first pass. We'll need more themes and a multitude of variants, finessed for region, language, et cetera."

Jann looked over at Nills, he smiled back. As she scanned the others, she realized they were all on board. No going back now. It was game on.

26

UN

After the initial shock, the UN had wasted no time in calling an emergency meeting of the general council. And, as Lane Zebos had reasoned, their thinking was, *what did they have to lose?* They could go though the motions, concede to the demands of Mars, until they could ascertain if the colonists really did have a solution to control the pandemic. Then they could simply backtrack.

Since all of the five permanent members with a veto were affected, and fighting a losing battle to placate their respective populations, there was no problem getting their vote. Once they were secure, enough of the others fell into line to pass the resolution.

But its success was in no small part due to the work that the AsterX lobbyists did on the ground. It couldn't have happened without them. Yet, the colonists did not have it all their own way. Some argued that Mars was effectively a rogue nation, that they deliberately infected Earth, that they were being ruled by a maniac demi-god hell bent on the destruction of the planet. Others simply found the fact they had a gun put to their heads intolerable. But in the end, the resolution passed. Mars and its moons Phobos and Deimos were declared independent. However, there were some caveats. But for the colonists, it was enough. Perhaps not all that they had wished for but they had, at least, won the battle, if not quite the entire war. There would be more to fight for in future.

The moment they verified the authenticity of the UN broadcast Jann released a file, detailing how the bacteria could be annihilated, to seventy-four carefully selected media outlets, complete with notes on all her experiments and an extensive explanation of how to synthesize the active compound. She wanted the information in the public domain, not the preserve of some government agency or corporate entity that could control or profit from it. During the two days that preceded its release speculation was rife as to what information it would contain. When the denizens of Earth were finally put out of their misery, its revelations caused a shit storm of unprecedented proportions.

Was she totally crazy? was the primary response from the vast majority of Earth's population. Leaders were quick to call for the instant negation of the UN resolution that had just elevated Mars' status to one of an independent nation. Nevertheless, those who had been fighting to contain the pandemic: doctors, chemists and the myriad of scientists working in labs all across the planet, knew instantly that what Jann had discovered could, at least in theory, work. You just had to get past its perception in popular culture and simply look at the science.

. . .

JANN DESCRIBED how it was that she came to discover it in many of the interviews she did after the pandemic had been brought under control.

"I always wondered what was so special about the biology of Nills Langthorp. My mission, the ISA, that is, was decimated by this bacterial infection. Yet, first officer Annis Romanov, working as an agent for the Colony One Mars consortium, had been tasked with bringing back to Earth the biological analogue of Nills Langthorp—even in the midst of this mayhem. Why? What was so special?

Remember, this analogue was a kind of living biological facsimile, used by the COM geneticists as a test bed for tinkering with the human genome, testing retro-bacteria... altering DNA. But it was free of the bacteria, and so was the real Nills Langthorp. All the rest of us, me included, had some level of it raging around in our physiology. How was that so?

I still had this analogue after the catastrophe of the ISA mission, but I did not possess the equipment to do any significant analysis on it. And, to be honest... I was a bit... preoccupied with being stranded alone, as I thought at the time, on Mars.

It was only after the discovery of the clone population in the mining outpost, and the upheavals that ensued, that I had the time and the resources to investigate it fully. We had extended the medlab in Colony One, and I had equipped a secret, subterranean sector with the necessary equipment. That's where I found the same Janus bacteria, still lurking in the soil processing facility. So now I had an isolated sample *and* the analogue. I could do my tests and try to get an understanding of its workings.

What came as a huge surprise to me was when I infected the biology of the analogue with the bacteria, it grew and multiplied just as in any other human. So there seemed to be nothing special about it. The only way I could control it, and kill it, was by pressure and oxygen. Then I would try again, and again, and again. But each time it was the same result.

Eventually I thought, *Maybe it wasn't Langthorp's analogue that was significant, maybe it was Nills himself. It was his biology.* That started me thinking about what environmental factors he had been exposed to—like low pressure, or saturated oxygen. I looked at his diet, what he ingested: plants, fish, the water he drank. Then it struck me. He was the only one of us to smoke a lot of weed.

There had to be some environmental factor that had eliminated the bacterial infection in him. And certain cannabinoids were known to have antibiotic properties. Particularly the non-psychotropic ones. Some studies I remembered had shown positive results against the superbug MRSA. So, it seemed like a distinct possibility that this could be effective. At that time we still had some growing in the biodome so I harvested a batch and set about breaking it down into the various cannabinoid elements. The one I thought most promising, cannabigerol, turned out to be the most effective, eradicating all traces of the bacteria in the sample within twenty-four hours."

IN THE END, the efficacy of Jann's breakthrough prescription was verified in a very short period of time. Within seven Earth days of it being revealed, the pandemic had virtually stopped due to widespread availability of synthetic cannabinoids. It took only a further twenty-one days to fully eradicate it, such was the global effort applied to the task. This made Dr. Jann Malbec a figure of heroic stature in the eyes of many. Savior of the planet. Calls were made for the highest honors known to humankind to be bestowed upon her. But others didn't quite see her in such glowing terms. To some she was a diabolical and duplicitous schemer. A person to be vilified, not hero worshiped. There were also those who felt that Earth had just been conned out of its dominion of Mars, and, true to form, agitation commenced to have the UN resolution reversed. But as Jann had correctly assessed, possession was nine tenths of the law. And, once a treaty was enshrined in the statute books, it was damn hard to undo it.

THE ONLY CAVEAT, if you could call it that, was that a representative of the new government of Mars would be required to accept the resolution, in person, at the UN general assembly, before conclusion of the current session. That gave the colonists about five months.

They had considered simply using an AsterX board member as a representative. But Lane was not eager to be seen to be so involved. The optics of such a scenario did not look good, too much corporate involvement. So, after much discussion among the council it was unanimously agreed, Dr. Jann Malbec would go. She would take off from Mars onboard the AsterX MAV, rendezvous with the now salvaged ISA Odyssey orbiter, and return to Earth. Rachel particularly liked this touch as she could spin the story as Jann, the ISA astronaut, finally returning from her mission to Mars.

However, Nills did not take this news very well.

27

A NEW FLAG

The main entrance cavern in Colony Two was a hive of industrious activity. Groups of colonists were knotted around several large fabrication projects. Jann could make out a new flying bed being built, its skeletal frame rising up from the workshop floor. It was the first of two projects being fabricated for AsterX, the second being a robotic exploration craft. It would launch from Mars and head out to the asteroid belt. Jann was not sure of the technical details of the mission, but she could see it was taking shape. On the side of the small craft was emblazoned the newly designed Mars flag. It was not unlike the Japanese flag, a red disk on a white background. However, this had two smaller disks, one on either side of the main one. These represented Phobos and Deimos.

Some were concerned that it was too similar to Japan's national symbol. But Rachel argued that to gain acceptance people generally acted more favorably to what was familiar. It would be like it had always existed. It seemed to work, as the emblem now popped up everywhere. A number of colonists had already scratched the flag out on the surface of the crater. Large enough to be seen by hi-res satellite. Images of the colony were now flooding back to Earth to feed the insatiable interest in Mars, which had now reached fever pitch since the UN resolution.

These craft, the flying bed and the robotic explorer, represented the first physical manifestation of their success in gaining independence from Earth. Already a new AsterX mission was departing Earth orbit with scientists and engineers as well as specialist raw materials and components to support the fledgling space industry that was now developing in the colony. Negotiations were also well advanced for a new batch of colonists for the red planet. Things were going to get very busy around here.

One of the rovers had been brought inside the main entrance cavern and prepared for the relatively short journey to the AsterX MAV. They had decided here was the best place to say their goodbyes as more colonists could be present to witness it than out on the surface.

Jann was already encased in her EVA suit. Over her left breast the new emblem of Mars had been stitched, beside the ISA logo. Xenon walked alongside, carrying her helmet and gloves. Jann shook hands, nodded acknowledgments and accepted the multitude of personal goodbyes from individual colonists. Rachel walked beside her holding Jann's holo-tab. It contained, among other things, the text of the acceptance speech she was to give at the UN General Assembly. Rachel had rehearsed it with her, over and over, stressing the need to pause after certain statements, slow down or speed up her pace, all crafted to emphasize certain points. How Rachel knew all this Jann had no idea, but she was a natural born propagandist, as she jokingly liked to call herself. Jann speech was a jumping off point for a barrage of finely tuned messages that Rachel and her team would unleash through their now extensive media networks. Rachel now had three other colonists working full time, doing nothing else but managing the message. Already the executives of AsterX were picking Rachel's brains as to how to do what she did. And to her great credit, she remained politely circumspect on her methodology.

In the background of all this was Xenon. His enigmatic personality left those who didn't know him wondering what the hell went on in his head. He seldom spoke, but when he did it was generally profound. He seemed to have an uncanny ability to know exactly what everybody was thinking and hence the best move to make. Rachel and he got along very well, she seemed to be the only one that Xenon would engage with in long conversations. So it came as no surprise to everyone when she proposed him for the title of President. No one objected, although some suggested Jann should also stand. But she declined. Her role, as she saw it, was as envoy. Nills also had no interest in such office, preferring instead to focus on the development of the colony as both a manufacturing hub for spacecraft venturing in to the belt, and as a processing plant for the refinement of returning ore. So the day-to-day management of the colony, was given to Nills and Anika. Xenon would be the face and voice of the colony, managed ever so precisely, by Rachel. There were others of course, but these were the first leaders on the now independent Mars.

AS JANN APPROACHED the rover she could see Dr. Foster and Chuck Goldswater were both fully suited up and waiting for her. Lane Zebos stood beside them, talking. But he was not going. He had given his place to Jann, preferring instead to spend more time here on Mars working with Nills to see their dream brought to fruition. When he saw her he approached, crossing the distance in a few long strides.

"Ready to rock?"

"No. Where's Nills?"

Lane pointed across the cavern to a small workshop at the back. "Last I saw him he was in his workshop."

"Okay, give me a minute."

Lane nodded. "Sure."

Jann pushed her way through the crowd and over to where Nills spent most of his time these days. The door was open. She walked in. Nills looked up from his bench. A filament of smoke corkscrewed up from a circuit board he was soldering.

"Oh Jann, sorry... I lost track of time."

Are you sure you're not trying to avoid me? she felt like saying, but resisted the temptation, it would serve no good purpose. They had been through all this, several times over the last few weeks, after it became clear that Jann was accepting Lane's offer to take his place and return to Earth. Nills of course knew why. His head understood the necessity for her to return, but his heart had a hard time accepting it. Not that it was any easier for Jann. She knew what awaited her on arrival, it would be challenging, to say the least. But she was thinking of the practicalities. Nills, on the other hand, was clearly deep in emotional territory, something he had difficulty managing. There was no set of plans for him to follow, no schematic to help him make sense of his feelings. This was new and he struggled with it. Already his mood had rippled through the rainbow of emotions associated with loss: grief, incredulity, anger and finally acceptance. So she forgave him for hiding out in here. Close enough to see her leave, but far enough away that he could handle it.

Jann looked down at an object on the workbench that Nills had been working on. She recognized it. "That looks like a part of Gizmo."

"It is. I've been working on him for a while... off and on... when I get the time."

"Him?"

"Ah... just doesn't feel right to call Gizmo an *it* anymore. I think he's earned the right to have a more personal pronoun... don't you think?"

"Do you think *he* can be rebuilt?"

"Yes, eventually. But, how much of the old Gizmo remains..." Nills gestured with a shrug, "...it's hard to know. His personality had been built up from countless interactions and experiences over a long time. I won't know until I finish how much is lost."

Jann picked up a charred component. It was a small square CPU, like a flat plastic millipede. Its outer surface coated with black soot, many of its pins were bent and broken.

"Is this from the old Gizmo?"

"Yeah, it's toast now."

"Can I have it, as a memento?"

"Of course."

There was a brief, awkward silence as neither knew quite what to say. "Are you ready to leave now?" was the best Nills could manage.

"Yes, they're waiting for me."

He stepped closer to her and held her arms. "I'm going to miss you around here."

She pulled him closer and hugged him tight. It was clumsy in a bulky EVA suit. They stayed like that for a moment until Jann pulled back her head. "Not too late to come with me."

"No, we've been over that. It's a bad idea. I'm a clone, remember. It would be a freak show back on Earth. No, this is your gig. I would serve no useful purpose." He smiled. "Anyway, who's going fix up Gizmo... and build all the machines that AsterX have ordered?"

"I know, Nills. But I had to ask, just one more time."

"Ahh... I'm sure the gravity on Earth would probably kill me anyway."

"Yeah, it's not something I'm looking forward to."

"You'd better go, don't want to miss your flight."

She was silent for a moment as she looked at him. "I have to do this, Nills. I have to go."

"I know." His voice was soft. "I always knew the sol would come when you would have to go home."

She lowered her head. "I'm not sure where *home* is anymore, Nills."

"Earth is your home, Jann."

"It *was* my home, now... I don't know."

She kissed him and broke away. "Remember me."

"You can count on it."

She walked out and tried not to look back. Jann kept her head down and pushed her way to the waiting rover. The rear airlock door was open. Dr. Foster and Goldswater were already inside. She stepped in and turned to wave back. A cheer went up. She sat down inside as the door was closed. The engine started and the rover lurched through the main entrance airlock and out onto the Martian surface.

Jann wept. No one spoke.

28

EARTH

Those on Earth that were infected and had survived would now have the same physical benefits that Jann and the colonists on Mars had, fast healing, longevity. They would presumably be the new elite. The bacteria had been eradicated but she had no doubt that samples had been saved and stored in labs all across the planet. How humanity would deal with the consequences of this event would be for historians to report. As of now, though, it was just speculation. Interestingly, those that had gone mad and were now free of the infection, gained none of its benefits apart from being simply normal. Of those that the bacteria had not driven insane, it had varying degrees of reaction. Some descended into the same depressive state that had affected some of the colonists, and became listless, even suicidal. But even those that had come out on top displayed varying degrees of biological alteration. Some healed quicker than others. These quirks of the infection had only become evident on Earth as the sample size was far greater than that of Mars. So now patterns could be seen.

Speculation abounded as to how this event could alter

the course of human evolution. Was this the point were the genus of Homo sapiens forked and diverged, with a kind of new *super race* branching off from its root? Who could say? But there was no question that things would ever be the same again. It was estimated that, at its peak, over fourteen million people had been infected. A significant number, but still less than 0.2 percent of the global population. Of that number, a significant portion had been radically altered biologically, upward of four million, and another six million to a lesser degree. The big question now was, could this superhuman trait be passed on, could it be inherited?

THESE WERE NOT the questions that occupied Jann Malbec's mind as she sat in the back seat of a very large, black, bulletproof SUV. Ahead of her and behind her were similar vehicles, all packed with government security agents and support personnel. Overhead she could hear the ever present thut-thut of a chopper, waxing and waning as it circled overhead. In the front passenger seat an armed agent sat on high alert, eyes darting this way and that, sometimes talking into his cuff, sometimes pressing the discreet earpiece closer to his eardrum.

Sitting beside Jann, who was now referred to as the Martian Envoy by the various officials, dignitaries and press, was Ms. Teri Denton, a high-ranking AsterX executive, who had been assigned to look after her. In reality that meant fending off the hordes of press, media and lesser mortals who wanted a piece of her.

From the moment that Jann landed back down on Earth, Teri had been glued to her side like a growth. And even before Jann had spoken her first words to the ground crew, Teri was answering for her. From that moment on it was clear that a battle was starting. On one side was Teri Denton, on the other was pretty much the entire world of press, government officials, media institutions, scientists, advocacy groups, lobbyists, celebrity agents, brand managers, commercial interests, hawkers, hustlers, fans, fanatics and straightforward crazies. She fought them all off with the help of a backroom team of well groomed professional stonewallers. Nothing got through this perimeter defense system that didn't meet the exact criteria set by Teri.

Outside of this ring of steel were even more defense systems, radiating out in ever increasing circles. So, to gain access to the inner sanctum, one would have to pass through a series of tests, each one more intimidating than the previous. The prize, if one succeeded, was an audience with the Martian Envoy, Dr. Jann Malbec. Few managed this herculean feat. And Jann was very glad of that.

Such was the zeal that Teri exhibited in her role as guardian of this precious resource, that she was always on the alert—and ever present. So much so that Jann was pretty sure that, if not for the fact that it may be viewed the wrong way, Teri would have slept in the same bed as her.

However, her role also extended to making sure that Jann had whatever she wanted. And what Jann really, really wanted was to pay a visit to her old family farm in El Dorado County, California. So Teri had made it happen. Not an easy task considering it seemed to involve mobilizing a security team to rival that of the U.S. President.

She couldn't just fly there and rent a car like a normal citizen. Her fame had denied her that. Nor could she simply do what she wanted anymore. Every tiny detail of her life had somehow become seismic. What she ate, how she slept, where she went, what she watched, how she looked—

particularly how she looked. Nothing was sacred, nothing was spared. She couldn't even stand and look out a window or her photograph would be on every media stream in less than five minutes. It was like living in a fishbowl. She had swapped one enclosed, encapsulated environment, that of Mars, for another, that of celebrity. And like Mars, moving outside the protection of the bubble could be perilous.

THE SPEECH HAD GONE WELL. Crafted to touch on all that was necessary, hit all the correct points. It was like some ancient diplomatic acupuncture, it soothed the body politic, delivered with minimal pain and maximum effect.

But what most animated the world's media was not the substance of the address, nor the seismic event that this moment in the UN represented for humanity. No, what garnered the column inches and screen space was her dress. A flowing scarlet number, replete with full length cape, accentuating her form, highlighting her mystique and captivating all to the point of distraction—which was the whole purpose of it. It was brand Mars: conceived, contrived and designed by Rachel and her team, it was meant to convey a mystical, otherworldly aura, and it achieved it in spades. Particularly with the addition of a tiara that looked like it might be capable of receiving a direct transmission from Mars. But this was all optics, designed to give everyone something to talk about that wasn't substantive. It was like a TV talent show, UN style. Nevertheless, how she looked mattered more than simply creating a distraction. After all Jann was now in her forties, yet looked like a fresh-faced twenty-five-year-old. She was the physical manifestation of the power of the bacteria to alter human biology

. . .

JANN GLANCED out the side window of the vehicle. They had been traveling for quite some time on a narrow two-lane blacktop, twisting and turning their way though the vineyards and ranches of El Dorado County. This stretch of road was cutting its way through a forest of pine. Every now and again the tree-line would abruptly end and the land would spread out in rolling hills planted with vines. All about was green and verdant and bursting with early spring life.

The agent in the passenger seat touched his earpiece, nodded to himself and swiveled his head around to Jann. "ETA in two minutes, ma'am."

"I hope it's not going to be another freak show." Jann directed her statement at Teri.

"Shouldn't be. It's not an official visit, all on the QT."

Jann looked out the side window again but this time she directed her gaze upward into the Northern California sky. "Assuming you're not counting the flotilla of news choppers that have been following us since the airport." She had counted four earlier on.

"Don't worry, they don't have permission to land. We'll get you inside quickly."

"You know, if I open my mouth wide enough I'm sure the lenses they have could look right down my throat and see what I had for breakfast." Jann took her head away from the window.

"We're here," said the agent.

They slowed down and turned off the road in through an arched gate. Above it, a sign read *Green Mountain Crematorium*. The driveway was long, and swept through a manicured landscape that would put the Augusta National Golf Club to shame. Up ahead, a row of low brick buildings came into view. The driveway opened out into a parking area. It was empty of vehicles, presumably cleared out by order of the security team. The motorcade moved up to the front entrance and came to a halt under the large canopy that protruded from the front of the building.

Jann could see several people standing at the doorway, immaculately dressed, hands clasped in front of them, waiting to be introduced. She sighed, "Here we go again."

But before she could exit, the security piled out of the ancillary vehicles and took up predetermined positions, holding their earpieces, talking into their cuffs. Only when they were all happy could Jann, otherwise known as *the package*, be extricated from the vehicle and escorted into the building.

Jann stepped out and was immediately beset by the funeral director and his wife, an elderly couple in their late seventies. She shook hands and nodded as they exchanged formalities. However, the last member of the welcoming committee she recognized. He was a good deal younger, in his early forties, short in stature with a strange scarlet birthmark extending from his left earlobe all the way down his neck, and under his chin to his Adam's apple. He made no attempt to cover it up, at least not anymore.

"Hello, Freddy. You're looking well," said Jann.

He shook her hand and smiled. "Not as good as you. You look just the same as the last time we met. You haven't changed a bit."

Jann laughed. "Looks can be deceptive, Freddy."

He gave a lopsided grin and he leaned in a bit closer to her. "I've been saying that very same thing to people for years." His voice was soft, as if what he was saying was meant for her ears only. He stepped back and extended his hand towards the interior of the building. "Come, this way, everything has been prepared."

They walked in through the front door into a wide, marble floored atrium, its tinted glass roof casting a kaleidoscope of colored light around the space. They moved to a large private office off the atrium. It was thickly carpeted with a wide oak desk dominating the central position. Around it were spaced several comfortable chairs. It was where the rituals of death were discussed as options in taste and affordability.

Sitting in the center of the desk was a modest urn. It contained all that remained of Dr. Jann Malbec's father.

Mr. Turlock took up his position behind the desk and placed a hand on the urn. "As requested we have extracted your father from his... resting place in the mausoleum."

Jann looked at him for a moment. "Thank you. You've been very kind. If you don't mind, though, I would like to conduct this business with just Freddy—for old times' sake."

Mr. Turlock looked crestfallen. He looked over at his son and like a fallen warrior passing the baton to his heir, he deflated and smiled. "Of course." He stepped out from behind the desk.

Jann swung around to the retinue of handlers and security agents. "Alone, if you don't mind."

Security staff talked into cuffs and Teri's face reconfigured itself into a look of utter rejection. She was being cast adrift from her charge. Her *reason for being* no longer wanted her around, albeit for just a few minutes.

"Certainly," she answered. "By all means, take as much time as you want." They were ushered out the door leaving Jann and Freddy alone. There was a moment's silence. "Drink?" said Freddy

"Really? You have alcohol here?"

"It's not against the law. And, well... a lot of people who

come and sit in here, really need a stiff drink. It helps to get them through it."

"Yes, I see what you mean. What have you got?"

He opened the door to a cabinet concealed behind the desk and lifted out a half empty bottle of Chivas Regal and two glasses. "Whiskey okay?"

"Perfect."

He poured two glasses and then produced a tray of ice, from a freezer underneath the desk. Jann dropped two ice cubes in her drink as Freddy sat in the chair opposite her. They raised their glasses and clinked. Jann sipped her drink, sat back and looked directly at Freddy. "I'm trying to remember the last time we saw each other. It was graduation day, I think."

"Yeah. Long time ago now."

Jann looked around the room. "So you never did anything with your college degree?"

"I worked for a while as an intern for a lab up in Seattle. But, my father got ill so I came back to look after the business. I ended up staying, even after he recovered." He gave a sort of shrug. "I know it seems a bit odd. Being a funeral director is not generally a career path for a biologist."

There was a silence for a moment as Jann cast her mind back to a simpler time, when exams were the only stress. She had never paid him much notice until their final year when they started to gravitate toward one another. He, like her, was a bit awkward, self-conscious of his birthmark. He kept to himself and had few friends. But, it was during some college get together that they struck up a conversation and realized they were from the same neck of the woods, and knew a lot of the same people. One thing led to another and Jann found herself waking up beside him the next morning. In the end, nothing really came of it and they went their separate ways.

Freddy nodded at the urn that stood on the desk between them. "So what's the plan?"

"Take him back up to the farm and sprinkle the ashes into the stream that runs through the property. It irrigates the vines, so he gets to be part of what he created." Jann touched the side of the urn. "It was his wish."

"Have you been back there yet?"

"Not yet. It's hard for me to do anything these days, without a major mobilization of troops."

"It's in a bad way. I took a trip up there a while ago, just to see. Everything is either overgrown, running wild or dried out to a parchment. I'm afraid the house has been broken into a few times. But Sheriff Morton informs me it's just souvenir hunters, nothing too serious."

They didn't speak for a few moments and Jann realized that he was used to sitting here with people who needed a moment to compose themselves. So he kept silent as Jann thought about what she was going to do. She had been putting this off for a while, but her father had made this request in his will, so she felt duty bound to fulfill it.

"Would you come up there with me, now, today?"

Freddy thought about this for a moment, and hesitated. Jann put her glass down on the desk and leaned in. "It would be nice to have someone with me who..." she looked away and gazed out the window across the gardens. "Well... someone who I actually know." She looked back at him. "Strange as it may seem, Freddy, but you are the closest thing I have to a personal friend on this entire planet."

He looked at her for a moment considering this request. "Sure, I'd be honored."

"Just so you know, as soon as you step out there with me, your face will be all over the news feeds in five minutes."

He smiled. "You forget, I'm used to people staring at me all the time." He turned his face and raised his chin to best display the birthmark down the side. "I'll make sure to present my good side."

"Thank you, Freddy. It's hard to do this on my own."

"No problem. Doesn't mean we're dating though."

Jann laughed. It was the first time she had done so since returning to Earth.

THE JOURNEY UP to the old vineyard was short, they were there in less than twenty-five minutes. Teri had been booted out of Jann's vehicle and Freddy installed in her place. As they traveled they pointed out places where people they knew had lived. Some were still there, but it seemed to Jann that almost everyone she had ever known here had either died or moved on.

The vineyard itself had formerly been part of a ranch that had been split up and sold off in lots. Her parents had come into some money and had had the romantically insane idea to move out of the hustle and bustle of the big city and engage in the agrarian lifestyle. But through a combination of naiveté, lack of knowledge and plain bad luck, that dream slowly faded into the harsh reality of subsistence fruit farming.

They turned off the main road through the gates to the property, and up the long drive to the house. Jann could see the effects of years of neglect. The plantings were parched and many were dead from lack of water. The olive trees seemed to have fared best and they were substantially bigger than Jann remembered. Already there were several security personnel dotted around. Presumably an advance party to check the place out before allowing Jann to set foot in such an open and unprotected space. Overhead she could hear the choppers circle around.

The SUV crunched its way across the gravel driveway and came to a halt in front of the house. Through the journey here she had rested the urn beside her on the back seat, cradling it with one arm. Now that they had stopped she brought it up and placed it in her lap and held it with both hands. The door was opened for her by a young and efficient security agent who stood back, motionless, one hand on the door handle, eyes darting this way and that as he waited for her to alight.

She turned to Freddy. "This..." she nodded at the urn, "...I have to do on my own."

Freddy nodded back. "I understand."

She stepped out into the afternoon sun, and made her way around the side of the house, through a small wooded area and down to the edge of the river that bordered the property. It was by far the best part of the place, and the reason that her parents had fallen in love with it. They spent many happy days here, fishing and swimming, when the river was high enough. She kicked off her shoes and waded in to the center of the stream. It was cool and refreshing. She lifted the lid on the urn and sprinkled the ashes into the water. It had been her father's wish, a romantic to the end. Perhaps he had some notion that he would be washed downstream and find his way into the vines that filled this valley. Maybe next year, when the new season wine was being drunk, the vintners and oenophiles would sniff its notes, taste its flavors and declare it an excellent vintage.

She stood there for a while watching the ash pool and eddy and slowly drift off with the gentle currents of the stream. She looked up from the water and took one last look around the home she grew up in. She stepped out of the stream, grabbed her shoes and walked back up to the waiting cars.

FREDDY WAS STANDING OUTSIDE LOOKING around when she got back. He waved when he saw her and then looked at her intently, perhaps trying to gauge her state. Careful to not say the wrong thing to her at this emotional time.

She waved back. "Mission accomplished. My father now sleeps with the fishes."

She sensed Freddy was somewhat taken aback by the glibness of her statement. She smiled. "It's what he would have said. He had many faults but at least he could see the lighter side of life. It was probably what sustained him."

"I can see what he liked about this place." Freddy scanned the landscape again.

"I can see the attraction, tending the vines, pruning, harvesting. Bringing life out of the ground sure beats the hell out of putting the dead into it."

He looked back at Jann. "Oh... sorry, I didn't mean any disrespect."

"None taken." It was now Jann's turn to take a more studied look around the fields. "Why don't you do it then, you know, get yourself a small plot, live the dream?"

"I would love to but... I don't have the money for it, and then there's the family business, commitments, duty. You know."

"Well then you can have this place." Jann spread her hands out.

Freddy looked at her and laughed. "I don't have the finances for anything like this."

"Freddy, I'm not selling it to you. I'm giving it to you."

He stood there in silence for a moment. Jann could see he was trying to figure out what her angle was, what trick she was playing on him.

"Freddy, I see the same thing in your eyes, that same look my father had. You would cherish this place, wouldn't you?"

Freddy was looking around again, but this time she could sense he was taking stock. Perhaps seeing what planting needed to be done, which areas could be expanded, how new irrigation could be set up. He was hooked. Then he shook his head. "It wouldn't feel right, Jann."

"I want you to have it, Freddy. It would make me happy, and my father, to know it was in good hands."

He just stood there speechless, for a few moments. "What about you? I mean this is your home."

Jann looked around again, slowly this time. "For a long time I thought of this place, this Earth, as my home. But now as I look around, all I see is what's not there anymore, what's gone. I now understand that home is not about place, it's about people. Coming here finally made me realize—my home is Mars."

THE END

Extract from the First Book of Martian Poetry, by Xenon Hybrid, President of Mars.

Extravehicular activity (EVA)

Enclosed, encased, encapsulated
No sound, save for breath and beat
No touch nor taste nor scent
Senses reflected
Like radar echo
Returned unanswered
By mylar and metal
To see, but not to be
To know through proxy only
This world, this planet
This Mars.

AUTHOR'S NOTE

I hope you enjoyed reading this story as much as I enjoyed writing it for you. If you did, then please leave me a review. Just a simple 'liked it' would be great, it helps a lot.

For notifications on upcoming books, and access to my FREE starter library, please join my Readers Group at www.geraldmkilby.com.

ALSO BY GERALD M. KILBY

You can continue the adventure with, Colony Mars 4, 5 & 6.

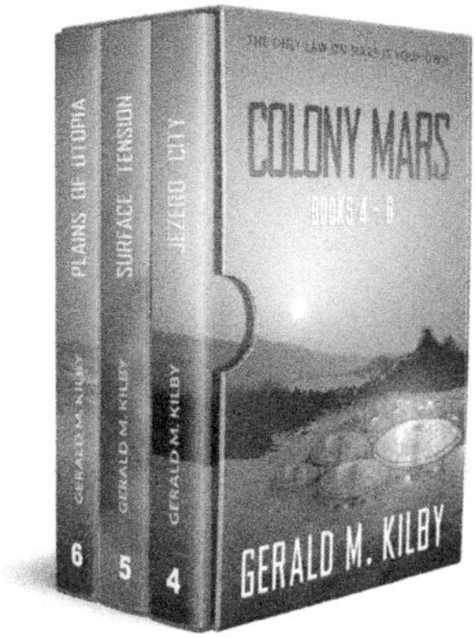

Jezero City *(Colony Four Mars):* When a colonist dies in tragic circumstances, just a few sols before a major terraforming experiment, Dr. Jann Malbec begins to suspect that all is not what it seems.

Surface Tension *(Colony Five Mars):* In the midst of the most devastating dust storm in the history of Mars, the survival of the half million people who call it home hangs in the balance.

Plains of Utopia *(Colony Six Mars):* When an Earth-bound ship explodes on the launchpad in Jezero City, and the DNA from two bodies recovered at the site are found to be an exact match, Dr. Jann Malbec is convinced that they are the product of a covert cloning program.

Made in the USA
Las Vegas, NV
28 September 2024

95913498R00361